Oliver August

was born in 1971 and grew up in Germany. He joined *The Times* after studying philosophy, politics and economics at Oxford University. In 1998 he won the journalism prize of the Anglo-German Foundation for a series of articles on Germany. He is now *The Times*'s China correspondent in Beijing after a spell reporting from New York.

OLIVER AUGUST

Along the Wall and Watchtowers

A Journey Down Germany's Divide

Flamingo
An Imprint of HarperCollins*Publishers*

Flamingo
An Imprint of HarperCollins*Publishers*
77–85 Fulham Palace Road,
Hammersmith, London W6 8JB

www.**fire**and**water**.com

Published by Flamingo 2000
9 8 7 6 5 4 3 2 1

First published in Great Britain by
HarperCollins 1999

Author photograph by Lindsay Maggs

ISBN 0 00 653111 3

Set in Simoncini Garamond

Printed and bound in Great Britain by
Clays Ltd, St Ives plc

For Tini, Erdmut, Florian and Mila

CONTENTS

ACKNOWLEDGEMENTS

I would like to thank everyone I met *unterwegs* for their help and untold acts of kindness. Furthermore, I would like to express my gratitude to: Jonathan Lloyd, my agent at Curtis Brown; Richard Johnson, my editor, Janet Law, my copy-editor, and Zoe Mayne at HarperCollins; Peter Stothard, George Brock, Patience Wheatcroft, Graham Paterson, Bronwen Maddox, Brian MacArthur, Erica Wagner and Adam Jones at *The Times*; Catherine Whitaker, Lindsay Maggs, Hillary Rosner, David Staton, Jennifer Schumacher, Melanie Entwistle, Sharon Krum, Caroline Wyatt, Peter Albrecht, Rachel DeWoskin, Stefan Oelze, Michael Braun, Cassell Bryan-Low, Niels Bryan-Low, Jonathan Turner, Stephen Grant, Andrew Butcher and Annette Swinburn; Mila, Tini, Erdmut and Florian; Pam Green, Michael Blütenberg, Bob Dylan, Cherry Garcia and Monsieur Claude.

During my research I consulted a number of useful sources. They include:

Jakob Arjouni, *Magic Hoffmann*, Zurich, 1997

Tom Bower, *Blind Eye To Murder*, London, 1981

John le Carré, *The Spy Who Came in From the Cold*, London, 1963

Gordon Craig, *The Germans*, London, 1984

Thomas Friedrich, *Who die Mauer war*, Berlin, 1996

Ralph Giordano, *Hier was ja Schluss*, Hamburg, 1996

Tony Grant, *From Our Own Correspondents*, London, 1995

Graham Greene, *The Lawless Roads*, London, 1939

Andreas Hartmann and Sabine Künsting, *Grenzgeschichten*, Frankfurt, 1990

Golo Mann, *Deutsche Geschichte*, Frankfurt, 1958

Jan Morris, *Fifty Years of Europe*, London, 1997

Jürgen Ritter and Peter Joachim Lapp, *Die Grenze*, Berlin, 1997

Matthias Röcke, *Die Trabi-Story*, Königswinter, 1998

Stanley Weintraub, *Albert*, London, 1997

Anyone who would like to contact me, please send an email to oaugust@hotmail.com.

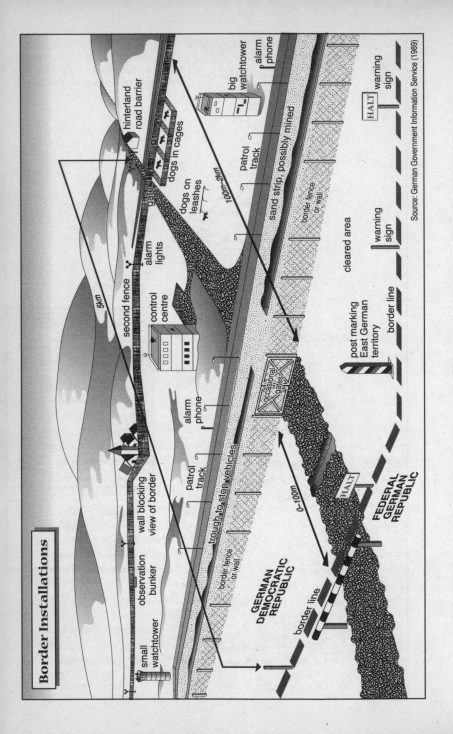

Border Installations

small watchtower
observation bunker
wall blocking view of border
5km
second fence
alarm lights
control centre
alarm phone
patrol track
trough to stop vehicles
hinterland road barrier
gate
dogs in cages
dogs on leashes
100m–2km
big watchtower
alarm phone
patrol track
sand strip, possibly mined
border fence or wall
occasional gates
post marking East German territory
border line
cleared area
warning sign
warning sign
HALT warning sign
border fence or wall
0–100m
HALT

GERMAN DEMOCRATIC REPUBLIC

FEDERAL GERMAN REPUBLIC

border line

Source: German Government Information Service (1989)

PROLOGUE

AT THE CHECKPOINT

M Y MOST PRIZED POSSESSION as a child was a rusty steel helmet with a bullet hole. It was heavy, with a sinister crack at the back. I imagined its last owner had suffered a demise of unspeakable horror.

I was eight years old when I found the helmet on an Easter-egg hunt. I beat my younger brother to it. We were on a family holiday behind the Iron Curtain. Our parents had hidden the eggs in the dunes by the Baltic Sea. If I remember correctly, we were visiting relatives in this breezy part of East Germany. To celebrate Easter, my mother had brought West German chocolate eggs across the border. That way, we wouldn't have to eat our relatives' artificially sweetened East German chocolate. My mother seemed keen to shelter us children from the grim realities of the Cold War.

The helmet lay in a boggy pit, covered with dirt. Only someone searching for West German chocolate eggs as eagerly as my brother and me could have found it. The rusty brown was barely distinguishable from the dark soil. In jubilant triumph I raised the helmet above my head and abandoned the hunt. Clambering down to the beach to wash out the soil, I noticed the bullet hole. My father said it was the helmet of a Russian soldier. Rather unnecessarily, he added that the soldier had probably died. The state of the helmet left us in little doubt as to the soldier's death. We ended the day by walking along the beach collecting stones in the helmet.

The next day we loaded up the car for the journey home. The helmet, still filled with stones, was packed into the boot between our suitcases. At the border, we encountered a longer wait than usual. Thousands of families from the west had been visiting relatives in the east. During the decades of division it had become a ritual: Easter in the east, a political act of fasting and atonement. Now we were all heading back to the land of real milk chocolate. One by one, East German border guards, known as *Volkspolizisten* or VoPos, stopped us and decided which cars to search. The VoPos took particular care when probing petrol tanks. Even to an eight-year-old it seemed incredible that a fugitive could hide there.

As we took our place in the queue of cars, my parents' thoughts turned to the helmet. 'I'm not sure it's a good idea to take it across the border,' my father said.

'Why not?'

'It's the helmet of a Russian soldier from the war. The VoPos will recognize that at once. Because they are like brothers to the Russians, they don't like admitting that Russian soldiers can get shot, too.'

I scowled at my own brother. We often had decidedly belligerent feel- ings towards each other. It can't have been easy explaining fraternal relations inside the Soviet bloc to us.

My mother was pragmatic. 'Let's just throw it out right here. We'll leave it in a roadside ditch.'

'But it's my helmet, not yours,' I sobbed, asserting my property rights.

'You can collect it when we come back next year. I'm sure it'll still be there.' But no amount of motherly reassurance could convince me to abandon my helmet. I began to punch the front passenger seat, at which point my parents realized they would have to risk a confrontation with the VoPos.

Sure enough, they singled out our car for inspection. 'To the right. Stop the car. Everything out.' My parents had to unload the entire boot and carry bags, half-eaten sandwiches, camping gear and left-over chocolate eggs into a small interview room. As he unpacked, my father whispered to us: 'Say nothing about the helmet.' After he had lifted the last suitcase out of the boot, he looked up at the VoPo and said: 'That's just stones. I won't bring them in,' and moved the helmet to the furthest, darkest corner of the boot.

In the interview room the VoPos sifted through dirty underwear. They tasted tooth paste and inspected personal letters. If this was meant to intimidate, they could not have failed more spectacularly. I grinned inanely. My helmet had made it through the world's most fortified border. Back in the car I celebrated, punching the front seats and howling with joy.

Further along the border on the West German side we stopped on a hill overlooking the fortifications. Down below, my father pointed out the East German village where he had grown up. It was a tantalizing 300 yards away. But we could not visit because it was too close to the border. The VoPos only allowed residents through.

My father had been fourteen when the war ended and the Allies drew a line across his father's tree nursery. The main house was in the Soviet zone while some of the fields were in the British zone. The border literally divided the property. Aged seventeen, my father hid a suitcase on a horse-drawn cart and drove west across the border on family property, leaving his parents behind. In the following forty years he was allowed to return only twice – for a maximum of three hours each time – for their funerals. He now pointed out the field where he had crossed the border.

When we arrived home from our Easter trip, the helmet took pride of place among my football posters. I would put it on my head occasionally to see if it was still too big for me. It would remain too big for many years to come. Slowly my enthusiasm for football faded, but the helmet remained on the shelf.

I was fascinated by the border. I listened to my mother's stories of her family's escape across borders. Her father, a German navy captain, had died towards the end of the war. His ship was torpedoed by a British submarine in the Mediterranean. His wife, my mother's mother, came from a Yorkshire family. When the Red Army advanced towards their Berlin residence, she decided to seek the relative safety of the British-occupied zone. During a dramatic flight she was captured and interned in a Russian camp. She managed to escape and eventually crossed the zonal border into what would become West Germany with her four-year-old daughter, my mother. Fifteen years later, my mother returned to West Berlin as a student. It was around the time the Wall went up. And as a naive twenty-two-year-old, she participated in a mission to smuggle a group of East Germans across the fortifications.

The more I heard about the Wall, the more I viewed my rusty helmet as a family treasure. Sneaking it across the border was an early rite of passage. My naive infatuation was further bolstered when as a teenager I read Graham Greene's *The Lawless Roads*, his account of a trip to Mexico. Greene wrote:

> The border means more than a customs house, a passport officer, a man with a gun. Over there everything is going to be different; life is never going to be quite the same again after your passport has been stamped and you find yourself

speechless among the money-changers. The man seeking scenery imagines strange woods and unheard-of mountains; the romantic believes that the women over the border will be more beautiful and complaisant than those at home; the unhappy man imagines at least a different hell; the suicidal traveller expects the death he never finds. The atmosphere of the border – it is like a good confession: poised for a few happy moments between sin and sin. When people die on the border they call it a 'happy death'.

Then, in late 1989, the border disappeared. The monstrosity built in 1961 fell overnight. A popular uprising succeeded where hundreds of Cruise missiles had failed. The Berlin Wall simply crumbled. The Germany I had grown up in disappeared.

Maybe coincidentally, I packed the helmet in a suitcase soon afterwards. I liked the idea of seeking new borders. I moved to England, a place I came to love.

As a child, I had spent two summers in England on family holidays. Even though it rained the entire time, I enjoyed myself; possibly because the rain gave me an excuse to lie in bed all day and read, rather than having to go on family outings. At the time of our first visit in 1979, I was eight years old and didn't speak a word of English. We stayed in a coastal village in Devon and my father read Dickens in German aloud in the evenings. When we returned six years later – this time to a house near Land's End – my English was passable. I ploughed through *David Copperfield*, understanding maybe every other word. My grades in English classes at school were barely average but I had befriended a number of British soldiers stationed in Osnabrück, the northern German city where I grew up. In the evenings we would meet in a pub by the barracks to play pool. On them I practised my classroom English, at least until they got too drunk to listen. Most evenings they had to be escorted back to the barracks by the Military Police. As far as my pool playing was concerned, I failed to learn a great deal from the squaddies. They had little incentive to teach me as the loser paid for the frame. But as a linguistic education, the pool lessons were priceless.

At the age of twenty, the year after German reunification, I went to Oxford after a stint at a Canadian high school. I was part of a sizeable group of German students, the second largest foreign contingent after the Americans. Unlike some of the other Germans, I had little trouble fitting in and making English friends. I shamelessly ingratiated myself by putting on an absurd English accent. My pool-table lessons came in handy. Friends suggested that with my accent I should become a spy, a double agent even. Sadly, I had to discount that idea since – nominally at least – Germans and Brits were supposed to be on the same side. But my English accent saved me from a lot of ridicule. Germans, even in Oxford, or perhaps especially there, were routinely teased about 'The War'. When a German walked into a student pub he or she might be greeted with: 'Two world wars and one world cup, doo dah, doo dah!' or with the even less imaginative, 'Don't mention the war.'

Occasionally, I would think it was cowardly of me to ditch my German accent. It had the whiff of desertion. But for the most part I was happy. I had avoided a peculiar dilemma. If Germans didn't laugh at war jibes then, obviously, they had no sense of humour, confirming an old stereotype. But if they did laugh, they were masochists. As a German, you couldn't win. Better to be incognito.

After finishing university, I decided to stay in England. My new friends were all moving to London to become sharp-suited yuppies. I followed them and – polishing my English accent still further – persuaded *The Times* to give me a job. Graham Greene had also worked for the paper as a young man, I modestly told myself. I was even happier than in Oxford.

But while I spent wondrous days in the Fleet Street jungle and endless nights in London's clubs, Germany was never completely out of my mind. I had a sneaking suspicion that the border – fragments of it at least – must still exist. Could something so powerful be erased as easily as a pencil mark on a map? I doubted it.

From afar, I wondered how reunified Germany was shaping up. Could the two halves simply be welded back together? Were fears about the rise of a Fourth Reich as ridiculous as they sounded? My curiosity eventually inspired the idea of a border journey. What better way was there to find answers? Had not borders and the expansion of borders played an important part in German history? Paul Theroux said Britain is defined by its coast; nowhere in the 'Kingdom by the Sea' is further than 65 miles from the ocean. By the same token, Germany is defined by its borders and the struggles they ignited. Placed at the centre of the European land mass, its borders have continually shifted over the centuries. German school books show page after page of maps tracking the different shapes of the fatherland. The Romans sliced Germany in half when they built the Limes defence wall that stretched from Scotland to the Black Sea. Two millennia later, Hitler tried to push back borders in his quest for *Lebensraum*. And with every border revision, the seeds of a new conflict were sown.

Theroux wrote that if you want to learn about Britain you have to travel its coastline. It attracts all that is best and worst about the country – from Belfast to Butlins. Equally, Germany reveals most about itself at the seams, where history is a constant reminder. Thus, I set off. By now a correspondent for *The Times* in New York, I armed myself with an American Youth Hostel pass and a raft of tourist maps. This is my account of a trip all along the *Antifaschitischer Schutzwall*, the anti-fascist protection barrier, as its East German builders liked to call it.

1

ON THE
BEACH

THE SHABBY HOUSE ON the edge of the ocean had been the last watering hole in West Germany. Or the first, if you came across the border from the east.

The tavern was called *Bei Mecki*. It stood where barbed wire once cut across the beach. Not far from here the Iron Curtain had run into the Baltic Sea. A sign by the door said: '*Achtung!* Dangerous dog.' The landlord kept a chart purporting to show how often his dog had repelled 'intruders': postmen – 13 ticks; burglars – 7 ticks; cats – 11 ticks; car tyres – 17 ticks. There were no ticks for East German border guards. They had been gone for a decade.

I wrenched open the door. A gale of smoke and laughter blew in my face. Lunchtime drinkers crowded the aisles. 'Come in, young man, and close the damn door.' The juke box drowned out chatter. The tavern was dingy, more like the sleeping quarters on a submarine than the ballroom of an ocean liner, but I felt at home nevertheless. Like a dog returning to his territory, I recognized the distinctive smell of a German tavern, a *Kneipe*.

I hovered by the bar. The landlord's face was scarred with red wrinkles. His Adam's apple bobbed up and down like a buoy. He was drunk and sentimental.

After the second beer, I mentioned my quest for the Iron Curtain. He told me he missed the border.

'You what?'

'I really miss it,' he said without a hint of sarcasm. The border had been such a convenient excuse for failure. Anything and everything could be blamed on it. 'If you lost your job, it was because the border suppressed trade. If your wife cheated on you, it was because of the psychological strain of living in the shadow of border. In the old times, people sat at this bar and complained for hours about the border. But they can't any more. What is there to blame when things go wrong now?' he said. 'We lost our crutch.'

Stepping out into blazing sunshine, I spotted a sandy beach. It was covered with thick lines of seashells left behind by the tide. Nudists waded through the treacherous field of carapaces. East Germans prided themselves on not being overly body conscious; paranoia over waistlines was alien to a classless society that had too much else to be paranoid about.

The beach was dotted with sandcastles. I stopped to admire an intricate system of canals, bridges and towers. Herr Hausmann and his son Dietmar had spent all day carving out this miniature Venice. The portly Herr Hausmann was beaming – part sunburn, part pride. 'In every German, I show you here, there is an engineer.'

'And a poet,' I said.

Herr Hausmann explained that on beaches further west, castle-building was prohibited. '*Verboten*,' he chortled, 'just because the East Germans built that damn Wall. Nobody is allowed to build walls now. That's crazy, like outlawing railways because the Nazis used them in the Holocaust.'

I looked at him in consternation.

'Oh, God knows why you can't build castles over there.' He let his eyes drift over the beach. 'You can't build castles but you can go round naked. What logic?' He slapped his son. 'Dietmar! Don't look at that woman's breasts.' He turned back to me. 'But who can blame the boy for looking? The East German border guards always looked at our women. They were the biggest voyeurs. On a hot day you could see the sun reflecting off their binoculars. We showed them our best assets – no wonder they tore down the Wall and came over.' Herr Hausmann grunted.

As I walked away I stepped into a hole dug by the family team and came to a painful halt. I winced as I twisted my leg out. That's why castle-building is *verboten* on the beach, Herr Hausmann.

Limping east, I hoped to hit the exact spot where the Iron Curtain ran into the Baltic Sea. After a mile I still hadn't encountered any derelict fortifications. I expected to see steel-reinforced concrete bunkers. I harboured fond childhood memories of play-fighting with my brother in

Hitler's fortifications along the French Atlantic coast. It was the most memorable part of that particular family holiday. Our parents, however, had been appalled by our war games. They deemed water pistols to be the first step towards genocide. In reformed postwar Germany, children were not supposed to play soldiers.

I lumbered along the beach. I now felt the distinct need to go to the toilet. Between the low dunes stood a 'nature reserve' sign. Perfect, I thought. A sandy path, fenced in on both sides, led into brushland. I climbed over the fence to find a secluded spot between bushes and birch trees. Fifty feet away a 4-foot-high UFO had landed. On closer inspection it turned out to be a giant fuse box. Cables had been cut, fuses ripped out and the door was missing. I checked for signs of live electricity – a vital issue when it comes to toilets. Grass was growing inside the box and a bird had made a nest. The cables were enormous. What *was* this? The word LIGHTING was scribbled on the side.

A policeman strolled up the sandy path. 'Get back here. You're disturbing the wildlife,' he yelled. 'And don't touch those border installations.' I quickly made off into the brushland behind the dunes. I was embarrassed, not because the policeman had caught me relieving myself in a nature reserve – what could be more natural? – but I had completely failed to see that I had found the Iron Curtain. I had travelled thousands of miles to see border fortifications, only to piss on them without actually noticing.

Looking around now, I expected to see some kind of memorial saying: 'Here began the world's most fortified border' or 'Evil Empire, free admission'. But there was nothing to tell visitors they had just crossed the former frontier. They would blunder across like I had. No tipped-over watchtower, no graffitied piece of brickwork. All traces had been removed and paved over. A smooth new road stretched across the unscarred land. The past was already fading.

I walked past a row of holiday cottages by the beach. They had sentimental names like *Gemütlichkeit* (Cosiness), written on wooden signs. Garden gnomes stood guard under German flags. The country's new flag was identical to the old West German flag. With unification, East Germans had inherited not only the deutschmark but all other western symbols of nationhood, including the flag and garden gnomes. By the roadside I found a memorial stone at last. 'Never divided again,' the inscription read. I imagined adding two garden gnomes holding hands.

*   *   *

The town of Travemünde lies a mile further west. It takes its name from the river Trave that flows into the Baltic Sea here. Travemünde is a German Brighton rather than a Blackpool. It is crowded in summer – but people buy their lunch in cafés rather than bringing soggy sandwiches from home. The town's main attraction is a casino built in 1833. Curiously, casinos are called *Spielbanken*, play banks, in German. This play bank was frequented by famously obsessive Russian gamblers at the turn of the century. After the Cold War interlude, when gambling as well as travelling was prohibited at home, the Russians returned.

Travemünde's biggest hotel, the Maritim, is a thirty-five-floor tower right on the beach. It had been the highest tower along the border between the two Germanys, higher than any watchtower, and doubled as a lighthouse. At night, a rotating red light atop the tower guided ships out at sea. The Russians at the casino, however, thought the red light advertised a giant brothel.

I inquired about accommodation at the tourist centre. The manager tried to be helpful. Her accent suggested she was Eastern European. She said: 'You must stay in this hotel. View is beautiful. And, of course, room has toilet and shower. This one has toilet and bathroom as well. Very nice. This one, not so sure about toilet. But this one, very nice toilet and bathroom.'

The woman had probably spent her entire childhood in a Warsaw or Budapest tower block where she would have had to run up three flights of stairs to use a non-flush toilet or wash with cold water in the middle of winter. A room with its own bath seemed the height of luxury to her. But I had grown up in affluent West Germany where people had more bathrooms than friends. I cared not one iota whether I would be sleeping near a sink. Most likely it would be dripping all night anyway. I didn't even want to stay in a hotel. I had imagined spending the night in a cosy bed-and-breakfast. I wanted to see the soft underbelly of united Germany.

'Please, no hotel room. I want private accommodation.'

'But no bathroom in private accommodation.'

'I don't want a bathroom.'

She sighed and flicked through the brochure, slapping each page. Then, with an unexpectedly triumphant cry, she turned to use the telephone. 'Private accommodation with private bathroom,' she announced. But nobody picked up the phone at the multi-bathroom mansion. She went back to slapping the pages. 'We have hotel with small apartments, like private accommodation. You know aparthotel? Bathrooms much bigger than in normal hotel.'

I said my good-byes and took the brochure with me to find a B&B on my own. The streets and cafés of Travemünde were pleasant if a little pretentious. Bacon with salad was called 'Rucola Salade with Crôutons and Bâcon'.

A wind-worn house on the banks of the Trave was listed in the brochure as 'home of an old Travemünde family of seamen'. The front door clicked open but there was no answer from inside. With a second knock I pushed it further ajar. I found myself staring at a stuffed shark's head. A voice croaked: 'We want no magazines, no Greenpeace, no Bibles. There is nothing to steal in this house. The money is in the bank, the jewellery with my sister. My husband is coming home any minute.' An elderly lady was holding a broomstick at the top of the stairs.

'Excuse me, I am looking for a room.'

'First you break into the house then you demand a room. Get out.' She came racing down the stairs, wielding her broom.

My inquiries at a second B&B were no more successful. One Herr Gerth said through the half-open door: 'We prefer not to.' That was all he said. I checked the name by the door again. It said Gerth, not Kafka. All my attempts to find a B&B in Travemünde were unsuccessful. The clipped explanations for rejecting me varied from 'It's not worth it for one night' to 'We only have double rooms'.

What good was speaking the local language when nobody wanted to talk to me? People weren't even opening their doors wide enough to let me have a sneaky look inside. I had imagined my journey would be effortless. Now I was forced to sleep in a hotel like a stranger just off the ferry from Scandinavia.

The Landhaus had been among the hotels suggested by the Eastern European bathroom obsessive. I knocked at the door. There was no answer. In pitch darkness, I went around the building via a car park. A woman stood on some steps, cutting bedsheets into small rectangles with a foot-long kitchen knife. She would make a small cut in the sheet, then hold the knife between her teeth and rip the sheet from end to end with a raspy roar.

I did not dare ask for a room straight out for fear of rejection. 'The sign says you are a hotel,' I ventured.

She cut into another sheet. 'Rest day today.'

The expression on my face must have spelled utter misery. The woman looked at me. Without saying another word, she put down her knife and unlocked a door behind her. She double-locked it again from the inside.

'Always keep it locked,' she said. 'You won't have a bathroom in your room, OK?'

I nodded gratefully.

My mother had kindly loaned me her car. The radiant red Toyota was slowly falling apart, but no more so than a decade ago when I received my first speeding ticket in it. I pointed the Red Racer down the autobahn. The city of Lübeck was ten miles away. The highway followed the Trave all along the border.

Lübeck has to be the Siena of the north. The Trave metropolis may be lacking Tuscan *esprit*, but the two cities share one style of architecture. Ornately decorated red-brick houses surround Lübeck's central square. Set at odd angles, they form a large, asymmetric space. Historic Lübeck was built in red brick, including the cathedrals. Even some cobblestone streets were paved with red bricks. If only architects in postwar Britain had been given the chance to visit Lübeck. Here was a textbook example that red bricks could be assembled to form something other than hideous tower blocks.

During the Cold War, Lübeck had received government subsidies to prop it up as a frontier post. It bore all the hallmarks of West German affluence. The shops along the pedestrian zone sold British shoes, French perfume and American sportswear. The military occupation of West Germany may have ended but the Allied retailers had certainly not vacated their bastions.

I passed a beggar with a neatly trimmed punk haircut. A crest of symmetrical spikes ran across his shaven head. The paratrooper boots were carefully laced up all the way. 'Would you excuse me, *mein Herr*,' he asked earnestly. 'I was wondering if you would have a small number of spare coins.' I was too perplexed by his verbosity to answer. 'Well, thank you anyway, *mein Herr*. I wish you a pleasant day.' With his grace and courtesy he would have made a good door-to-door salesman. Were times really so bad he could not find work? I retraced my steps to ask him. He was now talking to an art dealer across the street.

'You're the first beggar I've seen in a gallery,' I said.

He grinned. 'I'm an art student. I only beg for inspiration. I really don't need the money. My capitalist father has a whole bank vault full of the stuff.'

I had arranged to meet an old schoolfriend in Lübeck. Valerie studied medicine at the local university. She lived on a street called Engelswisch, or Angel's Wipe, in a maze of cobblestone streets. Even by the standards of England's medieval university towns, her abode was stunning. The afternoon sun gave the red bricks a glow of Tuscan gold.

At school, Valerie and I had sat next to each other in German literature classes. She hadn't forgotten. 'Do you remember we read Thomas Mann in class?' I had found Mann unreadable at the time. He was regarded as Germany's most gifted writer of the twentieth century, but to my schoolboy mind his texts seemed stale, tortured and convoluted. He exemplified everything about Germany that made me uncomfortable. Mann was constantly wrestling with his heavy soul, striving for profundity where he should have been sniggering. But Thomas Mann does not snigger. Give me Martin Amis any day.

Valerie said: 'Thomas Mann lived around the corner from here. You should visit the house. It's a museum now.' I was not convinced. We ate at a restaurant called Schiffergesellschaft (Seamen's Club). The long, dark room looked like below-decks on an old schooner. The ceiling was held up by large oak beams. Paintings of storms covered the wood-panelled walls. Food was served at five tables stretching the entire length of the room. Most of the food was pickled. Like an eighteenth-century schooner put to sea, the Schiffergesellschaft had to stock up only once every couple of weeks. The preserved food came in two varieties: salted herring called *Matjeshering*; and *Sauerfleisch*, pork in a jelly marinade. They were both served cold.

'Thomas Mann must have eaten here before he moved to America,' Valerie said. I was surprised. Not by the fact that Mann ate *Matjeshering* and *Sauerfleisch* – the dishes rather suited his prose style, I thought – but I was stunned to hear that Mann had lived in America. The land of the brash must have been entirely alien to his character. Intrigued by his Atlantic crossing, I was persuaded to visit his house.

It was actually called the Buddenbrooks House. *Buddenbrooks* is the title of Thomas Mann's first novel which describes the mid-nineteenth-century life of the extended Buddenbrook family in Lübeck. It is a barely disguised portrait of Thomas Mann's own dysfunctional family. Like generations of Manns, the Buddenbrooks are small businessmen and local politicians. The parents force their children into loveless marriages. The slavish children are destroyed by their obedience to the family. The *Sunday Times* called *Buddenbrooks* 'arguably the first great 20th century novel – despite the slightly inconvenient fact that it was actually published in the 19th century'. All I remembered from reading the book as a teenager were the convoluted passages on the first few pages. I never got any further.

The Buddenbrooks House at Mengstrasse No. 4, a three-storey building in a row of elegant town houses, stands opposite one of medieval Lübeck's seven red-brick churches. Thomas Mann modelled his fictional residence on the house he grew up in. The gabled roof is decorated with a statue of a scantily-clad woman at a Roman feast. On the ground floor used to be a shop run by the Manns. Since 1991 it has housed the museum. The Mann family tree shows Thomas Mann had six children, all of them published writers.

The most remarkable of Thomas Mann's children was Golo. As a historian and political commentator, he surpassed even his father. Famously, in *Deutsche Geschichte* (1958), he described the German national character as ✱

> a life in extremes. From apolitical calm Germany turns to overexcited political activity, from colourful multiplicity to radical uniformity; from utter weakness it rises to become an aggressive power, sinks back into ruin and works its way up again with incredible speed to new, hectic affluence. It is open, cosmopolitan, full of admiration for all things foreign; then it despises and disposes of the foreign and seeks salvation in an exaggerated nurturing of its own peculiarities. The Germans are deemed to be the most philosophical, speculative people, then as well the most practical and materialistic, then the most patient and peaceful, and again the most powerhungry and brutal. Their own philosopher, Nietzsche, called them the 'Täusche-Volk' – the deceptive people – because they always surprise the world by doing what is least expected of them.

Golo Mann inherited an interest in the German national character from his father. Thomas Mann said in 1914: 'It is not easy to be a German – not so easy and comfortable as it is to be an Englander.' This was written across a wall in the museum in Lübeck. I understood what he meant. I too had cherished England's intellectual freedom and irreverence. But my favourite Thomas Mann quote comes from a 1939 text called *Brother Hitler*. In 1936, Mann had gone into exile as a Nazi enemy. From California (where, unsurprisingly, he did not fit in very well) Mann wrote about Hitler: 'The lad is a catastrophe; but that's no reason not to find his character and fate interesting.'

Herr Bäumler, a placid man with a home-made walking stick, was staring at Mann's text on the wall. Tentatively, I pointed a finger. Herr Bäumler shook his head: 'Easier to say from California than the trenches.'

I said I agreed with Mann. The warning implicit in his text was truer than ever in unified Germany. To apologize publicly for Brother Hitler had become the norm, and rightly so. But anyone discussing the figure of the Führer in anything other than comic bogeyman terms was marked down as a supposed neo-Nazi. The Führer's character was still somewhat of a taboo.

Herr Bäumler said: 'We have to strengthen democracy.'

At the expense of free expression? He wouldn't say.

Incredibly, the text of *Mein Kampf*, Hitler's autobiographical manifesto and possibly the most important Third Reich document, is still banned in Germany. People are simply not allowed to print, buy or sell a copy. What a godsend to neo-Nazis; the ban signals that their ideas are so powerful that the government dares not let them be aired.

Herr Bäumler said he wasn't sure, but he thought that the copyright to *Mein Kampf* was held by the Bavarian state government. He recalled Bavaria staging a legal *Blitzkrieg* when the son-in-law of playwright Bertolt Brecht attempted to publish the text on CD-Rom.

I said Thomas Mann surely would have sided with Brecht's son-in-law. Herr Bäumler nodded.

I was beginning to like Thomas Mann. I bought another of his novels, *Doctor Faustus*, in the museum shop. In the far corner, a wild-haired customer rummaged through some books on her knees. She was talking to herself: 'Oh, no, stupid, you can't have that . . . oh, I'm sorry.' She had knocked over a pile of biographies but didn't look up. 'I wonder if they've got a version with nice pictures in it, yes, of all the main characters. Oh, I don't know.' She stood up and yelled across the shop to the cashier: 'Ex-cuse me. Do you have an idiot's guide to Thomas Mann?'

I had tea at the Café Niederegger. Sated and silent, burgher families digested afternoon refreshments. They loaded up on Black Forest gateau, shovelled in coffee-cream slices, and weighed themselves down in their comfortable chairs with apple cheesecake. Anyone still moving ordered an extra portion of *Rote Grütze*, red-berry jelly with whipped cream. A woman suddenly leaned forwards and berated her daughter: 'If I hear the name of your stinking boyfriend one more time I'll slap you.' The Buddenbrooks' combination of affluence and ugly family life had not died out after Mann's departure.

The Café Niederegger was a family business, I read on the menu. For seven generations, the Niedereggers had made Germany's finest marzipan.

The mixture of sugar and almonds – once called 'harem's delight' – was Lübeck's biggest export. Along with its growing business success, the Niederegger family had developed political connections. It exerted pressure on the city council to allow the café to serve coffee and cakes outside on the market square. Chancellor Kohl even sent Niederegger marzipan to German troops stationed overseas.

I met Holger Strait, the sharp-suited managing director. I asked him if the Niedereggers were the new Buddenbrooks. He thought that the Niedereggers were more famous. After all, Harrods in London stocked their marzipan.

I drove out of Lübeck on a street named after Count von Moltke. He had participated in the 1944 revolt against Hitler. I noticed the name. It was still rare to laud the resistance.

The suburb Schlutup (Old German for 'to unlock') had straddled the Iron Curtain. The border checkpoint at Schlutup had been the northernmost gap in the curtain. It was mainly used by West German holiday-makers, and perhaps the odd spy. I remembered that it was here at Schlutup that my father had smuggled my Russian helmet across the border almost two decades ago.

The border arrived with an unexpected suddenness. The Red Racer was climbing up a hill through rows of houses, affluent dwellings with plush gardens, four cars upfront and probably even more bathrooms inside. The last house on each side of the road was capped by trees. Beyond that the landscape opened up into a wide valley, devoid of anything but grass. No traces of Stalin's mighty curtain. Just a drab emptiness. Again, I had expected a little more: a map at least. Perhaps one with self-important statements from politicians, to which someone might have added drawings of the silly VoPos sifting through shipping containers filled with dirty underwear. But all I saw was a yellowing valley. To the north, water led to Travemünde and the Baltic Sea. To the south, the valley stretched 800 miles to the Czech border.

I parked the Red Racer with a distinct lack of enthusiasm. Visiting a non-existent border reminded me of school excursions where we would stare at an empty field. Studiously, the teacher would explain that Romans and Teutons had battled there with rusty swords and wooden shields. Meanwhile, bored pupils tried to poke each other's eyes out.

The last houses on the West German side overlooked the valley. Standing in his back garden, Herr Mauersberger wore cotton balls in his ears and a seaman's cap on his head. 'Is this where the border was?' I asked. It had to be, according to my map, but the question seemed a good gambit. He took a long drag on his cigarette and chipped it over his garden fence as if he was throwing it overboard. 'No,' he said.

Flustered, I tried to explain that I was hoping to travel along the border and apologized for disturbing him. He wasn't really listening. 'This is not where the border was,' he said. He had been pointing at his feet, now he moved his hand towards me. 'That's where it was. You are on their side. I'm not.' I must have looked even more puzzled. 'Well, you wanted to know, didn't you?' he said. 'The end of the garden was the end of the country. The fence was the border.'

And what was it like here back then? 'Quieter. A lot quieter. You want to know, don't you? The VoPos sat in their bunker over there, all gone now of course. They'd come right up to the fence, but never said a word. Living here was like life on Noah's Ark. Wonderful birds nested in these trees. Ducks would come flying over the border. One morning I got up early and found five deer between the flowers. They'd jumped over all the fences. More than any man ever managed. Today, the valley is a big carnival. People come here to have barbecues and go camping. They smash beer bottles, repair their cars, play loud music, walk their dogs and the dogs piss against my fence. You didn't see the VoPos doing any of that. It was just a lot quieter.' As I walked away I could hear him berating a woman with a dog. 'I hope that mongrel steps on a mine.'

The first thing motorists notice when they cross the post-unification border is the difference in tarmac. Schlutup has grey and smooth tarmac, spotless enough to satisfy Formula One racers. In the empty valley, the tarmac turns black and is littered with potholes, provisionally fixed but crumbling nevertheless. A few hundred yards into East Germany new, western tarmac has been laid, as shiny as the tarmac in Schlutup. It takes only a few seconds to drive over the dark, potholed border asphalt. But the gap between the two tarmacs is a visual as well as a symbolic jolt to the senses.

My plan was to head due north to the Baltic coast on the eastern side of the Trave, and then turn around to make the long trek south. I hadn't been in the area since the helmet incident when I was eight years old; there had been too many other inviting travel destinations.

Outsiders usually found East Germany disturbing. Jan Morris, the Welsh world traveller, wrote:

The Iron Curtain was hundreds of miles of barbed wire, watch-towers and minefields, with an awful sameness to it. Travelling from west to east through it was like entering a drab and disturbing dream, peopled by all the ogres of totalitarianism, a half-lit world of shabby resentments, where anything could be done to you, I used to feel, without anybody ever hearing of it, and your every step was dogged by watchful eyes and mechanisms.

To me, socialist East Germany seemed not so much a disturbing dream as a cruel joke. It was a banana republic that couldn't afford bananas. The government in East Berlin did not have enough hard currency to buy tropical fruit. When the border was opened East Germans spurned *foie gras* and headed straight for the fruit section in western supermarkets. Driving east now, I stopped at a corner shop in Selmsdorf, a few miles across the border. The bananas in the fruit basket had gone from yellow to brown.

Along the water I saw my first East German watchtower from up close. Perched on the Trave's edge, it could be mistaken for a life-guard post. The window glass had gone but otherwise the tower looked operational. The concrete had withstood the weather and the vandals from nearby Dassow, a bleak fishing village which endured a forty-year ban on fishing. The socialist party feared an exodus across the water and took away the villagers' livelihood. A curious step, to say the least, in a workers' and farmers' state. At a fast-food stand by the village entrance called the Sprinting Pig, a well-spoken woman gave me directions to the youth hostel. I had called the hostel in advance to avoid the drama of Travemünde. Bathrooms were not an option.

The sun had long set and the roadside woods had turned into a shapeless black mass. A white sign marked the way to the hostel down a narrow forest path. I was surprised to find it so far from the sea. Didn't people come here to swim? The concrete buildings stood forlornly in a clearing. There was nothing youthful about this hostel.

The door was not locked. 'Is this the hostel?' I called into the darkness. A young-sounding voice answered: 'Did you call earlier?' The hostel was run by two East Germans no more than twenty years old. One punched a light switch before I could answer. I followed him through a neon-lit corridor and handed him my American Youth Hostel pass. 'New York, huh. You got the pass in the States?' Huh. The guest book showed I was the only resident. In fact, nobody had stayed here for at least a week. We walked through a maze of corridors. Every light switch received a thump.

My room for the night was a cell in all but name. The windows were unusually high up and I had problems opening them. I noticed what looked like a speaker above the door. 'The building is Russian. Don't worry about the listening system. It's all been disconnected,' the young man explained. 'The Russians gave it to the East German border troops and they gave it to the secret police.'

Of course the youth hostel was empty. Who would want to sleep in a torture chamber? After a brief bout of melodramatic *angst*, I wanted to ask more questions. But my youthful host was already bashing the corridor lights again. I loosened some screws on a window and fell asleep in the fresh air.

It was still dark when I woke up to the sound of glass shattering outside. 'Hey, that was my beer.' The voice was under my window. 'Fuck the USA,' a second voice said. They started cheering and singing: 'Fu-ck the U-S-A.' They repeated the line half a dozen times with diminishing vigour to the melody of the Bruce Springsteen song 'Born in the USA'. Then they giggled.

I departed in the Red Racer at first light.

The village of Pötenitz sprawls high above the East German coastline. Travemünde is visible in the distance. A gigantic sign towered over a building site promising 120 'generous family castles'. Half a dozen 'castles' had already been built. Semi-detached seaside villas, they had about as much charm as Ikea furniture. I decided to be naughty and pose as a potential buyer. Using subterfuge on estate agents was as morally justifiable as cheating a conman, I thought.

I knocked on the door of the model house. Herr Heins peeked out. He tucked his grey turtleneck under his neon-yellow blazer and whispered: 'This is ideal for you. Twenty-four carat, I promise.' It was eight in the morning and we were alone, but Herr Heins insisted on whispering: 'See these pine floors – Finnish, straight off the ferry.' I inspected the 'castle' in haste. 'Think of the location, close to Hamburg, he whispered. 'Your wife will love it.'

'My girlfriend lives in another country.'

'Well, at least you're not divorced.'

I had heard enough. I paid the universal price for getting away from an over-eager salesman and accepted pamphlets, brochures, leaflets, prospectuses and a business card.

On my way out of Pötenitz I stopped once more at the big sign. I tried to strike up a conversation with Herr Dürner. His eyes looked as tired as his rusty bicycle.

'Wonderful project, isn't it?' I ventured.

'No, it's not.'

'OK, they're not really castles, just tacky semi-detached cottages.'

'No – look at the building companies involved. They're all West German. A western architect, a western engineer, a western builder, and probably western cleaning ladies as well. None of the money will go to East German firms.'

'But at least your people will have somewhere nice to live.'

'Now you really are pulling my leg. Do you think anyone in Pötenitz can afford this? Nobody in the whole of East Germany can. These houses are for fat Hamburgers with their fat wives who come here on the weekend in their fat cars. They will sit in their new luxury villas and get even fatter. These houses are not for Ossis.' He cycled off.

An Ossi is an East German. West Germans are nicknamed Wessis. Reunification has spawned its own vocabulary. The fall of the Wall is commonly known as the Wende, the turning point.

Before finding out just how much of a turning point the Wende had been, I made another pitstop at the Sprinting Pig fast-food stand. One more pork sausage for the road south. I was already starting to conform to Herr Dürner's stereotype of the fat Wessi. But I liked *Bratwurst*. I gorged myself with a guilty grin.

2

BY THE
LAKES

I HAD BOUGHT A SELECTION of maps fearing the embarrassment of getting lost in the fatherland. Spread out on the car roof, they showed a bewildering obstacle course of lakes and pools. The more detailed the maps, the more they looked like something designed by Jackson Pollock. They were all drips, splashes and sprinkles. The hapless border was forced to flip-flop between the lakes and on occasion cut right through them. From the maps at least, it looked as if the natural obstacles in the way of fleeing East Germans had been far more formidable than any man-made barrier.

I drove around aimlessly. Out of the corner of my eye I saw a road sign but failed to decipher it. In a fit of panic, I repeated to myself the names of the last two East German villages I could remember. Raddingsdorf and Carlow. But Raddingsdorf and Carlow quickly became needles in my haystack of maps. A prudent driver would have stopped and retraced the route before losing all sense of direction. But I was now too preoccupied with narrow roads curving around lake shores. Or rather, with the oncoming cars on those narrow roads. They were just about wide enough for one car. On either side of the road was a potholed shoulder. Where two cars met, one was forced on to the potholes. The Red Racer went into a huffing fit as the suspension bobbed over holes the size of a small grave, throwing up clouds of dust from the unseemly patchwork of botched repairs.

Occasionally, aggressive drivers would attempt to avoid the shoulder by engaging in an elaborate game of chicken. When they spotted an oncoming car they moved over to the wrong side of the road to stake their claim. Then they moved back almost on to the shoulder on their side. But no further. They stayed where it was still comfortable to drive. They seemed to be saying: I have done my bit, now you move over. *'Los, mach schnell!'* The other car, in this case the Red Racer, was groaningly forced on to the shoulder.

A hitchhiker was raising his thumb near Demern. I suspected an act of desperation. The odds of hitching a ride in this desolate landscape must have been minimal. Feeling charitable, I told Herr Lauterbach I would take him anywhere as long as it was south. Before we had a chance to discuss routes, I was already involved in the next game of chicken. A black Mercedes was laying claim to the road. 'The beach towels are coming out again,' I said. He gave me a blank sideways glance and I realized he had no idea what I was talking about. I explained that Britons had a common perception about German tourists always reserving the best spots by the pool for themselves, sneaking downstairs in the wee hours and spreading out a towel. 'That Mercedes did the same sort of thing.'

Herr Lauterbach spat: 'The whole concept surely is based on national stereotypes.' The thirty-year-old sounded just like his description of himself as: 'a schoolteacher with higher qualifications.'

I told him about a Carling Black Label advert on British television a few years ago. It showed a group of holidaying 'Krauts' being beaten to their spot in the sun by an early-bird drinker from Britain. Standing on his balcony, he throws his beach towel (rolled around a Carling can like a bouncing bomb – added insult) across the pool on to a deckchair. The defeated Germans mope while the Carling logo is shown.

'Quite funny, I guess.' Herr Lauterbach did not look amused. 'But you just cannot generalize about national characteristics. Every individual is always different and cannot be judged as a member of a race. Otherwise, the Holocaust would make all Germans genocidal maniacs.'

He made a reference to *Hitler's Willing Executioners*. This book by Daniel Goldhagen, an American historian, had suggested something similar. Published in 1996, it triggered a bout of national soul-searching and tortured debates about Holocaust guilt in Germany. Foreign commentators had welcomed the debates as a useful exercise. On the other hand, there were few things more typically German than an intense bout of national soul-searching; apart, maybe, from tortured debates that reached no conclusion. But Herr Lauterbach refused to acknowledge there could be anything 'typically' German.

To restart the conversation, I mentioned Golo Mann's description of

Germans that I had read in Lübeck. Thomas Mann's son wrote that to be German meant being poetic and pragmatic, soulful as well as systematic, aggressive yet caring. Did Herr Lauterbach agree with that?

'A very superficial summary of the German identity problem,' he sighed. 'Its broadness is bordering on vacuity.' He proceeded to give me a full-blown history lesson on how generations of Germans had failed – at least in Herr Lauterbach's eyes – to define a German identity. The problem was rooted in Germany's troubled birth as a nation-state, he said. For most of the nineteenth century, 'Germany' was made up of hundreds, and later dozens, of individual states and principalities. At the same time, centralized government in Britain and France had long matured.

Without wanting to antagonize him, I suggested that 'Germany', accordingly, was an umbrella term for poetic Bavarians, pragmatic Hamburgers, soulful Rhinelanders, systematic Swabians, aggressive Prussians and caring Saxons. *Richtig?*

Herr Lauterbach failed to humour my 'gross oversimplification of such complex people as the Saxons and the Bavarians'. He said unification of the German statelets around a Prussian core in 1871 did not solve the identity problem. If anything, the culture clash between Bavarians, Hamburgers, Rhinelanders, etcetera, only exaggerated the problem. Germany's worst atrocities of the last hundred years were committed in part to set in stone one or other idea of what it meant to be German. From late colonial efforts in Africa and China to Hitler's quest for racial purity and East Germany's incarceration of its own people behind a wall, grand schemes were hatched to construct a New Germany. And the failure of each and every one of these atrocious schemes served only to deepen the nation's insecurity.

I agreed. 'I regularly receive calls from British friends upon their return from Majorca or Florida. They tell me that by breakfast time half the deckchairs are already covered in Adidas towels. "It's been getting worse in recent years," they say. Our nation is worried about its place in the sun. Don't you think?'

Herr Lauterbach decided he had reached his destination and got out.

I might have been a little harsh on him. Admittedly, I had baited him. But I didn't feel the slightest bit guilty. I could not stand obsessive babbling about identity. For my money, Germany had been handed the grand prize of late-twentieth-century history in 1989. Reunification was the great gift the country had pined for all along. Now that its wish had come true, the time for self-indulgent identity crises was over. Or was it?

*   *   *

The roads were clear and I stayed off the bumpy shoulders. I hadn't encountered another car for miles. The Red Racer was zipping around lakefronts like a bird out of its cage. Some lakes were coloured a minty green, dotted with floating logs like chocolate chips. Others were a leathery brown, shiny in parts, and wrinkly as the wind brushed over them. Others still were covered with a smooth silver skin, languid yet awkward. Every blemish inflicted by the weather showed up all the more clearly.

I travelled unobstructed around bend after bend. This is what it must feel like to be let loose in a museum after hours. The paying visitors had been sent home and I had the place to myself. I could slow down and step back from a vista to improve my view. Or I could speed through willy-nilly. No snob would call me an ignoramus. Traffic had died out. There were no ramblers, no bikes, no farming vehicles, no train tracks. The lakes, too, were unpopulated. I had expected the shores to be infested with anglers at the very least. But they had been sent home along with everyone else. Or had they finally got bored?

I passed derelict villages in abundance. They were perfect pictures of decay. The seamless composition of broken windows, missing doors, rotting roofs and cracked walls was surprisingly artistic. Mother Nature was reclaiming her territory in many small steps. Grass would creep over a fence, slip through the missing front door and make a new home inside. Other vegetation followed. Ivy climbed the drainpipes and took up residence on the roof. Eventually whole trees would grow inside the house. Their seed had been swept in by the wind through a broken window, found fertile ground inside and, over the years, pushed its way through successive floorboards. The trees had it easy in places where houses had burned down. The roofs soon fell in and took rows of bricks down with them.

Some home-owners had boarded up doors and windows in the vain hope of protecting their property. What for? Were they planning to come back to this derelict cemetery? By the time they return, ivy will have mounted even the most spirited fortifications.

Thatched cottages stood forlornly by the roadside, bullet holes in the outer walls, I noticed. The first few holes looked like marks of decay. Or maybe they were the results of sloppy building work. But the scattering marks of a shot-gun and the pockmarks of a machine gun were unmistakable. These holes had not been made recently. They were remnants from the last war that had never been wiped away. The bullet holes gave the houses an appearance of historical importance. They reminded me of Bosnia with its perfectly bland villages that had been turned into backdrops for documentaries in just one night of fighting. I stared unenthusiastically. The area had little to offer beyond its grim desolation.

Between Thurow and Dutzow I overtook a young boy walking a pig along the road. Neither pigs nor young boys are, of course, an unusual sight in the country. But these two were the first living beings I had seen for at least an hour. I parked the car and slowly walked back towards them. As I rounded a corner I saw the boy being dragged across a field by the galloping pig. The boy was desperately trying to hang on to its leash. In between gasps of exhaustion he tried to yell at it. But the pig with its snout barely above the ground only made the boy run faster.

I laughed and returned to the Red Racer, but the trusty vehicle would not start again. As much as I willed it and cursed it, the engine would no more than whimper. With every turn of the key, the whimpers sounded tinnier. Looking under the bonnet seemed pointless; I was more likely to turn the mechanical equivalent of a cold into full-blown lung infection. And didn't people die from lung infections? Nevertheless, I stuck my fingers through the slits in the front grill and tried to find a catch that would release the bonnet. I scratched and dirtied my fingers but the bonnet remained tightly shut.

How I envied the boy with the runaway pig now! Not a single car had passed while I grappled with my misery. The chances of help offering itself seemed slim at best. I set off to find someone with mechanical skills superior to mine, however unlikely the prospect in this forgotten land. After only a mile I reached a farm building. The door was wide open as on most old buildings here. But the house was not derelict. The smell of fresh food came wafting out and a modern telephone stood near the doorway. My knocks met with no response. In desperation I made two uninvited steps into the house and used the telephone to call the ADAC, the German equivalent of the AA.

The service engineer in a spotless yellow overall arrived within half an hour and quickly unlocked the bonnet. Unlike me, he didn't try to finger the grill but simply reached for a lever below the steering column. I kept my surprise about the lever's existence to myself. The engineer probed and searched and fiddled but couldn't find a fault. In the end, he got behind the wheel, turned the key and – as if nothing had happened – the engine resumed service. Now I felt doubly embarrassed for having called out the man in the no longer spotless yellow overall.

*　　*　　*

The Schaalsee is Germany's deepest lake. So said my guidebook. The border had cut right across the water, making it a doubly formidable barrier. VoPos patrolled the eastern shore.

From a cliff, the villagers in Lasahn have a perfect view of the western shore of the lake, but only a decade ago they might as well have looked at the Statue of Liberty. It had been equally inaccessible.

A Protestant church dominates Lasahn, a copper weathercock crowning the spire. Frau Kerner, a slovenly lady with a ring on every finger and wrinkly skin like crumpled paper, stepped out of the church. She saw me twisting my head to study the weathercock. 'We only got that in 1980,' she said. 'We hadn't had a weathercock since 1945. The Brits shot it down after they took the village. The British soldiers were rampaging around and decided to celebrate their success by having a shooting competition. *Bravissimo*, they shot the cock down.' I felt like saying: But the British army brought you freedom, well, at least peace, even if peace meant defeat. I stopped myself, amused that I should feel compelled to defend the British army.

Frau Kerner was spinning a ring around her index finger like a Wheel of Fortune. 'The Brits didn't stay long,' she said. 'Their generals in London and the Russians and the *Amis* [Americans] renegotiated the zonal borders. The Brits moved further west and the Russians took over the village. They were no better.'

I took a stroll along the shore. The old border patrol path had been turned into a walkway for weary city-dwellers and their dogs. All the watchtowers had been removed by an agency conveniently named *Gesellschaft zur Beseitigung und Verwertung von Altlasten und Altanlagen* (Demolition and Removal Company). The lake water was clear. The sun's rays bounced off the waves with a gentle glare. Herr Magnusson, a university teacher from Berlin, sat on a bench with me. He emphasized that he came from East Berlin. He was balding and a last puff of fizzy hair hovered at the back of his head like a speech bubble. 'Being a border guard seems not so bad after all.'

'Are you submitting a late application?' I stammered.

'Hardly. But sitting here, it doesn't seem all that bad. Sure, there was the blatant perversity of locking up sixteen million people. But pragmatic souls, or insensitive ones, might manage to forget, given the overwhelming beauty of their place of work. What a splendid way to spend your days – strolling along the lake shore, watching the birds. Only a spoilsport would say that Auschwitz was also in one of the prettiest parts of Poland.'

I hurriedly checked we hadn't been overheard. He laughed. 'For a Wessi, you are pretty paranoid. Looking around like that was such an Ossi thing to do.'

The road pulled away from the Schaalsee and wound its way through thick woods. Trees stood so tightly that the sun had failed to clear the fog in the undergrowth. The countryside north of Lasahn had been desolate, now it was outright lonely. There were no villages, not even pockmarked forgotten cottages. Every few miles the woods opened up and in narrow, dark clearings stood East German barracks. From here the border guards had swarmed out to patrol the lake shores. After the Wende they were forced to help with the removal of the fortifications. The irony of it was probably lost on them. I couldn't help but think of dogs being house-trained. The VoPos were caught making a nasty mess and their noses were pushed right back into it to teach them a lesson.

The barracks were in a sorry state. Any semblance of military discipline had long gone. The perimeter fences were still intact but behind them decay and destruction reigned. Roofs were sloping, window frames missing, walls had cracked like eggshells, parking lots were overgrown, entrance ways filled with litter and heavy steel doors had found their final resting place cocked half ajar. I felt almost grateful that the barracks had not been removed along with the border fortifications. Germans had coined the word *Schadenfreude*, and there was no better definition than the *Freude* (enjoyment) I got out of the *Schaden* (damage) inflicted on cosy VoPo forest retreats. This was a sentiment that some of the locals must have shared. The sorry state of the buildings was not entirely due to the voraciousness of Mother Nature. Hooded youths armed with baseball bats had lent her a helping hand. The steel doors bore their jackboot marks. Who ever would have guessed that thugs had emotions as subtle as *Schadenfreude*?

Closer to Zarrentin, the road became pitiful. The tarmac fizzled out and from underneath cobblestones emerged. The stones were the size of skulls. There was no cement or gravel in between them; cars bobbed up and down like ships in heavy seas. The Red Racer was not happy. The suspension gave off a low rolling groan interrupted by occasional cracks of thunder. All other sounds were drowned out by the noise. The Via Regia, the Roman highway that had crossed Germany two millennia ago, was said to have run down the east side of the Schaalsee. The possibility that I might be ruining my mother's car on a Roman highway made the ordeal only fractionally more tolerable. My mother did not speak much Latin.

I spotted more barracks. Approaching them, the road surface changed back to tarmac. It was still potholed East German tarmac but in comparison to the Roman road it felt like the thoroughfare of a highly advanced civilization. It was smooth and almost inaudible. The barracks were, of course, derelict. That was the real difference between East Germany and the Roman empire. Caesar's roads may not have been up to scratch, but his barracks had developed into cities, leaving a permanent mark on history. Cologne and London had grown out of legionnaires' camps. The only thing growing out of East German barracks were trees.

The tarmac ended and the skull road re-emerged as soon as I lost sight of the barracks. The self-serving VoPos had paved only the stretch of road they were using for their patrols of the nearby border. For a few seconds while travelling past the barracks I had enjoyed music from the car radio. It was music I recognized. The local radio stations played British and American Top 40 songs. They made me feel at home. Or maybe they just dulled the loneliness. In the middle of this train of thought, the tarmac had run out and the skull stone road cut off the radio.

Zarrentin lies at the southern tip of the Schaalsee. Travel books and leaflets at the tourist information centre spoke of Zarrentin's 'remarkable recovery'. The town had been so close to the border, and the water offered such an easy escape route, that East German officials all but ordered its mummification in the 1950s. Nobody was allowed to move here and residents were encouraged to vacate the town. Where friendly encouragement had not been enough, a lorry would arrive early in the morning and residents would be given an hour to pack their possessions. No new homes were built and none of the houses had received repair work for forty years.

Following the opening of the border, efforts were made to revive Zarrentin. A businessman from Hamburg donated money to build new piers and boat-houses along the lakefront. New residential buildings were erected and streets repaved. A 'nature walk' was created that stretched along the lake and through adjoining meadows. But to me Zarrentin still looked drab and depressing. The new prefab buildings only made the town look worse. They were ill-fitting, like mail-order dresses. I imagined town officials – probably socialist stalwarts – going to a trade show for prefab homes. Used to planning without interference, they would wave their arms and yell to salesmen: 'We'll have a couple of two-roofs, half a dozen of the two-garage model, then some with shop space on the ground floor, and one of the winter garden variety.' In an aside, the mayor would say: 'The winter garden is for my daughter.' For the journey back to Zarrentin, the new homes would be loaded on to lorries now no longer needed for deportations.

Of course, this was unfair. The riverside walk was pretty, even if so straight and flat that it attracted hordes of cyclists who forced pedestrians off the track. The rest of Zarrentin was not criminally ugly, just charmless. It had lost all the ghost town mystique. Today it had the atmosphere of a giant DIY store. That was as good as it got around here.

Longing for some West German sophistication, I headed towards Ratzeburg. This magnificent town has a fine cathedral and a reputation as a rowing mecca, a German Henley-on-Thames, though the former's annual regatta is not so famous. Boating conditions on Lake Ratzeburg, however, are infinitely superior. The town was built on an island at the southern tip of the 6-mile-long lake. Bridges and pathways on three sides connected it to the mainland. The centre is dominated by designer boutiques while the red-brick Gothic cathedral occupies the highest point on the island.

If Ratzeburg is the German rowing mecca, then the loftily titled Rowing Academy is its main temple. It sits by the water's edge, stretching out its landing stages like octopus arms. The academy is a national training centre for Olympians, with a fully equipped boat-house, high-tech gym, video monitoring facilities and bedrooms for the athletes. As a teenager, I had trained here twice a year with my school team during vacations. The trips often ran into terse opposition from left-wing teachers. To them we were continuing where the Hitler Youth had left off. Rowing trained one to be obedient and to value bodily fitness above individuality or creativity, they claimed. Competing in national championships was denounced as a form of élitism. We schoolboy rowers were suspected of being more interested in attracting hero-worship than in developing critical faculties.

The left-wing teachers were even more critical of professional sportsmen. Cheering for Boris Becker or Jürgen Klinsmann was frowned upon. The teachers wanted Germany to be a hero-free zone. It was their response to the Nazis' exaggerated sense of German heroism. By banning the idolizing of sports figures they believed Führer cults and talk of master races could be banished for ever.

As I parked the car at the water's edge, I recognized that in Ratzeburg at least these sentiments must have changed. Germany's national colours were everywhere. Rowers wore black-red-and-gold tops and their oars were similarly painted. At the back of the boat-house, windows and cars were draped in German flags, including one pre-war flag with the Reich's eagle.

I walked up to Ratzeburg's cathedral, towering high above the Rowing Academy. In all the years I had come here, I had never made it up the hill. The concerned teachers had probably suspected as much. A Bach recital was in progress behind the thick red-brick walls. Blond choir boys were rehearsing for a Good Friday concert. A note on the church door said the concert would start 'at 15.30, the hour of the Lord's death'. The adjoining cemetery offered a splendid view of the lake. Like the Schaalsee, Lake Ratzeburg had been cut in half by the border. The surrealism of eight boys and a cox rowing in a no-man's-land, watched by armed guards in ugly watchtowers, had made our outings seem a little more thrilling.

I decided to give youth hostels another chance – never mind the miserable time I had had in Dassow. The hostels are quintessentially German in their sullen hospitality. There are 620 hostels in Germany, the highest number worldwide. Sweden comes second with 310. England and Wales together have 214 hostels, according to a brochure in the foyer. I slept very well.

The Red Racer lumbered up a hill on the outskirts of Ratzeburg. At a red light, I spotted the barracks of the *Bundesgrenzschutz*, a special West German police unit. Until 1990, the unit had patrolled the border. Following reunification, it assumed responsibility for the new eastern border *vis-à-vis* Poland. So what was the *Bundesgrenzschutz* still doing here, several hundred miles from Polish soil?

I spoke to a moustachioed major at the gate. 'Under no circumstances could our regiment move from Ratzeburg,' he intoned. 'We are an important economic factor in the region. We create many jobs, even for foreigners. We need a lot of cleaning personnel. Most of the cleaning we do ourselves, of course. But now that the Cold War is over we have relaxed some of the drills like making recruits clean vehicles with toothbrushes.' He seemed particularly pleased with this humanitarian gesture. The barracks looked spotless. The freshly painted off-white walls framed net-curtained windows. What a contrast to the derelict VoPo buildings.

I headed back to the border to look for more fortifications. After my brief glimpse of the land border at Schlutup, all my encounters with watchtowers had been by the water. An uneasy suspense built up as I approached the dividing line that was still marked on the road atlas. Unthinkingly, my father had given me a 1988/89 edition when I asked to borrow his atlas. This turned out to be a fortuitous mistake. The thick red line running through Germany north to south like a river of hot lava was unmissable, making the atlas an invaluable guide for my venture. With my eyes trained on the countryside to spot any slight difference in the lie of the land, I steered the Red Racer towards Stalin's giant garden fence. And past it, as it turned out. I missed the only clue to the exact location of the border and hurtled on for a good few miles. The clue was the roadside line of trees. Beech tree-lines were very common in northern Germany and highway B208 was no exception. But near the village of Mustin, the line was interrupted for a few hundred yards and then started up again. Staring into the middle distance I hadn't noticed the interruption. All other traces of heavy fortification had gone. It was as if the division of Germany had simply been erased. The gap in the tree-line was the last reminder of division. When the VoPos erected the *Antifaschistischer Schutzwall*, the trees must have looked like a disturbing connection between the two Germanys, a natural bridge between the people they were so desperately trying to prise apart, a threat to the higher goals of Marx's historical materialism and an all too visible bond with the capitalist neighbour. Or maybe they were just in the line of fire. Whatever the reason, the trees had been removed by the border builders.

When I pulled over, I found another leftover from the Cold War. The VoPo patrol track was still faintly visible in the muddy ground. It ran parallel to the border line and looked rather more inviting than it turned out to be. The Red Racer was wailing as I zigzagged between the puddles. The wheels were kicked deep into the suspension every time I hit a crater.

I carried on for several miles, chiefly because trying to turn round in this muddy mess promised to bring an early end to my journey. Much to my surprise, I stumbled upon a tiny watchtower. This wasn't a concrete tower of the brutalist variety I had encountered so far but a rather slight and rusty metal frame, only about 15-feet high. The tower wouldn't have looked out of place in a playground between swings and slides. With misplaced boyish enthusiasm, I began to climb the steel ladder. Unfortunately, ten years of acid rain and world peace had had a distinctly corrosive effect on the little tower. My hands were soiled with splintery rust and the whole structure creaked unnervingly. But the view from the top made up for much of the discomfort. The VoPos couldn't have guarded a more serene composition of groves and thickets. I was not sure they had particularly appreciated it. One didn't have to be Sherlock Holmes to imagine how the guards had spent their time up here. The floor of the observation post was covered with hundreds of cigarette butts and shredded cigarette packs. A whole tobacco harvest must have been consumed in the tower. East German citizens may take some comfort from the fact that many of the guards that once imprisoned them will now be coughing in a cancer ward.

Bracing myself for a small disaster, I turned the Red Racer around. But without a hint of drama I managed to circumnavigate the tower and head back towards the B208. The guidebook had promised a memorial stone close to the border. The book called it an 'interesting monument'. Was this a rare admission that most monuments are pretty dull? I spotted the monument between two beech trees. The dark stone was predictably sombre. The inscription, visible to motorists going west, read 'Unity and Justice and Liberty', the motto of the Federal Republic. Interestingly, however, a cardboard sign had been attached to the back of the stone, visible to motorists heading the other way. It read: 'Division and Deutschmarks and Loneliness'.

Bent over my various maps, atlases and guidebooks I spotted Mölln. The name itself sounded odd enough to merit a visit. Mölln is a smaller version of Ratzeburg. The centre is wedged in between the School Lake and the Town Lake, or Schulsee and Stadtsee, on a narrow peninsula. Mölln has a pretty cathedral and wonky half-timbered houses. Most people come to this sleepy West German town in the first place to see the birthplace of Till Eulenspiegel, the practical joker who lived here in the sixteenth century. Eulenspiegel amused himself – and generations of German children – by taking people all too literally. When he worked as a barber's assistant, he was sent on an errand. The master barber told him: 'See that house across the street with the high window? Go there.' Eulenspiegel proceeded to break the window to enter the house.

The town enthusiastically embraces the joker even though it had been the butt of many of his jokes. The *MS Eulenspiegel* cruiser takes visitors on tours of the lakes. At the Eulenspiegel museum, Eulenspiegel's deeds are inevitably subjected to tortured analysis. One note read: 'Eulenspiegel wanted to show people that steadfastly sticking to the letter of what was said is harmful. People should instead use their own minds.' Never mind that fables and sagas were meant to be self-evident. In Germany, Eulenspiegel's tales – understood by every child – had to be subjected to an official interpretation.

A lady at the museum told me the spirit of Eulenspiegel lived on in Mölln. Local West German youths had fooled a twenty-year-old Ossi right after the Wende. He had asked why there were so many animals on Mölln's streets. The group of jokers said that it regularly rained cats and dogs here. The Ossi had been so overwhelmed by the luxury in which West Germans lived that he didn't question the explanation.

The eight-foot concrete post sparkled black, red and golden. It stood by the roadside on a farmer's yard in Lehmrade. I probably would have missed it, if it hadn't been for my interest in the border. Similar posts had once marked the entire East German frontier. Each bore a metal plaque inscribed with hammer and sickle.

Frau Brüggemann watched as I got out of the car. She was a short and rugged woman who had probably worked in the fields all her life. I thought the border would be a universal topic of conversation around here and asked her what it was like to have the Iron Curtain run through one's carrot garden.

'The border? That's five kilometres further. At Gudow. Our fields hardly touched the border.'

But what was the border post doing here then?

'The post?' She seemed unsure of my intentions. 'That post, yes. My son bought it when the border was removed. Lovely, no?'

Why did he buy it?

'You know what – someone had to keep them. You couldn't throw them away. We lived with the border for forty years. We didn't like it but we lived with it. It meant something. Now the posts stand on the border between us and the neighbour. Some borders are removed but most stay.'

How much had he paid for it?

'I have no idea. But he would probably sell it to you for 150 marks.'

I crossed into East Germany at Gudow, recognizing the border easily enough now. The gap in the line of trees was unmistakable. This Cold War scar had become something of an unofficial memorial. The trees on both sides were unusually high here. I was reminded of walking down the centre aisle of a cathedral. As I passed the gap at the border, the view was unobstructed for a few seconds. Then the tree-line started up again. Interrupted by the trees, the fields and the sky flickered past in jerky movements as in an early black-and-white film.

Traffic on the road south was negligible. People crossed the border to work in the east or shop in the west, but few wanted to drive along the border now that it was open. By the time I reached the village of Gresse I was bored and looked for a cross-border route. My map showed a straight road leading from Gresse directly to the border and across it. On the 5-mile journey I passed Heidekrug, Schwanheide, Zweedorf and Dalldorf. Before the Wende, this road must have been one of the world's longest cul-de-sacs.

Now, following the arrival of the deutschmark, it had acquired a uniformity that surpassed even the results of forty years of socialism. New homes were being built from Gresse to Dalldorf, replacing the squat brick edifices that had been amended and extended throughout the Cold War. Next to the new deutschmark homes, the socialist botched jobs looked almost charming. Everything on the Ossi houses seemed expandable. Roofs had been raised, bathrooms added, new kitchens attached, winter gardens tacked on, balconies appended. The new deutschmark homes, on the other hand, were uniform and bland. They had red walls, red roofs and white doors and windows. The red was of a uniform hue and the windows and doors all came from the same manufacturer. The pattern was repeated in every village. Some front doors were brown rather than white. That was the height of East Germany's new-found individualism.

Following the opening of the border, a salesman for red houses with red roofs and white windows and doors had cleaned up here, Herr Beuter said. He was leaning against his grey, decrepit concrete box. He had resisted. The sales pitch for the deutschmark villas was always the same. Herr Beuter put on what he thought was an oily West German accent: 'My dear Frau Schmidt, times have changed. Nobody wants to live in a grey old box with funny extensions in this day and age. Look, all your neighbours have already bought this red model with white luxury features. You can't let the community down.' The appeal to communal solidarity was guaranteed to close the deal in a formerly socialist society, Herr Beuter said.

I crossed the border at Dalldorf. The first house on the western side was also a red-red-white-white construction.

3

UPSTREAM

THROUGH THE CAR WINDOW I watched a choir of eight homeless people in Lauenburg. They sat at a rickety bus shelter on a cliff high above the River Elbe in a downpour and whiled the hours away merrily. They sang Russian folksongs and sentimental German *Lieder*. Sometimes they would hold hands and sometimes they were even in tune. One man with a half-buttoned-up cuff-link shirt was conducting the choir with a rolled-up newspaper. Or maybe he was just waving his arms around to keep warm.

Near Lauenberg, the border hit the Elbe and for the next hundred miles ran along the river. The Elbe had become a symbol of German division. All through the Cold War, Bonn and East Berlin argued over whether the border was in the middle of the river or on the eastern side. The conflict was never resolved and for forty years there was hardly any traffic on this most German of rivers. The River Rhine had always been a European river, flowing through Switzerland, France, Germany, Belgium and Holland. Thomas Carlyle even called the Rhine his 'first idea of a world river'. But the Elbe was undeniably German. Every ancient map of Germany, in whatever guise, has incorporated it. The Elbe ran through Charlemagne's Holy Roman Empire, the German Reich of 1871 and Hitler's Third Reich. In 1945, Allied and Soviet troops first met and shook hands at Torgau on the Elbe. Neither side crossed the river and soon enough they fortified their respective riverbanks.

The Elbe marks not only a political but also a cultural divide on a par with the English Channel. The stream formed the western frontier of

Prussia – the source of all German evil, according to Rhinelanders and Bavarians. Konrad Adenauer, the first West German Chancellor, was from the Rhineland. When Adenauer took a train from Bonn, the new capital on the Rhine, to Berlin, the old Prussian capital, he pulled down the blinds in his carriage as the train crossed the Elbe and said: 'Asia starts here.' Recounting this anecdote, Jan Morris remarked: 'The English, in their jingo days, meant the same when they said that wogs began at Calais.'

Through my car window in Lauenburg, I could see the newly resumed river traffic on the Elbe. In a not so stately procession, the heavy container ships and freighters with exotic flags pushed their way upstream from Hamburg to the nether regions of Prussia. They were enveloped in clouds of rain but nevertheless jockeyed for positions in the fast-moving middle of the stream.

I followed the run of the Elbe. At Boizenburg, a border crossing point had operated next to the river. A surprising proportion of the fortifications still existed. They consisted exclusively of concrete. I was reminded of P. J. O'Rourke's trip to Warsaw in the early 1980s. He was baffled at how so many Poles could live in concrete houses and tower blocks devoid of any vegetation. 'Commies love concrete,' he concluded. The border at Boizenburg displayed a similar love of cement. I passed concrete terraces, concrete road lamps, concrete boulders used as crash barriers, and concrete fence posts shielding a concrete watchtower. A sign on the tower advertised: Checkpoint Harry, Restaurant & Partyservice, Rex Pilsner. The chips 'n' sausage fast-food stand was built into a concrete hut once used by VoPos to check passports. I ordered a cup of soup. Harry told me he'd bought this concrete wasteland in 1990. Business was good. The East German pilsner he sold was more popular than Wessi beers like Becks.

Bizarrely, there were no hotels in Boizenburg, an important rail, road and river junction. A pub landlord suggested looking for bed-and-breakfast signs, I was sceptical. Ten years in a market economy, I groaned, and you still haven't built a hotel. I kerb-crawled through Boizenburg with my headlights full on. It was a miracle I didn't get arrested. Maybe Boizenburg had neither hotel rooms nor prison cells.

On Schwanheider Weg I eventually found Frau Fröhlich who rented out rooms in her three-storey house. The word *fröhlich* means cheerful, and Frau Fröhlich was the embodiment of merriness. Her B & B business was going very well. It gave her something to do now that the children were gone and her husband was away during the week, working in West Germany. It was fun to make your own money, said the youthful forty-year-old. When I asked her about the time before the Wende, she became nostalgic. 'Until 1972, access to Boizenburg was totally restricted because we were so close to the border. We were a little bit sorry when the restrictions were lifted. Inside the restricted zone you got extra rations. When everyone received two bananas in the winter, then the people in the restricted zone got four. Oh, well, now we can have as many as we want.' The next morning Frau Fröhlich served six different types of ham at breakfast. I told her it was the best breakfast in the whole of East Germany. 'Thanks. I get the ham from a private butcher. We want to enjoy life, don't we?' I promised to come back, or at least to enjoy life.

Driving out of Boizenburg, I heard the most peculiar announcement on the radio. Following the news, a panting reporter rattled through the traffic bulletin. Then he stopped to catch his breath and said in a decidedly solemn voice: 'This evening we expect a strong increase in toad migration on the roads. The police have asked motorists to be especially careful.' I was sure that's what he had said. Images came to mind of giant toads leaping down a motorway and devouring articulated lorries, King Kong-style. It seemed too ridiculous. Had I become incapable of understanding my mother tongue? I banished the toad exodus from my mind.

The Red Racer zipped along the western riverside. A mountain range snaked its way along the Elbe. The hills reached right down to the water. The hilltops afforded magnificent views of the flat wetlands in the east. Hemmed in on the western side, the Elbe regularly flooded the eastern river basin. The west had the geographical as well as the moral high ground, I thought smugly.

I climbed a wooden observation tower on a hilltop. The planks were sodden and slippery but the view was a royal reward for the moments of panic. The silvery river glistened in the rain. Its majestic bends wound their way around the hills. Placidly, it lay between the mountains and the wetlands like the strong arm of a father keeping his warring children apart. The river still had the appearance of a border, if no longer between two countries then at least between two ways of life: the hunters of the hill range and the gatherers of the marshes.

The Elbe had been a border that East Germany did not find difficult to guard. Keen swimmers might have made it through the fast-moving stream, but the boggy lowlands alongside it are a formidable natural barrier. Thanks to biannual floods, the river basin is wet all year round. From my wooden tower I could see ten miles into East Germany. Lagoons by the river gave way to reservoirs. Further back was a maze of pools and ponds. The area was dotted with glistening waterways as if someone had drawn lines and spots with a silver crayon. It was too swampy and messy for an escape route.

At Bleckede, I waited for the ferry. Dozens of small ferry services had sprung up along the river after the Wende. It was clearly a good business in an area where the few existing bridges were destroyed during or after the war.

I ate apple-cake in a small café by the ferry terminal and watched a man standing at the bar with a beer in one hand and his head resting on the other. He was fast asleep, probably the first man I had seen sleeping upright. Occasionally, he would snore with a jolt. Otherwise he was entirely stable. After a few minutes the waitress came over, looking embarrassed. 'His name is Bernhard,' she said. Did he do this often? Yes. We stared at him for a full minute. His head jerked sideways but the beer glass didn't move. When his snores became more frequent, the waitress said with heightened embarrassment: 'I was wondering if you could persuade him to leave.' She flicked her hand, suggesting he might have hit her before. Outside the ferry sounded its horn as it was docking. I got up and quickly called out in passing: 'Herr Bernhard, sleeping is best done at home.' He lifted his head and gave me a hazy stare. I hurried out the door. Herr Bernhard hurried after me. Fearing grevious bodily harm I locked myself in the Red Racer. Herr Bernhard came blundering out. He grabbed a bicycle leaning against the café door and struggled to get on the seat. He flip-flopped across the road and cycled straight on to the ferry. The choreography was masterful but I decided to wait for the next ferry.

Ten minutes passed before it returned to pick me up. When I finally made it across and rode along the dyke, I overtook Herr Bernhard no more than two hundred yards from the ferry terminal. His cycling style had become even more erratic and error-prone. It seemed he had fallen asleep again.

At Neu-Wendischtun, I passed a mean-looking watchtower on the dyke. It was much higher than the specimens I had previously encountered and its orange-tinted mirror-glass windows looked like motionless bug eyes. The tower was spotless to the point of seeming to be still in operation. Part of a master race of watchtowers. Then I saw a hand-written sign on the door: 'This border watchtower from the wretched past of German division and distress has for ever lost its malign function. It is now in private ownership and is only used for peaceful and humanitarian ends.'

I considered ringing a doorbell at one of the surrounding farm buildings to visit the tower. While I pondered whether my journey qualified as either peaceful or humanitarian, Herr Bernhard came back into view. He was in serious distress, lurching dangerously close to the water. And it was all my fault that he was out here rather than peacefully standing at the bar. I was definitely disqualified from claiming humanitarian status, I decided, and sped off.

Further upstream at Neu-Darchau I passed farmhouses that stood directly behind the dyke. I was driving on the narrow VoPo patrol track on the dyke, level with the first floors of the houses. I could easily look into the farmers' bedrooms, but, having made enough mischief for one day, I turned off the track. Immediately I hit the worst bit of road since the muddy patrol track on the border near Ratzeburg. At one point I was forced to back into an entrance to a marshy field to let a slow-moving tractor pass. When I tried to pull out again the wheels span. The Red Racer failed to move. No amount of gentle nudging of the clutch would propel me out of the mess. I could still see the tractor at the end of the road and decided to cut my losses. I sprinted after it, only to find myself being chased by the farmer's dog which had been trotting next to the tractor. I jumped up to the cabin as the dog snapped at my heels and begged the farmer to pull my car out. He seemed taken aback, by my appearance as much as by my request. He had not seen me coming up behind him, nor had he seen me getting stuck. But he took pity on me. Or maybe he was just glad I was driving on the road rather than the patrol track atop the dyke where I could spy like a VoPo.

One of the joys of travelling along the Elbe was the multiplicity of rare birds in the river basin. I came to this conclusion not as a seasoned birdwatcher but as a reader of noticeboards. I grew up in a city and can barely tell the difference between a mouse and a rat. I had no idea if the beaky animal winging its way over the river was a duck, goose or swan, let alone a crane or stork. I did, however, recognize the sight of clever noticeboards, and a great number of them here extolled the area's multiplicity of rare birds. If the birds were anything as multiplicitous as the boards, then I had stumbled upon a hotbed of feathery flapping.

Apparently, the Elbe basin is the bird equivalent of a spaghetti junction. The noticeboards explained that swarms of ducks, geese and swans use the marshes as a pitstop on the way to their Scandinavian breeding grounds in the spring and again in the autumn on the way back to their Atlantic winter camps. They congregate here for a while before setting off for their various destinations. I imagined it as somewhat similar to west London's Hangar Lane gyratory system where bleary-eyed drivers congregate in the morning rush hour and again in the afternoon on their way back to base camp. Of course, the birds had picked a prettier spot. It was much quieter than Neasden. For four decades, the VoPos had kept out traffic, rowdy kids and poisonous factories. The area was effectively cut off during the Cold War, creating ideal conditions for the birds.

Noticeboard writers possess a universal gift to bore. I found this favourite prejudice of mine amply confirmed. The Elbe basin harboured past masters. Curious visitors were informed on various boards that 700 varieties of butterflies lived by the river. Many were threatened with extinction, including the *Hipparchia Statilinus*, the *Syntomys Phegea* and the *Cucullia Argentea*. Could anyone remember these Latin names long enough to petition politicians or write angry letters?

According to the boards, there were a total of 151 species of birds. My interest was aroused by the *Raubwürger* ('Thieving Choker'), or *Lanius Excubitor*. Sadly, there was no picture of this charming fellow. There were, however, pictures of some of the 1,050 different types of grass.

Herr Mahlzahn had been standing by the noticeboard for some time, clutching a pair of binoculars and sketching feathered wings with a stubby pencil. Reluctantly he let himself be drawn into conversation. I remarked that birds and bureaucrats had been the only beneficiaries of the division of Germany. He agreed, calling the untouched strip of land running along the border East Germany's 'green unification dowry'. Did he want to award the bird lovers in East Berlin medals for their conservationist efforts? I didn't dare ask and instead said: 'Wonderful.'

'Wonderful?' He looked angry and dropped his pencil. 'The situation is not wonderful. It's terrible. It's a crime. The cars are disturbing the *Remiz Pendulinus* and the *Athene Noctua*. The *Asio Otus* is in serious danger and I won't even speak of the *Anthus Pratensis*. The opening of the border has the potential to create an animal holocaust. The farmers are now allowed back on their fields and have nothing better to do than to cover them with dung. The tourists are chasing the birds away as soon as they arrive.'

I muttered, '. . . guess that's the way it goes.'

'That is not the way it goes. We will not tolerate it. We are actively pursuing the creation of a nature reserve covering the whole of the Elbe basin and we have made excellent progress.' Herr Mahlzahn explained that, after the Wende, East Germans and West Germans had formed an environmental group to save the marshes for the birds. He said it was the region's most critical election issue in recent years. Hard campaigns had been fought and ministerial endorsements had been won. An area covering 24,000 hectares had already been given special status and soon UNESCO would be petitioned to declare the whole Elbe basin a 'biosphere reservation'. But the crusade had not yet reached its goal. Environmentalists wanted to convert several smaller nature reserves into one Über-reserve. The flooding areas must be extended to create new swampy nesting grounds for our feathered friends, Herr Mahlzahn demanded, and hunting had to be banned along the former border. West German hunters had apparently invaded the marshes after the Wende. Herr Mahlzahn called them 'crane killers'.

'This evening we expect a strong increase in toad migration on the roads. The police have asked motorists to be especially careful.' I was listening to the radio news in the car. The mystifying announcement was repeated. So I had not misunderstood the bulletin in the morning. Hordes of beady-eyed King Kong killer toads would indeed be dining on articulated lorries.

The situation took on an extra air of crisis when I spotted an unorthodox sign by the roadside. Below a red triangle were the hand-painted words: TOAD MIGRATION. An exclamation mark hovered clumsily on the edge of the sign. Were neighbourhood watches and vigilantes preparing for an imminent attack?

The sign was leaning against a roadside crash barrier. Underneath the barrier ran an 8-inch-high strip of plastic parallel to the road. After driving along the plastic barrier for several hundred yards I pulled over. The back of the strip was crawling with insects, worms and, yes, toads. They were, however, ordinary toads. In a rush, several of them would run against the plastic barrier, bounce back and try again. So this was the toad migration.

A passing cyclist said the barrier had been erected to protect the poor buggers from being squashed on the tarmac by passing cars. Herr Schuster had a flat tyre and was pushing his bike. Nevertheless, he seemed in high spirits. He said East German officials in the environment ministry were probably responsible for the toad wall; they had plenty of experience of stopping mass migrations. He put on a Saxon accent: 'We do the following: first, build a wall, then, monopolize the media for propaganda reasons. We can use radio and television announcements to curb the migration. Just like the old days.'

I told him West German officials would most likely answer: 'Typical. You Ossis will never change. You only know one answer to a problem, that's building a wall. Freedom and environmentalism are inseparable.'

Herr Schuster's Ossi official replied: '*Bitte, bitte*. I think after closer scrutiny you will find that this is a perfect example of the dialectic of walls. They can serve good purposes as well as bad ones. The toad wall is a step forward in the historical development of walls.'

My Wessi official was getting more irate: 'So you think you know what's best for the toads? You just want to lock them up like cattle!'

'*Ja?*' challenged the Ossi official defiantly. 'What would you do instead? Tear down the wall and let the toads run free? They will waddle right on to the road and get run over by some fat Mercedes.'

We giggled like schoolchildren.

'But honestly,' Herr Schuster's voice took on a more earnest tone. 'Environmentalism is actually one of the few issues that Ossis and Wessis don't argue over. The environment is not controversial – it affects both sides in the same way. It's quite apolitical. And Ossis and Wessis are grateful to have something they can agree on. Hence everyone embraces environmentalism. The Green Party is sometimes even outflanked by right-wingers. Environmentalism is the new German panacea.'

I told Herr Schuster that most of the land along the border from the coast down had been returned to natural use. Some meadows were left to their own devices, others had become full-blown reserves. Forests were always preserved. In the clearings, however, new homes quickly went up.

'That doesn't surprise me,' said Herr Schuster. 'If cornered, it has been said, a Frenchman will flee to a salon or start a revolution. A German will withdraw to nature.'

We shook hands conspiratorially and said our good-byes.

A flag beckoned me to the forest's edge. The bright red, yellow and blue fabric sat awkwardly in the greenery. I didn't recognize the colours of the flag but remembered the Cameroon football team had worn similarly garish garb. By an opening in the thick pine curtain stood a sign: 'Village Republic Rüterberg. For 22 years, the 150 inhabitants of Rüterberg lived totally locked up between two fences. A single gate was the only entrance to the village. On 8 November 1989, the inhabitants declared their community a village republic.'

Rüterberg is an East German river village with a fascinating history and a magnificent view. During the Cold War, a metal fence kept inhabitants away from the Elbe. The same was true for most river villages, but Rüterberg had suffered doubly. It was deemed to be so close to the water and so difficult to guard that East Germany's wall builders fenced in the village on all sides. Between 1967 and 1989, Rüterberg was a riverine Alcatraz. It was cut off from both West Germany and East Germany. Heavily armed Ossi soldiers guarded the only gate in the fence. Visitors needed special permits to enter the village. Inhabitants had to undergo strict checks before they were let out for a few hours.

Decades of incarceration had eliminated all commerce in Rüterberg. Its brick factory was destroyed and farming made almost impossible. The inhabitants became dependent on hand-outs from their captors. Rüterberg was turned into a totalitarian showcase.

On the day before the Wall collapsed in Berlin, human spirits re-awakened. Buoyed by the demonstrations in Leipzig and East Berlin, the imprisoned villagers, symbolically at least, freed themselves from their captors with a declaration of independence. They created Germany's first village republic since Bismarck's unification of fiefdoms and statelets. Party officials and soldiers were so demoralized by events in the capital they put up no resistance. Two days later the guards at the gate were withdrawn, opening up the village for the first time in twenty-two years. It took the villagers another two years of bureaucratic wrangling to get the title 'Village Republic Rüterberg' recognized in German law. Since 1991, the republic has had its own administration and its own red, yellow and blue flag. The villagers celebrated with delegations from New Zealand, America, Norway and Uzbekistan. President Nelson Mandela of South Africa sent his personal greetings.

I learned all this from the republic's official history. The author, Herr Rasenberger, had witnessed life in Rüterberg before the fence came down. 'We had invited my parents,' he recalled. 'Six weeks in advance, as was demanded, we sent in a form asking for them to be allowed into the border area. After a while we received an answer. Their entry would not be permitted.' Herr Rasenberger fought a war of nerves with party officials but their refusal was steadfast. Visits would be approved only on two occasions, he was told: major anniversaries and life-threatening illnesses. Herr Rasenberger's father was finally able to visit the village after he had fallen ill with a heart problem.

On 14 July 1991, the day Rüterberg was officially granted its independence, Herr Rasenberger wrote: 'This day was a celebration of our love of life. In all humility, the day should be seen as an act of providence.' His book, *The Village Republic*, was published soon afterwards. But Rüterberg's love of life seemed to have taken a beating since then. I entered the village on a crumbling road. Rüterberg now had to maintain its own roads as a supposedly sovereign entity, but had no money to do so. There were still no jobs in the village. The only source of income was from visitors. The local pub earned a few deutschmarks during regular tourist invasions. Poles and Dutchmen descended by the busload. They eagerly peered through every window and subjected the villagers to an intense scrutiny not experienced during twenty-two years of being locked up. Flower pots were knocked over and vegetable gardens trampled in stampedes to get close to the dyke where the fence had stood.

To guard their properties against visitors, the villagers employed some of the techniques they had been subjected to before 1989. Sturdy metal gates closed off most driveways. Shepherd dogs on long leashes patrolled backyards. One sign depicting a menacing dog read: 'I watch here.' Rüterberg's VoPo watchtower was fenced in especially high, bearing a large 'Private' sign. The tower had been converted to residential use but the orange-tinted mirror-glass windows still looked terrifying. The house opposite and a few others bore 'For Sale' signs.

Most Rüterbergers I approached seemed fearful of speaking to strangers. The few I spoke to in the Elbklause pub said they were glad the fence was gone, 'The security then was phenomenal.'

I met Rüterberg's head of state at his riverside cottage. Mayor Schmechel was a brutish man. He had transformed himself from a farmer into something more intellectual with the help of half-moon glasses. I asked if I could attend the meeting of the village council that day. He shot a sceptical glance over the rim of his glasses. I persisted. 'After all, if Rüterberg is a republic, the council must be your parliament. And in republics, parliaments meet publicly.' Reluctantly, he agreed.

I entered the dingy meeting room through a side door and took a seat at the back. Herr Schmechel sat at a large desk covered with official papers. Three 'parliamentarians' were seated in front of him. The first was a woman with black hair and piercing eyes. I guessed she was about thirty-five years old and probably a former border guard. She eyed me suspiciously. Next to her was a fifty-year-old man with a shaggy beard. A teacher, I decided. Next to him sat a farmer in his sixties who kept mum for most of the session.

Herr Schmechel began the democratic procedure with the words: 'Well,

guys, looks like the other three won't show up.' Three heads nodded in
agreement. 'Today we have a guest. What to do you think? Should we let
him stay?' I tried to smile. The teacher turned to Herr Schmechel: 'What?
Can anyone just walk in and watch? Ten years ago, that's for sure, we'd
know exactly why he was here. But with the Stasi gone, you never know
any more what side they come from.' The others nodded. But the mayor
allowed me to stay after I repeated my little speech about the village being
a republic and holding parliamentary sessions in public. 'Of course, we
are a republic. No question,' he said.

The first item on the agenda was the annual budget. Herr Schmechel
handed out several pages filled with spread sheets and pointed to the
federal subsidies. 'We'll keep quiet about this one. Not for the public.'
He threw me an icy glance. My smile turned into a nervous grin. Soon
the four were involved in a passionate debate about dog taxation. Had
everyone paid the tax? What about the new couple and their dog? Were
there twenty-nine or thirty dogs in the republic? Did everyone who had
two dogs declare the second one? Herr Schmechel turned to the silent
farmer: 'What do you think – is it twenty-nine or thirty?' Resting his head
on one arm, the farmer maintained his silence. He had fallen asleep. Herr
Schmechel grew agitated when the council failed to make any progress in
the dog taxation debate. 'We're just not getting this done. God, why can't
everyone agree on something? I hereby move the item on the agenda to
the non-public part of the meeting. We'll sort this out afterwards.' This
solution pleased him.

Next on the agenda was changes to building regulations. The teacher
and the border guard immediately asked for this item to be moved to the
non-public part of the meeting as well. But Herr Schmechel said: 'Just
quickly, let's do the new tower.'

'What new tower?' the border guard asked.

'The observation tower that'll be put on the dyke to watch the river
birds.'

'But I thought it'll be built on the rubbish dumping ground. Why
should it be on the dyke?' she insisted.

'It must be on the dyke. The people from the environment office in
Boizenburg were here and said we won't have to pay a single mark for it.
They'll build the tower and everything. Isn't that great?'

The border guard shook her head. 'But you never told us it'll be on
the dyke directly in the village. That will mean more cars coming through.
More visitors running around. We need to protect the village.'

'But Boizenburg will pay us 3,000 marks for every car parking space. It'll look great in the budget.'

'That's a one-off though, isn't it?' she asked. 'It'll only help us next year.'

Herr Schmechel stared helplessly at the walls. He seemed to be counting the fake flowers in the room – and there was no shortage. The debating chamber was decorated with flowery curtains, flowery wallpaper and a flower motif tablecloth. Finally he spoke: 'OK, it's a one-off, but I think it would be best if we now moved to the non-public part of the meeting.' Four pairs of eyes turned towards me. I picked up my coat and gladly followed their invitation to leave. I had seen quite enough of East German republicanism.

Further upstream at Lenzen I sighted another watchtower on the dyke. Someone had scribbled 'WC' on the outside of the concrete observation post. How apt, I thought. But when I opened the tower's door I was surprised to find that it actually had been converted into a public lavatory. Brand-new toilets and washing facilities were awaiting sweaty ramblers and cyclists. The shiny white tiles contrasted markedly with the shabby exterior. The stainless steel toilet bowl and the gleaming wash basin were made in Italy and had the self-assured elegance East Germany was so desperately lacking.

Still on the eastern riverside, I stopped in Dömitz to find a hotel. Until 1945, a railway bridge and a car bridge had spanned the Elbe here. The retreating German army destroyed both to slow down the Allied advance on Berlin. During the Cold War there seemed little point rebuilding the bridges, but unification had sparked a desire to reconnect the two river banks. In 1992, a new arched steel bridge was unveiled. The obvious symbolism of physically rejoining east and west attracted politicians and celebrities to the opening. Pictures of the festivities even appeared in my guidebooks.

However, the bridge was empty when I crossed it, and so was Dömitz. The town was lifeless. The Kaufhaus building had been leased to one West German department-store chain after another over the years. None of them could turn a profit in Dömitz. Now the empty shell of the building hovered over the town centre like a messenger of doom. Few other shops were open.

Standing at a bus stop, Frau Belzer glanced at me, uncertain whether I wanted to snatch her purse. 'Dömitzers must be self-sufficient,' I remarked. 'Nobody seems to go shopping here.'

Frau Belzer smiled. 'Dömitzers? Oh, there are so few of us nowadays,' she said and her smile faded. 'The young people are all leaving. This is an empty land, dear, a very empty land. Before the Wende, the authorities occasionally forced people to leave. Undesirable subjects, you know. They didn't want them close to the border. Today, our youngest and brightest leave without force. As soon as they finish school – some even before – they take the train to Berlin or Hamburg. Some go to work, some are into drugs. But they all go and they won't come back.'

She said there were no prospects here for the young. There had been no prospects here before the Wende either. Then, though, they had nowhere else to go. Now the big cities had so much to offer. We talked about the new bridge. Her eyes lit up but she agreed the bridge had done little for Dömitz. There was a toad wall on both sides of the bridge, she said. I asked if she could recommend a hotel.

'A hotel in Dömitz? There aren't any. We Dömitzers never shop and we never have guests.' She smiled wickedly. I waved good-bye.

I never liked visiting relatives while travelling. They offered cheap lodgings, but at a price. One invariably ended up regurgitating family stories about a wedding cake that collapsed or a drunk uncle at a wake. The stories held all the excitement of a sitcom rerun. You already knew the plot. And you knew exactly at which point the canned laughter piped up. No fly-ridden slum hotel could inflict such agony.

I was, however, keen to visit Karin Kreissl, nee August. She was a distant cousin and her husband Manfred had briefly worked as an East German conscript border guard on the Elbe.

Karin and Manfred had both been socialist believers. They labelled themselves *Überzeugungstäter*, conscientious offenders. The collapse of the border entailed the collapse of their world-view. Karin said: 'The Wende was the defining moment of our lives. Like the war was for our parents. We identified with the socialist state. Then our dreams fell apart. We eventually made peace. But we had really thought we were part of the better half of the human race in East Germany.' She giggled.

Manfred was silent and positioned himself away from my tape recorder. Then he got up and fled to the kitchen to make coffee while Karin continued. 'I am not sorry at all the old regime collapsed. I sometimes wonder what it would be like to be back for four weeks – the old cars, the old supermarkets, the old problems. I can be a bit nostalgic but if I'm honest with myself, I've had it. Never go back.' The thought of having sworn allegiance to the workers' and farmers' state made her laugh. Karin combined moral strength and good looks in unusually large amounts. She grew a little taller with every past folly she recounted.

Manfred occasionally peered out of the kitchen to listen in, clearly drawn by the subject. But he quickly retreated again as memories flooded back. He made Condo Melange coffee, an old East German brand that was now marketed by a West German company to Ossis. Finally he came and joined us. 'There is still a subconscious feeling of loss,' he said reclining in his chair. 'Everything has changed in our lives. You are a stranger in your own country. You can't even get the same rolls at your old bakery any more.'

Manfred became more animated when we talked about the border. He had 'only' been an army driver, although he had built part of a front-line fence. A friend was a real guard. 'The border – say what you want – it was done perfectly.' He told me that old East German maps were deliberately misprinted to confuse anyone trying to cross the border. Roads that ostensibly led to West Germany brought the fugitives straight to the nearest VoPo barracks. Even the course of the Elbe had been changed on paper. People would swim through the river, wrongly believing the water's edge on the other side was in West Germany. Overjoyed that they had made it, the fugitives would give themselves up to uniformed officials. The officials turned out to be VoPos with accurate maps.

After conscription, Manfred trained as an engine driver. For fifteen years he drove East German trains. After the Wende he was forced to switch to West German technology under West German management. 'Driving trains was a very honourable job under the socialist government. The status was comparable to that of an engineer, and so was the pay. Now I get treated like a prole, I'm lower class. That's hard.'

But the loss of social status wasn't what really irked Manfred; his main heartache was the switch from Ossi engines to Wessi engines. He had been very proud of East Germany's technological progress. His heart broke when West German managers threw it all out. 'We had great technology. Witnessing that was the high-point of my career. I saw the great changes . . . In 1975, we had steam engines like the '01 and everything was dirty. By the end everything ran electronically. In many ways, our technology was more advanced than in the west. When I was in Russia I saw East German technology everywhere, whether it was trains or machinery. Like the 143 – great power, great steering, very reliable. I remember how proud I was the first time I drove the 143 with 8,000 horse power right behind me. Wild. Then the Wessi train drivers came after the Wende and took one look and said: what kind of a model train is that? It really hurt. I had been so proud. From one day to the next, all of our technology was consigned to the scrapheap. All rubbish, they said.'

After finishing the Rondo Melange coffee, the Kreissls took me on an excursion to Schnackenburg, a village on the western river shore. Schnackenburg sat on the thin end of a West German territorial wedge that reached deep into East Germany. This furthest outpost of civilization, as the Wessi train drivers would no doubt have called it, had been pinned in by VoPos on all sides except in the west. Today it was the site of a museum about the border, the first I had seen on my trip.

Situated in a timbered-framed manor house, the museum was filled with memorabilia. I saw VoPo uniforms, photographs and reconstructed fortifications. Manfred was preoccupied with the cars, lorries, motorcycles and boats of the border patrol force. 'A fine vehicle,' he marvelled, pointing at a bucket car. 'This boat, used up and down the Elbe, could do 60 kilometres per hour. That's an incredible speed. No digs from Wessis about that technology.'

Returning home, I noticed a family photograph of the two parents and their three children, lying naked on a pier. Karin laughed when she saw my surprise. 'Before the Wende, East Germans were not very uptight at all. Things were uncomplicated in our society. People stripped off in fields without a care. Nobody would go to a beach to goggle at naked women. There were no porno magazines. Maybe a few erotic pictures, that's it. Now things have changed. Western body consciousness has swept the land. New magazines show incredibly skinny people, and every woman is suddenly starving herself. The need to be slim is already affecting thirteen-year-olds. Anorexia didn't exist before the Wende; now it's a big problem. I had never even thought of shaving my legs. It didn't make a difference what you wore. Now I have to use all the weapons available to me. Make-up, short skirt. I think we've made an evolutionary step backwards.'

I brought the family visit to an end after a few more cups of Ossi coffee. 'There is so much more to tell,' Manfred said wistfully and gave me the number of his friend Ralf Pötter who had been a 'real border guard'.

A few days later, I met Ralf at the train depot where he and Manfred worked. Ralf showed me the last few East German engines, sumptuous tanks destined for the scrapyard. I liked the look of them, sleek but not streamlined. The engine technology was still good enough today, he said in the car on the way to pick up his children. The two boys went to a day-nursery after school. German schools finish at lunchtime. Day-nurseries had only ever existed in East Germany where the proportion of working mothers was much higher. Their continued existence is a rare example of a surviving East German institution. The other notable example was a green arrow sign on traffic lights that indicates motorists may turn right on red if there is no oncoming traffic. Together these two practices form the administrative inheritance of the socialist era. Everything else has been scrapped by the West German government.

The Pötter children played in a park by the nursery while I chatted to Ralf and his wife Gitta, who rendezvoused with her family in the park every day after work. 'Nurseries are not political. The east just got it right.' They never wanted to go back to socialism, she said, but the perks had been great.

Ralf had been a conscript guard, serving in Rüterberg. He had little patience for the new-found republicanism of the villagers. 'When I was a guard we sat in the pub with the locals. They knew us and we knew them. We played cards together. Many of the supposed captors and inmates were neighbours. The higher-ranking guards in the area lived in Rüterberg. In fact, anyone who was allowed to live so close to the border was in some way connected to the state. Otherwise you were deported.'

Ralf witnessed one major breach of border security. 'Once, three people got to the last fence at the river. Two were caught but one made it over the fence. The search continued through the night for eighteen hours while the fugitive was hiding somewhere in the grass by the water. We used dogs and boats and helicopters but it still took eighteen hours. And for the whole time, the same team of soldiers stayed in position. When the fugitive was found by a young soldier the frightened man was immediately handed over to the secret police.' The young soldier went back to the barracks and committed suicide by throwing himself on to the bayonet of his gun from a bunk bed.

Ralf said he did not enjoy being a guard, but I thought I could occasionally detect an adventurer's romanticism. The camaraderie, the excitement of the chase, the big motorized toys. It all sounded a little too indulgent. Maybe that was unfair. But, in any case, I could not fault him for his romanticism – if it existed. I had often wondered whether I would have joined the Hitler Youth, had I been born fifty years earlier. Aged fifteen,

I probably would have found the glorious music, the bustling camp fires, the play fights and the camaraderie irresistible.

The Pötters and the Kreissls lived near Wittenberge, a railway crossing point. All the shops were closed on Saturday mornings. The town was empty. I couldn't even buy a newspaper. My only choice for breakfast was McDonald's. The English menu had been adapted to suit Ossi eaters whose only foreign language was West German. The Big Mac had been renamed the Big Mäc. A veggie burger was called a Gemüse Mäc. A cheeseburger, or Royale With Cheese at French McDonald's, was a Hamburger Royal in Wittenberge. Next to the napkins and straws were copies of McDonald's 'environment prospectus'. It stated: 'We take our ecological responsibilities very seriously. We feel obliged to act environmentally friendly to preserve and take care of the natural basis of life. Guided by the motto Avoid, Reduce, Recycle, McDonald's takes a step in the right direction every year.' On the next seven pages, the world's biggest food company detailed how it only used wooden rather than plastic coffee spoons and that all its ice cream cups were eatable. The glossy brochure was illustrated with recycling diagrams and photos of the Golden Arches on green lawns.

McDonald's betters all other multinational companies at adjusting to local idiosyncrasies and vernacular. In China, the fast-food chain has tailored its marketing strategy to one-child families. When parents walk in with their only boy, the little tyrant is greeted personally at the door. A programme called 'Little Emperor' keeps track of his birthday and a McDonald's employee sends him a birthday card every year. In Wittenberge, the fast-food chain served a clear conscience to post-tyranny eco-warriors. The burgers sold faster than they could be fried. No VoPo brigade could have held back the hungry horde.

I expanded my family visitation programme on the West German side of the Elbe in Hitzacker. My father had spent some of the dark war days here. He swam with distant cousins of the Schneeberg family in the river.

Now, over lunch with Gisela and Hartmut Schneeberg, I mumbled my way through a discussion of the exact branching of the family tree. They were brother and sister. That much I remembered.

After the war, Gisela had married Fritz Möllmann, who owned a local cement business. I asked Fritz whether he would have supplied concrete to build the Wall, if he had been asked in 1961. 'I would have rejected it,' he said. 'An order of that size would have been far too big for us at the time.'

Hartmut Schneeberg, Gisela's younger brother, used to run a clothes store. In retirement he had developed an interest in machinery. He had nothing but scorn for East German technology and engines: 'You can forget about the cars.' He said that the speedy VoPo boats that had captured Manfred's imagination were worthless. 'Sixty kilometres an hour? Never.' His wife Elke said: 'Directly after the Wende, we went on lots of cycling tours over there. But not any more.' The way she said 'over there' made it sound as if she was referring to Poland.

The two husbands dominated the conversation while their wives periodically disappeared into the kitchen. With the Kreissls or the Pötters it would have been the other way round.

After lunch I climbed Hitzacker's *Weinberg*, or vine hill. It towered over the town directly on the Elbe. Its steep slopes made it an ideal vantage point from which to control the river. The view of the eastern basin and the last few watchtowers was stupendous. I wasn't surprised to read on a neat noticeboard that the hilltop ruins dated back to an eighth-century Slavic frontier post: 'The biggest part of the archaeological findings was bones (more than 90 per cent domestic animals) and pottery. From fragments a development can be traced from early, unsophisticated pottery to richly decorated late Slavic vases.' The pottery hadn't been found until 1960, when E. Sprockhoff and B. Wachter excavated the site.

I looked down on the lush basin as the Slavs must have done and as no doubt West German border guards did only ten years ago. It had taken 1,200 years for archaeologists to put up a sign explaining the hill's historical significance. I wondered how long until we could read by the river banks: 'The biggest part of the findings was bones (less than 10 per cent human) and cigarette butts. From the filters a development can be traced from early high-tar cigarettes to late Soviet menthol cigars.'

4

ACROSS THE
FOREST

SHOOTING MUST BE ONE of the few sports where obesity is an advantage. Inertia steadies the aim, said Herr Schönfeld. A car mechanic from Lomitz, he chaired the village *Schützenverein*, or shooting club. He had a big beard and an even bigger body. The pistol champion with his own weapons cabinet at home was a solid man and a solid shooter. He fired with the steadiness of a freight train on a straight track.

But when it came to forming bonds with Ossis, he was nimble. Within days of the border opening, he joined forces with a *Schützenverein* in Wittenberge. His small West German village club linked up with East Germany's national training centre. The Olympic medal mint in Wittenberge had the biggest shooting range east of the Elbe. The link was a real coup for the club and its chairman. Herr Schönfeld created the first ever military alliance between East and West Germany. I suggested his action had foreshadowed the eastwards expansion of NATO.

The bearded mechanic smirked. 'It all started when a Wittenberger shooter came over to buy a western car. After the Wende, every Ossi wanted a Volkswagen or Audi or an old Mercedes. This shooter wanted my VW Polo but didn't have enough deutschmarks to pay for it. We started talking about shooting and he offered me a swap. In return for the Polo, he gave me two complete rifle ranges including targets. He said they were spare. After the Wende, they were selling everything over there: rifles, pistols, amunition. The VoPos had stockpiled the stuff.'

Following the swap, Herr Schönfeld helped the Wittenbergers to set up their own club. There were no shooting clubs in supposedly pacifist East Germany before 1989. All shooters were either obese professional athletes or gun-toting border guards.

Many of the new club members were former guards. 'But we never talk about that,' Herr Schönfeld insisted. 'The biggest problem for them was choosing a club uniform. Most western clubs have green uniforms. Green is the colour of the shooter and hunter. But some of them moaned: we can't have green, we'll look like VoPos. Now they march in grey uniforms.'

The village of Lomitz is buried in a sea of trees. South of the Elbe, the border ran through impenetrable woods. My maps showed acres of tree symbols dotted across the landscape like a monosyllabic alphabet soup. Not a stream or a field. Just a spiky green carpet cut up by the Iron Curtain. This woodland had the lowest population density in West Germany. A mere 47,000 people lived in the remote county of Lüchow-Dannenberg, an area bigger than Greater London.

Elsewhere in Germany, Herr Schönfeld and his club members would be typical residents – car mechanics, foresters, landlords and shop-keepers – but in Lüchow-Dannenberg they were a minority, the token locals, the ground crew caterers. After the Wende, the county was overrun by city-weary artists. A dribble turned into a mass influx. The artists brought canvases and paint pots and, most importantly, money. They purchased the more imposing local farms and today dominate public life in Lüchow-Dannenberg.

Why did they come? I asked a group of paint-smeared young women at a café in Jameln. They introduced themselves as Katja, Sabrina and Verena. Surnames weren't even mentioned. They were the first strangers on my trip to drop the Frau and Herr titles. We addressed each other with the informal *Du*, rather than the more formal *Sie*. Katja was a sculptor from a family of Hamburg tradesmen. 'The land here is incredibly cheap,' she said. 'Or at least it was before my whole art school class decided to follow me. You could pick up a barn for no money. Everyone helped to restore it. Places were cheap because the border made the area a dead-end, properties were worthless. It was cheap, cheap, cheap. I should have bought a whole village then. I'd be richer than my father now.'

Sabrina interjected: 'Katja, we didn't come here for the money. Remember?' She was a little shorter and not as pretty as Katja. She said they had come here for the freedom, the adventure, the '*Romantik*'.

Eager to use my threepence-worth of art history I chipped in: 'So you are a romantic painter? I thought that movement died when Caspar David Friedrich stopped painting those portentous big skies in the nineteenth century.' The three women gasped. I had made a fool of myself trying to show I knew my Monet from my Manet.

'You're talking about historical romanticism,' Sabrina explained. 'I meant our romantic *Lebensgefühl*.' The word *Lebensgefühl* is one of those wonderfully rich German linguistic creations, sired by the downtrodden *Leben* (life) and *Gefühl* (feeling). Amalgamated, the two words described the complex sum of our emotions at a particular stage in life. The English word 'lifestyle' is a poor cousin once removed.

The women's reasons for moving to the forest included, in no particular order: to express themselves and reach a 'higher form of being'; to flee the capitalist pig state with its endless rules and petty squabbles; never to have to look at a wristwatch; to opt out of the Fourth Reich; to have a lie-in; not to be forced into marriage and the drudgery of 'having one in the oven every other year'; to avoid Rotarians; to experience lust and pain and wonder; to paint 'true life' outside imposed mechanical arrangements; to avoid all clubs, especially the Rotary Club. The list was considerably longer and included several mentions of masturbation. But the three couldn't quite agree whether Onan was the hero of all adventurous spirits or the embodiment of isolationist and soulless city culture.

They lived in a converted farmhouse with a winter garden where they grew untreated vegetables. The paints they used were environmentally friendly; the heavily insulated roof apparently had an incredible heat retention factor. Verena, a red-head dressed in wellington boots, claimed she could only exist close to nature: 'We are rebuilding life here from the bottom up. Pollution is removed from every layer. It starts in the home and with the food.'

The women were devouring tofu burgers and wholewheat pasta. I confessed to having a craving for a deliciously fatty battery chicken with spotless potatoes instead of wrinkly eco-spuds. Despite their enlightened *Lebensgefühl*, they failed to find this funny. They recognized me for what I was: not a kindred spirit spouting art history trivia, but a confirmed city-dweller. We parted company.

Across the county I passed art galleries, publicly displayed sculptures and fine restaurants in abundance, though mostly of the tofu variety. Lüchow-Dannenberg was more urbane than the entire East German desert I had crossed. In the town of Lüchow, I went to a bravura brass concert.

A group called SKF performed the eighteenth-century folksong 'Kein schöner Land':

> No more beautiful land in this time
> Than thine, far and between
> Where we may find ourselves
> Under a lime
> At evening time.

The song dated back to the Wandervogel movement, an early German forerunner of modern environmentalism. It can still be heard in fields or around camp fires. Families will sing 'Kein schöner Land' on long walks.

I learned from Herr Neumann, who sat next to me at the concert, that the post-unification influx of artists was actually the third such wave. 'The woods have been an escape for romanticists through the ages,' he said. In the aftermath of the Great War, nudists, health campaigners, craftsmen and practitioners of holistic medicine came to Lüchow-Dannenberg. In the empty county they found a safe haven from conservatism and industrialization. Behind the protective hand of the woods, they spread their ointments and dropped their trousers. After the Second World War, the area effectively became a Cold War cul-de-sac and attracted West German 'Aussteiger', or drop-outs. They saw a chance to live self-sufficiently, far away from the industrial society they despised. The deep forest was an ideal setting in which to practise free expression and free love. Only lunch wasn't free, as the bespectacled agrarians soon found out.

Before our century, the area had been a retreat for another reclusive tribe. The county of Lüchow-Dannenberg was also known as the Wendland. The Wends were one of the many hundred of peoples that formed the splintered, pre-Bismarck Germany. They were pagan Slavs in a land of Teutonic Christians. As such, they were excluded from all guilds and repeatedly persecuted. Much like the latter-day drop-outs, they lived agrarian and self-sufficient lives. The Wends enjoyed a period of calm during the reign of George II, the English king and Elector of Hanover. He felt flattered that such wondrous people should be among his subjects and admired the ornately stitched folk *Trachten* they wore. But by 1800, the Wendish language, a Slavic variant, was extinct. And the Nazis' zeal to impose racial purity on Germany extinguished any surviving Wendish *Lebensgefühl*. 'The Wends had once been a powerful group of tribes,' Jan Morris recounts, 'so irredeemably heathen that in the 12th century the

Roman Catholic Church authorized a crusade against them. This culminated in the destruction of a gigantic figure of their god Swiatowit. The image stood at the tip of the island of Rügen, and the soldiers of Christ toppled it ceremoniously into the sea.'

What remains of the Wends are their Tolkienian place-names – Satemin, Mammoisel, Gohlefanz – and their dwellings. They had lived in villages called *Rundlinge* (roundlings). A dozen timber-framed brick houses were arranged in a circle facing each other. The round village green in the middle was used to keep animals and for celebrations and festivities. The *Rundlinge* operated as rural communes. All twelve families shared duties and supplies. Only the church was kept out of the inner village, which itself lay hidden from highways behind a thicket. Many of the villages survived the persecutions. Artists and intellectuals bought them in the 1960s, as the idea of the commune was once again in vogue. They restored the timber-framed brick houses to their original splendour and added roof insulation with high heat-retention factors.

I passed one such eco-roundling in Lübeln, just outside Lüchow, on a Saturday and attended a wedding. An uncharitable soul might have said I gate-crashed but, thankfully, there is no word for such caddish behaviour in German. As far as the other guests and the dictionary were concerned, I was simply attending.

The bride wore a traditional Wendish wedding dress covered with flower motifs. George II's wonderment at the Wends was easy to comprehend. The bridal outfit included a fabric crown reminiscent of an Indian turban and satin bands instead of a veil. A bunch of thorny flowers had been stitched to the bride's chest. While she was so attired the bride must not look in the mirror, according to Wendish custom. What punishment awaits her is not known, because no bride in the Wendland has ever broken the rule. So said the master of ceremonies. Rather more conventionally, the gangly groom was draped in an oversized morning suit.

Bride and groom arrived in a horse-drawn carriage, staring straight ahead. They were not allowed to turn their heads, the master of ceremonies explained: '*Dei sick umkiekt, dei kiekt sick noa ein anna um*' (Who looks around, is looking for someone else). After exchanging their vows, the pair stepped into a circle formed by the guests on the village green. To drive away evil spirits, the newly-weds were pelted with linseed and the groom drank a muddy love potion.

Afterwards, the romantic drop-outs who owned the village showed their mettle as hard-headed bottom-liners. The groom's bill was 500 marks for use of the bridal dress, 120 marks for the carriage and 150 marks for use of the village, excluding clean-up costs. I felt guilty for being a free-loader. But at least the romanticism of gate-crashing was otherwise untainted.

The song sheet from the wedding ceremony fell to the bottom of the rubbish bin. I was aware of being watched as I walked away from it. Then a chilling cry rang out: 'What do you think you are doing, young man?' An imperious pensioner was clutching the bin with one hand. The other rested on his hip. Flippantly, I said I was being a good citizen, putting litter where it belongs.

'Ha. That is precisely the point. You did not put this where it belongs, young man.' He picked out the sheet with his thumb and index finger. 'This,' he said waving the sheet, 'is old paper. You,' he pointed at me, 'put it into the yellow bin for recyclable packaging.' I snatched the sheet from his stiff fingers and walked off.

Of course, I knew I was committing a heinous misdemeanour by throwing paper in the bin with the yellow label. But I had rather enjoyed it. Germany has the world's most complicated refuse system. Households are forced by law to separate rubbish into four categories. There are colour-coded bins for old paper (blue), yoghurt pots (yellow), nappies (green) and Coke cans (red). The bins are emptied on a rotating weekly schedule. If you miss the green, bio-degradable bin collection one week, you are stuck with the stinking nappies for four weeks. Or, you put them in between the newspapers and wedding song sheets the next week. But don't get caught. Rules are applied strictly. And, while we're on the subject of rules, never mow a lawn between 1p.m. and 3p.m. That too is *verboten*. However, you may operate the lawnmower to your heart's content in the middle of the night, a period not covered by the rules.

I got lost in the forest. I was surprised it hadn't happened earlier. Plotting a course on the network of forest tracks seemed simple enough. They ran for miles without a turn or twist. Occasionally they crossed one another, usually at right angles. The network had the navigational logic of a chessboard. I got lost nevertheless. All forest tracks look identical. Seas of trees hurtled past. I would gaze out of the car window in much the same way that a farmer might on his first visit to London or New York.

Soon I was most definitely lost. I had forgotten whether I wanted to turn left at the second crossroads or right at the third. So I kept going. The rush of the trees gave off such a tender, burbling, gay, effervescent, sweet cry. It was the fervent music of nature, I told myself dreamily. Then the trees suddenly stopped. I was in the middle of a long, narrow clearing that reached from horizon to horizon. Thank God for the border. I awoke from my romantic musings and quickly pinpointed my location on the map. The Iron Curtain was an unwavering signpost among all the fuzzy Nature. For a moment I had indulged in something faintly familiar.

The sight of a forest – more than mountains, oceans, rivers or green and pleasant lands – brings out the romantic and mystic in a German. Even some city-dwellers recognized the *Wald* as their true spiritual habitat. The nineteenth-century Romantic writer Bogumil Goltz said in his book *Die Deutschen*:

> Of all of nature's scenes, it is the Wald in which all of her secrets and all of her favours are found together. [. . .] What the evil, over-clever, insipid, bright, cold world encumbers and complicates, the Wald – green, mysterious, enchanted, dark, culture-renouncing but true to the law of nature – must free and make good again. Whoever has a heart in his body must regret that he cannot stay in the Wald and live on berries.

Personally, I preferred to spend the night at the house of the forester rather than in his *Wald*. The forester's residence in Wirl was down a bumpy track five miles from the nearest houses in Prezelle. The potholes were horrendous. The moaning and groaning of the Red Racer drowned out any 'fervent music of nature'. But I was excited to see animals sipping from the water-filled holes. Most were scared away by the Red Racer's roar. But two deer (or venison, if you are a city-dweller) gamely stood by the roadside.

Otto von Wahl, the local West German forester, was away but his wife Reinhild showed me to their guestroom. She suggested a drive through the forest, though even she might not find the way back. We got into the Land Rover. Wasn't this a very lonely place to live? 'We're used to it. Ten years ago, when Otto started here, we had just come back from two and a half years in Togo. Before that, we were in Senegal. And anyway, since the border opening it's not so quiet any more.' Reinhild catapulted the sturdy vehicle through the potholes with scant regard for gravity. 'We are now approaching the Wirler Tip. The border makes a 90 degree turn at this point. There used to be a secret gate in the fence.' We stood at the tip, looking down the cleared rows to both sides. A strip, 50 yards wide, had been hacked out of the woods. And nothing much had changed in the last decade. A few bushes grew in the sandy strip but the pesticides used over the previous four decades had lost little of their deadly power.

Reinhild kept the Land Rover on the VoPo patrol track for fear of setting off forgotten landmines. She said there was a lot of speculation about the secret gate. East German agents may have used it. The gate had also been linked to West Germany's Red Army Faction. The leftist terrorists may have camped in the remote woods. Lately, though, the forest has become quite busy, at least by local standards. 'Cyclists come along the border track, and farmers and commuters take short-cuts across the border through the woods,' said Reinhild. 'Since the border guards on our side left, we don't feel so safe any more. Thirty border guards used to live in a wooden hut next to our house.' Reinhild crossed the border weekly to go shopping, sing in an East German choir and get her hair cut. Even a decade after the introduction of a uniform market economy, Ossi hair-dos are still cheaper.

Back at the house, she kindly tried to introduce me to an eco-commune of thirty-five Berliners. They called their farm the Lomitzil, for Lomitz domicile. One Herr Lutz told Reinhild on the phone he had to consult his fellow drop-outs. Later, he said, they would debate at a special commune meeting that evening whether or not to meet me. I could call back the next day to hear their decision, he said. I declined, citing 'bureaucratic reasons'.

Instead I had dinner with Reinhild, her visiting brother and his family. Hubertus von Beloh was an eye doctor from Dresden in deepest East Germany. His young children continually talked about 'my West Germany'. It was the Ossi children's play name for a paradisaical place where they had total freedom. 'In my West Germany you can put your feet on the table and eat with your hands,' the youngest said. In this mythical West Germany, children could stay up as long as they wanted, fart in the living room and ride on the dog's back. Herr von Beloh was bemused by his children's innocence.

He had studied at Moorfield's Eye Hospital in London. Throughout, he endured Nazi gibes from fellow students. At his graduation dinner at the In & Out Club on Piccadilly, he finally ignored the *Fawlty Towers* diktat and returned fire with his own war story. 'The RAF was preparing for a Luftwaffe raid on a British airfield. The ground troops had just enough time to build a few life-sized model planes from wood and deposit the dummies on the runway before the raid began. The real Lancasters were hidden away from the airfield. The RAF officers sat in their bunkers, slapping their thighs. The Luftwaffe squadron circled over the airfield for a while, then one plane buzzed over the runway and dropped its load – a wooden bomb.' Apparently, the Moorfield students didn't enjoy being bested at their own game.

The woods in the western Wendland have been owned by the family of Count Andreas von Bernstorff since 1694. An ancestor bought the forest from the von Bülow family for 50,000 Reich coins. With Otto von Wahl's help, Count Bernstorff was trying to make enough money from forestry to support his castle and his philanthropic interests. Reinhild arranged an audience with him.

Before I made my way through the woods to the castle, she gave me a quick lecture on how to address him. He was 'Count Bernstorff', not Herr Bernstorff or Herr von Bernstorff. And he was most definitely not Herr Count, which translated into German as Herr Graf. Steffi Graf was a vulgar tennis player. Her father, Herr Peter Graf, was in prison for tax evasion. Never say Herr Graf. The lecture sounded well rehearsed. After Bismarck effectively abolished aristocratic rule, Germany forgot how to address its landed gentry. Germans were baffled by the British honours system. How could a man called Sir John turn into Lord Smith?

The Bernstorff castle hid behind three pairs of white columns on the edge of the woods. The Count was in his late fifties and with his stripy shirt, red jumper and Barbour jacket he looked the very model of a British lord of the manor. His philosophical home, however, was closer to Islington. He mused about the compatibility of ecology and economy. 'There is no conflict between the two. What's good for nature is good for the purse.' I demurred. But forestry was not his main interest in any case. He left both ecology and economy to Otto von Wahl. He spent his time on philanthropy.

Count Bernstorff was the biggest patron of the arts in the Wendland. He supported the local artistic community with grants and nurtured their escapist enclave. Every year he invited a group of sculptors to display their work on his land. In 1992, a French artist took a watchtower from the border and sank it into marshland until only the top observation platform was visible. The view from the platform was considerably diminished. Jean-Lucien Guillaume told the Count: 'At its new place, the tower makes no sense. In its senselessness it has lost its military ugliness.' If Germans can be bested by anyone blowing esoteric speech bubbles, it has to be by the French.

I was about to disembark from the Wendland Ark. This was a beautiful stretch of land – one hardly ever sees venison quite so fresh. But in between extracting wholewheat pasta from my teeth and getting lost again, I decided to depart.

Not, though, before I had seen the black sheep on the Ark. Deep in the forest near Gorleben was a nuclear storage facility. Sensibly, the German government had decided to stash its nuclear waste in the least populated part of the country. It chose an old salt mine in which to store contaminated fuel rods.

The government had, however, made one miscalculation. It was dumping the most toxic of excrements on a community that cherished nature above all else; a community that had come here to be far away from the toxins of modern civilization; that would feverishly fight the loss of its paradise; and that had the guile of Robin Hood. Before even the first rod arrived, more than 5,000 eco-warriors occupied the clearing around the mine shaft. Nine years ahead of the Rüterbergers across the Elbe, they declared independence. But the wooden shanty town of the Free Wendland Republic lasted only two months before the government sent in 10,000 policemen to rough up the artists and drop-outs, and destroy their dwellings. It was the start of a battle royal that reached its height after unification when Ossi and Wessi protesters united.

The storage facility was finally finished in 1994 and the first nuclear fuel rods were driven to Gorleben. In the woods, the lorry convoy was ambushed. I had heard Katja, Sabrina and Verena talk about the battle. They had braved the police truncheons and water cannons. Or at least Verena had. Sabrina joined a bored Katja at a mobile tofu stand. 'This nuclear war was terrible,' Verena had recounted. 'We were sitting on the tarmac, clinging to each other. First we heard the police helicopters, then the convoy arrived. The police water cannons blasted us in the freezing cold. But most people wore raincoats. So the police prised us apart with truncheons. They beat children and pensioners. But it took them hours to advance maybe 50 metres. What an elevating feeling! I felt so at one with the others. Shame only that we didn't get on television.'

At the time, a reporter described the scenes as reminiscent of the tales of Tacitus. The massed forces of the state stood on the north German heath. In serried ranks and body armour like so many Roman legions, they confronted and vainly sought to tame the Teutonic tribes emerging from the forest to thwart the would-be occupiers.

I began my tour of the battlefield with a visit to the Info-Haus, the local propaganda outpost of the nuclear industry, stuffed with brochures and models. The timber-framed brick house in lovely Gorleben bore its share of battle scars. A red paint-bomb had been thrown at the door.

A nuclear spokesman bellowed, '*Mein Herr.*' Frenetically, he extolled the safety record of the CASTOR metal cylinder used to transport the fuel rods. A replica formed the centrepiece of a small exhibition. The yellow box was Dr Strangelove's favourite exhibit. 'We have tested the CASTOR extensively. Accidents are impossible. We have dropped it from 9 metres on to a concrete surface and from 1 metre on to a 15-centimetre-wide steel pin and put it into an 800 degree fire for half an hour. Nothing happened. We have simulated car crashes, train crashes, even a fighter jet loaded up with weapons falling out of the sky straight on to the CASTOR. Boom. Nothing. Nada. Indestructible.' What would happen if one dropped the *Titanic* on the CASTOR, would both stay afloat? He didn't know. 'We never did that test.'

The nuclear compound around the mine shaft was a bastion, an Orwellian model of fortification, a modern version of the impenetrable crusader castle Krak des Chevaliers in Syria. The ubiquity of barbed wire, fences, spikes, closed-circuit video cameras and high beam lights made the Iron Curtain look like a toy barrier. The Berlin Wall would still be standing if it had been built by West Germany rather than East Germany, I conjectured.

Protesters had sprayed '*Stoppt CASTOR*' on traffic signs, walls, trees and the tarmac. I met a group of them at a rest area not far from the compound's front gate. Sven was holding forth: 'We have this mess thanks to the Nazis. Schacht nationalized the energy sector in 1935 to prepare it for war. Now we have our own eco-Auschwitz.' The history student had grown up in the Wendland but studied at Hamburg University. At weekends, he returned to plan upcoming protest events.

One of every three German lightbulbs was powered with nuclear energy. What was the government supposed to do?

'Well,' said Jörg, a fellow student. 'It can't be right that Germany has enough nuclear material to make its own warheads.'

Sven nodded furiously. 'The bottom line is, the nuclear waste endangers lives. And if our lives are not valued then we can't value the laws.'

Weren't these the same arguments used by right-wing anti-abortionists?

The two were more interested in actions than justifications. Their protest tactics were remarkably sophisticated. When a nuclear convoy approached, the students used CB radio to co-ordinate flying squads armed with petrol-bombs. Hay barriers were wired up and could be lit by remote control. Steel cables were fastened across roads and protesters would hang from the wires as human barricades. The students seemed keener on urban class war than rural romanticism.

Not so Count Bernstorff, who owned the forest around the compound. He too was opposed to nuclear energy. But he chose weapons more suited to his class, namely, applying the law to fight the government. According to German property laws, using land for mining always had priority over storage use. Hence, the Count founded a company called Salinas to mine salt in Gorleben. Five hundred years ago, when the crystals were as valuable as gold, salt mining was the region's main source of income. Today, the white gold was a loss-maker, but the Count reached deep into his pockets to exploit the loophole. The first Gorleben Salt was now on supermarket shelves. The label assured consumers that, of course, the environmentally friendly salt did not include any 'chemical additives'. Never mind radiation.

Recently, however, the government moved the goalposts. It rewrote the law to allow nuclear storage. Would the Count now climb the barricades? I doubted it.

The castle of the Bismarck family was an hour away from the border in the town of Schönhausen. A visit promised a deeper look into the once 'evil', now mostly empty, empire. Maybe I hadn't seen the Ossis' true colours while I clung to the border.

I headed east on a perfectly straight forest highway. Traffic was light; the Red Racer purred. Yet, my progress was somehow thwarted; my fellow motorists seemed to be conspiring against me.

Bad drivers came in two variations in East Germany: those trying to break a land-speed record and those being overtaken by cyclists. The combination of the two on one road warranted a warning on the radio traffic bulletin.

Directly in front of me was a smoke-belching Trabant. This East German box car, dubbed Trabbi, was still the pride and joy of many Ossis, regardless of its technological inferiority. The old communist production lines had been so slow that delivery took an average of fifteen years. The lines were closed down soon after unification; nevertheless, the Trabbi became a symbol for everything East German. It was decrepit, smelly and slow. Trabbi jokes soon mushroomed. How do you double a Trabbi's value?

Fill the tank. Why didn't the Trabbi move when the lights turned green? Because the tyres were stuck on a piece of gum. Why do luxury Trabbi models have heated rear windows? To keep your hands warm when you push them.

Yet, as a motorized David on an autobahn filled with pristine western Goliaths, the Trabbi had a certain charm. Many long-suffering Trabbi owners steadfastly refused to trade in their shoeboxes for a beamer or a beetle. Never mind that the Trabbi was only half the size of a beetle and could be overtaken at top speed by a reversing beamer. The Trabbi enthusiasts didn't care. One such nostalgic Ossi driver was travelling right in front of me. He would slow down inexplicably – as if there was a temporary fuel shortage because comrades operating the Siberian oil wells were on strike – and then speed up again. Two minutes later he slowed down again as plumes of greasy smoke spluttered from the exhaust.

I tried to overtake but was continually thwarted by Audi and BMW sports cars. The souped-up space ships were rushing west. As if engaged in a video game, the wide-eyed drivers shifted to a lower gear for extra acceleration and tried to overtake in a single lane. I was not surprised East German car crash statistics were off the scale. To these Ossi drivers, the main benefit of unification must have been the introduction of West Germany's glorious freedom to drive without speed limits. I eventually arrived in Schönhausen, drenched in sweat. Maybe the billions of deutschmarks in economic development aid to East Germany would have been better spent on free driving lessons.

The birthplace of Otto von Bismarck is featureless bordering on grim. His estate lies hidden behind concrete monstrosities and is not signposted. The medieval castle has gone. West German builders were restoring what little was left of the building. It had been razed to the ground by Soviet forces – not during the war but thirteen years after it had ended. On 2 August 1958, most of the castle was dynamited. On the same day, Berlin's royal palace where German kaisers had resided, and Puttbus castle on the Baltic Sea were flattened. The Soviet leaders wanted symbolically to destroy the Prussian Junkers. They blamed the 'Iron Chancellor' and his ilk for the exploitation of the working class and Prussia's bloody territorial expansion.

Frau Neumann, a tour guide at the estate, said Bismarck had been a taboo subject before the Wende. 'We simply would not talk about him. He was *persona non grata* even though everyone in the town knew the history. And outside, we were tainted by association. Being from Schönhausen counted as a slur.' As a child, Frau Neumann told a teacher

her grandmother had been a kitchen help for the Bismarcks. The teacher punished her for this 'moral failing'. She was ordered to stand in a corner for an hour. 'I had no idea what I'd done wrong.'

Today, Frau Naumann was helping to rebuild the castle, including a Bismarck museum. The impetus seemed to be economic as much as historical. Schönhausen desperately needed money and tourism was its only hope. After the Wende, unemployment soared and the population shrank from 4,000 to 2,000. While many locals moved west to find jobs, tourists with an interest in history went on pilgrimages to Schönhausen. Even without a museum or a signpost, 6,000 visitors turned up in one year. Spurred on by this, the town decided to turn the Iron Chancellor into a cash cow.

The old Soviet antagonism towards him was still deeply ingrained. I overheard a group of Saxon academics who were touring the estate.

'Herr Kollege, I agree. Bismarck was no angel.'

'We agree on something at last.'

'Should Bismarck be an angel, then Engels has to be something even higher, a god.'

I suspected their West German colleagues would not quite agree.

A. J. P. Taylor said Bismarck was Germany's political 'barometer, the test of what German historians think of themselves and of the world'. The English equivalent would be Henry VIII. Generations of Oxbridge historians have pegged their view of good and evil with a judgement of his deeds. In Germany, Bismarck has been portrayed either as a rogue or a hero. Nationalists praised him as Germany's greatest statesman. Left-wingers criticized his supposed immorality. The man who said politics was the 'art of the possible' might have taken that as a compliment.

I walked past the castle into the gardens. By a wooden bridge over a canal stood a statue of Hercules. The Roman was immensely tall and muscular, but when I inspected his backside at the urging of Frau Neumann, I found some curious pockmarks. The Roman's buttocks were covered with holes. Apparently, the young Bismarck used to take potshots at the statue in frustration when he returned from unsuccessful hunting trips.

5

OVER
FIELDS

A MAN CALLED SCHMIDT TOLD me to expect a fork in the road. He cautioned me against veering left. His warning did not include an explicit reason for staying on the right, but he had run his index finger across his throat, slowly, like a willing and able executioner.

I never reached the fork in the road. Or maybe I passed it without noticing. The country lanes rarely crossed and daylight had gone from a fickle pink to red and then to the colour of embers. The sky stayed dimly aglow for hours over the flat land. But between the hedges in front of me darkness washed over the road like an incoming tide. I was lost somewhere on the East German side between Arendsee and Salzwedel. I knew just carrying on would not deliver me to safety. There were no natural barriers to the east from here. The land was flat all the way to the other end of the Russian steppe. I might end up in Stalingrad if I didn't stop soon.

In my headlights I spotted a man walking in unkempt grass by the roadside and slowed down to ask for directions. His flat cap looked familiar. I recognized Schmidt as he slowly turned his head. Under the flat cap lurked a toothless grin. 'I warned you not to go left. It's just one big loop and you're back on the same road,' he said. I told him I was lost but instantly regretted being candid with this man. He hadn't even listened. 'You can stay at the farm,' he volunteered. 'My Frau won't like it. But one more in the barn won't matter.' Before I could respond Schmidt had walked around the car and settled himself in the passenger seat. He smelled of hay, and with the overhead light on his rugged face he reminded me of the maverick MP and historian Alan Clark. 'We'll just stop at the gates and check they're done up, then we'll say *Prost.*'

He made me stop every few hundred yards so that he could get out and check padlocks. I sat in the car contemplating what would happen if I drove off without him. Naturally, the open passenger door was a problem but what worried me even more was that I might bump into him a third time tonight. I waited patiently. After the last gate, he pulled a flask out of his coat. No alcohol in the house, he said, and shared his schnapps with me.

'It's my father's farm. We're lucky to have kept it out of Russian hands.' The tall buildings were handsome and I told him the farm had the air of being profitable. He laughed. 'It used to be. East Germans may not have been the better half of mankind but we certainly had the better farms. All the land was pooled in professionally managed co-operatives. Many of the smaller unprofitable plots were shoved into one big plot. They pulled out hedges and tree-lines with just as little respect for nature as they had for people. It did us a lot of good.'

He got out of the Red Racer one last time to lock the farm gate behind us. I was now confined to his company for the night.

Frau Schmidt was watching television in black and white. The living-room lights were switched off. The film flickering across the screen could have been shot in black and white or the television set may have been prehistoric. There was no telling in the dark. She failed to look up, even when her husband announced they had a guest. 'Your problem, Schmidt,' she said. 'He's not staying in the house. But you know, the barn is all yours.'

We sat outside the kitchen door and shared the rest of the schnapps. The day glow had receded to a ragged silver-blue horizon. An evening breeze swept across the featureless fields, encountering not a whimper of resistance. The Schmidts were not sleeping in the same bed, not even in the same building. He was vague as to the reason for their separation. I had asked, emboldened by liquid confidence, but he only ventured: 'How many reasons do you want? Barbados, Cape Cod, Great Barrier Reef . . .'

We walked over to the barn. Ten feet up on some timber-covered beams, Schmidt had built himself a little bedroom. A lantern was dangling over several stacks of mattresses and a carefully constructed bookshelf. We inhaled the smell of dry hay and I heard an animal scraping on the floor below. Schmidt did not listen. With his head thrown back and a faint smile on his face he looked fragile and broken.

'Dreams are my reality,' he hummed. 'What song is that from?' I didn't know. 'Travel, far-away places, that's something to dream about,' he said. A few years after the Wall came down, Schmidt had loaded up his tractor with his favourite foods and driven through the farm gate heading west. His destination was Biarritz on the French Atlantic coast. He had packed tinned ravioli, Paulaner beer, hard-boiled eggs and smoked sausages. The trip was well-planned and Schmidt estimated it should take him no more than a week to reach Biarritz. He would stop only to sleep. The tractor featured such luxuries as a special magnetic strip on the dash board, so Schmidt could have a tin-opener at the ready for the ravioli. He chose to travel by tractor even though he owned a car. 'It was my first trip so I wanted to go really slowly. I had memorized the name of every town along the way and I wanted to put a mental picture to each name.' Near Aachen on the Franco-German border, Schmidt drove through a vegetable garden, reckoning it was a scenic route. The owner called the police, who followed his tyre tracks. The tractor was finally impounded after Schmidt crashed it into a stream while the police were pursuing him on foot. He took a train back to his angry wife.

'I had offered to take her with me to Biarritz. But she only said I was taking the silly dreams too far.' I asked why Biarritz. The chic French resort was unlikely to welcome tractor-drivers. 'Biarritz was only the first stop. There were so many places I wanted to visit. But most of them could not be reached by tractor. And I honestly thought my Frau wanted to go, too. While the border was shut we always repeated to each other magic names like Biarritz, like Barbados, like Rio. We never really thought about going there, at least not realistically, not even longingly. We didn't feel incarcerated here. Biarritz, Barbados, Rio – we talked about them as if they were places in a novel. Fascinating but in another realm.' Schmidt's eyes were wide open and he seemed ten years younger now, maybe no more than forty.

He had begged his wife to come travelling with him after the border was opened. But Frau Schmidt was scared. 'She wanted to hang on to the images of Biarritz, Barbados and Rio. Going there would destroy the make-believe world we had created.' Schmidt said he still didn't understand her. So he went alone and she had a nervous breakdown while he was munching tinned ravioli on his tractor seat. 'We drifted apart after I came back. She blamed me for wrecking the safe little fantasy world we had inhabited. So we each chose our own new fantasy world. She television, I the bottle.'

I fell asleep fully clothed on the stack of mattresses. The next morning a cacophonous pounding disturbed my slumber. I suspected a vicious hangover boxing its way through my subconscious. The stench of schnapps compounded the feeling. But the hammering came from outside the barn. I gazed out at an apathetic Schmidt. He was chopping firewood with an unwavering regularity. He would place a log in front of him with his left hand and in one motion bring down the axe in his right. As the wood splintered and fell apart he would reach for the next log. He was sweating profusely and didn't stop to return my greeting. It was still early but the farm gate was unlocked. I accepted his unspoken invitation to leave.

After a few more miles of driving aimlessly I parked the Red Racer. Today I would give up early before I got lost again. The sky seemed limitless as it reached further and further over fields and farms. A few clouds were drifting playfully, chasing each other and melting into new formations. Horses galloped noisily. After the confined forest world of the Wendland, the open expanse presented a picture of joyful release.

I abandoned the car to roam across the pastures on foot. Country walks are a wonderful opportunity to soliloquize – no raised eyebrows or shaking heads would stop me from talking to myself at leisure – and they have the power to give gravity to even the most empty epigram. Poems learned by heart in primary school re-emerged from memory with an effortlessness that made them sound meaningful. The lack of company seemed to banish all reticence.

I was trying to coax a few lines from Goethe's *Faust* from my brain when I realized I had miscalculated. At the far end of the track a couple were walking a dog. The wind was blowing in their direction. *'Erkennst du mich? Gerippe? Scheusal du? Erkennst du deinen Herrn und Meister?'* As they came closer I shut up and fixed an embarrassed grin on my face. They smiled back. Suspiciously, I thought. Had they heard me? Walking down a noisy street they would have remained oblivious. 'Let the doors be shut upon him, that he may play the fool nowhere but in's own house. Farewell.'

At a tavern, I sat down between groups of farm hands. The tables stood on a lawn under scrawny umbrellas, covered with beer bottles. The eager lunchtime drinkers fell silent upon my arrival. In a monosyllabic twilight one of them volunteered, 'The beer's good,' followed by a burp. It earned him a laugh.

When three stragglers sat down at my table, conversation seemed out of the question. But one asked me: 'Ossi or Wessi?' I talked about London and New York and the conversation became lively. We compared notes on air travel, English weather, American food, trips to Spain and keeping in touch with holiday sweethearts. As we mentioned various destinations, other farm hands joined in. One overheard a mention of Oporto and gave a rendition of a Portuguese song learned on holiday. With our travel talk we had found something in common. We shared a bond not as countrymen but as travellers. I was reminded of Schmidt and many similar travel conversations on my journey.

After a while the conversation drifted to television programmes and football players, and I was once again clueless. The stars' names meant nothing to me. I was mixed up. I was back in my timewarp.

During a lull in the conversation I asked if foreign travel was everything they had expected it to be when the border opened. 'The biggest shocker was you couldn't go naked,' said one. 'I went to Florida in 1994 and thought, America, land of the free, but think again. The women weren't even going topless. The Americans would have thrown us in prison if we dropped our pants.'

One by one, the farm hands went back to their ploughshares. They left behind Herr Ritzke, the foreman. A burly man, he was quietly sipping his beer. He hadn't said a word since I arrived. Now it was his turn. 'My boys have no idea what they're talking about. They rushed overseas after the Wende and now they think they've seen it all. But all they've seen is Majorca. Freedom is a funny thing; it goes stale so quickly. The boys go back to the same tacky Spanish hotel every year.' I asked if he was a bitter man. No, he said, but travel had broadened his mind too much to be charitable.

All I asked from Salzwedel was a clean and affordable hotel room. It did not have to have a bathroom; just my own four walls, instead of a hay-filled barn. On paper, an easy enough request in a big town. But so far I hadn't found a single hotel in East Germany. And not for lack of trying.

Opposite the Salzwedel train station I spotted the Bahnhofs-Hotel. Reception was at the smoky bar. I asked for an 'affordable single room, nothing fancy'. The barman demanded 80 marks, more than I had paid anywhere in West Germany. I walked out, but at the car I changed my mind and returned with my bag – a clear sign I was prepared to pay his price, one would have thought. Yet, without further negotiating, the barman said I could have a room for 45 marks. I was beginning to understand why hotels were a rarity east of the border.

When I walked in the room, though, I realized the last *Lacher* was on me. My temporary abode was undoubtedly affordable. I would, however, be sharing it with two spiders staking out the door frame.

The town of Salzwedel is built around a decrepit Gothic church called St Mary that had been crumbling ever since the little known Beer War of 1488 during which brewers and politicians nearly came to blows over what substances could be included in the brew. (The German Purity Law [Deutsches Reinheits Gebot] was agreed in 1516 and is still in force today. German beer drinkers pride themselves on the superior quality of the domestic brew.) The church has the haunted look of a monastery fighting a losing battle against the seven deadly sins. It fits in rather well with the Stalinist architecture of the new town. There is nothing sinfully indulgent about the concrete tower blocks, but they share the church's bleak look of dereliction.

With my back to St Mary, I walked down Jenny Marx Street. What a surprise to see the name Marx had not disappeared from the city map after being banished from the political landscape. Jenny Marx was Karl's dutiful wife. She tirelessly transcribed his notes, a task not to be underestimated. Edmund Wilson noted that Marx's prose 'hypnotizes the reader with its paradoxes and eventually puts him to sleep'. Him, but not her. Jenny Marx was the Virgin Mary of communism, the woman who turned *Das Kapital* into legible (if not intelligible) script.

Her birthplace was a sleepy town house with a commemorative plaque by the door: 'Jenny Marx Haus, baroque building from 1737.' The heavy wooden doors were more suited to a manor house than to the cradle of communism.

A lady by the door charged two marks admission and explained that a room at the back was dedicated to Jenny. 'The whole house used to be a museum just for her. The workers and farmers came by the busload. But after the Wende we were given new instructions. You know, with the new circumstances we cut Frau Marx back to one room.' I was intrigued to taste the local brand of revisionism. Had the Marx exhibition just been reduced or completely rewritten? Did Salzwedel have the courage to acknowledge past follies or had communist diehards preserved a beachhead?

Behind the door to the Jenny Marx Room hung an oil portrait of the woman known as Jenny of Westphalia. Karl had a rather bourgeois taste in women, it seemed. Doughy-eyed Jenny wore a ball gown and carefully curled hair. She was the busty daughter of a Salzwedel district president.

I wondered if the oil portrait was a new addition to the house to make Jenny more acceptable to today's district presidents.

The room still reeked of hero-worship. One note read:

> The achievement: Jenny Marx was outstandingly intelligent and revered beyond her circle of friends. She did not approach the public with historically important achievements of her own. But as secretary to her husband, she supported him by copying out his unreadable hand writing for publication, and answered his correspondence. Karl Marx pursued his goals without compromise. Subordinated to his life, Jenny Marx existed in the shadow of the great revolutionary.'

This barely deserved a pass mark in revisionism class, even if it showed 'the great revolutionary' to be an exploitative husband.

There was a picture of Eleanor Marx, the daughter who joined the British trade union movement. She, too, worked as Karl's secretary. A pre-Wende plaque gave the name of the house as 'Museum of the Marx Family', even though nobody called Marx had ever lived here. Jenny left Salzwedel long before she met Karl and never returned. The street outside had been named Jenny Marx Street in 1948, two decades before the house was turned into a museum. With regards to the changes made in 1990, it was noted: 'The former Marx Memorial received the name Jenny Marx House. The content profile was changed completely.' A concluding evaluation of the pre-Wende years suggested that everyone knew at the time that the Jenny cult was humbug. The note read: 'All efforts to justify the existing political circumstances and to depict the development of the Communist society as the only true society did not go down very well.' And, of course, none of the members joined the party voluntarily but had membership forced upon them.

The garden at the back was dominated by a bronze statue of an exceedingly busty Jenny. She was fenced in by a 15-foot brick wall. An example to postwar Marx disciples?

Not far from Jenny and St Mary, I walked into a travel agency. The farm hands had inspired me to research favourite Ossi holiday destinations. Frau Krämer said there was an insatiable appetite for Spain, Italy and France. But not Yugoslavia or Turkey. Too far east. The Black Sea was impossible to sell. Same for the Baltic. England was unpopular because people were sick of queueing. Short trips to Munich or the Rhine did pretty well. What really concerned her was how few Wessis wanted to visit East Germany. I mentioned the lack of hotels, but she insisted there would be hotels if only enough Wessis wanted to come. Instead of holidaying at the Schaalsee, they flew to the Maldives. I couldn't blame them.

Frau Krämer was engagingly candid. She said her customers had reacted to the Wende like a cast of Woody Allen characters. Some were intensely miserable when they went from their protected East German cocoon to the unbridled razzmatazz of the Costa del Sol. Many would have been better off not going at all. That way, at least they could have continued to dream about white beaches and bronzed bodies. Other Ossis travelled obsessively to overcome what Frau Krämer called *Mauerkrankheit*, Wall sickness. Years of relative isolation had turned them into hypochondriacs. The enviable cure was a year-round programme of skiing in Switzerland, swimming in Spain, snorkelling in the Seychelles and sinning in Sweden. A third group of customers liked to travel to the few remaining communist countries for a last glance at the Utopia they once enjoyed. Unfortunately for Frau Krämer, their first trip to Cuba or China was also usually their last.

Customers had walked in while we spoke and stuffed brochures into bags. They didn't sit down for a sales chat. But at every mention of a foreign destination, they shot envious glances. Clearing her throat, Frau Krämer said, matronly: 'Many, of course, cannot afford to go anywhere. They just look at the pictures. Just like the old days.'

The fields had been flat and featureless. Further south, sturdy trees sprouted and crests rose ever more cockily. It was as if the landscape had suddenly hit puberty here. Bosomy hills stood erect and earthy skin broke out with spots of weedy green. Where the landscape had been even and smooth twenty miles up the border, it was now stubbly and studded.

Near Henningen, a farmer had dressed up a scarecrow as a VoPo. He had draped a military jacket over a wooden cross and crowned it with a rusty People's Army helmet. A pair of soggy marching boots leant against the base. The adjoining field was empty. The Cold War posture was as chilling as ever.

The church in Henningen was facing west, as were most churches in the area. I remarked upon this curious fact to two Ossis at the church gate. 'Shielding the altar,' said Herr Bussmann. 'Evil spirits rise when the sun sets in the west. The tower protects the church.'

The occult answer didn't convince Herr Durowski. 'It's the weather. The worst storms always come from the west. The tower stops the wind.'

'*Nein*', insisted Herr Bussmann. 'Bad spirits come from the west. When the sun dims and falls behind the western fields the spirits come out.'

Herr Durowski quoted peasant weather maxims in support of his case.

However strongly they dissented, the two Ossis unquestioningly agreed on one thing. Evil – whether metaphysical or meteorological – always came from the west.

On Henningen's village square stood a black, red and golden border post. In neighbouring Barmebeck I saw another. Both had been carefully repainted from top to bottom. Prominently displayed in the village as they were, the posts looked like totem-poles. Taken from the happy hunting-grounds of their forefathers, the posts might be used by Herr Bussmann and his ilk for pagan rituals on May Day morning. Alternatively, Herr Durowski could put a weather-vane on top.

By the early afternoon I had crossed countless meadows and spotted several more brightly decorated totem-poles. Marching on an empty stomach, I began combing villages for a shop. But it was Sunday, a day when even pagan Ossis stayed at home. If East German villagers engaged in commerce at all, they certainly weren't doing so on weekends. After vainly banging on the few shop and pub windows to be found, I faced the inevitable truth. There was only one place where food could be procured, namely, in the land of fat-free, free-range, feel-good milk and honey across the border. West German villages generally sported at least one Turkish grocer, Greek restaurant, Italian ice-cream parlour and British petrol station at each end. Western shop-keepers operated on the simple premise that if Christianity can ply its trade on Sundays then so could capitalism. Anything else would constitute a breach of fair competition rules. Sundays were often the busiest days at the village shop – conveniently located next to the church.

In the first village across the border, Bergen, I found the most urbane eatery one could have asked for. The Antiques Café was a coffee-house inside an antiques saleroom. The interior resembled an estate agent's wet dream. Some oleaginous fellow might have purred: 'This exquisite property exhibits period features including hand-cut beams and wrought-iron door hinges.' The food was refreshingly hearty. A lady in a rustic apron served apple-cake (not-so-secret ingredient: butter) with double whipped cream and extra vanilla sauce on the side. Many a harvest will be brought in before the same fare is on offer across the border.

After my third slice of apple-cake, I settled down to write in my note-book. Restaurants were my favourite place to take notes. The proprietor was guaranteed to send over a complimentary drink or extra dessert, fearing the presence of a restaurant critic. Writing was lucrative after all.

Heading back east, I passed yet another former border checkpoint. The vainglorious East German regime had erected a white column reaching a hundred feet into the sky to display its coat of arms. Presumably, the column was for the benefit of visitors rather than returning citizens. Today, the hammer and sickle had long gone; but not vainglory. The local district coat of arms had taken pride of place atop the ungainly concrete column.

I steered the Red Racer on to the border patrol track which had been widened into an agro-autobahn. At three times its original width, the track was operated as a multi-lane trunk road for combine harvesters. The red threshers crawled along the dusty track like giant mechanized lobsters. In comparison, my car was a mere baby shrimp. I cowered behind the wheel as they passed. Among the gently undulating fields, I stumbled upon the village of Hestedt. It hovered precariously close to the border, but not quite close enough to have received Rüterberg's extravagant treatment. Hestedt had only faced a fence on one side rather than all around. In some ways this was a worse fate. While Rüterberg had attracted international attention and developed a sense of identity through the overthrow of its captors, Hestedt knew only apathy. The cemetery appeared to be the liveliest part of the village. For every new house there were five decaying barns. As I sat in the car looking at a For Sale sign, a group of youths on bikes circled the Red Racer like Indians around a barricade of waggons. After a few moments, they withdrew without a word.

I left the car and walked towards Eversdorf where I crossed a field of orange blades. They stood several feet apart and looked quite miserable from up close. The weasly amber stalks were barely tall enough to be swayed by the light breeze. Yet, as I lifted my eyes, the colossal field glowed orange. Like the many small dots in a television picture, the meek orange blades added up to a strong image. An invisible sun had lit up the vast sunset-coloured carpet.

I endeavoured to learn the name of the strange orange growth. Herr Jürges stood by his front door next to the field. He clutched an orange stalk between his thumb and index finger and slowly shredded it. The stalk crumbled and flakes drifted to the floor. 'This is not a real plant but a weed that was sprayed. We kill it off, otherwise we have to plough it under later. Now it's dried out. Sunburn has turned it orange.'

Herr Jürges was the manager of a farming business. Following de-collectivization in the early 1990s, when family farms were returned to their old owners, he gathered 500 cattle and set up his own agricultural empire. Judging by the ornate grandfather clock, oil paintings and leather armchairs in his living room, he had done well. 'The Altmark was always a cattle area. My father was forced to put his land and his cattle into a co-operative after the war. It worked quite well for a while. My father's generation of farmers still felt responsible for what they had put into the co-operative; they cared and worked hard. But when they retired or died, farming co-operatives turned into holding pens for the lazy and unemployable in the socialist state. Chaos reigned. Then the border fell in 1989, thank God. It was clear to me things would change dramatically. To become profitable, 80 per cent of the people had to go. You couldn't hold progress back. You had to adapt to the market economy, quickly.'

I had met a truly zealous convert. Herr Jürges rented fields on the other side of the border, directly taking on West German farmers. He seemed to relish the chance to prove himself in the bustle of the marketplace. 'There was a gold-digging atmosphere, a Yukon in the east. And there was a lot of trouble with charlatans. You had to fight back suddenly. We weren't used to that. You have to get lawyers. We never knew people could simply not pay and get away with it. You have to be careful whom you give a dozen cows to and at what price.'

Herr Jürges was a model capitalist. 'I believe risk-takers deserve to make money. But EU farming subsidies should be abolished. Let the market regulate prices. We produce quality and that sells. It's crazy the EU pays farmers to let land lie fallow while some people starve.' But the forty-year-old could not hide his last few remnants of Ossi pride. 'I was at a trade show in West Germany and saw this combine harvester. The shape looked just like our old ones. But the harvester was blue instead of the familiar red. I scratched the paint and under the blue, surprise, was a coat of red. A western company had bought up the production facilities and now manufacture our top threshers under their name. East Germany really had some wonderful technology.'

I asked if he missed the good old days. Of course not, he said. 'But people are less sociable today. In the old days, boy, did we party. You could drink all night and take all day to recover. Legendary stuff. Nobody cared if you slept in the fields. Now everyone has a full diary, too much overtime, people fear for their jobs, pressure from the boss, I guess from people like me. Everyone is tense. Always tension. People go consumption crazy, then they spend the next year worrying about repayments for the house, the big car, the stereo television.'

Herr Jürges suggested I visit Herr Ranft, a friend in neighbouring

Sieden-Langenbeck. I took a short-cut across the fields and was greeted with a black coffee and home-made cheesecake. Herr Ranft agreed that partying had never been the same again after the Wende. He grew up with Herr Jürges. The two childhood friends went together on their first trips to West Germany. 'A great bonding experience. We drove to Hamburg where he had a cousin; later we went to the Alps. The first trip – that was special for every Ossi.'

The phone kept interrupting our conversation. From the fragments I overheard I figured out he had just got married. Reluctantly so, because he didn't want to give up the sense of freedom he experienced when the Wall came down, and he was still living with his mother rather than his wife. 'We didn't even tell our parents . . . it only took fifteen minutes . . . we had to wait until the officials had emptied their Champagne glasses before we could leave . . . it's only a piece of paper . . . yes, me, the eternal bachelor . . . now we can send our regards to our respective wives . . . I held out a long time . . . we don't even have the same name . . . marriage means rings and rings mean chains and who wants to live in chains?'

Herr Ranft was a free spirit. So free, in fact, he preferred unemployment to taking an 'alienating job'. He and his mother lived in a house frozen in time. The East German plywood chairs and the formica kitchen had yet to be replaced with designer furniture. The car outside was a Trabbi not a Volkswagen. Herr Ranft had studied economics. But since Marxism's stock had been marked down, his qualifications were a liability not an asset. Was he bitter? 'Never. Life's too short to be bitter. What's the best way to ruin a company? Alcohol. What's the most enjoyable way of ruining a company? Women. What's the quickest way of ruining a company? Give it to a Wessi.' My smile must have encouraged him. He followed up with a second joke. Out at sea, you spot two castaways but you only have room for one. One castaway is black, the other white – who do you rescue? The black, he's guaranteed not to be a Wessi. 'Nor an Ossi,' I said. He squinted. 'Oh, yeah, I guess so.'

With lots of time on his hands, Herr Ranft had become a lover of the good life. He couldn't afford caviar but he had poetry. Herr Jürges had warned me about his passion for reciting verses. Herr Ranft attributed his inclination to the influence of Goethe who said 'no day is complete without singing a song and reciting a poem. It keeps me happy and it doesn't cost a single mark.' Herr Ranft also delved into art history and bee-keeping, but his jovial nature could not conceal a certain bitterness over what had happened between him and Herr Jürges. They hardly ever saw each other now. Many childhood friendships break up, I suggested. But not when you are in your mid-thirties, he observed melancholically. What happened? 'One night a few years ago I met Frankie Boy in a pub. He was drinking with another friend and we started to argue about what we were doing with our lives now. Frankie Boy was very proud of running his own business. He said the unemployed were *Schmarotzer*, parasites. I was living off their hard-earned deutschmarks, he said. I replied, so you think I should receive nothing, maybe get sent to a concentration camp. They screamed yeah, yeah. Send them all to the camps. The other friend later apologized but Frankie Boy never did.'

Herr Ranft said Herr Jürges had been corrupted by the new system. As a manager, he was constantly making deals with cattle feed salesmen and butchers in cordial but brutally calculating meetings. 'If you do that for years, you start applying the same harshness when you meet your friends. It's impossible to separate work and private life. When we switched to a market economy it didn't stop at the garden gate.'

6

THROUGH THE HISTORY BOOKS

I HAD NOT FOUND A single museum documenting life along the border from the Baltic Sea to Schnackenburg. Now suddenly there was a museum every few miles. In Brome, the local shrine to the Iron Curtain was in the dungeon of a castle. A picture of what a typical stretch of border had looked like was painted on a wall at the far end of the cellar. The fuzzy watercolour showed two watchtowers. In front of the painting stood an original piece of East German border fence. This collage actually worked well as a reminder of how West Germans had experienced the border; the first hurdle – the fence – was very real, the country behind it remained shrouded in a fuzzy haze.

The exhibits bore all the hallmarks of over-eager amateur historians at work. They loved displaying photographs of themselves shaking hands with visiting dignitaries or in front of cranes tearing down the last pieces of the Iron Curtain. Exhibits such as medals for attending May Day parades and old East German passports were often their own. Amateur historians also had a good eye for exposing the ridiculous slogans of the old regime. A sign once mounted on the world's most impenetrable border read: 'Only under socialism can freedom and humanity blossom!'

Brome was a West German town inside a mile-wide land pocket that reached three miles into East Germany. The town had been a peninsula, surrounded on three sides by walls and watchtowers. After the Wende, the amateur historians tried to convert the fortified ring around Brome into an educational trail. They wanted to keep parts of the fortifications intact as a memento mori. A legend mysteriously noted: 'For various reasons the plan was dropped and the fortifications were destroyed.'

I wonder why, I mused aloud. 'Isn't it obvious?' a mother with two aggressive young boys chipped in. 'It would be very divisive. Why make Ossis feel inferior by reminding them of the border? Why give Wessis another opportunity to point fingers at Ossis? It's time to make up.' Was she an Ossi or a Wessi? I didn't dare ask after her appeal for unity. I said, what about learning from history? 'Oh, Germany's libraries were full of history books in 1933 – did that stop Hitler?' With a sigh of resignation she turned to her ever quarrelling sons.

Her view that 'it's time to make up' was shared by the amateur historians. In a note describing their aims they said: 'The exhibition must not be one-sided. While showing the inhumanity of the border, the exhibition should respect the dignity of the soldiers who worked there.' Dignity?

At the admissions desk I picked up a brochure listing twenty-six Iron Curtain museums along the border. A map showed that I had not over-looked any museums north of Schnackenburg. There simply was none. From here south, however, amateur historians in every little town had kept themselves busy collecting signs saying things like 'East Germany – our fatherland, land of freedom, of humanity and of dignity'.

I was fascinated by pictures that showed how comically unsightly the border was. Even Nikita Khrushchev had once remarked on its ugliness. The walls and watchtowers looked like something from a giant Fisher-Price play set, a childish fantasy poured in concrete. A perfectly raked sand-pit ran along the entire 800-mile death strip so guards could spot the footprints of fugitives. Every morning the young recruits were sent out to perform their socialist duty with a rake. How very German.

From Brome I drove to nearby Schnega to visit another Cold War cabinet of the macabre. I had phoned ahead and was greeted by Herr Ritzmann at the door of his windowless barn. Inside he had built a life-sized replica of the border, complete with 10-foot fence and sand-pit. He grabbed a bamboo pointer and strode on to the death strip. 'Right now, we are crossing the inner German border,' he announced and took a long step over a scotch-tape line on the floor. He pointed at the sand-pit. 'Always raked perfectly. The rake was for East Germany what the Ausch-witz train timetables were for the Nazis.' He pointed at a black, red and golden border post. 'Note the small metal pin on top. It's there to prevent birds from sitting on the post and shitting on the hammer and sickle just below the top.' He pointed at a small flap in the fence at ground-level.

'This is a wildlife gate. The flaps existed along the entire border to allow rabbits and wolves to cross over.'

In schoolmasterly fashion, he marched up and down the barn, pointing at beer mugs with East German insignia and VoPo uniforms. After explaining what each uniform was, he gave me a little test. 'First uniform on the left: major, lieutenant, corporal, sergeant, sergeant-major, lieutenant-major or officer. Which one is it?' he barked. I failed. Our next subject was acronyms. 'What's a BT11?' *Betonturm*, concrete tower, 11 metres high. 'BT9?' Nine metres high. 'SM70?' A spring gun mechanism. 'Yes, but with how many projectiles?' I didn't know. 'The standard version has 118, but one would, of course, be enough to kill you.'

Herr Ritzmann had been investigating the border since his early childhood. 'There is something mystical about all borders,' he said. Aged thirteen, he started trekking along the fence near his parents' house. During years of observation and research he developed a near encyclopedic knowledge of border trivia. The fence was made in Sweden not the Soviet bloc. Eight hundred people died trying to cross it. An average of ten VoPos patrolled one mile of border. Erich Mielke, East Germany's Minister for State Security, decreed: 'The border must be clean and lit up at all times.' And so he went on.

On his treks, some lasting days, he took notes on upgrading work and tried to befriend East German guards. Once, when they were repairing a fence, he drove his car right up to them. Knowing the East Germans' interest in technology, he offered to let them look at the car engine. 'All they had to do was take one step across the line.' They didn't take him up on the invitation and instead reported him to the Stasi. When Herr Ritzmann inspected his Stasi file after the Wende he found a note saying he had encouraged desertion among VoPos.

Whenever he appeared at the border, the guards would photograph him. In retaliation, he began photographing them. Now he was displaying the pictures on two walls of the barn. He brought the pointer down on two black and white shots and, putting on his public prosecutor voice, he said: 'Herr Krause. Herr Henschel.' The two butch VoPos were depicted pointing their cameras at Herr Ritzmann. 'They were the star photographers. Wherever I went, they were there. We saw each other almost every day. One day, some time after the Wende, I bumped into Herr Krause. He said: Guten Tag, Herr Ritzmann. They knew exactly who I was, probably from spies on our side. Herr Krause joined the West German police force but then they found his thick Stasi file. Now he guards nuclear waste in Gorleben.'

Herr Ritzmann spent his personal savings on building the museum. 'After I had done all the work, there were lots of politicians offering their support at the museum opening. They waxed lyrically about how wonderful and important such a museum was for unified Germany. Then, three days later, I received a letter from the local authorities telling me I had to shut down immediately. I had no permission to operate a public facility without a toilet on site, they said. No toilet, no museum. And they fined me 500 marks. So I got myself my own toilet.' Herr Ritzmann opened a door to a dingy room and sat down on a plastic box, clutching the bamboo pointer. 'There is no running water in the barn so I got this disposable toilet. The chemicals kill the smell. It's really great. And it's definitely much better than the VoPo toilets.'

The village of Zicherie-Böckwitz had been famously sliced in half by the border. Some 200,000 visitors came to the western part every year until 1989. Michael Foot, the Labour Party leader, and Robert McNamara, the US Defense Secretary, had stood at the end of the high street, cut off between the village pub and a farm. From Zicherie in the west, they could hear conversations across the narrow gap in Böckwitz. But if Foot or McNamara returned today, they wouldn't find a single brick of wall. The 300 villagers voted to tear down what had divided them after the Wende. The gap left by the border was turned into a park and given the name Europa Meadows, nicely cosmopolitan and uncontroversial. The tightly mown lawn was framed by scrubbed garden fences and tidy backyards. The village had not yet lost the feel of an orderly border town.

In the evening a bonfire sizzled between the houses. Dozens of people were drinking beer, dancing, singing songs. They eyed me suspiciously when they saw me writing in my notebook. In West Germany and most other parts of the world, the use of television cameras is seen as the most intrusive form of journalism. In East Germany, notebooks had a much greater power to frighten people.

'It's still the same old notebook from my Stasi days,' I said. The young couples didn't laugh, but at least it gave me a chance to ask questions. Had it been easy to fit the two halves back together?

'Sure. You just look around the fire tonight. Böckwitzer and Zicherier, happy together in equal numbers.'

'But don't start arguing again about the tower.'

'It's not me who started that argument.'

'So, now it's my fault?'

Trying to intervene, I asked them to explain the issue.

'I'm from Zicherie. He's from Böckwitz. There was a watchtower right in the middle of the village. For the border obviously. The Zicherier wanted to keep it as a memorial. But the Böckwitzer said it had to go.'

'Yeah, we had lived behind the tower for forty years. That's quite enough.'

'But you can't just bulldoze history aside.'

'You mean, in the same way that the Zicherier Wessis bulldozed their way back into Böckwitzer? Only a few days after the border was opened some came over and squatted in empty properties.'

'But the houses were legally theirs,' the Zicherier said. 'Many were forced to leave farms behind after the war. They still belong to them.'

I scribbled furiously as they continued to argue. When I later asked them for their names they declined. The Zicherier said: 'No names. Zicherie was full of spies during the Cold War. Most were sent over from Böckwitz. We know who they are. But they didn't get us then and they're not going to get us now.'

Another group told me that several former border guards still lived in the village. They married local women and stayed for good. There was no animosity towards them. A rotund woman suggested: 'They only did their job. Many were actually afraid of the work. If the guards saw fugitives and failed to shoot them then the guards went to prison.'

I said this merely showed they were selfish, or at least calculating. They would obviously rather kill someone than suffer themselves. Very human, but still beastly.

'You cannot blame the nineteen-year-old recruits,' the woman said. 'They are guilty of nothing. But whoever gave them orders to shoot, they should be shot. Of course, nobody can remember now who gave the orders.'

The next morning I stumbled upon yet another border museum. It was run by Willi Schütte, a West German farmer who had fled Böckwitz in 1953 and repossessed his family's farm two months after the border opening in January 1990. The farm stood directly by the border, next to the pub that had disappeared in the border gap.

Herr Schütte gave up farming after unification and turned his barns into an exhibition space. He had been inspired by the dozens of visitors roaming around the village every weekend. 'Some people travelled all the way from England. They wanted to see the border but there was no more border. So we had to get it back.'

In addition to the now familiar collection of uniforms and SM70s, Herr Schütte had also preserved an original watchtower on his land a mile outside the village. Painstakingly, he rebuilt the fortifications: a 100-yard stretch of fence, a sand-pit and a trench designed to stop cars and tanks. He was creating the educational trail that had been vetoed in Brome. Along the trail was also a memorial to the journalist Kurt Lichtenstein who was shot by VoPos near Zicherie in 1961 when he approached the border from the West German side. 'A German shot by Germans,' the inscription read.

Herr Schütte, the spitting image of Boris Yeltsin, said: 'The children are the most interested in the border. The first post-Wende generation has no experience of a divided Germany. The museum is for them. Unfortunately, not many Ossis come to see it.'

Two observations struck me with regard to the border museums. First, the museums were run by Wessis for Wessis. So far, all of them had been on West German soil. Second, local authorities were not very keen on them. Herr Schütte had encountered problems similar to those experienced by Herr Ritzmann in Schnega and the amateur historians in Brome. 'The authorities told me it would take two years to approve the museum. They asked, why do you want this? It's superfluous. I thought: I'll show you.'

Then, when Herr Schütte opened the museum in 1997, it was such a success that the local district decided to open a rival museum next door with more money. The authorities that once rejected him were now trying to take over his hobby horse.

South of Zicherie-Böckwitz, the swampy borderland had been converted into the Drömling Nature Reserve. I crossed waterlogged ditches and fields in a rain storm, and came to a railway bridge. Below lay a huge, derelict train station. Oebisfelde had been the main rail crossing point between East and West Germany. Trains to West Berlin passed through here. VoPos checked every passenger and every carriage for fugitives, clinically probing hidden cavities. Today the border station was completely deserted – the tracks stretching to the horizon; the decaying but nevertheless menacing buildings; the single, dark watchtower. Its zealous orderliness made it seem familiar. How could one not think of Auschwitz? I didn't want to but the resemblance was overwhelming. I walked through the ruins and saw padded, windowless interview cells. I left, glad that travelling was no longer a blood sport.

*   *   *

There was a question I had been bursting to ask East Germans all along. Why didn't you at least try to run away, to cross the border alone or in a mass break-out? What kept you? Had Moscow's puppets really invented an impenetrable border? In fact, a small number of the sixteen million East Germans had attempted to cross the Iron Curtain. They tried on foot; across rivers, lakes and the sea; by plane and balloon; or hidden in a vehicle. The western media celebrated their attempts while the eastern media ignored them. Every attempt was an encouragement to kindred free spirits. And every crossing symbolically chipped away at the fortifications.

How many East Germans successfully negotiated the barbaric obstacle course is not clear. Probably around 40,000. The number of people who died at the border is better documented. *'Die Grenze'* (*The Border*; 1997), by Jürgen Ritter and Peter Joachim Lapp, reveals that most of the deaths were not known or confirmed until years after the Wende. As relatives slowly gained access to secret files and confronted former guards, the number rose from 197 when the Berlin Wall fell to 916 in August 1997. Other statistics in the book's appendix reveal the chilling precision with which the Eichmanns in East Berlin chronicled what they called 'border safety measures'. On 30 June 1984, an unusually remote, 100.6-kilometre stretch of border was guarded by 1,181 attack dogs on long leashes. The dog runs had been expanded to 128.2 kilometres but with only 1,163 dogs the next year, before being cut back to 71.5 kilometres and 886 dogs by 30 June 1989. Ten years earlier there had also been a 292.5-kilometre minefield and a 393-kilometre stretch fitted with spring guns (apparently invented by SS concentration camp guards).

Crossing the border was evidently dangerous. But I didn't feel this entirely explained why so few people had tried to escape. At the very least, East Germans must have thought about it. According to the statistics their chances of survival were 40:1. Did they never fantasize about Steve McQueen's motorbike stunt in *The Great Escape*?

'Nein. Kein Thema.' Not a subject for discussion. 'We knew too little about the border to imagine elaborate escape scenarios.' Herr Kirstner lunched on chips and *Currywurst* at a fast-food stand. The fried sausage was covered in ketchup and curry powder. I explained my travel itinerary and, after ordering my own *Wurst*, I asked why people hadn't collected information on the border to prepare an escape.

'There was no information; all a big state secret. Most people never saw the border until the Wende. Kept in the dark, precisely to prevent escapes. We knew not to go there. But the nature of the fortifications were a mystery.'

What about help from the West?

'Maybe, if they had shown border maps and descriptions on western television instead of the night-time test card, East Germany would have fallen ten years earlier. Who knows?' Like all their neighbours, the Kirstner family had eagerly watched western television. No fortifications could stop the airwaves. But *Dallas* reruns hardly encouraged them to climb over barbed wire and join the capitalist tribe.

If any ordinary East German citizen had known the specifics of the border, it would have been Herr Kirstner. An engineer, he described his job as a mix of home insulation and installation. He was a fiddler who could not look at something without trying to understand how it worked. When I arrived at the fast-food stand, he was kneeling between gas tubes to check for a suspected leak while waiting for his lunch. The plump stand owner had mentioned an unusual smell. Rather than investigating the leak further while Herr Kirstner ate, he was now following our conversation. 'It's all because of the five-kilometre zone,' he suggested.

Herr Kirstner agreed. 'We just couldn't get close enough. Everyone was stopped at a road block five kilometres from the border. Beyond that was a heavily policed exclusion zone. No knowledge, no escape. Only residents were allowed in there.'

So why not become a resident?

'They wouldn't let you.'

Even without knowing exactly what the border looked like, people might have harboured escape fantasies, I mused while chewing on curried *Wurst*. People dreamt of travelling to far-flung, sci-fi galaxies. What would be more natural than imagining a journey to the unknown, distant and mysterious west, maybe in J. R. Ewing's Mercedes or a Trabbi spaceship?

'I know what you mean. I have those fantasies now. But not then. I needed to see what the border looked like – a graphic memory – to imagine escape. Nowadays, I sometimes think: You could have made it. There is a weak point in every installation. But I still haven't figured out the best route.'

Flying had to be the ideal way to cross the killing field, the higher the better. But Herr Kirstner shook his head. This was the Warsaw Pact's front-line, peppered with even more radar than watchtowers.

Maybe drive an articulated lorry through a checkpoint; one with barri-caded windows, steel-plates over the tyres and a plough welded to the front to clear away obstacles? My escapist enthusiasm was undiminished despite the culinary time-bomb now lodged in my stomach.

'You have to understand the complex anatomy of the border.' My engineer took three napkins to represent the five-kilometre cut-off and the two fences or walls that formed the actual border fortifications. Lining up the napkins parallel to each other, he explained that West Germans only ever saw the first fence, directly on the demarcation line. The second and more hazardous one was a mile back. It represented the real challenge. Ten feet from top to bottom, it was covered in alarm wires in addition to the V-shaped crown of barbed wire. On occasion, a third fence had been erected an arm's length beside it. In between the attack dogs roamed.

'This was only the start.' There was no hint of horror in his voice, just quiet pride in his new-found knowledge. 'In between the two main fences was the guards' hunting-ground. They had from the moment someone crossed the first fence and triggered the alarm until he or she was over the last fence. It was a question of speed. How quickly could he or she run and climb? How long did it take the guards to arrive at the spot and pinpoint their target?'

Herr Kirstner picked up the three napkins, carefully folded them and said he had a free half hour to show me everything 'in flesh and blood'. I followed him in the Red Racer to our first stop, the 5-kilometre road block. Even in this flat landscape, three miles was too far to make out any fences, walls or towers right on the border. The ordinary citizen really wouldn't have known what to expect.

We parked two miles down the road where the first fence had stood. All physical evidence had been removed. But listening to Herr Kirstner, I felt as if I was being transported to the Normandy beaches or Gettysburg or the Somme.

'This is where the race began. From here you had no more than ten minutes, depending on how long the guards took to get into their vehicles. There were a number of things to watch out for.' We started walking west through open terrain.

'Obviously, you had to pick a fence segment furthest between two watchtowers. But there were also guards in hidden bunkers strategically placed in this strip. Some people made the mistake of trying to hide rather than run straight for the final fence. They would trek sideways to cross the final fence where the guards didn't expect them. Chances were they got spotted. Dozens of guards would swarm out and, in any case, the final fence was lit during the night.'

Without noticing at first, our pace had picked up. We headed through brushland that offered little opportunity to hide or move stealthily. Herr Kirchner warned me to stay away from dwellings. Local residents often co-operated with the guards and reported anyone unfamiliar to the police. During the night, vigilantes patrolled the streets. It was difficult to imagine the resulting atmosphere of suspicion being removed as surgically as the physical fortifications.

As our pace increased further, my stomach was beginning to revolt. My digestion struggled to win the fight with my fried lunch. When I was nearly at the point where I'd rather have sat in a Stasi dungeon than carry on, Herr Kirchner announced we had reached our destination.

'The border evolved over the years.' He was dripping with sweat. 'The spring guns at the final fence here were removed after massive international protests. Same for the minefields in the mid-1980s. Instead, they installed more sophisticated alarm systems. Some of them really innovative.'

'Must have cost a few roubles.'

'The tit-for-tat fortification of the border was a smaller version of the superpower arms race, you might say.'

We stood by an unusually deep creek running parallel to the border. 'This is the *Kfz-Sperrgraben*.' The trench with its angled sides lay beyond the last patrol tracks, forming a vehicle barrier. It was the penultimate obstacle. Most of the border was fitted with fences rather than walls. Only where the border cut through populated areas, such as Berlin or Zicherie-Böckwitz, had walls been erected to prevent visual contact.

Having recovered somewhat from our hike, I flippantly remarked, 'If you can't use a vehicle to escape and can't make elaborate plans, then what you need is a ladder and a good pair of Nikes.'

Herr Kirchner entered into the spirit of the discussion. 'Maybe Nike also make rope-ladders. They'd be much easier to carry than wooden ones when you're running.'

'What about pole-vaulting equipment?'

'Or a big trampoline? One for each fence?'

We were drifting into fantasyland and we knew it. It was liberating. It was a show of non-acceptance, of protest and defiance against the grotesque. I now understood why Herr Kirchner had never entertained any thoughts of crossing the border before the Wende. One needed the inspiration that comes with detailed knowledge. Without a mental image of the fences and dog runs, it was impossible to pin one's hopes for a better future on crossing it.

It seemed, the most important element of fortification along this border was ignorance. In people's minds, the death strip had existed only as a black hole. That made it all the more impenetrable.

The Hotel Schönitz opposite the train station in Helmstedt was disturbingly chintzy. Flower motifs and figurines adorned the rooms. Oppulent pink curtains gave the smoky dining room the air of a brothel as imagined by a virgin. The bathrooms reeked of sickly sweet perfume. Hence I was all the more baffled to find what can only be described as a mechanized, self-cleaning toilet. Behind the seat (it clicked into a fixed position if lifted up) was a plastic case three times the size of an ordinary cistern. The logo read 'CleanSeat' and a green light was flashing next to the inscription 'disinfected'. If you sat down, the green switched to red, blinking 'please flush'. I dutifully followed the order. A plastic arm reached out from inside the box and gripped the toilet seat tightly. Then the seat began to move slowly, completing a 360-degree clockwise rotation in about 20 seconds while the grip wiped the surface. As the arm creaked back into the box, the red light switched back to green, 'disinfected'. A third light indicated 'service' (room service here?), a fourth 'trouble' (stomach trouble?).

However automated the East German border had been, I smirked, West Germany was still one step ahead. Here alarm systems and mechanization extended to the most private chambers.

Helmstedt had been West Germany's main passageway to the east. The autobahn that crossed the border at neighbouring Marienborn was the artery that connected West Berlin to the rest of the country. West Germans could travel on it without a visa. To monitor the transit traffic, the VoPos had erected the biggest control post along the entire Iron Curtain. One thousand guards checked papers and cars around the clock on several square miles of concrete. Dozens of lanes of traffic snaked through the labyrinth of probing stations, waiting for a grim face under a green cap to lift the final barrier. And on the return journey, the same procedure again in Berlin.

Today a new stretch of autobahn channelled traffic around the grey complex. Most of it had been converted into a museum. But the wide open tarmacked space had not lost its menace. Like the set of a horror film, it looked both comic and ghoulish. One plaque said: 'This building was used by the German Red Cross. Ambulances and hearses were checked here, and sometimes dismantled. The procedure also included coffins. This was aimed at preventing the smuggling of goods and persons.'

I climbed up inside the highest observation tower. From here the barriers and lighting system were controlled via two antiquated switchboards.

A television reporter was interviewing Herr Fricke, a lorry driver who had once tried to break through the checkpoint in a tanker. 'I thought they wouldn't shoot at a full load of petrol.' The trick had worked at first. Herr Fricke made it past the controls. But a guard in the tower activated a battering ram that shot across the autobahn and ripped the carriage out from under the lorry's cabin, travelling at 70 mph. Then, with the chase already over, the VoPos started shooting.

A miraculously unharmed Herr Fricke went to prison like all other *Republikflüchtlinge* (fugitives from the republic) – the oxymoron East Berlin used for the escapers. Those unintimidated by such words went to a dark cell. The standard prison term for *Republikflüchtlinge* was increased from three years when the Wall was built, to eight years by the time it came down.

The television team was filming a segment for the evening news to be shown the next day when the German President came to visit the new museum. I decided to return.

Herr Herzog swept down by helicopter under a clear sky. A white-haired former constitutional court judge, local government minister and church official, he would have been called an apparatchik in socialist days.

Blotches of sweat sprouted on his shirt. The 'channels of fear', as the control lanes had been called, didn't seem to induce terror in this visitor but the shabby VoPo cubicles turned into glass houses on hot days. Herr Herzog wanted to get through this as quickly as possible, handing out platitudes. 'These exhibits can show youngsters what freedom means.' He mopped his neck. 'Many things are being forgotten.' A glance at his watch. 'The divisive nature of the border fortifications must be made clear to future generations.' He was looking for one of his aides. We brushed past a noticeboard where visitors wrote down their impressions. 'Rebuild the wall, but ten metres higher this time', read one note. Another said: 'I am an Ossi – but I'm still alive.' Herr Herzog asked his aide about the next stop on his whistlestop tour, the annual meeting of the Friends of the Garden Club in Dessau-Wörlitz.

Then he stopped, standing in the middle of the vast tarmacked space surrounded by grim control towers. 'Is all of this real?' he asked. For the first time it seemed to occur to him this was not another flower show or school play put on especially for his visit. He shuddered. Later I asked him about his own memories of border crossings. 'They always gave my wife a hard time,' he said looking deflated. Then the President plodded off to his helicopter.

7

BEYOND CONCRETE
AND STEEL

A GUST OF WIND PUSHED the letter across the pavement. I noticed its
exotic stamp and reached down to inspect the philatelic treasure but
couldn't determine its origin. The letter was addressed to someone called
Schneider who lived around the corner. The postman must have dropped
it on his round, I thought. Rather than putting the letter back in a box,
I decided to deliver it personally.

Herr Schneider lived in a small house on the outskirts of Braunschweig,
a city 15 miles west of the border that early German immigrants to Canada,
Chile and Ohio had translated as Brunswick. Everything about Herr
Schneider's house was small. The roof barely reached over the walls, the
door was made for midgets and the narrow strip of garden surrounding
the house was short like a mini-skirt. I had plenty of opportunity to survey
the property while waiting for a grumbling Herr Schneider to find the
key that unlocked the door.

He was still grumbling when I handed him the envelope. He checked
it for a sender's name but it was blank except for the colourful stamp and
his address, written in large, uneven letters. Bowing his head and stepping
out of the darkness of his house, he ripped open the grey envelope with
barely contained excitement. Tugging and tearing, he seemed completely
oblivious to my presence. He pulled out a single sheet of paper filled with
crayon drawings, but it was clearly not what he had expected. His body
froze for a second before sinking down on a small garden wall.

'You thought it would be something else?'

'Yes.'

'But those are pretty drawings.'

'My grandson.'

Herr Schneider wasn't looking at me. He stared straight ahead, unaware he was talking to a complete stranger.

'What were you expecting to receive? Money?'

He shook his head but remained silent. Maybe it was time to go.

'For a moment, I thought it could be a letter from Brigitte. The funny stamp. The clumsy handwriting.' Forcefully, he shook his head again, trying to rid himself of a bad memory. 'But Brigitte is not your problem.' The sentence sounded less confrontational in German than in English. He didn't mean Brigitte was none of my business; she just wasn't a good topic for small-talk on the doorstep.

Herr Schneider looked out across his skinny lawn and I looked at him. He had dressed ambitiously. His silk shirt, dual-tone loafers and corduroy trousers did not go together, no matter how much money they had cost him. His receding hairline, however, gave him a look of honesty. I wanted to hear his story.

I sat down next to him on the low wall – not too close – and asked, 'Was Brigitte your girlfriend?'

He sized me up with a fleeting glance and nodded. Then he hesitated. 'No, she wasn't.' He shook his head vigorously. 'Not quite. She was supposed to be my girlfriend, my future wife.'

I hadn't yet gained his confidence and filled the renewed silence with the words: 'I'm not from around here. I travel.'

'Have you ever been to Russia?'

'No.'

'That's where Brigitte is from.'

'Brigitte? That doesn't sound like a very Russian name.'

'There you have it. She's probably a big fraud.'

Brigitte was Herr Schneider's mail order bride. A year ago he had responded to a newspaper advertisement. 'Russian women are real goers!' it promised. 'Humble, domesticated and lithe.' An agency sent Herr Schneider a number of photographs, plus some biographical information. With a hint of disgust in his voice, he described the pictures as pin-up shots. But Brigitte's *curriculum vitae* caught his interest. She had a university degree. In his eyes that lifted her above the sordidness of the love-for-sale business.

He wrote her a letter that was passed on by the agency. The response he received a few weeks later arrived in an envelope similar to the one I had delivered. Brigitte wrote she was looking for a new beginning. Germany was a country that had always interested her. She would like to see a photograph of Herr Schneider. Would he consider coming to Russia to meet her? She couldn't afford the ticket to Germany. That was unless he would pay for it. And, yes, she was very serious about finding a husband.

I could only imagine what the picture she received from him must have looked like: Herr Schneider wearing a mismatch of patterns and fabrics only too appropriate for the cross-cultural relationship he was hoping to form. But he wasn't a vain man. He tried hard because he was desperate. I liked him.

'What happened next?'

'We exchanged more letters. They were fairly short but seemed genuine.'

'Did you meet?'

'I made plans to visit her. Everything was arranged. We even spoke on the phone before I left. She actually speaks German. That really convinced me I was doing the right thing. Her German wasn't perfect but good enough. Then, a day before my flight, my holidays were cancelled.' The building company Herr Schneider worked for had to rush through an important contract. 'If I had insisted on going away because I was meeting my future foreign wife, they would have laughed and laughed. After that Brigitte and I spoke one more time on the phone. I told her I would pay for her flight to visit me. I sent her a cheque but didn't hear from her after that. Of course not, you might say. The strange thing is, the cheque was never cashed. I still haven't cancelled it. I thought I'd wait and see what happened. Then you came with this envelope.'

Herr Schneider stood up and smiled. 'I have to go to work now. But thank you very much for delivering the letter. Please, come back and visit me if you are in the area again.'

'I will, Herr Schneider. And maybe Brigitte really wasn't a fraud. Maybe she fell ill or has to care for sick relatives.' I surprised myself when I said those last words. His desperate hope was infectious.

A few days later I passed through Braunschweig again and looked up Herr Schneider. He was wearing linen trousers with a sleeveless denim shirt, looking as forlorn as on my first visit. But his smile ignited when he opened the door. (I could see only the bottom half of his face as he stood in the tiny door frame.)

'I got a letter from her.'

'That's wonderful.'

'*Ja*. Well. The news isn't all good.' He invited me in. 'Mind your head.' Most of the ground floor was taken up by one smallish room. 'She wrote me this strange letter. She says she found a husband at home.' Herr Schneider showed me a single sheet of paper with uneven handwriting. 'The funny thing is, the letter wasn't posted in Russia. The postmark says Postamt Magdeburg.' Magdeburg was a city 40 miles away on the other side of the border.

'You mean she could be here?'

'I don't know. She always said she wanted to come to Germany. Something about old family links.'

'Why would she come but not see you?'

'She probably got lots of responses from German men. I know I'm not the only one. Russian women are very popular here. They are beautiful. She might have had several offers and decided to keep all the suitors going until she selected the lucky prince.'

'You mean, she could be living with another man in Magdeburg? You're saying she lied to you about her location but admitted to being engaged to someone else? A man in Magdeburg?' It all sounded odd. I asked Herr Schneider if he still had her photograph. Most certainly. A thirty-year-old bottle blonde peered out from the expensive black frame. Behind the garish make-up I saw a woman both good-looking and kind.

'It just doesn't make sense.'

'No, it doesn't.'

I expected Herr Schneider to be lonely and dejected, but he still had a glint of hope in his eyes, reignited by Brigitte's first communication in months. 'Will you come to Magdeburg with me?'

'*Wie bitte?*'

'Come to Magdeburg with me. I want to find her. Just to take a look at her. Maybe then the whole thing will evaporate and I can go back to looking for a humble, domesticated and lithe German Fräulein.'

We drove to Magdeburg in the Red Racer. Who knew if I would be back to Braunschweig following this adventure? Herr Schneider's posture was relaxed but a desperate man might commit desperate acts.

To calm the air of expectancy, I asked him about cars. Two Britons would have chosen the weather. For two Germans, the automobile was the natural topic of conversation.

When we crossed the border I took the opportunity to tell Herr Schneider more about my trip. I said the border still seemed very present, and not just because of the museums; differences between the two sides were easily recognizable. He said 'that shameful construction' was now fading. The Wende already seemed a long time ago. He squinted out of the window. 'They did a very good job building the fortifications. I should know as a construction manager.'

'But the Wall fell nevertheless.'

'You cannot blame the construction workers for that. Buildings don't usually fall down by themselves. This thing – all the concrete and steel – was built for eternity.'

'And that's how long they thought it would last. With enough concrete, the wall-builders believed they could cement their rule for ever.' The conversation died down and we boarded our separate trains of thought.

What delusions had befallen East Berlin's corridors of power when the Wall was planned? Did the apparatchiks really think they could incarcerate an entire population in perpetuity? What arrogance to attempt a feat tried in vain by leaders through the ages. 'Nothing anywhere has ever been successfully defended,' noted General Patton. The Roman Limes crumbled brick by wonky brick. Jerusalem, regardless of the Crusaders' divine support, remained indefensible. And the Maginot Line, outmanoeuvred by the Panzers, stands to this day as a monument to transience. But Herr Ulbricht, the first East German leader, thought he could safely base the future of his state on a concrete wall.

Or were we the delusional ones, thinking the human spirit could only be subdued for so long? In Rüterberg, I thought I had found answers. The villagers' uprising suggested, even in allegedly order-loving Germany, that man was indomitable. But the new village leaders were almost as intolerant as the old ones. Maybe Rüterberg had swapped one tyranny for another. Maybe Herr Ulbricht's heirs had simply been unlucky.

Our hotel was as charmless as the rest of Magdeburg. The net curtains in the bare rooms had soaked up Trabbi exhaust smoke for forty years and the odour was now slowly working its way back out. If you closed your eyes, you could see VoPos directing traffic below. On my night table, I found a copy of the New Testament, probably the only recent addition to the room.

Magdeburg was a war victim on a par with Dresden. Some 90 per cent of the city had been destroyed. To rebuild it, the mayor must have employed the same architects that designed the concrete border. Hundreds of tower blocks ringed the centre like a medieval city wall. They were the most desperate and soul-destroying kind of quarters. Where grand façades on a tree-lined chaussée may lend a spring to strollers, the streets of Magdeburg could prolong winter until July. This was the Cold War's frosty legacy. Not all of East Germany had been cemented and frozen in time, but only because time ran out and a few timid flowers basking in the political thaw flourished in the cracks between concreted Utopia and tarmacked wasteland. Hammer and sickle had been chosen as the country's emblem with rare but chilling honesty. Nowhere was the cult of cement more ubiquitous than on Magdeburg's stony acres. Even the old socialist regime had admitted this garrison of cell blocks was no landmark. 'Attractions in the common sense, there are relatively few in Magdeburg,' recorded an official, pre-Wende travel guide.

Herr Schneider wanted to start combing the concrete desert immediately and was nice enough to ask if I was ready. I had to admit I harboured an ulterior motive for accompanying him on this trip. Brigitte's story had awakened my curiosity about Germany's growing immigrant community. One out of ten residents in the reunified country were Ausländer. Millions of refugees, asylum-seekers and guest-workers from Eastern Europe flooded into Germany following the implosion of the Soviet empire. Newspaper editorials claimed the country might turn into a US-style melting-pot (*Schmeltztiegel*). What made Brigitte so desperate to be part of it?

Herr Schneider decided the register office was an obvious place to search for clues. If Brigitte had married a Magdeburger, the authorities would have paperwork with her name on. I didn't share Herr Schneider's confidence in German bureaucracy. The government employed more than five million people, making it Europe's biggest employer, and the system's inertia was legendary. If Brigitte's name was on file we were unlikely to be told for weeks.

Champagne flowed inside the register office, but there was no wedding party in sight. One of the officials was celebrating a birthday. This seemed to absolve all of them of their duties. Herr Schneider eventually attracted some attention by asking for a glass of bubbly. A surly official told us data protection rules prevented him from divulging any information.

Next we tried the registration office. By law, every resident in a German district has to register with the authorities. To foreigners, this may confirm suspicions about the German love of control and order, but my guess was that the government needed to find something for its millions of civil servants to do, hence the extra paper work. Another clever trick from the same drawer was the lack of metal-detectors at airports. Germany distinguishes itself as the only industrialized country that employs hundreds of armed policemen to bodysearch passengers before they board aircraft.

An administrator at the registration office eyed us suspiciously. 'We only have one list you can use. It's called the phone book.' The words slithered tartly from her mouth. After our failure at the register office, we hardly expected more help here. The steely-eyed grandmother behind us in the queue, however, was outraged, calling the official's behaviour a 'bitter cocktail of arrogance spiced with arrogance'. She suggested a trip to Olvenstedt, a northern suburb where many Russians lived: 'They all know each other; they still live as a community.'

Olvenstedt presented itself as not so much a concrete jungle as a concrete cemetery. The architects had lined up tower blocks at right angles like tomb plates stacked high. Mediterranean people buried their folk like this.

Herr Schneider fell silent as I parked the Red Racer. He clutched Brigitte's picture, his last connection to her. He had brought the whole frame, unwilling to release her from the tight grip of the non-reflective glass and backboard.

Finding Brigitte's countrymen was easier than we expected. They congregated in lazy circles between the buildings and basked in the warm afternoon haze. We swanned from group to group showing the photograph and trying to avoid looking like policemen on a search mission. Had they seen this woman, we asked. Then Herr Schneider would tell his story. How he had hoped to marry her. How he would still marry her if she was single. One group of women with toddlers wanted to hear more. They giggled nervously until Herr Schneider finally interrupted his self-absorbed monologue. 'You think I'm ridiculous . . . stupid?'

It couldn't work, they said, Russian and German, '*kaputt*'.

'But Brigitte said it could work. She wanted to come to Germany and be with a German man.'

'Many Russian women want German man. But when they arrive here, Russian and German don't mix. Like milk and lemon.'

Herr Schneider seemed mystified by the reference, or maybe the fruitlessness of the search had dawned on him. I quizzed the women about their relations with Germans. They said they didn't know any. None of the Ausländer – Russians, Georgians, Ukrainians, Armenians, Africans – were integrated into daily German life. Ausländer drank in their own clubs, shopped in ethnic stores and soon stopped learning German. The image of a melting-pot was misleading. Germany – in Olvenstedt at least – looked more like a *solyanka*, a fatty Russian soup bristling with diced meat and vegetable leftovers.

We regrouped at a Chinese restaurant. Herr Schneider's enthusiasm was severely dented. I tried to cheer him up with an analysis of changing culinary tastes in East Germany. Sweet and sour chicken was the new national dish, I suggested. Chinese restaurants had quickly opened up across the country after the Wende. All other overseas cuisines were shunned. Every village now had a Red Dragon or Mandarin Palace. Was it not ironic that East Germans should forgo *solyanka*, the Soviet culinary staple, but embrace the kitchen of the only other communist superpower? Or maybe the choice reflected how East Germans felt about the Wende – sweet *and* sour?

My feeble attempts at humour served only to deepen the furrows on Herr Schneider's pained forehead. 'Or maybe there's a much easier explanation. Chinese food is fatty like *solvanka*. It suits the fat-loving palate of glutinous German eaters.'

Herr Schneider was irritated. 'Why are you so negative about German food?'

'The food's wonderful,' I said.

Cracau was another area of Magdeburg where we had been told to look for Russians. One out of eight residents in Cracau was an Ausländer and everyone supposedly knew everyone else. A group of swarthy men shared spicy Georgian food between dustbins. After much bemused questioning – 'Why a Russian woman? Russian women not beautiful, Georgian women always the best in Soviet Union' – the eldest pointed us towards Katja. The men nodded in a quiet acknowledgement that although she was Russian, given her beauty she could have been Georgian.

Katja refused to make her story sound sad. She didn't like sad Russian stories. Run-down Russia needed happy stories and happy people. She stood in her shoebox flat and played with the pigtails of a neighbour's daughter. Katja was a year younger than Brigitte and had sought the same short-cut to fortune. She had picked a Bavarian farmer from an agency list, but the marriage fell apart after less than a year. 'We were like stone and water,' she said without further elaboration. To avoid going back to Russia, she moved in with relatives in Magdeburg. Forestalling a plea from an increasingly desperate Herr Schneider, Katja offered her help. She would introduce us to friends.

When we returned the following day, Katja was standing on a box in her kitchen and belly-dancing in front of two of her friends, Nadja and Frau Meiser. Their laughter drowned out our entry through an open front door. Katja jumped off the box and introduced us. From the reaction of the two women it was obvious they already knew of our search. Suspicions as to Brigitte's whereabouts clouded the room. Herr Schneider had probably hoped for more. The most tangible result of the conversation was a suggestion to phone the agency again. 'You have to be tough with them. Threaten them. Say you'll go to the police.' Katja ranked Russian marriage agencies somewhere on a par with the Russian mafia. Herr Schneider shuddered but eventually picked up the phone and did his best to intimidate. He was told to call back later.

Katja's friends left and we lunched with her. I wanted to know more about the Bavarian husband. Had he been abusive? Was that why she came to Magdeburg? 'The shopping is quite good here,' she frowned. 'Why shouldn't a woman come here for the shopping?'

Herr Schneider phoned the agency again. 'You must tell me where she lives or where her new husband lives . . . I know she's here with him . . . No, I don't want to receive a new list.'

I had arranged to meet Katja's friend Frau Meiser without Herr Schneider. She was a self-appointed Samaritan trying to make the city a less forbidding place for Ausländer. The main task she set herself was fighting attacks on foreigners and helping them in their dealings with the local bureaucracy. 'An Ausländer gets ignored without someone to translate or explain in German,' she said.

We passed a charming sign by the roadside: 'Ausländer Free Zone'.

Frau Meiser toured the city like a historian striding over a battlefield. On this corner an Armenian had his jaw broken by someone wielding a baseball bat. In Olvenstedt a man from Angola was beaten in his own home. When he escaped the two intruders set his bedroom on fire. Here, a group of eighteen young right-wingers chased a family from Togo that was lucky enough to be carrying a starter gun to scare them away. At the McDonald's restaurant on Breiter Weg, an Ausländer was kicked by a neo-Nazi and later arrested by a policeman whom he had asked for help.

The man was forced to sit naked in a police cell for two hours and held until the next day without charge.

'This makes me very angry. It's so primitive to equate foreignness with being guilty.' She wanted to give me reports on many more such cases.

She said Magdeburg had become a tribal society. Not in the African sense but every splinter group looked out only for its own people. There were the well known divisions between Germans and Ausländer, but the Armenians and Turks and Afghans and Sudanese also fought each other. To a Russian, for example, a Palestinian and a German were both foreigners. 'Ten years ago we lived in a very homogenous society.'

The long shadow of the border was looming once again. The government in East Berlin had claimed the border was built to keep West Germans (and Nato tanks) out, not to prevent East Germans from leaving. Everyone knew that to be a lie. Few West Germans had the slightest desire to forgo bananas to join the socialist experiment. But an unintended side-effect was an almost complete block on immigration. Most East Germans had never seen a dark face before the Wende.

'At the very least, there must have been Eastern Europeans from your socialist brother states.'

'We saw quite a few Russians in Magdeburg. But they weren't popular then either. They behaved badly.' She sighed. 'I shouldn't be telling you this. It'll only cloud your opinion of Magdeburg.'

Frau Meiser's earnest local pride was endearing. She wanted to show me what remained of the original centre, the 10 per cent that had survived the Allied bombers. 'When the city was founded a millennium ago, it stood above petty racial hatreds.' Otto the Great, a contemporary of Charlemagne, created the Moritz Abbey that grew into the city of Magdeburg. The old stonework was raw and convincingly medieval in its cragginess. The abbey was named after Mauritius, the Moor, slayer of pagans. Skin colour and blood lines were irrelevant in the old Magdeburg as long as you believed in Jesus Christ.

I asked Frau Meiser if she had any further inkling about Brigitte's case. No, but she promised to find those reports on other Ausländer cases.

Rain accompanied Herr Schneider to a Bierkeller where he waited for me. Two phone messages had reversed his melancholy. The agency now said it could help with a new address for Brigitte in Germany. He brandished a half-empty glass of Pils – by no means his first – and held up his index finger. 'But,' he wagged his finger, 'that's not all. Katja, dear Katja, also has a firm lead. We're getting close.' His smile reached around his head and stretched his skin so tight the furrows on his forehead momentarily disappeared.

I dragged Herr Schneider out of the beer-hall. The first setback waited for us at the hotel. The agency had left another message. It gave Brigitte's address as a post office box in Berlin. Herr Schneider knew the address. It was one of the boxes used by the agency.

When we arrived at Katja's flat, she was with another girlfriend. 'I would like you to meet my friend Brigitte.'

At the kitchen table sat a blondish woman. She looked Russian but could have been Polish. I noticed her friendly smile but quickly turned to Herr Schneider to read the expression on his face. The beer-hall flush evaporated, leaving behind ashen wrinkles.

'Brigitte is one of my German friends. I thought you might want to meet her.' Katja's confidence wavered. 'She is German . . . you are German. She just finished her divorce.'

Her eagerness to find a partner called Brigitte for Herr Schneider was touching. To her it must have made perfect sense. This Brigitte was blonde like the one we were looking for, and, even better, there would be no nationality clash.

Herr Schneider bolted from the silent kitchen; I caught up with him on the stairs. He had fallen into the same absent-minded state I had witnessed on the day I first knocked on his door. Once again, he had been presented with the wrong envelope.

'I suspected from the start that my Brigitte was involved with the Russian mafia; something had to be wrong with the whole thing; maybe it is a prostitution racket, or worse; you read so much about what that mafia does, like transplant organ smuggling and drugs. Who knows?' Herr Schneider ranted, with no evidence to support his suspicions. He was not amenable to reason. Hope had been his only currency and he was flat broke.

At the hotel I found an illegible message from Frau Meiser. Later we were joined by Jusuf, a Turkish building contractor who occasionally worked with Herr Schneider. Jusuf seemed to be the source of his Russian mafia suspicions. In Jusuf's mind, the mafia was already running Germany. 'What's biggest business in Germany? Cars. Germany makes best cars in the world. Who sells 'em? Russian mafia. We Turks make good living from building. But never work with Russians.' Herr Schneider didn't listen to his business associate. He had already stepped back through his small doorway into a world where he dressed alone in front of a mirror.

Then Katja came to apologize. She felt guilty but didn't know what for. Her eyes searched the lobby in vain. On his strict orders, I told her that Herr Schneider had already departed. 'I don't want to see Katja; I don't even want to see Brigitte any more,' he sighed. I drove him back to Braunschweig and dropped him at his home where he took the picture of the blonde out of the frame and ripped it up before ducking through his front door.

Back on the autobahn, the Red Racer sounded like the empty tin can that it was. I had enjoyed having a passenger. Chatter and heartache had banished all mechanical tribulations. The car had seemed quieter, the engine more powerful for a short while. Now arthritic clanking accompanied my travels once again.

Even without Herr Schneider and Brigitte, though, I felt I was not finished in Magdeburg. Jusuf's talk about the Russian mafia seemed a trifle melodramatic, but it fitted in with Frau Meiser's argument that Germany was dissolving into a 'tribal' society in which all ethnic groups distrusted each other and carved out their separate spheres: Turks in the building sector; Russians in the car trade; Vietnamese in cigarette retailing. And so on.

Beyond Braunschweig by the autobahn, so I had been told, there was an open-air market for second-hand cars. Russian mafiosi were rumoured to be the organizers. Who knows, they might offer me a fist full of deutsch-marks for the clapped-out red Toyota. Jusuf's little diatribe might yield a useful result after all.

Suspicious locals directed me to a field filled with car wrecks. Grass grew out of mangled metal heaps in a green moonscape surrounded by an earth wall. Intermittently, disappointed customers showed up with similar tales. They had hoped the market would still be in operation 'despite all the trouble'. For years, Russian dealers had congregated here to buy vehicles of almost any condition and ownership status to export them east as far as Siberia. Everyone became rich. The Russians' insatiable demand sent second-hand car prices at registered dealerships through the sun roofs. Allegedly, the mafiosi offered to buy the market site for 10 million deutschmarks. But the farmer who owned the field found it more lucrative to continue charging them a fee for each vehicle. Two years ago, the enterprise was ruled illegal by the police after the Russian entrepreneurs diversified into the pharmaceutical sector. But trade continued, protected by the embankment. The police finally closed down the commodity exchange a few months ago following a machine-gun battle.

Jusuf felt vindicated. I caught up with him in Magdeburg where he was entertaining Kemal whom he called a *Gymnasiumtürke*, or grammar school Turk. Kemal held square, horn-rimmed spectacles in hands that had never touched a brick in anger. The three of us drove to a kebab house in Jusuf's Mercedes ('bought from an official German dealer').

'If it's not the Russians smuggling cars, it's the Vietnamese with contraband cigarettes or the Poles with booze.'

'. . . or the Turks taking over a building site. Not a very peaceful Germany, you describe. How about sharing?'

'You can't mix oil and water.' (I remembered what the Russian women in Olvenstedt had said: Germans and Russians were like 'milk and lemon'.) Jusuf sounded worldly-wise to himself, judging by his smile. Kemal did not smile but evidently shared his views. He didn't conform to Jusuf's picture of a good Turk, having swapped bricks and mortar for the mortarboard. But he employed an intelligence that lent force to Jusuf's blunt tribalism.

'So how would you share?' he asked.

'Make you feel at home in Germany, maybe.'

'You want Ausländer integration?' Kemal was baiting me.

I fell into his trap. 'That would be nice.'

'Very nice. First, the Germans try to get rid of the Ausländer in gas chambers. Didn't work so well. Now you think you found a better way of keeping Germany German. You want Ausländer to wear *Lederhosen* instead of yellow stars. A few years of integration, some Pumpernickel bread, reciting Goethe, drinking beer brewed according to the 1516 purity law, each family member showering in their own private bathroom, *Gemütlichkeit*, order, order, order – and *Kabumms*, little Kemal has turned into Klaus.'

Ausländer-bashing right-wingers would have agreed with every word of Kemal's blather. But he was good. He obviously didn't mind a few years of integrated German grammar schooling.

The two Turks concentrated on their pitta bread. 'No Pumpernickel on the menu. I'm sorry.' I ventured to change the topic of conversation. Probably out of habit, I began to ask them about Brigitte, but changed course halfway into the first sentence. It wasn't the fact that Herr Schneider had given up the search. I didn't want Jusuf, his business associate, to blab about his love life. I arranged to see Kemal on his own. Maybe then

I would ask him, even if he was likely to disapprove of such liaisons as yet another integrationist trick.

Magdeburg seemed all the more derelict without Herr Schneider. Nobody bothered placing flowers between blocks of flats. People put flowers in cemeteries, yes, but not in their living quarters.

Katja flitted around out of reach, chasing a new lover. In her flat I found Frau Meiser. A file with reports on right-wing attacks was waiting for me at her house, she said. I offered her a lift home. On the way, we stopped at a police station. Walking in, I counted more filing cabinets than cells.

Frau Meiser had heard an Ausländer and a *Fascho*, or young neo-Nazi, were arrested after a fight. A police officer was trying to interview an olive-skinned man called Mirko. The grinning *Fascho* sat on a bench, boots neatly laced and arms folded. Mirko struggled to pin assault charges on him.

Policeman: Why did he hit you? You must have done something to provoke him?

Mirko: Provoke who? You *Arschloch*.

Policeman: Shut up and answer the question.

Mirko: *Schweine Fascho*. Is gay.

Policeman: Do you have a statement to make, no? I'll throw both of you out.

Mirko: You *Arschloch*, talk here. Listen, you *Scheisskerl*.

Fascho: I would guess, he is angry and tries to show remorse for the attack on me.

Mirko: Angry. *Scheisse*, you gay, *scheiss Schweinehund*.

Policeman: Last chance. My colleague said he saw this clown baiting you. If you wish to make an official complaint I will fill out the appropriate paper work. You will have to sign it. Then it will be dealt with in an orderly procedure according to the rules of my country not your country. For that, we need your disciplined co-operation.

Mirko: Discipline, Hitler, *Scheisse*.

Policeman: He ... You ... Boom?

Mirko: Speak Deutsch, *Arschloch*.

Policeman: OK. Fine with me. No paper work.

Fascho: What if I want to make an official complaint against him?

Mirko: *Scheisse* on your complaint, *Schweinehund.*
Policeman: Get out of the station.
Mirko: *Fick* police station.

We filed out behind the *Fascho* and Mirko. I had expected Frau Meiser at least to approach Mirko, seeing that we were here because of him. But she wore a disdainful frown under her African shawl. 'You know, sometimes the German police can really be awful to Ausländer. They punch them and keep them in prison for no reason. Doctors see broken bones and choke marks. Amnesty International has condemned the German police.' It was a bizarre apology for having wasted time on this detour. Frau Meiser had wanted me to see an abusive police officer.

She lived in one of Magdeburg's few old town houses, far away from the unseemly bunkers. The airy rooms were filled with 'ethnic' clutter. I rested my hand on the shaven stone head of a man from Africa.

She handed me her file. It contained the assortment of crimes I had come to expect. The likes of: 'Skinheads yell Heil Hitler after stabbing Ukrainian.' The perpetrators usually sipped from cocktails of hormones, unemployment and sadism. But one case stood out. The local government had asked the hamlet of Gollwitz to accommodate a group of immigrants. The 800 East German villagers were up in arms when they learned fifty Russian Jews would move into an empty manor house owned by the local government. They had hoped the 'castle' could be turned into a hotel. The guests they longed for were well-heeled West Germans. The village council voted unanimously against the immigrant settlement, apparently not for anti-Semitic reasons but to 'protect the Jew from local baseball bat owners'.

The most perplexing thing about this case was Frau Meiser's interpretation. 'You have to understand what type of people live in Gollwitz.'

'You mean they are neo-Nazis'.

'No, no. They are ... I don't want to be rude, they are simple people. Really quite simple. No education, no jobs, no contact with the outside world. They are not like our *Faschos* in Magdeburg.'

'They don't stab people, so you sympathize with them?'

'Oh, I don't like them at all. They are peaceful but in many ways worse. Unlike the *Faschos*, they fear foreigners. They can't bear the fact that these Russian Jews are much smarter than them. One day soon after their arrival, the immigrants will try to teach the villagers how to speak proper German, so they think. Like the Turks who speak without an accent, almost as university professors. Like the Turkish builders who know their way around the village lanes better than they do. The villagers are scared of questioning the way they live their ignorant lives, scared of losing their identity.'

As I was leaving, Frau Meiser mentioned that Katja wanted to see me.

I was late for dinner with a radiant Katja the next day. She had waited an hour, but nothing could wipe away her smile. She had played with the loose threads of her frayed jeans, humming high-pitched melodies.

We talked about her new Russian boyfriend, Igor. Her feelings of guilt towards Herr Shneider had gone. She was back to belly-dancing. She said she was in love. I ate while she extolled the many qualities she had in common with Igor. How they would dance and sing and cook together.

Then I asked about the Bavarian ex-husband. What had happened between them? Was he abusive? Her smile collapsed before I had realized the cruelty of my question, given her current mood. 'I divorced him because he had none of the things that Igor has. None. Empty.'

She had told me a few days ago the marriage was like 'stone and water'. What did she mean?

'Igor holds me up, lets me float on water. My husband, my ex-husband, let me drop like a stone. He didn't understand me.'

Wasn't this a risk one took when choosing a catalogue lover?

'Igor understands because we are both Russian. No German husband can match him. I didn't want to say anything like that in front of Herr Schneider. I just wanted him to be happy. He could never have been happy with the Russian Brigitte.'

'How do you know?'

'He wouldn't. And if we asked Brigitte, she would agree.'

'But we can't find Brigitte. Herr Schneider tried and gave up.'

'We can probably find her. I just didn't want Herr Schneider to find her. It's better for both of them.'

Kemal was simultaneously smoking two cigarettes, drinking tea, coffee and beer, tuning a radio to a thumping hip-hop station while flicking through CD cases, trying to wiggle into a pair of Adidas trainers, hitting the redial button on his mobile phone and carrying on two conversations, one with me, the other with a friend in another room. We were off to a football match in Salzgitter across the border. He grabbed his car keys, still holding a shoe in one hand, when finally he got through on his mobile phone. He was cut off immediately as we climbed into his car outside the crepuscular tower block to join a convoy of Turks in Mercs.

'I hate these Wessis,' he screamed over the drumbeat.

I couldn't tell whether he meant to offend me. I remembered Kemal had grown up in the Rhineland and moved to Magdeburg only after finishing his grammar schooling.

'The Ossis are pretty straightforward racists. The darker you are, the more they beat you. But at least it's honest.'

Well, hardly.

'Ossis are straight with you. Totally. You know where you are. Black means stick?'

And Turk means?

'People in Turkey hate the blacks as well. Nobody likes foreigners. Can't blame the Ossis. They didn't have many Ausländer before the Wende. Why start now?'

His mobile rang. The Turkish driver in front was calling. Their favourite hip-hop song was playing on the radio. Kemal sang along to the black American slang over the phone and gave a Bronx ghetto salute out of the window.

'Yeah, man, I really hate those Wessis, man. No honour.'

What's so honourable about beating people? My responses sounded as flat as his incendiary patter.

'Honour means unity of words and deeds. The Ossis say they don't like the foreigners and they act like it. That's honourable.'

And Wessis are racist without admitting it?

'No, man. They want to sucker you in, make you a dark or black Wessi. The Ossis beat you but at least they otherwise leave you alone.'

Had Kemal ever been beaten?

'No, man. But worse things can happen to you. My Wessi teachers tried to turn me into a clone. Dress like this, think like that. You should read this book not that.'

During a lull in the music, he told me Turkish teachers and pupils were not allowed to wear their traditional headscarves in many West German schools. Wessi parents feared their children would get the wrong signals from the headscarves – which in their eyes were a symbol for the oppression of women in Islamic countries. Wessi mothers said they had fought decades for equal rights, now they didn't want their daughters to experience renewed oppression. Hence they insisted on curtailing the rights of Turks who wanted to wear their traditional clothing.

Kemal turned up the car radio to listen to a song with American police sirens.

'Maybe the people at your school were scared of you.'

'Why, man?'

'Well, I met a woman who campaigns on behalf of Ausländer. She translates for them and so on. She said some Germans are scared of people like you who could be smarter than them and influence their lives, even take their identity.'

'That's bullshit, man. She sounds like a softy. I call them Ausländer-catchers. They want to help us and integrate us. Makes them feel better about the Holocaust or something, the whole guilt-thing.'

'That's possible.'

'They are the ones who are really scared, scared that we don't want their help and protection. That we don't want to be part of their wonderful new Germany and kill their guilt.'

'Possible, too.'

'It's the same with the younger Wessis, the schoolgirls. They want to be so politically correct they have to have a boyfriend who is an Ausländer. The darker the better. You wouldn't believe how much the boys from Ghana and Sudan get laid. A Latin lover is good, like a Turk or Italian, but nothing beats black skin for them.'

I was reminded of Brigitte and how keen Herr Schneider had been on lithe Russian women. His fascination with having a foreign wife hardly seemed to stem from political correctness. My thoughts drifted to whether Katja could actually find Brigitte in Magdeburg. If I met her what would I tell Herr Schneider?

'Of course, the whole thing – black and German – never lasts. Can't work. I once had a German girlfriend. Do this, don't do that. I could have killed her. The bitch had no honour. She went off with a black guy in the end.'

It didn't seem a good time to ask whether Kemal had heard of Brigitte. Maybe later, but then we arrived at the football ground where two Turkish teams battled in the rain, and soon Kemal was smoking and drinking and screaming over the music into a mobile phone, discussing a referee decision with a friend at the other end of the pitch.

*　　*　　*

Katja was toiling away merrily in her kitchen when I walked in. I sank into a chair, exhausted from a long walk up the grim staircase. She wore the prissy grin of a head girl at boarding school. 'I have something for you,' she announced while reaching for the phone.

There was no warning; no sign that the invisible sun our acquaintance had revolved around would finally rise. After our last meeting had ended in tears, I was surprised to meet again at all. Katja gave no clues as she waited for a dialing tone. All the shoe leather and tyre rubber of the chase, now for the finale. A short dance of her fingertips on the dial, a momentary pause as she waited for an answer, a staccato burst of Russian, then she handed the receiver to me. 'It's Brigitte.'

I gripped the phone suspiciously. She had actually found her. I covered the mouthpiece with my hands. 'How did you find her?'

'Talk to her. She will tell you.'

'I want to hear it from you. How do I know it's the right one?'

'You will know it when you talk to her.'

'But how did you find her?'

'It was easy.'

'How?'

'She's Russian. Our people stick together. Now speak to her.'

Our conversation lasted almost an hour but Brigitte remained as elusive as she must have been for Herr Schneider. I invited her to lunch with me after making sure she understood who I was, but she declined. This was to be our only conversation. However much I tried to understand her, she remained as two-dimensional as Herr Schneider's picture of her. She was forthcoming yet seemed detached. I could blame the physical circumstances of our conversation. The phone line crackled terribly; her German was grammatically correct but otherwise bare; Katja practised bellydancing moves in the kitchen; a haunting music was playing in the background wherever Brigitte was speaking from. She could be in Russia; there was no knowing.

The difficult physical circumstances were augmented by her unwillingness to talk about her family and friends, her hair, her past, her life. It was almost as if she felt a duty to set the record straight about her dealings with Herr Schneider. But no more. During the hour, I learned a little about her movements and motivations but nothing that would have helped the naive hopes harboured by Herr Schneider. She said not one memorable sentence. I was talking to the corporate spokesperson for Brigitte plc.

I found out she did have a university degree in politics but an illness impaired her handwriting. Her blonde hair was not from a bottle. She was offended when I told her about Herr Schneider's suspicions about the Russian mafia. She had liked him but received a 'better offer' just before her trip to Germany. This offer was not from another Russian man as she had suggested in the letter but from the German government. It had offered her a German passport. Now she didn't have to marry to leave Kazakhstan and come to Germany. After receiving the passport she moved to Magdeburg because Herr Schneider had praised the area's beauty.

Why did the government offer her citizenship? Brigitte said she was an ethnic German. Her family had moved to Russia at the invitation of Peter the Great in the eighteenth century, or maybe it was Catherine the Great, she had forgotten. Both tried to people the Russian south with German farmers to reap the benefits of the fertile flatlands north of the Caucasus. At first, the Germans preserved their culture and language. But successive terror regimes wiped out their German identity. Stalin persecuted them in the 1930s and then deported the million-strong community in cattle wagons to the Kazakh steppe when Hitler's army invaded Russia, fearing the ethnic Germans would collaborate.

As long as our conversation revolved around her people rather than herself, Brigitte spoke fluently. Later, I read more about the ethnic Germans.

When the Soviet Union collapsed, Kazakhstan faced hardship. Subsidies from Moscow were cut, collectives collapsed. Soon the ethnic Germans called for autonomy to gain control of their affairs. But a long-standing offer from the West German government to give a passport to anyone of German blood undermined their efforts. As more and more ethnic Germans emigrated, the autonomy movement fell by the wayside. Now over half of the one million German Kazakhs have left. Few speak any German – unlike the millions of second- and third-generation Turks – but the Kazakhs received a passport nevertheless. Germany is the last western nation where nationality is passed down by the parents. An imperial law from 1913 enshrines the blood code. Kemal could not get a German passport, but Brigitte's whole Kazakh village did.

So did she enjoy living in the country that was so generous to her people? A little, Brigitte said. She didn't want to talk about herself. Was she married? No. Would she want to see Herr Schneider? No. How did she feel about him? She felt pity. I suggested she could write him a letter, then we hung up. This is how Herr Schneider must have felt.

Katja was anxious. 'Will you tell Herr Schneider that you spoke to her?'
'No, I think not.'
'Good.'
'I wouldn't want to raise his hopes again.'
'Oh, yes, it could never work between two people like them.'

8

UPHILL

THE *LANDSTRASSE* ROSE WITHOUT making any great demands on the Red Racer's engine. The r.p.m. metre had died somewhere north of Lübeck, but the purring sounded reassuring. The straight strip of tarmac lazily pulled itself up to the apple trees atop a hill seemingly of no geographical significance. For the last few hundred miles I had encountered no more than the occasional small rise in the North German flatlands.

The coastal region from east to west was as even as the Ordnance Survey maps used in Yalta to carve up Germany. The flat-chestedness of the country's top half had inspired Stalin to suggest the division of Germany into north and south. The Americans – familiar with such a split at home – applauded the idea, but Churchill objected to a Soviet presence deep inside western Europe. Thus the two Germanys were divided lengthwise and shared the same geographical make-up. If one travelled south along the border, it was uphill from the clusters of lakes by the sea, over the forests and fields, and into the mountains that now lay in front of me; travelling in the reverse direction it was, of course, downhill, while going across the border meant battling uphill whatever the direction.

As I approached the apple trees, the road changed. The gentle slope abruptly veered upwards. The engine squealed with the inadvertent intake of breath of someone about to sneeze violently. We had barely reached the top and passed through the apple tree gate, when the Red Racer was thrown towards the first serpentine in a convulsive lurch. The *Landstrasse* had become a *Bergstrasse* and I had crossed the line Stalin had originally wanted to draw across Germany, between flatland and *Bergland*.

I permitted myself the occasional upwards glance while steering through the curvy new surroundings. A wide front of rocky crests rose from east to west. The Harz was Germany's northernmost mountain range. The wooded canyons and ski slopes had straddled both sides of the border. The SM-70s, watchtowers, patrol tracks and alarm fences snaked across ridges. Viewed from a hilltop, the sharply twisting fortifications were reminiscent of coffee-table pictures of the Great Wall of China.

Educated Germans called a region of historical interest a *Kulturraum*, or cultural space. The Harz earned the term from the many bloody rulers who reigned from high up in the mountains. Early Celtic and Teutonic mountain tribes were the first to seize the commanding heights. They were succeeded by Kaiser Heinrich I who first united Germany a millennium ago from his castle on the Harz's northern edge. Wilhelm I, Kaiser in Bismarck's time, later converted a castle in nearby Goslar into a nationalistic shrine. And Hitler formed his right-wing alliance with the Deutsch-Nationale party that eventually delivered the Weimar parliament into his hands in nearby Bad Harzburg. All in all, the Harz was a rather dark *Kulturraum*.

Inspired by such precedents, much of the Harz's culture tended towards the realm of the occult. In countless fables as well as works of literature, including Goethe's *Faust*, the mountains were peopled by dwarfs, witches, princes, demons and fairies. On 30 April, Walpurgis night, amateur pagans converged on Harz hilltops to await May Morning. Every year, neatly dressed devils and witches danced around camp fires. Yearning for the emotional intensity of their fable-filled childhoods, the witches dragged around factory-new broomsticks and the accountant-devils dreamed of mythical fireside orgies before the May Queen arrived at midnight.

The two main ingredients of Harz fables were death and wild animals. Both were captured perfectly in the story of the witch-cats that I had memorized as a child. Accelerating towards a sinking sun, I could readily imagine how the lone patrolman was accosted by a black cat one night. It purred and begged, sweeping around his legs from side to side. 'You've not had a crumb this day?' he asked and tossed her a piece of bread. The next night she came back and he fed her again. And so the night after that. But then further up the mountain road a second black cat also begged a piece of bread. And the next night a third black cat joined in. They begged so insistently he could not refuse. Angry with himself, the patrolman by day drove nails into a club and by night attacked the first black cat without mercy. It fell to the ground with a tortured cry, alerting a whole horde of black cats. They scratched and bit, and in the morning there was little left of the patrolman. Villagers suspected local witches. One was seen wearing a head-scarf, going to the doctor to have bandages put on her head. Apparently, there were as many holes in her head as there had been nails in the patrolman's club.

Entering the Harz from the open flatlands now, it was easy to understand fears that death and animalistic evil lurked in the mountains. The evening sun projected long, craggy shadows. The impregnable forests, dark canyons, wild rock formations and harsh winters made the Harz immediately mysterious and sinister. Hence the legendary place-names such as Hexentanzplatz (witches' dance floor), Wildemann (wild man) and Teufelsmauer (devil's wall) in this most storied part of Germany. Devil's Wall – even Ronald Reagan never had the temerity to use that term to describe the Evil Empire's border.

The downpour stopped and the people of Wernigerode emerged from doorways and bus stops. Lightly dressed shoppers shot uneasy glances into the dark sky. Limping pensioners eyed the next shelter should the rain return. A waiter took a peek to check if the competition next door was already resetting tables outside. Life resumed, umbrellas folded away and eyes fixed on traffic. But there remained an air of suspicion; that quick glance over the shoulder lest one turned out to be the hindmost.

If I had met Herr Zimmermann and Herr Vogt upon arrival, I would have understood immediately why Judas seemed to loom larger in Wernigerode than any occult figure. The two men were East German agents of betrayal. Their power had waned but not the fear they had inspired. They had snooped and spied for many years. 'We were a good team.' The conspiratorial meeting places ('*Konspirative Wohnung* = KW') were obsolete now, the letter drops (*tote Briefkästen*, or dead letter boxes in German) comically extinct; but the legacy of fear lived on.

When we met, they tried to explain, tried to rationalize, but they could not understand the lingering impact of their dirty work. 'It was just a job. No more. Now it's over.' The men had been foot soldiers in one of the government's many spy legions. After the Wende, unemployment, that dark leviathan of the industrial age, swallowed them up like many of their victims. In the eyes of the two men, the loss of paid work made everyone equal. Stasi or not, they now faced a new, a common, enemy. Their victims disagreed. They still looked over their shoulders. Meeting Herr Vogt and Herr Zimmermann explained many a fearful glance. But I didn't meet them until later.

From the rain-swept shopping streets in the medieval centre I walked to the tower blocks in the suburbs. The coarse concrete slabs lay ahead of the first range of Harz hills. Wernigerode hovered on the edge of the mountains. The tower blocks were yet another barrier on the way south.

Intrigued by the life I had seen in Magdeburg, I combed the barren landscape of cemented windows and staircases. The locals called a tower block *Plattenbau*, literally, plate or sheet building. It was constructed like a house of cards, made of vertical and horizontal sheets of concrete. A dozen ceilings were slotted on top of each other and fronted by concrete squares, each with a hole for a window. When the inhabitants felt charitable, they called their homes rabbit-hutches.

I walked through the canyons. I tried to approach a middle-aged man coming back from a trip to the supermarket. '*Entschuldigung*,' I called out with as much warmth as I could muster without sounding like a weepy beggar.

He glanced and then hurried into a doorway. One of his shopping bags ripped on the handle. He retrieved a few tin cans and shut the door as I came closer.

Another man crossed the street after he had watched me approaching. A grim woman spat out: '*Nein*. I don't want that.' Another woman shook her head with her eyes averted.

To avoid seeming even more sinister, I would duck into doorways when taking notes. Facing a wall, I scribbled. Could there be anything more suspicious?

In one open doorway stood a broom and leaning on it idly was a tall man in a yellow shell-suit who mumbled his name. It sounded like 'Reineke'. Any excuse was good enough for Herr Reineke to prolong his break from house-husband duties.

I said I'd seen a lot of twitching curtains in his street.

'There is a lot of looking and checking to be done.'

Like what?

'Like checking that everyone takes their turn sweeping the stairs.' He laughed.

What else?

'There is also the matter of sweeping the front of the house. And the back. Everyone has to take their turn. So says my wife.'

'It seems you don't like doing it much.'

'Well, everyone has to take their turn. Except for my wife, of course.'

'I'm sorry. Is she ill?'

'She has a job and I don't.'

I asked him if there was anyone else who might speak to me without a court summons or a gun at their temple. Herr Reineke pointed towards three women on a street corner.

One was blonde, one brunette, and the third wore a wig. They declined to tell me their names but acquiesced to my company.

'The Heinemann is always behind her curtains.'

'She's not as bad as the Dehnert.'

'But the Heinemann has experience. Did it before the Wende, for the good of the *Volk*. At least, I think.'

'She'll call the *Ordnungsamt* if you put plastic in the *Biotonne*.'

A curly-haired woman stopped on the corner, hovering on the edge of our conversation. The three women exchanged glances and switched to discussing their children.

The curly-haired woman was walking away. I caught up with her. She complained about the thin walls in her *Plattenbau*. The outside walls may be concrete, she explained, but all dividing walls were made of cardboard. The buildings seemed to share a set-up with the socialist regime – a rotten centre surrounded by a concrete wall.

The woman said one could overhear every noise, every television, every argument in the building. 'When people weren't supposed to watch western television, they kept the volume down. Now it's crazy.' She pointed at dozens of satellite dishes fixed to windows and balconies.

What would she watch on satellite? Did they have CNN?

'My husband and I watched some Dutch pornography last night.'

'Really? Interesting.'

'We are not ashamed to talk about it.'

'Obviously . . . I mean, of course not.'

'*Ja*. My husband said it's good for morale.'

'Sure.'

'Watching the skilful love-making shows people here that not everything they did before the *Wende* was wrong, says my husband.' She ruffled her curly hair.

'So. The thin walls in these buildings, did people use them to spy on neighbours?'

Her features hardened. 'You mean . . .'

'Stasi.'

'There is nothing more to say now.' She turned away.

I had done my homework on the Stasi. East Germany used to have more spies than doctors, cabinet-makers or plumbers. Its spooks and informers outnumbered the Gestapo and other Nazi secret police units by around 10:1. This curious fact inspired little confidence in the Stasi. Was there enough for them to spy on? Thanks to its more than 100,000 contributors, East Berlin had probably created the world's biggest sociological research facilities. Women recorded how often children visited bottle banks; sweeping schedules for entire suburbs could be analysed for class differences; and records of sexual activity in tower blocks aided population growth projections.

Not surprisingly, the Stasi itself became the single most investigated subject after the Wende. Daniela Dahn, an East German political commentator, complained that 99 per cent of all published material about the *ancien regime*'s injustices concerned the Stasi. Revelations of past spying – whether on family, friends or colleagues – turned into one of Germany's most divisive issues. Ossis complained they were all being tarred with the same dark brush; some wanted the Stasi files destroyed. Wessis responded, ironically, by insisting the postwar failure of denazification in West Germany should not be repeated. The divisions were not always so clear-cut. But when the curly-haired woman said there was nothing more to say, she left no doubt as to where her sympathies lay.

Before travelling to Germany I had tried to contact the 'Stasi'. This was not as ridiculous as it sounded. Of course, there was no longer a ministry of *STAatsSIcherheit*, state security. And in any case, the spooks had never been very partial to interview requests. But being good Germans, they had created a new organizational structure, entirely legal, part lobbying group, part trade association. It would have been fun if they had adopted the old Stasi nickname: *VEB Guck und Horch*, Peep and Eavesdrop Public Company. Instead, they opted for *Initiativgemeinschaft zum Schutz der sozialen Rechte ehemaliger angehoriger bewaffneter Organe und der Zollverwaltung der DDR e.v.*, or ISOR. I found this organization no more helpful than the old Stasi would have been. I might as well have put my correspondence in a 'dead letter box' at Checkpoint Charlie. Nor were its two sister clubs any more forthcoming: *Gesellschaft zur rechtlichen und humanitaren Unterstutzung* (GRH) and *Gesellschaft zum Schutz von Burgerrecht und Menschenwurde* (GBM).

Hours spent flicking through pamphlets finally paid off in Wernigerode, however. I knew I recognized the newsletter the man with unusually long hair was reading. It could have been *Cattle Farmer Weekly* or *The Butcher's Gazette*, judging by format and print quality, but in letters big enough to be deciphered from my seat at the bar it said: *ISOR Aktuell*. Herr Vogt, as I would learn to call him, was reading the Stasi trade association news-letter. I had found a paper trail.

Herr Vogt nervously brushed his long, reddish hair out of his face every few seconds. He would turn a page, then flick his hair. I stared at him via a wall-mounted mirror. He sipped from his coffee and flicked his hair again. He didn't seem to notice it any more. The short jabs came at orderly intervals like the trains of the Deutsche Bundesbahn.

How does one approach a member of the spook trade union? Would this man respond only to a secret password? Maybe I should get the waiter to send over a conspiratorial message written on a beer mat.

I sidled up to him in an not entirely inconspicuous fashion. A sachet of sugar fell under his table. '*Entschuldigung.*' I picked up the decoy. 'Oh, you too are reading *Cattle Farmer Weekly*?'

'*Nein.*'

'It looks deceptively like it.' I picked up the cover page. '*ISOR Aktuell.* That must be interesting reading.'

'One could say so.' He brushed back his hair.

'*Ja.* One always wonders what happened to the more sophisticated parts of the East German workforce.'

'Well, the most skilled find work eventually.'

'I guess the market economy is very good at picking out people with valuable skills.'

'And there really were some very skilled people.'

'Sure. And why shouldn't skilled people have their own publication.'

'We need it. One has to stay in touch. Skills are a rare commodity.'

Our little charade carried on for several minutes. Herr Vogt, as he introduced himself in between flicking his hair, included himself in the class of master tradesmen. But he didn't detail the nature of his skills.

'So, who were the skilled Ossis most in demand after the Wende?'

'The police force has a lot of skilled people in its ranks. Of course, the bosses don't always know quite how skilled some of the officers are. I guess it's better for both sides if they don't find out.'

'You mean, the police is full of . . . of skilled people who disguise some of their skills?'

'They have to disguise themselves. The whole system is hypocritical.

The market economy is failing to follow its own rules and allow the most suited candidates to fill certain posts.'

'Luckily, your people have the skills to fix this aberration in the system.'

'Luckily, the private sector is not as hypocritical as the public sector. After the Wende all the most skilled people lost their jobs because, you know . . . Everyone started from scratch, whether you were skilled or not. After a while western companies recognized where the most skilled people came from.'

'And they advertised for "skilled people" in the appointments section of *ISOR Aktuell*?'

'*Ach nein*. Nothing so crude. They would test you in the interview, ask you how many people lived in East Germany. It's roughly sixteen million. They would jokingly say: "Do you know their names and addresses?" Then it was up to you to indicate you were highly skilled.'

Desperate to take notes, I excused myself to go to the toilet. I jotted down everything I could remember. But I didn't dare stay too long. The techniques practised by spooks and investigating writers were all too similar. If Herr Vogt was as skilled as he claimed, he would surely become suspicious.

The bar filled up with lunchtime drinkers, disrupting our resumed conversation. Herr Vogt flicked his hair with increasing vigour. He said he worked as an insurance salesman. Seemingly bored with the veiled references to 'skills', he mentioned colleagues who had worked in West Germany before the Wende. Apparently, they faced difficulties when claiming their pensions. Having worked 'undercover', sometimes under various different names, they had problems proving they had paid contributions. Some were forced to 'expose' themselves to substantiate their claims. Herr Vogt's hair was thoroughly unruly by now. I feared he would leave soon and decided to take a gamble. 'Herr Vogt, I'm writing a book about the "anti-fascist protection barrier". I am interested to hear more about the skilled work involved.'

Herr Vogt stopped halfway through adjusting his red mane. 'Have to ask my boss.'

'Sure. But what does the insurance company care?'

'My old boss.' He said the two of them might come back the next day.

Herr Vogt was late. The lunchtime drinking crowd swung through the café doors. Plates of *Schnitzel* and chips piled up. The smell of bubbling fat invaded the dining room.

I guessed that Herr Vogt fell into the category of *Informeller Mitarbeiter*, or *IM*. These 'informal employees' made up the bulk of Stasi informers. There was nothing informal about their work. Most of them had signed contracts and received money or favours in return. Herr Vogt's 'boss' would most probably be the handler who had recruited him. I thought it more likely a witch-cat would show up than either of them.

At the next table sat a group of ladies who looked like veterans of at least two world wars. One held a shiny Cartier watch in her hand.

'My daughter in the west sent me this.'

'How delightful.'

'Oh, I carry it around with me every day.'

'And what did you do with your old watch?'

'I still wear it, of course. The Cartier is too precious to be worn. I would only get it dirty. Much better to keep it in my pocket.'

Murmured consent rippled around the table.

When Herr Vogt stepped through the doors he cut a miserable figure. His hair fell in his face as soon as he had brushed it aside. Declining to sit down, he clung to the bar unsteadily.

'How is your boss?'

'Healthy. But please don't call him boss to his face.'

'Is he joining us?'

'No. And I can't stay. He thinks it's not good for me to talk. But he will meet you.'

'But it's OK for him to talk?'

'Herr Zimmermann is Herr Zimmermann. That doesn't change.' Herr Vogt let me buy him a beer. For a few minutes he entertained himself with anecdotes about the fate of various famous spooks. He was bemused by the recent wedding of the son of spymaster Markus Wolf to an Israeli. The secret ceremony, attended by the Stasi godfather, had taken place after the son converted to ultra-Orthodox Judaism. 'It makes perfect sense. Mossad has the best agents in the world.'

Given his new-found candour, I felt free to ditch our silly code calling his ilk skilled workers. 'You sound well informed. Were you formally or informally employed?'

'*Ich bitt' Sie*, Herr August.'

'And Herr Zimmermann?'

'Herr Zimmermann cannot disclose any personnel matters.'

'And what can he disclose?'

'You ask Herr Zimmermann.'

*   *   *

Ilsenburg is draped around a soapy pond at the entrance to a narrow canyon. A gourmet spa restaurant and a tourist office sit between newly opened shops by the water. Ramblers mingled hesitantly before setting off with sticks and packs. Soon they would hit the border patrol track, easily the most convenient path.

I passed the ramblers after leaving the Red Racer in a car park at the canyon's mouth. Scanning an urbane restaurant menu, I wanted to ask someone how much Ilsenburg had changed in the last decade, but the answer seemed too obvious. I had seen plenty of East German towns and villages close to the border; none offered food that was either French or healthy, let alone both.

As arranged, Herr Zimmermann and his dog waited by the pondside bus stop. He greeted me as if I was doing him a favour by turning up. 'What a pleasure.' But there was no mention of the pretext for our meeting. He wore a jacket and tie even though it was the weekend. In his hand he held a leash and a tartan cap to cover a big balding head. 'I like dogs. How about you?'

I contended I was more taken with cats – black ones in particular.

'You are in the right place; though you can't take cats for a stroll.'

'Is that what you are here for?'

'We're on our way back. I like to go early to avoid the family outings.'

The small-talk ebbed and flowed. He praised the quality of West German dog food. We exchanged views on the cleanliness of cats. Maybe I had accosted the wrong man, a rambler with his proverbial best friend waiting for the bus home. Stretched out on the tarmac, the Alsatian looked exhausted. His snout rested on his front paws.

Herr Zimmermann, who had not introduced himself by name, put on his cap. 'I didn't forget. You are interested in the covert measures that helped to protect the border.' His debonair tone of voice remained unchanged but the sentence sounded alarmingly like an afterthought, as if he was ready to depart.

I offered an account of my trip and expressed the hope that, as an insider, he could shed light on suggestions that Stasi agents worked alongside the VoPos.

He asked a string of questions about who had made these suggestions, before concluding: 'Even if I was an insider, one's *Tscheckisten* oath would remain binding long after one is relieved of one's duties.'

'But were you an insider?'

'I don't mean to be patronizing but it's an impossible question. The answer must always be *nein*. Either one wasn't, or one would have to lie about it.' A poodle came strolling along the pond. Herr Zimmermann merely locked eyes with his Alsatian to restrain him.

'But was the Stasi involved at the border?'

'That's no state secret. I would say *das Organ* played an integral part in making the border safe.'

'Safe?'

'Yes. This was not the monstrosity described in the western media. The formal fortifications brought order to the zonal border after the turmoil of the postwar years.'

'You mean, the way Hitler brought order to German roads by building the *Autobahnen*.'

'That seems an unfair comparison. Undercover operations on both sides of the border were necessary to stamp out crime.' Herr Zimmermann rattled off the titles of books and reports, both East and West German, that attested to the falling crime rate along the border after the massive fortifications went up in 1961.

From Herr Zimmermann's references, I later reconstructed one case that had especially excited him. The details were gruesome. There could be no doubt the border had been a killing ground long before the planting of minefields. Books and newspaper cuttings from the 1950s told the story of Rudolf Pfeil, a serial mugger, rapist and murderer. He preyed on lone women who crossed the border on forest tracks high up in the Harz. In the poverty-stricken years before the *Wirtschaftwunder* (economic miracle), the mountains were teeming with smugglers and black market-eers, many of them war widows. They carried coal, foods and gold in and out of the Soviet-occupied zone. Pfeil would offer to guide them. On a deserted hilltop or in a dark valley, he killed them with a single blow to the head. Then he acted out necrophilic fantasies and fled across the border with the loot. His more than forty murders inspired such fear in the smugglers that the black market was temporarily paralysed. In 1958, Pfeil committed suicide in prison after a failed attempt to castrate himself.

Over the years, the memories of Pfeil have been embellished with many an outlandish detail. He is variously described as a communist campaigner, a wily Nazi, a double agent, a Saxon and an Austrian. Pfeil and the border crossings had entered the realm of myth and legend. Some day, the entire Iron Curtain might follow.

Benevolently, Herr Zimmermann looked down on his dog at the bus stop. I asked if the Alsatian had been one of the guard dogs that ran along the border on a long leash, chasing the odd *Republikflüchtling*.

'*Ach Gott, nein*. Those dogs went crazy after a while. Most of them were put down after the Wende. They could never adjust to the new life.' Herr Zimmermann tipped his cap. The Alsatian jumped up and followed his master to the gourmet spa where they both disappeared.

It seemed silly to feel frustrated. I had been lucky to recognize Herr Vogt's *ISOR Aktuell* newsletter in Wernigerode. Ex-Stasi men – if that's what the two really were – preferred an elusive retirement. They had never known the limelight. My meetings with them lasted no more than twenty minutes. I tried to squeeze everything out of these encounters, remember every sentence, but in the end I knew almost nothing about their work. (They, however, learned a lot about my trip.) Their dark presence was feeding my curiosity rather than satisfying it. What part had the spooks really played at the border? I decided to stay in Ilsenburg and explore the hilly patrol tracks on foot. Signing into a hotel, I found a copy of Tom Clancy's latest spy novel in a stack of books for bored guests. The blurb spelled out the magnitude of recent changes in the world of intelligence-gathering. Missing from the Clancy plot were exchanges of political prisoners at the Berlin Wall, casual double-crossings over a glass of Pilsner in a cosy *Kneipe* and the smuggling of microfilms across the Iron Curtain. Europe no longer existed on the maps of the alphabet soup agencies in Washington and Moscow. The new baddies were much swarthier: Arabs, Latinos, Chinese – now it was their turn, their border disputes.

Carrying a borrowed backpack filled with lardy *Schnittchen* – white bread sandwiches filled with Harz cheese – I joined a group of about a dozen ramblers the next morning. I was lugging everyone's lunch. The pack's straps were digging into my shoulders like barbed wire.

Our guide advanced speedily as if fleeing a whole VoPo division. Gladly I fell in with a divorcee at the rear. The broad-shouldered lady said she had not sweated this much since being married. And we were still within Ilsenburg's town limits.

Water rushed down the side of the road. We followed the stream up the narrow canyon under a green roof. We changed directions several times and my companion drowned herself in memories of married life.

The patrol tracks I had expected to encounter remained hidden. Apart from me, no one in the group seemed bothered. The border was not an attraction they had come to see. On the whole, it wasn't clear what attractions interested these teachers and salesmen from East Germany's industrial heart in Saxony.

'This place makes you thirsty.'

'There must be a bottle opener in your jacket.'

'Why do you say must?'

'I know. I put it there. You must have nicked it. Is this the Harz, or Poland?'

'No Polish jokes, please.'

'Who said I was joking?'

The divorcee and I fell back further. 'Surely you weren't married to one of them?'

'No. My husband was more of a quiet *Kerl*.'

'And how do you know that bunch?'

'Some are colleagues. Colleagues, wives, friends. A colleague's wife's friend and so on. It's the third or fourth year we do this. You've been here before?'

'Once, travelling along the border.'

'Was the border near here?'

'Not far.'

'Really? I had no idea.'

Another straggler joined us. The divorced lady introduced the corpulent man snacking on a Mars Bar as 'the one who's responsible for choosing this route, though he might already regret it'. The man tried to hide the chocolate. 'The young man says the border cut right through the Harz here, did you know?'

'I think it was further west, but I don't know exactly.'

'Who wants to see that anyway?'

I said I had travelled a long way to find what was left of the *Antifaschistischer Schutzwall*, but I sounded strangely nostalgic to myself and fell silent. My fellow ramblers had already lost interest in walls and watchtowers; their conversation drifted off to wallpaper and watching television. 'Wouldn't it be nice to decorate the living room as if it were a forest?'

'Better tree wallpaper than a beach scene.' The chocolate-eater turned to me. 'Are you sure the *Schnittchen* will be OK?'

At the bottom of a steep incline, the stragglers staged a revolt. Arms flailing, brows streaming and coughs begging for sympathy, we demanded to take a gentler path circumnavigating the rocks. The suggestion of an early lunch clinched victory for the new path. An ideal picnic setting soon presented itself by a dam, the Eckertalsperre. We rounded the water and found a walkway on top of the dam. Hundreds of feet below on one side were a few houses in a canyon shaded by trees. On the other side, waves lapped the dam, seemingly ready to overwhelm the narrow concrete wall any moment. One was walking on either water or a tight-rope, depending which way one faced.

The dam had a remarkable history. It was built between 1941 and 1943, right in the middle of the war. Why were German engineers constructing dams during the Blitz, while British engineers were building dam busters? 'Not total war,' declared one rambler, 'but total nonsense.'

After the war, the Eckertalsperre was cut in half. The zonal border sliced through the lake and the dam. A black, red and golden East German border post remained today as the only sign that the walkway across the water had been barricaded and draped in barbed wire. The setting would have been ideal for a Clancy or le Carré novel under patrol-boat lights and snipers' sights, prisoners might have crossed the dam in a night-time exchange.

We settled down at the water's edge. The *Schnittchen* gave off a sour stench. The cheese had melted into the backpack. After the food had been shared out, the group fell silent. Everyone seemed to be concentrating hard, as if it was their first ever meal. With customary precision, the German language offered the term *gefrässige Stille*, or voracious quiet.

I tried to start a conversation about the border and the Stasi, but lazily tossed out suggestions lingered unanswered, almost eerily so. My fellow ramblers seemed too voracious to break their silence.

I glanced across to the concrete barrier and the several hundred thousand tons of water it dammed up. A picture similar to this had been used to describe the psychological situation of East Germans. Hans-Joachim Maaz, an Ossi psychotherapist, studied the long-term effects of the Stasi and other forms of state-sponsored terror. His study was titled *Gefühlsstau* – dammed-up emotions.

On jolly walks over several days I tried to puncture the emotional dam. I groped my way south through craggy valleys and over wooded ledges, always seeking the company of rambling folk. At Torfhaus, I joined Herr Karmanski from the Ruhr Valley. We admired the distant peak of the Brocken, the highest mountain in the Harz. During the Cold War, Torfhaus had been the major western vista for viewing the Brocken across the border. Deprived of the macabre barbed-wire spectacle, the tourist stalls now sold postcards of witches in patchwork skirts riding on thorny broomsticks.

Herr Karmanski had a fondness for standing with his hands on his hips, elbows out. The old gentleman could hardly walk fifty yards without striking a new pose. 'Thank God that wall is gone.' He pointed to somewhere near the bottom of the Brocken. 'It felt so creepy looking across from here.' He pointed to the peak. 'And up there, the Stasi put its listening station; listening to private conversations and who knows what else.' He shuddered.

The town of Braunlage – more witch postcards and mugs – was balanced on the western edge of the border. I bumbled down from Torfhaus in time for a late lunch. The Greek restaurant, Palladion, was trying very hard to be palatial. Copious columns adorned the beer garden. Compliantly, the rustling of the wind and the rushing of a stream combined to conjure up images of distant Mediterranean holidays. I lunched at a long bar, reciting Greek vacation destinations to the waiter. When I disturbed the idyll with suggestions that Stasi spies might have operated here, he flinched. Might they not have tried to scupper rescue missions from the western side of the divide? The waiter couldn't understand how this could be more interesting than discussing bronzed bodies.

Braunlage nestles at the bottom of the Wurmberg, the highest western Harz peak, straight across from the Brocken. Through the summer months, a bubble ski-lift ferries visitors up to this former western spy post. While the Stasi listening station on the Brocken had intercepted westbound radio traffic, the CIA *et al.*, did the same from the Wurmberg. The two peaks were less than a mile apart. The patrol track ran, like a scar, through the valley below. The two superpowers had stood not so much eyeball-to-eyeball as ear-to-ear. Both sides had since cleared out their arsenal and the Brocken had been reopened.

Atop the Wurmberg, an overweight couple pointed at the Brocken ridges. 'They behaved like Philistines.'

'They turned the mountain into a rubbish dump – typically East German.'

The two, who obviously preferred eating rubbish to dumping it, were standing on a ski-jumping platform pointing east. From the top it seemed a good ski-jumper might have made it across the border. But who would have wanted to?

To stand on top of a ski-jumping tower on top of a mountain was to gaze in all directions and straight into the blue and green hues of a painter's palatte. The eye roamed fifty or more miles into the distance, but the view across to the Brocken remained the most compelling. Below us, between the peaks, had been a stretch of border guarded by vicious dogs on long leashes. All the sophisticated spying gear could not replace their crude blood-lust.

The journalist Ralph Giordano stood here in 1978 and watched the dogs. In his book *Hier war ja Schluss* (This Used to be the End), he wrote: 'By chance we witnessed the feeding of the border dogs. There was no regular schedule. The dogs, chained to ropes, ran along a stretch of eighty metres parallel to the fence. Their task, to bark at fugitives and attack them.' The ropes were measured so as to let the dogs come within an inch of each other; close enough to leave no gap, but far enough apart to prevent these modern witch-cats from mutilating each other as they endlessly raged along the fence.

Below the tower, a professorial figure peered over a small fence surrounding a circular ruin. His limply outstretched fingertips bobbed up and down. I asked what he was counting.

'The stones; some went missing when the Witches' Stairs were excavated.' He pointed to an uneven stone staircase. 'The site is prehistoric but it's long been destroyed.' Herr Dr Rittbaum explained local witchcraft had fallen victim to the *Malleus Maleficarum*, a fifteenth-century canon of laws persecuting the occult. This so-called Witch Hammer dictated that occultism stemmed from the female gender. Witch trials were conducted based on the flimsiest of rumours. Anyone could give evidence against women suspected of conducting rituals on mountain tops. The excommunicated were allowed to give testimony, even heretics and other witches, or husbands against their wives and children against their mothers. The trials all followed the same gruesome procedure: no interrogation without torture, no verdict without fire and death.

I was reminded of another, more modern witch-hunt. I suggested to Herr Dr Rittbaum there might be parallels between the Stasi and the executors of the *Malleus Maleficarum*. 'Of course, the allegations of torture and death in Stasi cells have never been proven,' I added, sensing his discomfort.

'I'd rather say – and I say this not as a Dresdner but as a German – there still is a witch-hunt on. Not the one you're referring to, though. There is a wholesale presumption of guilt by many West Germans when they travel east. Every Ossi is a potential Stasi informer. Given the informers' ubiquity, everyone is suspect. I wouldn't be the first to say East Germans feel like second-class Germans.'

'Have you ever been suspected?'

'It's usually a look. The look says: wonder what he did before the Wende. Apparently the Stasi liked employing academics.'

'Might there not be an element of paranoia, ingrained over the years?'

'You could be right.'

Rather awkwardly, I asked Herr Dr Rittbaum if he knew anything about Stasi activity along the border. His despondent look said to me: you Wessis never give up, do you? Or was his Ossi paranoia rubbing off on me?

In Schierke, I found a clue to the Stasi work from a pre-Wende leaflet that had been distributed to East German holiday-makers in the Harz. They were warned never to enter the 5-kilometre exclusion zone. 'Your holiday will end immediately. You can count on criminal proceedings and the notification of your employer.' There was no doubt who could best administer the sinister punishment: the mighty octopus of darkness.

From Schierke a steam engine went up to the Brocken. The top was bare and hostile, wholly unlike the rest of the wooded, shrouded Harz. Not a single tree could withstand the unrepentant blowing. The Langenscheidt dictionary translates *Brocken* as lump, hunk or chunk. Witches had not been linked to the Brocken until Goethe set the Walpurgis night here in *Faust*, written in the late eighteenth century. If witches had existed they would have been unlikely to choose this icy rockscape for their roaring outings. To conduct a Cold War, however, there could be few better places.

Intrigued by their names I took a stroll between two little towns further south along the border. They were called Elend and Sorge (Misery and Anxiety, in German). The patrol track wound its way through a tight valley. Fish splashed in a spindly stream. Steep slopes of pine trees lined a flat meadow of sodden green. This was an ideal location for inter-agency romance in a spy thriller; or just the most scenic part of an ugly border, a rare delight between east and west, between misery and anxiety.

I alighted upon a further clue here. To be between misery and anxiety – that's how the Stasi had wanted its citizens to be. Between fear and despondency. Between obedience and accommodation. Between submission and suspicion. That was the Stasi aim. Miserable and anxious citizens lacked the will to climb over barbed wire and brave the dogs. No border could be made impenetrable – unless people were too demoralized to approach it. Fear was the best fortification.

And as long as misery and anxiety were still alive, the divide between east and west would continue to exist.

9

DOWN A
MEADOW

IT IS PERHAPS A question every precocious child asks: What if my parents
had never met? Would I still exist in some form? If not, who could
possibly be in my place?

I was reminded of such short-trousered soul-searching in the village of
Ellrich. I had plenty of reasons to visit Ellrich. It straddled the border,
for one, on the East German edge of the Harz. More importantly, though,
my father, Erdmut, was born here in 1931. And as a skinny seventeen-year-
old, he fled across the then only moderately fortified border. If he had
been caught by the Russian guards who patrolled the Allied zonal border
before Germany's definite division in late 1949, he would never have met
my mother. And, presumably, I would not be standing here.

Long since out of my short trousers, this thought now amused rather
than bothered me. I felt we had cheated a higher power. By making his
way through the Iron Curtain, my father had snuck me into this world
against Stalin's will. The mighty Red Army had defeated Hitler but failed
to stop my father. I laughed as I stood in Ellrich's decrepit centre. I
revelled in the pathetic glory of the lucky underdog.

Admittedly, I was glad my parents had met and procreated elsewhere.
The streets of Ellrich appeared woefully ancient, its windows left unre-
paired. Some sorry streets looked just as they had when my father had
left them. 'I bought my shoes here as a schoolboy,' he said pointing at an
old shoe shop in dire need of a good shine.

We were retracing the escape route he had taken one winter morning during the bleak Cold War years. Joining me on my travels, today was his first return in fifty years to the very meadow that, to me, represented a family triumph over the moustachioed monster in the Kremlin. To him, the story seemed to belong on a dog-eared page in someone else's biography, someone he knew but no longer resembled. It simply hadn't occurred to him to come back by himself, he said, but he liked the status I accorded him as glorious victor over the Red Army.

He played tour guide in a museum that exhibited fragments from his past. It was a role he embraced with gusto, clearly enjoying narrating his own story. We began where his parents' house had stood in the centre of Ellrich; it was demolished after the war. He suggested I take photographs as we walked towards the border. Occasionally he would hide behind a tree, pretending to evade Russian patrols while smirking conspiratorially. Then he would resume his animated narration.

'That morning I put a suitcase with a few possessions on a horse-drawn cart. I piled cow dung on top until the suitcase was fully covered. My father – your grandfather – then helped me drive the cart out of the village, right along this street. Both of us were dressed in farming clothes. Ellrich and our house, of course, were in the Soviet zone but we owned a field that reached across the border. And with a special permit from the Russians we were allowed to farm on both sides in the early postwar years.'

We walked along narrow streets lined with fruit-trees. 'The roadside trees are typical for the region,' he explained. His father had run a tree-nursery. We left Ellrich's village church behind. Houses stood further and further apart. Erdmut gestured towards the house of childhood friends. As far as I knew he had never seen them again after his flight. 'Every house has a story. In this one here lived a Marxist family. The father was a factory-worker. My father would never allow me to play with the sons. For a while I thought they must therefore be my best friends. But they were much rougher than me and hated me and our family. You know, my parents joined the NSDAP [the Nazi party] in 1933. It could have been 1934.'

I had never heard my father talk about his parents as Nazis. In fact, we rarely spoke about them at all. They remained absent from our family life even in their old age. Between my father's flight in February 1949 and their deaths in the mid-1970s, contact was made impossible by the border.

When my father uttered 'NSDAP', arguably the most paralysing acronym any language has known, he didn't sound disturbed. He talked as a tour guide. He was still reading from someone else's biography. But I sensed the impact of our excursion. Not only did he talk freely about his parents' party membership, but he suddenly remembered intimate details. 'When I was four years old, my mother took me to a local NSDAP meeting. I see myself sitting on her lap. She wore a fur coat with big buttons. I faced directly into her furry collar. While the fire-brand speaker roused himself to one oratorical climax after another, I played with the top button. I struggled terribly to fit it into the button-hole. It was stitched very tight. Then, in a rare moment of complete silence, I finally pushed the button through the hole with my clumsy little fingers. Into the hall packed with Nazis hanging on to the speaker's every word, I yelled: "Now it's in."' He laughed triumphantly.

By now we had left the last houses behind. Our destination, the point where Erdmut had crossed the Iron Curtain, was no more than a half-mile outside Ellrich. The tree-lined road rose up a hill next to derelict railway tracks. We came to the brow of the hill and Erdmut led me over a wooden foot-bridge that crossed the tracks. 'The bridge used to be wider. At that time, we took the cart across the bridge.'

Another set of railway tracks ran through the valley below. Now the dash for freedom. The tracks marked the border. In between lay a befittingly romantic meadow. Undulating pastures sloped gently downhill, partly overgrown with brambles. We had arrived. My father posed for another set of conspiratorial photographs.

'At the time, we had to stop the cart at the Russian checkpoint by the bridge. But there was no problem. As soon as we got to the field, we started distributing the dung. In a straight line we headed towards the bottom of the field where the border ran. Soon I unearthed the suitcase. We turned the cart around and I pulled the suitcase out. The Russians could hardly see us.'

Erdmut and I now stood in a trench. I assumed it had formed part of the later fortifications. His *Camel* boots grappled up the slope ahead of me. 'There was only a brief moment when the Russians could have stopped me. The last stretch was in a blind spot. And anyway, smugglers crossed the border daily. On his way home, my father had no problems getting past the Russian checkpoint without me.'

Erdmut and I vaulted to the top of the slope. Time for more photographs. 'When I was standing here,' he pointed to his feet, 'I had already made it. My good fortune was certain.' He made a victory sign and amusedly raised his arms. I snapped away.

'Did you know then you would not come back quickly?'

'I didn't even think about it at the time.'

'There was no tearful departure from your parents?'

'It wasn't unusual then to cross the border between provisional Allied zones. Germany was still one country. From here, I walked along the railway track, through a tunnel to Walkenried. In the following years, I worked in Meckenheim near Bonn and later abroad, in France and Britain. And all the while the border fortifications were tightened rather than relaxed as we had expected.'

I took a few more photographs of Erdmut walking along the tracks, re-enacting his escape and waving good-bye. He smiled with no hint of a heavy heart. I imagined him exactly like this on a wintry morning in 1949, enveloped in a cloud of frozen dung, as he unwittingly closed the door to his childhood.

I had yet another reason for visiting Ellrich. Not only was the village my father's place of birth and escape, but it had also harboured a Nazi concentration camp. The remains of the KZ Dora stood directly on the border. The camp had burrowed deep into the southern foothills of the Harz.

For the first time on my trip I was truly shocked. If ever there was any question whether one could compare the East German leaders to Hitler, it was answered here for me. The Iron Curtain was manifestly unjust, but it never matched the barbarism of the camps. Especially not of this one. KZ Dora was set up in 1944 in a labyrinth of tunnels. In great secrecy and protected from air attacks, the Nazis manufactured the V2 rockets that rained down on London in the dying days of the war. Jews, communists, gypsies and prisoners of war were worked to death in the process. Conditions in the freezing tunnels were atrocious. The lightly clothed workers never saw daylight and had an average life expectancy of only six weeks once they entered the camp. Some 20,000 died.

The rockets were uniquely deadly. They killed not only the people they were aimed at, but also the poor souls who made them. And my teenage father had grown up right next door. Should one feel guilty about that?

We parked the Red Racer near a rusty railway carriage. Barbed wire covered the doors. The darkness inside was oppressive. This was one of the original carriages that Adolf Eichmann had sent to Auschwitz. A year ago, someone found it on a dilapidated side-track. Now it marked the entrance to the camp.

Before the Wende, the deadly tunnels had not been open to visitors. East Berlin deemed the labyrinth too close to the border and the site too sensitive. The Red Army took over much of the Nazi machinery following the war. In 1948, the Russian forces detonated the tunnel entrance after they had removed every last blood-stained piece of equipment. Only workers' tobacco boxes, diaries and glasses stayed behind, seemingly locked for ever in the mountain. But volunteers successfully campaigned for a reopening of the tunnels after the Wende. More than 150,000 people a year now visit the draughty underground chamber of horrors.

Frau Lehner was one of the East German volunteers who had worked against the rule of ignorance. Even today at seventy-three, she spent every weekend at the camp. 'When I'm not here, I feel something is missing from my life,' she announced with a cheeky grin, dressed in a stripy T-shirt. She first visited the camp in 1944 when she smuggled in aspirin and vitamins and brought out letters from workers. In 1945, she accompanied American soldiers on a tour of the liberated camp. 'Under socialism, there was little interest in all this. Paradoxically, the military used the camp to swear in recruits,' she said. 'People's senses were dulled. Today, eighty per cent of visitors are Wessis.'

Tagging along with a group of visitors, we passed through a fence (guarded by a security company calling itself Plato) to the tunnel entrance. We huddled together in the chill of the dark air. Everyone talked intensely. We felt a need for companionship. In the utter darkness, the sound of our disembodied voices was comforting, no matter how horrible the subject of conversation.

'Apparently, the inmates had to sleep on the floor.'

'And food was scarce.'

'I read, an SS doctor once came to visit and said this was the worst camp he'd seen.'

We had walked several hundred yards, inhaling rather than seeing the chalky mountain. A dim light now illuminated a vast tunnel, big enough for ballistics experiments. The domed space stretched into the unknown. Smaller side tunnels split off at regular intervals. The main tunnel had been the rocket assembly line, fed with wings, engines and impact detonators from the flanks.

'There's a rocket part here,' I heard Erdmut say.

'It doesn't seem big enough for a V2.'

'Probably the stump of a V1.'

'Over here is definitely the engine of a V2.' The rugged jet engine lay beached on a slab of cold stone. It was heavy enough to destroy several terraced homes in Hammersmith or Islington or Bloomsbury with or without its customary 1,500 pounds of explosives. Its mass alone seemed enough to wreak mayhem.

We ate lunch with Erdmut's brother and his family in Ellrich. Steaming dumplings and crispy hunks of beef were carried out from the kitchen, later followed by home-made cakes and plenty of whipped cream. For the special occasion of our visit, gold-rimmed crockery adorned the table.

My uncle was the only one of Erdmut's six siblings who returned home after crossing the border in the postwar years. He came back across the Iron Curtain to run the family tree-nursery. He now lived in a simple house on the edge of the village. The original parental home in the centre of Ellrich where Erdmut grew up had been lost. After the war, the Red Army ordered the summary expropriation of the assets of the landowning upper class. My father's family hardly fitted that description, but the expropriation committee of local comrades that executed the order included the Marxist factory-worker with whose sons Erdmut had not been allowed to play. The unjust expropriation still rankled. Erdmut's brother was forced to live in a ramshackle house with a leaking roof. What was left of the tree-nursery barely supported his family. The sumptuous lunch they gave us was all the more special for it.

Stop. I hesitate to write down the name of Erdmut's brother, or the names of his wife and their five children. The eldest son explicitly told me he did not want to be named in my book. He angrily declaimed over lunch that he wanted nothing to do with my *Unternehmen*. The other children showed a strong sense of wonder, but they too seemed reluctant to be quoted. I was struck by the contrast to Erdmut's boyish enthusiasm in retracing and recording his escape route. As I looked around the lunch table, the image of native Indians who shied away from being photographed for fear of torment sprang to mind.

At the end of the meal, I made another attempt to open my notebook. I asked my uncle and aunt if they minded me posing a few questions 'on the record'. Politely, they declined. And yet I feel compelled to paint at least a tentative picture of their lives, for they are an extraordinary family. If this constitutes a breach of familial trust, so be it. It is committed out of nothing but respect for how they weathered the political storm that raced – and continues to race – through their home.

After lunch, we took a stroll together. I wanted to find the spot by the border where I had stood as a child and looked down on Ellrich; the place we had visited after smuggling the helmet through the checkpoint. I remembered clearly how Erdmut had pointed at the village, so close yet so irrevocably part of another world. If only I could conjure up this surreal view once more.

We started at the railway tracks which I knew marked the border.

'These ruins here belonged to the KZ Dora.'

'The basement and walls are one of the few leftovers in Ellrich. The workers were shipped from camp to camp on trains that ran on these tracks.'

'Before the Wende, of course, this whole area was no-man's-land.'

'For forty years it was all *terra incognita*.'

'Around the corner there's a memorial put up by a group of Belgians.'

'And there's a drawing by a Frenchman.'

'Look, you can see the meadow where I crossed the border,' said Erdmut. 'And over here is an old pond. I played by the water as a child. In April 1945, days before the end of the war, the SS hunted down two escaped KZ inmates here. Because of their stripy livery we called the inmates "zebras". The two escapees were hiding in the water. But the SS nevertheless found them and forced them to run through the streets of Ellrich completely naked. The SS men chased them in a lorry. The inmates ran for their lives.'

I shuddered. Was I supposed to feel guilty that my father had been a bystander to such events? That seemed ridiculous. He was thirteen years old at the time. Yet, I felt irked. I was caught in a very German guilt trap. I felt guilty because I couldn't summon up the pangs of war and Holocaust guilt still expected of every good German at every opportunity. 'The horrific scene from April 1945 has nothing directly to do with you,' I told myself. But this sounded as if I was belittling the event.

We scrambled up a wooded incline above the pond. The place where I had peered across the border and down on Ellrich as an eight-year-old was called Juliushütte, I was informed. Below us the SS had plied its evil trade. We passed obscured tunnel entrances.

Then we reached the Juliushütte. I failed to recognize it. Foliage engulfed the lookout spot. Trees had grown wildly, fences were broken and benches had gathered moss. The view had disappeared. When Ellrich awoke from hibernation, the lookout lost its popularity. It went back to being a hilltop path. The village was hidden once again.

*   *   *

We returned to the house exhausted and hungry. I was to stay the night in the bedroom of my young cousin Dorothea. She was the only one of my uncle's five children absent today. By her bed I found a leaflet that she had apparently left there for me. It described the work of a youth group dedicated to preserving the KZ Dora as a memorial. The group organized visits by former inmates to the camp. Every year, the students brought back ageing survivors. They discussed life in the tunnels and, hopefully, the survivors came away convinced such evil would never be repeated here.

The main text on the leaflet – signed *Dorothea August, Chairman* – read: 'I have been coming to the KZ Dora for several years. Something started here that changed my life. The more I learned about the inmates from across Europe, the more I wanted to contribute to keeping alive their painful memories. This desire culminated in the founding of the group "Youth for Dora."' I was overwhelmed. It seemed to me, Dorothea had discovered an enviable way out of the German guilt trap.

Dinner started with a prayer. In West Germany this would have been nothing unusual, but East German leaders had for four decades denied their subjects what Marx called the 'opiate of the masses'. The socialist party had taken over many church functions. It offered trips and counselling. Faith mostly withered away. In the August household in Ellrich, however, the children had been brought up as Christian believers. Every meal started with a deeply-felt prayer.

The clash between religion and ideology had made my uncle and his family outsiders in the socialist society. Before the Wende, he regularly defied the local party hierarchy, telling the apparatchiks his children would not attend socialist summer camps or work groups. For him, there was no substitute for religious belief. And to be an outsider seemed not to trouble him. He was a proud man and had no wish to be too closely associated with the people who had expropriated the family's property and forced him to live camped in a field.

All this I could understand. In fact, who wouldn't admire such strength of conviction? But I was surprised that my uncle and his family seemed to be outsiders once again today. The socialist party and the quasi ban on religion had been defeated. But new adversaries had risen, the Wessis. Over dinner, conversation highlighted the animosity some family members harboured for everything West German. Snippets stuck in my mind. A story was told of two men meeting in West Germany. They awkwardly introduced themselves. Then, recognizing the accent, one said: 'Seeing that we're both Ossis, you may call me by my first name.'

Later, it was remarked that, apparently, 'ninety per cent of East German capital is already in West German hands. When the last Ossi has sold his property to a Wessi, then Germany's reunification will finally be completed.'

The reference to property was pertinent. It reminded me that a family property in the centre of Ellrich had been sold by a state agency to a Wessi after the Wende. A reversal of the Russian-inspired expropriation was vetoed by the government in Bonn, dominated by Wessis. The property now lay derelict while my uncle struggled to keep his tree-nursery in business.

After my father's departure the next morning, my uncle introduced me to Herr Fischer, who had commanded the local stretch of border for sixteen years. He greeted me cautiously across his garden fence.

I wondered how the formerly imprisoned villagers now treat the retired 'warden'.

'The people of Ellrich don't bear a grudge,' he said. 'I've lived here since 1952 and I still talk to everyone in the street. Nobody points a finger at me. Sometimes I'm asked – do you feel ashamed about having been the border commander? I say *nein*. I still wear the same old service jacket. I haven't found a better jacket in the new shops.'

We sat down at a table in the garden he now tended full-time. Herr Fischer had a friendly grandfather face. I asked a question about his life in retirement. It was the only question I asked him. For the next two hours, clipped fragments spluttered forth as quiet anger engulfed him. 'The people of East Germany may have wanted freedom to travel. *So*. But they were not told it would cost them their jobs. That's a fact.' He brushed his white hair from his forehead. 'There is no German unity. We're a colony. Fact. This is supposed to be a democracy. *So*. But we have been incapacitated. *Fakt*.'

Throughout the monologue I thought what strange bedfellows my uncle and Herr Fischer made. Ideology had divided the two men for decades. While one had suffered under the border, the other had guarded it. And yet, they now shared many sentiments.

10

THROUGH A TREE

MY LAST VISIT TO the Barbarossa Cave had been on a trip with my old schoolfriend Peter. We were racing to a nearby railway station. We were late for the train, but stopped nevertheless.

We were always late. That's how we had become friends at school all those years ago. Usually, by the time we arrived in class, only the two desks at the back were unoccupied. Whether in chemistry, history or geography lessons, we slumped side-by-side, furthest from the blackboard. This, of course, suited us. It seemed an ideal place to practise some of the things preached at the front. In geography, Peter and I would play territorial board-games like noughts-and-crosses. In the chemistry lab, we collected powders to fabricate our own fire-crackers. Once we set off such a device during a history lesson. The cracker rolled down the middle aisle and erupted with a smoky puff by the blackboard. Frau Steiner, our pacifist history teacher, won our lasting affection when she finished reading her text on the Great War without flinching before looking up to seek out the perpetrators. Thankfully, lack of discipline was a common theme in our class. Peter and I hid behind a line-up of suspects.

Now, I once again passed the Barbarossa Cave. The stately grottoes and underground chambers, washed out by water, form one of Europe's biggest caverns and reach hundreds of yards into the Kyffhäuser mountains south of the Harz.

The car park was not nearly as big as the cave itself. I wedged the Red Racer in between bigger vehicles. On my right, a towering red *Bus* (the

German habit of capitalizing nouns seemed justified for once) had arrived shortly ahead of me. Its load of Ossi teenagers spilled out in an evenly paced stream. The tidy single file marched around the bus and lined up. They didn't mill about, start smoking or fuss over who stood next to the most developed girl or the best dressed boy. They simply awaited the teacher's next command in a disciplined fashion I had never experienced as a schoolboy.

Marshalled by earnest commands ('Remember your notebooks. It's for your own good.'), the class proceeded up a long stairway to the entrance of the cave. I traipsed up behind them, fascinated by their re-enactment of a clichéd Germanness that I had thought extinct outside the Kraut-bashing in British comedy.

The students were uniformly decked out in trainers, jeans and sweat-shirts. The trainers' multi-coloured laces were tied around their ankles. All of them. The sweatshirts served as walking billboards for their manufac-turers, who had inscribed their names in large block letters across the chests of both sexes. I counted more than half a dozen LEVIS. The tops were tidy, the creases neat, the trainers clean and the haircuts trim.

As the class spilled into the small ante-room by the cave entrance, a pecking order emerged. A few officious teacher's pets spat out instructions. 'Klaus, don't block the door.' 'Eberhard, move out of the man's way.' The teacher could rely on them to stamp out fire-cracker throwing in the back row.

Without haste or pushing, we filed into the narrow tunnel that led into the rugged underground empire. The cold and wet air clung to our clothes like an autumnal shower. A stream coursed through the stony halls. Muffled gurgles and the clak-clak-clak of dripping water lent a familiar sound to what was a world of unsurpassed complexity. The walls were covered in bizarrely intricate and brightly blinking stone formations reminiscent of spacecraft pictures of the earth. The half-moon-shaped ceilings gave the magnificent impression of walking in a riverbed turned upside down. As we silently, almost solemnly, strode through hall after hall, the ceilings rose higher, deeper, until we reached the main 100-foot dome.

The guide's hushed tones were hardly audible at the back of the group, yet not a word was spoken out of turn among the students. They had opened their notebooks and studiously recorded the guide's droning monologue about the types of gypsum and calcium sulphate washed out of the mountain. Eager pencils classified taxonomic groups, classes and subclasses, and categorized how the water had eroded the stone in 'series, sequence, succession and progression'.

We came to the so-called Barbarossa chair and table. Legend has it that Barbarossa, the red-bearded German Holy Roman Emperor Friedrich I, who died on a Crusade in 1190, sits deep inside the Kyffhäuser mountains, apparently waiting to re-emerge. He was expected to return Germany to greatness as soon as the black ravens stop circling overhead. After the cave was accidentally discovered by miners in 1865, a stone table and seat were built for him.

In narrowing intestinal twists the cave wound its way to an exit, spilling us back into the car park. The teacher arranged the students in a perfect semi-circle. 'Who has heard of Barbarossa?' Had the students known, they would have politely raised a hand and waited to be called. Pencils fidgeted idly over white pages, yearning to categorize one more gypsum fact.

The teacher's efforts were futile. 'Barbarossa stands for a strong Germany. In history and myth, he symbolizes the power of the Reich. The soldiers of World War One came here on pilgrimages. They were waiting for the return of the strong saviour who once led German soldiers towards Jerusalem. When the black ravens stop flying, they believed, Germany would reunite and rise once again. In the Third Reich, Hitler was seen as a new incarnation of Barbarossa.' None of this was mentioned in the pamphlet handed out at the entrance. The cave's political significance was still as awkward and inconvenient as before the Wende. Nobody dared to see if the ravens had landed. Safest to stick to geology; except for the teacher.

His colleague suddenly seemed beside himself with worry after looking at his watch. 'Hurry. We'll be late for the elephant toilet. Hurry, hurry. Our guide will be waiting for us at three.' The teachers marshalled their pupils back on to the bus. I followed at a distance. I knew their next destination, Bad Frankenhausen. The 'elephant toilet' was a gigantic, drum-like building that housed the world's biggest painting. En route to the railway station, Peter and I had stopped here, too.

In the 1970s, the leaders in East Berlin commissioned a museum to be built on the site where Germany's first revolutionaries battled during the Peasants' War. The war raged from 1523 to 1525 and was started by peasants in southern Germany who wanted to break free from their feudal masters. It quickly developed into a national movement. Four and a half centuries later, the communists staked a monumental claim to this almost non-existent German revolutionary past in the form of a battle pictorial.

Some 45 feet high and wrapping continuously around the hall over 400 feet, the panorama painstakingly depicts detailed scenes from the peasants' battle and their miserable lives. Legions of unarmed folk were slain while opulent feudal rulers gorged themselves on the fruits of their labour. It took one man ten years to design and paint this monumental bloodbath celebrating the popular uprising. And two years after its completion in 1987, Germany saw its first ever successful revolution. The museum's patrons were overthrown.

I caught up with the teachers and their flock inside the circular, windowless chamber. A guide reeled off yarns of convoluted earnestness. 'The picture's richness is constituted from the imponderable intellectual depth that manifests itself in the sensually concrete form.' Like flotsam, the mangled prose washed up unquestioned in the students' notebooks. '. . . theatrical effects in the context of concrete historically illustrative facts.' The students organized the colourful tapestry of gore, lust and domination into categories. Peering over one shoulder, I saw a notebook with a neatly drawn clockface listing the exact locations of the seventy-five key scenes. A slender boy sketched out battle formations of sword-wielding stick-men.

I wondered how the students would reconcile the two diametrically opposed notions of Germany they had seen today. Would they simply categorize Barbarossa and the peasant uprising, the strong Reich versus the popular revolution, the nationalistic, mostly western view versus the East German state doctrine and file them under different headings? Was there room for a personal view between the orderly columns of facts? When it came to analysis, I suspected the efforts of these seventeen-year-olds were close to break down – *kaputt*, 'on the fritz', as Americans curiously say.

Outside, I saw the first signs of the students' discipline dissolving. They cautiously mingled in the vicinity of the bus. The line that had formed by the door dispersed when the driver failed to open it. Boys played cards sitting on the tarmac. Two girls ran off to the toilets at the museum. A couple snatched a kiss from the jaws of self-restraint.

The history-minded teacher smoked obliviously.

'This doesn't look like a normal school bus,' I ventured.

'We rent it.'

'It's monstrous.'

'The kids really like it.'

'More than what they see when they leave the bus?'

'Probably. The bus is the closest thing to the milieu they come from.'

'What's that? You from a car-manufacturing area?'

'Yes, Eisenach. But that's not what I meant. The bus has several televisions. It's almost like a tower block on wheels.'

'They must want to get out occasionally.'

'It seems not.'

'Maybe someone was inspired to paint today.' I thought of stick-man boy. 'I did notice how amazingly restrained they are.'

'You should see their parents. Followed strict Party rules all their lives. The kids still live incredibly regimented lives at home.'

'Well, I hope they enjoyed their day of revolution and freedom.'

He took a lustful drag. '*Ja*. I told the driver to keep the doors locked for at least another hour. Let's see what they get up to.'

I pottered along for several days. A heat-wave loitered over the borderland. The oak beams of a country inn would satisfy my needs at midday. Before I knew it, my map was folded. Sheets on a shaded bed crinkled. It didn't feel as if I was giving up on travelling. I was giving in. I was slowing down. The whole country seemed to be slowing down with every step further south. The Med was just over the Alps. My days racing across the plain north were over. This at last felt familiar.

My home-coming sentimentality triggered a one-man retail boom. I would stop to shop at the unlikeliest places. I procured keyrings, candles and chains of river-washed pebbles painted by handicapped children. Nothing seemed too tacky. Not even a VW beer mug with wheels. In fact, the tackier the better.

The inn-keepers shared in the joy of my retail baptism. 'The tin-opener goes perfectly with that pocket knife.' As shoppers, Germans were a nation of collectors, not bargain-seekers. Tat comes in series, the same motif featuring on an unlikely panoply of utensils. The choice was splendid but prices non-negotiable. Sales, whether impromptu or linked to a bank holiday, *verboten*. A joyless canon of regulations permits two tightly regulated periods when prices can be marked down: one after Christmas, *Winterschlussverkauf*, and another to flog leftover bikinis, *Sommerschlussverkauf*. I had missed both. But price was the least of my concerns.

'Need a bigger room for this stuff? Won't cost you.' The young inn-keeper made the offer clearly not expecting me to stay. No guest with an out-of-town licence plate ever did. But I wasn't a travelling salesman; I was a travelling buyer. And I would travel only at the speed permitted by

Germany's strict shop opening hours. In my current state I could not go anywhere on Saturdays after 4 p.m. when deutschmarkland shut down. On Sundays, my sole retail window of opportunity was to buy incense candles at a church service. Without hesitation, I accepted the inn-keeper's offer of enlarged storage space.

Then, with retailmania in full bloom, the heat-wave blew out. The façades of village high streets sharpened again at the edges in the crisp air. The ripe ivy growth on fleshy oak beams stiffened. The lips of the inn-keeper thinned to form a tight bottom line. The Med was further away than I thought. I stuffed the smaller of my acquisitions into envelopes and posted them to appreciative acquaintances. At the *Postamt* in Sonder-shausen, a mother quarrelled with her daughter about how to spell a particular address. It evidently contained a double S, a letter combination the German language sometimes transforms into a single letter called SZ, a hissing hybrid which looks like a B with an elongated stem (β). It was on the brink of grammatical extinction. The lexicographical ivory poachers were winning. A controversial change in spelling rules had occupied news-paper editorials for years. Traditionalists fought against the abolition of the β as if it was their favourite 'Sesame Street' letter. But the rule-makers – presumably the same people who had restricted shopping hours – had prevailed again. The German alphabet was losing its most curious and exotic member. The courts had ruled in favour of bringing cleanliness and order to the fatherland's mother tongue. A similar standardization had been introduced after the last German unification in 1871. The Puttkamer Orthography devised by the minister of Culture Robert von Puttkamer in 1880, laid down a new common cannon of spelling and grammar. On that occasion the β had survived.

Stretched out in front of me lay the Eichsfeld (Oak Field), an area of 30 square miles. I stood on the edge of a garden, an enclosed homestead of wheat fields. There was no picket fence surrounding it. No plastic gnomes tending to the pond. The garden spread over hills and streams. Yet fields and farms locked into each other like the furrowed bark of an *Eiche*, an oak tree.

The lush Eichsfeld sits between the Kyffhäuser mountains and the River Werra in the south. For centuries, it had been ruled by the bishops of Mainz on the River Rhine as a satellite part of their electorate. The Eichs-feld was a religious oasis during a period rich in conflicts. Surrounded by belligerent Protestants, the local Catholic majority had developed a strong sense of community and faith. Then, in 1945, the Iron Curtain was ploughed across the wheat fields and oak groves. Some 130 villages and towns fell to the east, while thirty remained in the west. Early western attempts to maintain religious ties failed. The secularization of the socialist state permitted no cross-border pilgrimages.

I entered the Eichsfeld with a feeling of foreboding. Nowhere further north had such close cross-border links existed before 1945. If reunification could not be made to work here, what hope was there for the rest of the country?

I noticed the Eichsfeld air as I climbed out of the car. I had developed a routine of opening the door upon arrival and inhaling a deep breath. The air surged over the tongue, trickled down the tonsils and settled in the lungs with a thud that reverberated through the stomach and let the shoulders drop in one slow motion. The Eichsfeld air had a strength that would be called smoky in a whisky. I searched for oak trees. I thought I could taste their heavy scent and hear the rustling of leathery leaves. Northern sea air thickened as it brushed over these fields. Gone was the nervous industriousness that had enveloped the mountains. Heat burned rather than pricked; cold bit rather than nipped. Storms came from no particular direction. They were no longer easily divided into on- and offshore, down valley or across. Heavy storms unpredictably tore sideways. And heavy sunsets glowed auspiciously with the promise of sin and redemption. So, at least, I surmised.

I had another routine upon arrival. If it was evening, I would fetch myself a wheat beer in a tall half-litre glass and sit hunched over my notebook on a bench or a tree-stump. Between gulps of beer and night air I recapped the day's encounters. German brewing *Meister* commonly adopted religious names derived from the orders that nurtured the brewing techniques. Of the hundreds of wheat beers, all golden brown and cloudy, I favoured Paulaner and Franziskaner. My nightly sojourns in the company of St Paul or St Francis were the closest I have come to attending Confession.

I leant against the Red Racer. Tonight, I would not, nay, I mustn't, wait to find a bed before fetching my glass of *Hefeweizen*. The dying sun teetered on the branches of what I declared to be an oak tree, sight unseen. I purchased a bottle of St Paul's finest and unwrapped an emergency glass I hid in the boot. The trick to pouring a wheat beer is to turn the glass almost horizontal and insert the bottle. The bottle's mouth should rest inside the glass to minimize bubbling.

With my full glass, I sought a roadside tree-stump in the flaming evening air, ready to confess to almost anything.

There could be no better place to inquire about the reunification of the Eichsfeld. After a night with the Old and the New Testament by my hotel bed, I went to see the *Zwei-Länder-Eiche*. The Two-Country-Oak stood directly on the old dividing line. One section of trunk was solidly west of the border, the other in the east. They were joined at ground level and until a decade ago had belonged to different countries.

All sorts of metaphysical nonsense has been read into this tree, mostly in West Germany in the years before the Wende. Across the border, reunification was a taboo, but to western nationalists the tree was a gift. The symbolism was unbeatable. The forest, *der Wald*, made many a German knee wobbly. The mystical old oak exemplified how the country's two halves belonged together. Just look at the sumptuous heavy trunks; combined, they would dominate every tree in the forest.

I peered through the undergrowth. Coloured leaves in all stages of decay rested under a sun-lit canopy. Brittle branches hung from tall trunks. One could read almost anything into the Wende's *pièce de résistance*. Was the new Germany a brittle branch or a tall trunk? Was the reunited Eichsfeld a colourful patchwork or in a state of decay?

I circled the tree. On each round, a new cast of characters hopped out of limousines. 'What belongs together will grow together,' boomed a botanist. 'The roots go deep.'

'I feel like an Eichsfelder, always have. We're proud of the tree, always have been.'

'Right after the Wende I said, Hildegard, this tree has to be protected. It means something. *Stimmt's*, Hildegard?'

'That's right. But I said, the tree survived forty years divided. That was the difficult part. What's there to protect now?'

Most visitors said they liked walking here for this was a special place. Most also said the Eichsfeld again existed as a unit. But they could name few examples of joint ventures across the border.

I veered east to Heiligenstadt. A hearse driver told me that efforts to create a joint local government for the area had fallen through. 'But people pay the same on both sides when they die. And the coffins are the same size. We adopted West German funeral regulations.'

Herr Kuhnert overheard our conversation at the *Imbisstube*. 'Well, me, I'm in the transport business. It took a bit to reconnect the roads but is *klasse* now. The Eichsfeld has the best cross-border road network.'

'Thank God for that. The roads used to be so bad you could hear the corpse banging around. The stories, *Junge, Junge*.'

'Well, me, I've got some experience myself with this. I was on the B247, or it could have been the B80, it was somewhere near Leinefeld, at least I think, when . . .'

I reached Leinefeld, 15 miles along the border, probably before Herr Kuhnert had finished his story. By the town entrance I spotted a bunch of teenagers, bored and slightly bloated. I stopped the car. They had little contact with anyone of their age 'on the other side'. Sports clubs rarely competed far afield. And when they did play soccer in Duderstadt or Göttingen, nobody would remember their names, but just call them 'Ossi'. Club life, in any case, was no longer the same. For a few years after the Wende, they had carried over a strong *Gemeinschaftgefühl*, or sense of solidarity. Now players turned up for practice sessions, matches and club evenings only if they had nothing better to do.

Barrelling down Herr Kuhnert's B247 to Duderstadt, I passed the obligatory border museum and parked by the timber-framed town hall. I learned little from approaching strangers. Duderstadt was as silent as I had come to expect parts of East Germany to be. The one morsel I picked up led nowhere. Apparently, regular pilgrimages were being conducted to Hülfensberg, the Lourdes of the Eichsfeld. During socialist rule, the sacred hill had been inside the border exclusion zone and therefore out of bounds. But I could find no pilgrims on the tightly cobbled streets of Duderstadt.

I took the B247 back to Leinefeld a few days later. It was as splendid a road as Herr Kuhnert had promised. The students and soccer players I met had mentioned their upcoming *Jugendweihe*. The secular rite of passage was a pre-Wende leftover. Socialists had created the 'Oath of Youth' in the nineteenth century as an alternative to Christian Confirmation. The Nazis quickly adopted the oath for their own purposes. This did not stop postwar rulers in East Berlin from revamping the *Jugendweihe*. It formed part of the ideological indoctrination unleashed on even the youngest citizens. Every fifteen-year-old was encouraged to swear political allegiance and disregard Christian traditions. Anyone who failed to participate was marked down as an enemy of the state and was usually not permitted to go to university.

The oath-taking should have collapsed with the toppling of the Wall, but a mixture of *Ostalgia* and fear of the unknown ensured its survival. Tens of thousands of East German teenagers still took the oath every year. They now pledged to live a life mindful of the community. It was a cross between the boy scouts and New Labour. The old socialist vow to 'fight for the great and noble cause of socialism and honour the revolutionary heritage of the people' was scrapped. Rather than being party-sponsored, a private club now organized the *Jugendweihe*. The club's slick logo adorned pamphlets and stages, instead of the hammer and sickle. But the same torch was still being passed on.

In my previous conversation with the students, they had been preoccupied with the gifts they would receive on the festive day. Jakob, a cherubic left midfielder, hoped to get a mountain bike. Stefan, a lean goalkeeper, had missed out on a CD player on his recent birthday. Maybe the *Jugendweihe* would prove to be more fruitful.

Were they taking the oath only for the gifts, I asked, rather than to show they were team players off as well as on the pitch. 'I'm doing it because my parents want me to,' growled Jakob. 'It's only fair I get something back from them.'

I now saw him again at the ceremony. He had swapped his soccer shirt for a new corduroy jacket and stood lined up with his team mates as camera flashes rained down like penalty shots. Parents and grandparents held flowers and books. There was no sign of gifts.

Jakob and Stefan were called to the front. An official from the *Jugendweihe* club handed them a floppy certificate. The inscribed homilies were subsequently elaborated on by a guest speaker. He started: 'Dear youths, you, as young adults, are, herewith and from now on, and I say this with hope, joy and reflection, in our community, the difficulty of which . . .' The speech stumbled from subclause to parenthesis like a drunken sailor.

At the end, the parents filed out first, reminiscing about their own *Jugendweihe*.

'Then in those days we didn't get any big presents.'

I asked, was it not odd to continue a ceremony overtaken by political reality.

'The oath is part of our history and it's useful. What more do you want?'

Then why have Christian rituals like Confirmation faded almost completely?

My question was swept away when the soccer team burst out of the hall. They begged to know what their presents were. Judging by Jakob's and Stefan's goal-scoring antics, the mountain bike and CD player were in the net. With their arms locked, they soared into the Eichsfeld air. Parents cheered. The *Jugendweihe* had found its place in the consumer society between birthdays, Valentine's Day and Mother's Day. The Catholicism that held the Eichsfeld together before 1945 seemed lost for ever.

As a West German teenager, I had enjoyed what must have been the world's laxest school system. The unpunished fire-cracker throwing was no one-off. A few months later a religious service was transmitted live on radio from our school hall. Peter and I decided to carry out another chemistry project. This time the fire-cracker went out of the classroom window and landed next to the hall. Praying audiences across the country heard a muffled bang over the radio. It sounded as if the altar had collapsed.

Anti-authoritarian teachers and parents practically conspired to give us free rein. For years, we attended only half the lessons and still passed gloriously. We attended not so much a school as an educational supermarket. Nobody seemed to care that our trolleys remained empty. Least of all us.

But when it came to choosing a German university, I bolted. I disliked what I had seen of German universities. If there had not been the option of going abroad to England, I might never have seen the inside of a lecture hall. The local *Universität* in Osnabrück next door to my grammar school had none of the free-wheeling breeziness of our school lessons. Its campus was peopled by a joyless throng of eternal students. This stock character of German operettas was a beer-drinking, sabre-wielding *bon vivant* in the nineteenth century but, in more downbeat postwar West Germany, his zest had evaporated. Students combined a tedious subculture with the meticulousness of the East German pupils I had met at the Barbarosssa Cave. When they weren't dissecting methodology, they scribbled ideological mission statements on toilet cubicles. The lavatory at Osnabrück's university library featured a discourse on how Gorbachev had betrayed history, the Russian people, us all. Marxist tirades in the biro colours of the rainbow suffocated youthful exuberance.

I parked the Red Racer in Göttingen, twenty miles from Duderstadt. Bespectacled and besandalled students gathered in an airy campus. With its thirty Nobel Prizes, Göttingen University is what Americans call Ivy

League. In Germany, nobody would dare to be so 'elitist' or 'simplistic' as to rank venerable educational establishments.

I joined the queue at the campus cafeteria, here called Mensa. In front of me unfolded a conversation about Princess Di. 'She is a phenomenon. Her legend has become a folk myth. She fits into the analytical framework of my seminar.'

I picked up a handful of leaflets. A folded white sheet stood out for its promise of irony. '*Wer bin ich?*' it blankly asked. 'Who am I?' I giggled conspiratorially. 'Those who don't know who they are cannot find real joy or the actual meaning of life.' Monty Python seemed to be as popular as ever in Germany. '*Es geht also um die wichtigste Frage im Leben überhaupt.*' The authors promised to deal with life's most important question. The Quest for the Holy Grail II, surely. But repeated mention of *Bhagavad-Gita* soon made my heart sink. 'The body is like clothing or housing in which the soul, the self, the *atman*, lives.' The claptrap leaflet advertised the services of the Chaintanya Centre ('in principle free of charge'). It promised 'help to understand and live one's spiritual identity'. Irony would never win against the obsession with identity.

I also picked up a local student magazine. '*Training für 60 Paare*', announced the headline above a photo of naked bodies in bed. A psychologist at the university was looking for sixty couples with relationship problems. Instead of orthodox therapy he offered something called GOAL (Goal Orientated Action Learning). It sounded as if he had distilled the management lessons of Henry Ford into a programme for all-round sexual gratification. The action learning at the clinical psychology lab aimed to teach 'self-regulation of conflicts'.

Balancing free-range tofu on a tray, I negotiated aisles filled with receding hairlines and wrinkled skin. I had walked into a Mick Jagger lookalike competition. I was the only ex-student, but everyone in the cafeteria appeared to be older than me. There were women with children of school age. Göttingen's eternal students would soon share seminars with their sons and daughters.

Among the earnest chatter, I picked up flicks of English. Jamie and Jonathan introduced themselves as exchange students from the University of London ('UL, mate, not London University'). They were visiting Göttingen as part of a German language course, much to their regret. 'Can't understand a word they say. Honestly.' Jonathan was twenty, Jamie twenty-one. Their ages made them as conspicuous as their rugby shirts.

They had attended a business studies lecture in the morning.

'It was all compound nouns. The lecturer spent half the time writing out words that reached across the blackboard from one end to the other.'

'It's like, *Shareholdervaluetargetrangeprojection*.'

'We was sitting there and I felt this *Boredomattackpain* in me neck.'

'You had this *Foreverlastingemptystareface*.'

'Not as bad as your *Cutegirloverttherelook*.'

'Right. Where did she go?'

'Probably doing *Sharevaluehomeworksession*.'

The two had a mixture of intelligence and arrogance that only the English educational system could confer on someone their age. Jonathan declared the German language a paradox. Here was a people known for its order and organized efficiency, he said, yet these same people strung words together in the most convoluted fashion. The compound nouns were one of many anomalies. If only Germans constructed sentences the way they built cars.

After lunch, I went to the university library. The steel-and-glass building could have been an airport terminal. The high-falutin' might pronounce it a take-off ramp for the mind. It housed among its many volumes what I had hoped to find, *The Awful German Language*, by Mark Twain. Jonathan had reminded me of what the American master of punchy language had observed during a trip along the Rhine:

An average sentence in a German newspaper is a sublime and impressive curiosity. It occupies a quarter of a column; it contains all ten parts of speech – not in regular order but mixed; it is built mainly of compound words constructed by the writer on the spot and not to be found in any dictionary . . . ; it treats of fourteen or fifteen different subjects, each enclosed in a parenthesis of its own, with here or there extra parentheses which re-enclose three or four of the minor parentheses, making pens within pens; finally, all the parentheses and re-parentheses are massed together between a couple of king-parentheses, one of which is placed in the first line of the majestic sentence and the other in the middle of the last line of it – after which comes the VERB, and you find out for the first time what the man has been talking about; and after the verb – merely by way of ornament, as far as I can make out – the writer shovels in '*haben sind gewesen gehabt geworden sein*' or words to that effect, and the monument is finished . . . To learn to read and understand a German newspaper is a thing which must always remain an impossibility to a foreigner.

This quotation, was included in a book by a US Germanist who had taught my father at Berlin University in the 1960s. He recounts the story of an American visiting Berlin in Bismarck's time. Anxious to hear the Chancellor speak, she procured two tickets to the visitors' gallery of the Reichstag and hired an interpreter to accompany her. They were fortunate enough to arrive just before Bismarck intervened in a debate on a matter of social legislation. The American pressed close to the interpreter's side so as to miss nothing of the translation. But although Bismarck spoke with considerable force and at some length, the interpreter's lips remained closed. He was unresponsive to his employer's nudges. Unable to contain herself, she finally blurted: 'What is he *saying*?' 'Patience, madam,' the interpreter answered, 'I am waiting for the verb!'

Leine Hotel, said a rather plain sign. I expected dank rooms, sagging beds and a breakfast akin to a brief Formula One pitstop. On a mental television screen, I could see the seconds ticking away in the lower left corner.

The Leine Hotel was perched on the edge of Göttingen, close to the autobahn. The grey concrete front promised nothing. Tired travelling salesmen might prefer it to the darker grey of the autobahn's tarmac. I had turned up out of desperation. In the city centre, the worldly palaces offering beds for the night had taken in their *Zimmer frei* signs. I had looked into cosily lit rooms. Guests snacked on *Betthupferl*, chocolate knick-knacks on the pillow.

Of course, there were no *Betthupferl* at the Leine Hotel, but everything else was a surprise. The rooms looked cleaner and the service more efficient than anything. I had seen so far. Breakfast consisted of an elaborate buffet, crafted with precision. Tea came in neatly packed bags. The label read: 'Pompadour. Euro-blend. Strongly aromatic tea mixture. Weight 1.5 grams.' The hotel was run by Danny Ramsey, a burly Englishman with an immigrant's zeal for imitating local custom. Except, there were no books in the rooms, just television guides. 'I married a German,' he said in German with only a hint of an accent.

In the lobby, Herr Ramsey offered a wide range of newspapers. I avoided the big national broadsheets. More than a century after Twain's visit, they still served up grammatical cobwebs. Anyone wanting to see the difference between modern Germany and modern England should compare copies of the *Frankfurter Allgemeine Zeitung* and *The Times*. They are equal in status, but nothing else. The German Thunderer doesn't even have photographs on the front page. While *The Times* takes in news until three in the morning, the *Frankfurter*'s copy deadline is at sundown. I remember picking up the *Frankfurter* the day after the Oklahoma City bombing in 1995. Germany's journal of record made no mention of the terrorist attack that killed more than 150 people. Inconveniently, the bombers had struck just after 5 p.m. *Frankfurter* readers waited a further day for the news.

The local papers I picked up from Herr Ramsey's rack were different beasts. Being much closer to their readers, they pulled no punches and liberally employed the tabloid currency – the cliché. 'Climate of fear', screeched a headline. A group of teenagers had given the Hitler salute. A tape with Neo-nazi songs had been played in class. Using Fleet Street's name-and-shame tactics, the paper ran a picture of the headmaster who had failed to control his students. A banner caption quoted his defence: 'No right-extremist background at the school.' Presumably, jackbooted eighth-graders had raised their right arms to answer trigonometry questions.

I met an East German student back at the university cafeteria. He mumbled his name. It sounded like Jan. He preferred to be called John, he said. John Denver, John Cale, John Wayne – I couldn't think of a single German called John. Maybe that was his inspiration.

John hunkered in the sole company of a coffee cup. His sunglasses and blazer stood out among the dungarees and woollen patchwork jumpers. His demeanour was formal. When I asked to take a seat at his table he attempted to rise from his chair to greet me. He stopped himself from completing the effusive gesture. Rolling open a palm, he motioned me to sit down.

We talked about pranks in lecture halls and at school. I mentioned my enjoyable geography, chemistry and history lessons. He said, at his East German school, the teachers still used pre-1989 maps of Germany. A thin red line ran from the Baltic Sea to the Czech border. This was years after the Wende. There was no money to buy new maps. I chuckled. In him, though, the maps had inspired not ridicule but frustration. During one lesson, he told a teacher that under socialism at least the maps were right, even if the people couldn't go anywhere. After assurances from professors in Göttingen that the university's maps no longer showed an Iron Curtain, he matriculated here.

'You should ask them if they still use those maps.'

'I never see them when I'm home.'

'Why not?'

'Kafka,' he said cryptically. I probed a little. John had been an avid Kafka reader as a teenager. While others learned to handle guns and cleared drains, he read. For the most part he was left alone. The indoctrination system may have been oppressive but obvious loners weren't forced to join in. However, when he praised Kafka in class, teachers screamed at him. 'Decadent, bourgeois literature of the class enemy.' John was subsequently forced to participate in paramilitary exercises. Kafka faded from his world. 'I had read his books a dozen times, in any case. What did it matter.' After the Wende, Kafka returned. The same teachers who had denounced *The Trial* and *The Castle* now competed to be first to place Kafka on the syllabus. John called them *Wendehälse*, wrynecks. It was a wordplay on the Wende and the teachers' ability to unhinge their heads and turn with the political winds. 'I never thought that Kafka could make me feel sick,' said John.

Across the cafeteria, he pointed out Christopher Kopper, a famous young history lecturer. I recognized him from talkshows and newspaper profiles. Herr Kopper had recently published a damning study of the role played by the big German banks in the Third Reich. The book was based on Nazi documents stashed in East Germany. Before the Wende, Herr Kopper's requests for access had been denied. By the mid-1990s, his book was a bestseller. Partly, no doubt, because he was the son of Hilmar Kopper, the chairman of Deutsche Bank.

'And he attacked his father's bank?'

'Naturally, naturally. But he savaged Dresdner Bank even more.'

We watched Herr Kopper Jr get up from his blonde beehive of female companions. Behind round glasses, he carried a grin more relaxed than German academics normally permitted themselves. At thirty-five, he was barely older than his students.

'I don't think he's flirting with them. That's not why he's grinning. It must be his work that makes him happy.' John ignored my comment. Dealing with history was a serious matter. After all, Herr Kopper's work was conducted in the name of a fancy compound noun: the past-coping-process, or *Vergangenheitsbewältigungprozess*.

11

IN THE
VALLEY

IT WAS ARDUOUS FOLLOWING an arbitrarily drawn border. The Iron Curtain shadowed no coastline. There were no roads alongside it. Villages in its way had been flattened once and for all. Beauty spots which were deserted during the political ice age were only slowly being rediscovered. Tourist boards struggled to put up new signs. Occasionally, I glimpsed a watchtower; a toppled wall segment might fester in the undergrowth; but the trail would soon go cold again.

Maps slumped over the steering wheel, I planned the next leg of my journey. The list of border museums charted only a patchy course; the red line dividing Germany in my pre-Wende road atlas was scarcely more helpful. Newly inflated business parks and fresh coats of tarmac conspired to bury the unpleasant facts of history. Money, not time, was the country's healer.

The Red Racer was currently beached on a parking lot dwarfed by yet another superstore. The border was by no means invisible. In the *Hinterland*, differences remained on open display. The actual dividing line, though, proved to be elusive. Even patrol tracks had been scrubbed out.

Then I found a new guide. Over the next fifty miles, the border ran alongside the River Werra. At Wahlhausen, fences had come right down to the water's edge. I hitched my fortunes to the Werra from Oberrieden to Vacha.

Water and border shared a valley. It was remote rather than rural. Bumpy tracks beached visitors on sparkly pebble banks. Had Holly

Golightly been looking for a breakfast spot in Germany, the Werra might have served as her Tiffany's. The stream moved unburdened by floating *hoi poloi* under a brilliant blue sky. Farm hands were tying logs together. Motorized terror stayed out of view. The river was a narrow gash in a flat valley. It flowed as calmly as its bigger sibling, the Rhine, and glistened teasingly in the rising sun.

The water seemed unsullied. An angler with a broken leg disagreed. 'But it's not as dirty as it used to be,' he added. East German salt mines had polluted the Werra for decades, he sneered. Rhenian environmental rules now cut emissions. 'Most mines had to shut up shop.' Slowly, the fish returned.

The angler's main distraction was the occasional passing leisure cruiser. Lifting his crutch, he poked an imaginary boat. 'Even before the border opening the cruisers were allowed to travel here. They could cut through eastern parts of the river with impunity.' Every utterance sent his shoulders galloping. In unison, the rod in his hand bobbed up and down. 'The thrill of straying across the border is gone now.' And, much to his frustration, so was his bait. I suggested he should wedge the rod into the crutch and sit down.

According to my atlas, the lower Werra valley forms Germany's geographic centre. I had drawn diagonal lines connecting the country's furthest corners and found they crossed in the valley's grid square. Admittedly, I practised an approximate science, but the result of this little exercise was none the less a surprise. I had never heard of anyone visiting the Werra. For decades, the river had been perched on the border to nothing. With no official VoPo crossing point in the vicinity, the geographic centre became the ultimate periphery. Germans called it the land 'where the dog is buried'.

I let myself be guided by the hill ranges enclosing the canine cemetery. The Red Racer rolled towards the double town of Bad Sooden-Allendorf down a green aisle. My motorized beast had been utterly obedient recently. Earlier antics were forgotten. But a report on the radio seemed to be tempting fate. According to a new car survey, Toyotas had come out on top in a reliability test. I feared my moody Toyota could become complacent. I swiftly changed stations, only to be treated to one of the more obscure fixtures on German radio. The new station carried location reports of police radar traps. Following the news, the weather and the traffic bulletins, a cheerful voice announced: 'Blue BMW on the B27 near Bad Sooden-Allendorf, parked in a driveway. Looks like a hand-held radar. Ring us if you spot other police cars doing speed checks. Every hundredth caller gets a bottle of sparking wine.' I listened in bewilderment. This was neither Monty Pythonesque subversion nor Stasi-style denunciation.

I lunched in modest splendour. The chips were soggy. As usual, they came with mayonnaise. I gave the bottle a good wallop and doused the chips. Spread with a knife, it covered most of the chips. I thought this would ward off the waiter's inevitable Spanish Inquisition as to why I hadn't eaten my food. But instead, he asked why I had left so much mayonnaise. The restaurant called itself *Der Adler*, The Eagle. I told the waiter: 'You've got eagle eyes.'

'*Wie bitte?*'

'*Wie ein Adler*. You spot everything, like an eagle.'

'I don't want to hear anything more about eagles. I've had enough.'

'Why – have you been attacked by one?'

'There are no eagles in the area. But any damn neo-Nazi driving by comes in. They think, with a name like ours, we must welcome their lot.'

'And you don't? I thought you might.'

'Nowadays I throw them out straightaway. They come across from the east and try to sing fatherland songs. But not here. Our eagle is not the same as the one on the old Reich's flag. *Schluss. Aus.*'

I tried to give him a tip matching his courage, but he refused and grumbled on. It wasn't the first time I had seen a German waiter turn down money. Service could be slow but guests were never cheated. The only place where tipping was rigorously enforced was in autobahn toilets. Cleaning ladies stood guard by a sign demanding a specific amount.

In Bad Sooden-Allendorf, the mile-wide valley narrowed to a green garden cut up by the Werra. The hyphen connecting Bad Sooden and Allendorf turned out to be a concrete bridge across the river that divided them. Both towns were still in West Germany, but the eastern hills overlooking the genteel sprawl bore the familiar border marks. A stretch of fence ran along the green crest.

For the first time, I noticed that all nuts and bolts on the fortifications were facing west. The fence could only be dismantled from the class enemy's side. *Republikflüchtlinge* might otherwise have escaped using a spanner. Instead of a risky climb over the fence, they could simply have unscrewed it.

Whoever designed the border this way was a genius. He or she saved sixteen million East Germans from having their spanners confiscated.

The position of the nuts and bolts was pointed out to me by a group of cyclists. The six men and two women clad in spandex had stopped close by. They saw me scribbling. (On dry days, the car roof was an ideal place to rest a notebook and survey the surroundings. I could peer over the edge of the page, lining up reality and prose next to each other.)

'Are you from the municipal government office?' asked the spandex leader.

'Do I look like it?'

'We just thought you might be writing a checklist – oh, I don't know – on whether the roads and telephone poles are still in order. You kept looking around.'

'Not quite; but you're close.'

'Good. Because we need directions.' While consulting my maps, we discovered almost matching itineraries. They were heading north along the river and border. This was their third cycling tour partially retracing the Iron Curtain. The first had been along the Czech border. Last year, the group crossed the Harz. They had expected the Werra valley to be much less laborious than the mountains, but the local border patrol track was usually hidden or impassable. They kept having to scale the hill ranges.

I folded up the maps. We were standing on a high plateau. A single tree nestled in a yellow field like the last crumb on an empty plate. Clouds drifted in the valley below us. We looked down on the sun-gilded billows. I asked what attracted them to the border. 'Even now, the Wende and reunification seem like a miracle. It's a wonderful feeling, still, to criss-cross east to west daily, hourly.' They saddled up and rolled past the fence, plunging their spokes into an apple grove already enveloped by clouds.

Eschwege was a West German archetype. Decades of deutschmark grooming had bestowed a manicured beauty on the riverine town. Pristine timber-framed houses overlooked a canalized Werra. Windows displayed wares from catwalks rather than pet shops. Store-owners locked their doors at noon for a two-hour lunch break. Nobody expected them to operate at the convenience of customers. ('Closed on Saturdays.') Much could be said against Eschwege, but it surely was not the 'ugly face of capitalism' many East Germans expected to see across the border.

By the roadside, a radiant red Trabbi was parked in high grass. Painted across the doors, front and back, I read: 'bed, 35 marks including break-fast'. On the boot, a half-litre of pilsner was chalked up for 3.80. I headed east, chasing the Werra through a widening valley, only to be thwarted as the river wound its way out of the road network. To catch up with the water I climbed ever higher into the hills. I passed Rambach and Rittmannshausen.

At the entrance to Creuzburg I reached East German territory. It showed. Serpentines frazzled out. Crumbling old buildings and new architectural sins came into view. The gleaming roofs on sagging walls looked like fresh trimmings put on a leftover Christmas tree in March.

'This is all wrong. Wrong. Wrong. Wrong.' Herr Köster pulled packs of washing powder from the shelves of a supermarket. 'I never know what to get. Too much choice, don't you agree?' The pensioner didn't listen to my cautious appraisal of the consumer society. He was lunging ever deeper into the nether regions of the toiletries section. Bottles and multi-packs rattled off the shelf. 'What do we need all this for? Nobody would buy a dozen different products to wash socks.'

Herr Köster said it was all the fault of the greed-mongers, the market-hungry, the *Geldseligen*. Before the Wende, there had only been one washing powder. Rich and poor walked around in equally clean clothes. But it wasn't just a question of socialism. Having one powder was easier, he cried. Was one brand not enough? Who wanted to listen to all the loud advertising for different brands? In the old days, people could trust advertisements to give honest advice. And salesmen had real warmth and didn't try to con customers. 'Look at this. Omo, Ariel and all the other washing brands. Why can't we just have our old Ata powder? The shops have all this choice, but the one item you want, they refuse to give you.' I suggested that Ata's absence could be due to the fact it was not a washing powder but a toilet cleaner. 'Next aisle over.'

'Oh, God, yes.' The old man was crushed. It hadn't been my intention to be patronizing. Blotchy skin made him look all the more bedraggled. 'My wife would have known where to find the washing powder.'

'Why didn't she come shopping with you?'

'She's dead.'

I apologized.

'She's been gone for years. Heart attack right after the Wende. I lost my wife and my mistress at the same time.'

'Your mistress?'

'That's what my wife and I called the Party. Only at home, of course. I spent a lot of time on Party business. I could have made it to the cadre élite, you know. Now it seems I have lived for nothing. All our work . . . well, Omo and Ariel did a good job. Not a socialist mark in sight. Our biographies have been washed away.' He proceeded to the cash register with an indistinguishable powder brand.

I strolled down to the Werra, shrunk to a brook. Tarantulan diggers worked on a new road bridge. Upstream, a gritty overpass from the thirteenth century offered ramblers easier passage. The old bridge's reddish-blonde stones had recently been given a facelift. When I returned to Creuzburg, I saw the old man back at the shop. 'Look what you have sold me. This *Scheisspulver* is no good.'

'But it's a popular brand.'

'I don't know about you and your customers. *Zum Kuckuck*. Here it says the powder is not even for washing clothes.'

'*Ah, ja*. It is meant to soften the fabric.'

'But it doesn't wash socks.'

'No.'

'Your modern stuff does everything – except what you want it to do.'

'*Wie sie mögen*. If you want to wash, you need a washing powder as well.'

'Of course, you want me to spend more money.'

Some Ossis liked to say decidedly belligerent things about the new Germany. They missed the cosiness of a life behind walls. They felt cheated when western managers 'ruthlessly' cut jobs. With a snarl, market economics was still being called capitalism. ('*Sozialismus* got things right, too.') The murmurs of discontent could sound like a grumbling drum beat. Many Ossis seemed scared by what they had brought on themselves. Nevertheless, most believed life had taken a turn for the better over the last decade.

Herr Köster's abhorrence of the new Germany was different. Given half a chance, he would retreat to socialist rule, Walls and all. He would gladly wash his socks with toilet cleaner. He would not wait for the next advertising break on television to escape the world of multiple washing-powder brands. Initially, I marked him down as an aberrant loner, an understandably confused old man. But I was wrong. There was a whole class – how they liked that word – of deeply disaffected East Germans. He was the first of a cluster.

Leaving Creuzburg felt like a belated emergence from a boozy luncheon. Relief was mixed with surprise that daylight had not faded completely. Hoping to escape a cloud of rain, I raced along the valley. I tried an eastern route, but the Werra made a habit of escaping from my view. It slunk through steep, wooded slopes. When I crossed a bridge, my riverine guide hid behind a silky drizzle. On the western side, the path led straight to an autobahn. Four lanes of concrete had been extended across the valley to connect Berlin and Frankfurt. I was tempted to ask if the motorway was the only thing connecting them.

At a rest stop by the border, the thorny features of a military convoy peered over car roofs. A lorry carried a *Leopard*, a *Panzer* originally designed by Germans to kill Germans. The soldiers guarding it today were acting as curators. They carried adjustable spanners instead of weapons. Even driving a security van collecting petty cash would pose greater risks than their current duties.

The convoy stood beneath a voluminous tower that had housed East German border guards. The old checkpoint was converted into a rest stop. A service station inhabited the tower. The lanes for vehicle checks had metamorphosed from a patrol station into a petrol station, with queues longer than before. Leftover from the *status quo ante* was a smaller watchtower on the side. It alone could not be cannibalized. I suspected a case of concrete indigestion.

I approached the convoy. The unarmed men idly pursued the death most common among German soldiers, eastern or western. They smoked. About the border, they had nothing to say.

In the cafeteria, I met Herr and Frau Mankowski. Inspired by the military might outside, I ambushed them. I had overheard their conversation while searching for a table. 'Maybe a little walk later? The Werra has become so popular with ramblers.' With their saggy postures, neither of them appeared ever to have veered off the autobahn. I was keen to hear more. Unfortunately, there was a free table out of earshot but within sight. I feared Herr Mankowski would object if instead I sat down next to his wife.

The free table would have to be blocked. And the only weapons available were my apple pie and my 0.4 litre glass of Coke. The armour was laid out in front of me on a plastic tray. I made a mental note to buy another drink later and lifted up the apple pie. The shift in weight made the tray pivot. The Coke was catapulted on to the table, foaming darkly.

'*Entschuldigung.* The table over there is *schmutzig.* May I please . . . ?'

'Everything is always dirty. Who's doing this? Wherever you go there is litter.'

'Seat yourself, young man.' Frau Mankowski moved her coat to another chair.

'Watch out. That chair is probably dirty as well.'

I introduced myself and Herr Mankowski reluctantly followed suit. 'I'm sorry for interrupting your conversation. I heard you talking about the Werra.'

'The river's dirty as well. Didn't I say everything is dirty?'

'I was told by an angler the Werra is cleaner now. The salt inflow has been cut.'

'Maybe, maybe not. But the border opening has hurt the environment in the river valley. At least on our side. Our side was protected before.' I assumed this meant he was East German. 'The animals are disturbed. The forest ruined by ramblers.'

'You ramble much?' It had been Frau Mankowski who suggested a walk earlier.

'I don't have to, to know it's dirty, right?' he blurted.

'I don't ramble much myself.' I told them about driving along the valley and described the other river that shadowed the border, the Elbe. I dwelled on Elbe watchtowers being converted into a lavatory.

'These towers are historical monuments. The *Republikflüchtlinge*, they deserved to be shot. They tried to betray the economy of their country. Taking their skills away – that suited the west. That's why we built the wall in the first place. The west was committing economic plunder in 1961, drawing out all our resources. Freedom to travel? I laugh at that. What about freedom to walk into any bank vault? Are the walls and guards in a bank different? Are bank guards sent to prison when they stop a robber? *Oh nein*. But our border guards get dragged into political show trials. Greetings from Nuremberg. All just to make socialism look evil, once and for all. It's an attack on the life's work of everyone who laboured for a better Germany.'

Herr Mankowski flew into a rage. He wasn't loud, but his tirade welled with quiet disgust for my frivolity. I was reminded of something Herr Köster had said: 'It seems I have lived for nothing. Our biographies have been washed away.'

A forlorn Herr Mankowski went to the gents. Nodding her head in his direction, Frau Mankowski remarked that, strictly speaking, part of this watchtower, too, had been converted into lavatories. 'I won't bring it up with him though,' she whispered. 'But honestly, the border guards were not all bad.'

Frau Mankowski had grown up in a nearby village. The guards were friendly with the local girls. One got acquainted during music evenings and *belles-lettres* readings organized by the border commanders. Some girls even married a man in uniform. Frau Mankowski joked that girls had a choice between their cousins and the guards. I left ten minutes later. Herr Mankowski had failed to return from his watchtower window seat.

'Between you and me,' groaned the buxom young woman sipping coffee, 'sex was definitely better before the Wende.' We were sitting in the winter garden of the Pension Mahret in Eisenach, the biggest East German city directly on the border.

When I arrived at the hotel, she had said there was only one room available. I was happy to take it, sight unseen. But she insisted that I view it. She went up the stairs in front of me, her behind gently gyrating. I wondered if she was going to show me her own bedroom. But instead she unlocked the door to a decent broom cupboard overlooking the winter garden. There was standing room only. I liked the view. 'I'll take it,' I said. This seemed to displease or at least surprise her. 'But the room doesn't have its own bathroom.'

'I don't mind using the one down the corridor.'

She changed tack. 'I'm afraid, I'll have to check with the other guests if they're happy with that.'

Eventually, she let me have the room. I teased her that she didn't want me to stay. She took her coffee into the winter garden. 'Why do that?' The television was blaring.

'You might be saving the room for someone special.'

'Who, please?'

'Maybe your Prince Charming, a suave stock broker from Frankfurt with a Porsche and a villa in Tuscany.'

'I've seen the type. They're useless. At least in bed.'

'All of them?'

'Generally, the Wessi is ... they are ... they're so mechanical. It's all *bumm, bumm, bumm* – next. Unfortunately, Ossis are picking up selfish Wessi habits.'

'You mean a lack of passion.'

'Yeah. But Ossis are still the better lovers, really.'

'Wessis have been procreating at a decent rate for the last fifty years.'

'That's exactly it. Procreating! They have no imagination. You suggest maybe exploring something new. But all they come up with are these silly stunts, like, you know, doing it on the window sill. And as soon as they're done, I mean, they're really done. Finito.' She grinned broadly. 'So where are you from? Wessi, huh?' I volunteered a few personal details before escaping to my chaste cell.

The winding streets of Eisenach appeared to be thriving. I saw a replica of Osnabrück, the West German city where I grew up; the same bumbling attempts to create cosmopolitan chic. Medieval buildings were given designer facelifts. Tarted-up stores crammed carts with designer shoes in between the tables of outdoor cafés. Eisenach even had a 'British Shop'. A local English teacher, spurred on by her affection for Blighty, had opened a souvenir store. Britain's most important exports to East Germany, it turned out, were not parliamentary democracy or the game of football but spice racks, mugs, rugs and Crabtree tea. As a British garrison town throughout the Cold War, Osnabrück, too, had had its share of Crabtree bric-à-brac. We embraced it as if it came from Harrods.

Eisenachers, however, found little joy in the shop-keeper's efforts. Tourists eagerly inspected the wares of UK plc, but the locals were elsewhere – at a stall selling Thuringia *Bratwurst*, for example. In their nasal Saxon tones, the Eisenachers sounded doubly miserable. They complained that jobs were scarce, no matter how lavish the streets looked. The few people who did have jobs found them demeaning. ('I get paid but I get no *selfworthfeeling*.') All through the jeremiads, we wolfed down fried pork sausages. The long, white sausage tubes burst easily. Equal amounts of runny fat and shredded meat bulged out.

I followed the throng of tourists from the city centre uphill. Eisenach nuzzles against valley slopes. On a jutting rim high above the shopping streets hovers the Wartburg castle, where Martin Luther secretly translated the New Testament. The Wartburg is known as 'Germany's castle of destiny'. It looks not so much like a castle as a hilltop clutter of adjoining bastions constructed piecemeal over a thousand years. Medieval stone masonry is mixed with Bismarckian timber-frame walls and postwar roof tiles, mirroring a destiny equally cluttered and fragmented.

I climbed a draughty staircase to a room exhibiting knights' armaments. Before I had a chance to inspect the battle-scarred shields, I was accosted by a less than chivalrous attendant. '*I saw it exactly*,' she jousted, 'you came through that door.'

'Sure.'

'But you cannot.'

'But I did.'

'Leave then.'

'Why?'

'That door is the exit not the entrance.'

Inky clouds welled up. I passed them descending from the Wartburg. Eisenach would soon be thrashed by a heavy downpour. Oblivious, a hollering circle of pedestrians crowded around a stall on a street corner. They whooped conspiratorially. Questions were being bellowed out of sight.

'*Was macht man mit einem Kohl?*' (What do you do with a cabbage?)

'Slice it up.'

'Boil it for hours.'

'Or pickle it.'

I heard a thump. Coming closer, I made out a Punch & Judy show. A tiny stage was propped up on a trestle table. An obese figure resembling Helmut Kohl, the Chancellor who engineered Germany's unification in 1990, was being clubbed with a wooden spoon. Eisenachers cheered with rare enthusiasm. 'Give him one from me, too.'

The political overtones of the cabbage-beating were unmistakable. By the stage lay propaganda from the successor party to the once all-powerful East German Socialist Party (SED). Herr Köster's mistress was still a political force, but she had changed her name. After losing power, prestige and grand residences, the SED was reborn as the PDS.

In a rousing finale, Punch shoved and laboured and finally pushed the corpulent Chancellor off the stage. None too subtly he croaked: 'We'll do the same at the election.' More cheering. The crowd called for an encore. Someone even picked up the tubby Kohl and put him back on the stage. 'Push him off again.' But Punch was tired.

As the crowd broke up, I asked a middle-aged man with a bushy moustache if he thought the PDS could only be popular if it was funny. He was still chuckling, his twitching facial hair amplifying his hilarity. 'In all honesty, it's not just the cheap laughs that people were here for. You feel a certain camaraderie at the PDS. A revival of a long gone spirit, being together as a community.' But did he agree with the party's policies, did he want a return to socialism? 'The policies are almost irrelevant. The main thing is that someone speaks for us. East Germans get treated like stepmothers in all the other parties. The PDS is our preserve. Surely, no democrat could object to us having our own representation.'

The jovial crowd still milled around the stage when the downpour arrived. The sky had darkened with a swarthy five o'clock shadow. Winds picked up tablecloths from a street café and flung them over unsuspecting shoppers. The first pregnant drops splattered on cobblestones. I scarpered but the crowd's spirits could not be deflated. The socialists, reformed or otherwise, ignored their surroundings.

The sodden clouds lodged themselves between the Wartburg and an autobahn. The motorway hugged the opposite side of the narrow valley. Lorries drifted in and out of the rain as they passed Eisenach on the curiously elevated piste halfway up the hill. Caravans of red and blue tarpaulin sprung to life, only to be immediately gobbled up again by clouds.

In an attempt to stay dry, I sought out a dusty wooden hut in Eisenach's outskirts. The roof was supported by ageing beams. The whole structure seemed to be propped against a larger block of flats. Unimposing as it was, the hut nevertheless housed the local PDS office. Humour may have been one of the party's new secret weapons; glamour was not. This mixed strategy evidently worked. The PDS encompassed the biggest party organization in East Germany. Even after millions of party activists from the SED era had resigned, some 100,000 supremely dedicated PDS members were leftover.

The diminution in numbers shocked the stalwarts. Nevertheless, the PDS was still more in evidence than any other political club. 'That's our key strength,' said Frau May, a kindly woman with a librarian's short, flat hair. A decade ago, she would have been an apparatchik with an office larger than the average flat. Now she waded through election leaflets to find me a seat in the cramped quarters.

If the loss of privilege took its toll on her, she had long since recovered. 'We have a great network of contacts, an army of campaign workers,' she grinned. 'People really identify with us.' Eisenach was a PDS stronghold. The local constituency had one of the few directly elected PDS members of parliament. Frau Neuhäuser was a fifty-year-old career politician of undiminished ambition. She began climbing the greasy pole of socialist politics at an early age, becoming a party secretary in her student days. All this was mentioned in the first paragraph of her campaign leaflet, next to a picture of her children. The third paragraph read: 'I joined the SED in 1969. From 1979 to 1980 I took a training course at the district party school of the SED in Erfurt. After that, I became a secretary at one organization and party secretary at a publicly-owned watch-maker in Ruhla. For ten years, from 1970 to 1980, I was a member of the district council in Eisenach. And from 1985 to 1989, I was a candidate for the

Volkskammer [East German parliament]. In 1989, I was laid off.'

I asked Frau May why Frau Neuhäuser would mention such a dark past in campaign literature? Was this not political suicide and an embarrassment to the party?

'Absolutely not.' She seemed more surprised than irked by my question.

Given the way Frau Neuhäuser confidently mentioned her past, she obviously thought it was an asset. Frau Neuhäuser wanted to remind voters she came from the ranks of the Great and Good of the *ancien regime*. She seemed to say: huddle around me, I share your past and I know your pain. I, too, lost my job when our SED was toppled and our socialism was destroyed.

Undoubtedly, Eisenachers were proud of their socialist heritage. Even the official tourist brochures pointed out that Germany's Social Democratic Workers Party – the original Marxist seed – had been founded in the city in 1869. By comparison, the Wende in 1989 hardly merited a mention.

Frau May suggested I should see party work outside Eisenach. A few days later, I drove along the Werra to Gerstungen, a mile from the border. A hollow-eyed watchtower overlooked a new railway line. Lorries were unloaded between 'Spanish Riders', the unusually poetic name bestowed on anti-tank barriers. Frau May's directions led me straight to the Penny-Markt, one of the thousands of new supermarkets in East Germany. It stood half empty. This particular banana retailer struggled to fill its aisles even on a Friday afternoon, while the PDS effortlessly crowded out the car park.

I joined what looked more like a street party than a political party. Leaflets piled up unread on a trestle table. Party officials were dressed casually and blew very few slogan-filled speech bubbles. Friends and neighbours turned up to gossip. Children and party officials chased a leather football between parked cars. This was a far cry from the usually stolid German politicking.

An elderly lady wanted advice from party officials on how to fix her satellite dish. 'A fast-talking salesman persuaded me just recently to buy it. And it's already broken.'

'Broken? Maybe it's a problem with the satellite and its position.'

'There isn't much I can do about the satellite, is there, young man?'

'Not unless you learn to fly, granny.'

'The Russians sent the first man into space. I could be the first granny in space.'

Another woman asked a PDS functionary how to call her sister in Tunisia. 'And how much will it cost?'

A group of mothers talked about vacations in Bulgaria and Hungary. They welcomed the street party. Most husbands were unemployed and apparently drunk on Friday afternoons. 'There used to be a time when the Party took care of the men and organized social outings. But this isn't bad.'

In the car park, a group of merry but sober men fiddled with a Trabbi. From the open hood rose a whirring cough. 'We still have something in common,' said the car owner. 'It's easy to become isolated now. So we try to keep up the old camaraderie.'

I asked the party workers if they did any actual campaigning. Quietly, they listed the afternoon's tally. A doctor agreed to put party leaflets in his waiting room. Car owners offered to drive elderly voters to polling stations. Shop-keepers volunteered to host hustings on their premises. This was hardly revolutionary electioneering. West German parties, though, were in no position to match the PDS. They had arrived here after 1989 and few shop-keepers cared even to speak to them.

The PDS functionaries in Gerstungen and Eisenach were backed up by a surprisingly crafty party leadership in Berlin. Every village and town along the Werra was plastered with campaign posters. Gregor Gysi, the PDS leader and arguably Germany's wittiest public speaker, smirked at passers-by from glossy pictures. The posters proclaimed in red letters: 'Cool! PDS' and 'Sexy! PDS'. Gone were the SED's turgid Marxism debates. The PDS wanted to be hip and human. And as an underdog, I had to admit, the party had my sympathies, even though I didn't agree with any of its policies. *That's just what they want you to think*. Conspiracy theories rumbled through my mind. *The class enemy must be beaten with its own weapons*, whispered little red devils in my head. No matter. The party's modest national success was admirable, regardless. German socialists had been nearly extinguished by the end of the Weimar Republic, in the Third Reich and in the Bonn Republic. Yet here was a party led by a witty man eager to listen to the public. By contrast, West German parties of the left and right had lost touch with voters. Decades of convoluted coalition government and paranoia about creating another Führer cult had made politics in Bonn utterly dull. While the PDS embraced popular democracy, West German politicians often sounded uncannily like the speakers in East Germany's Volkskammer.

I left the Penny-Markt and crossed the border for probably the thousandth time. The West German village of Obersuhl was really only a 'foreign' extension of the last houses in Gerstungen. The string of dwellings was almost seamless. Eastern blocks of flats merged into western two-room villas. I wanted to know how the party was regarded over here. From the papers, I gathered the PDS was about as popular as the Monster Raving Loony Party in the UK, but the degree of hostility nevertheless surprised me.

Outside a *Tante Emma Laden*, an 'Auntie Emma' corner shop, I brandished PDS leaflets. One proclaimed, 'Five expensive years: German unity – costs and benefits'. I wasn't pretending to hand out the leaflets, but merely tried to fish for comments. A gardener took one look and said: 'Everything you always wanted to know about socialism but were afraid to try out. *Pfui.*' An insurance broker with proudly displayed chest hair said: 'The PDS doesn't exist for me as a political party. They have no place in our system.' His peroxide wife lifted her head, affording me a view into her nostrils. She compared PDS leaders to Nazi criminals who had escaped prosecution. 'For every Mengele, there's a Gysi.' The arrogance was breathtaking. She strode off like a football referee tucking his red card back in his pocket. I was dumbstruck.

The British historian Tom Bower has painstakingly documented the failures of de-nazification. In *Blind Eye to Murder*, he wrote of postwar West Germany: 'Those who gave the orders for murders, deportation, plunder and slavery not just survived; they had in many cases returned to their desks and were again in a position to give orders.' The same was not true today. Whether the imprisonment of senior SED politicians amounted to 'victor's justice' – as many PDS members claimed – remained debatable. But it was certain that East German malefactors would never be allowed back into public employment. There was plenty of anecdotal evidence showing that strict new rules succeeded in weeding them out.

I was reminded of the case of my father's secretary and her dubious past. My father had moved to East Germany shortly after the Wende. He assumed the artistic directorship of a state-owned theatre in the city of Stendal. In his new office, he kept on his predecessor's secretary. She adapted quickly to the western management and won praise. Years later, though, a note was found that indicated she had once cooperated with the Stasi. She lost her job immediately. No such misdemenour was small enough to escape punishment. Much could be criticized in the new Germany, but the failures of de-nazification were not being repeated. Unlike the old Nazis, few PDS members even wanted to hide their past.

I felt dizzy. Here I was, defending the socialist Wall-builders.

*   *   *

Did I want to accompany him to the hardware store, asked my host. Of course, of course.

Herr Kaiser and his family lived in what must be described as a villa. It featured a winter garden, a new balcony overlooking a new pond, sliding glass doors partitioning off the designer kitchen, newly fitted bathrooms and colour-coordinated extensions on both sides of the front entrance. A wobbly bar dominated the living room. My guestroom resembled an exhibition of different wood-panelling techniques. What once was a modest house – even by East German standards – had grown into a splendid residence, all thanks to Herr Kaiser's frequent trips to the hardware store. He had spent most evenings and weekends during the last decade building his little empire. Every screw and every nail, every square inch of wood-panelling, had been fitted by him personally. He embraced a methodical perfectionism. Not a speck of the old grey and concrete was allowed to poke out. But the DIY make-over was not finished. And judging by Herr Kaiser's *esprit*, it probably never will be. He took me on a tour of the corridors, outlining his plans for yet another extension. Maybe he will combine the two upstairs bathrooms into a sauna and jacuzzi.

He was on his way to the hardware store now. Did I want to accompany him? I eagerly accepted. I had practically been waiting for this invitation. Ever since reading that Germans spend twice as much as Britons in hardware stores, I had been the Cinderella of DIY. I wondered, what were my countrymen up to? According to the research consultancy Corporate Intelligence, per capita DIY spending in the UK was £170 per annum compared to £340 in Germany. Americans spent only £110 a year. Tool and timber retailing was one of the fastest-growing businesses in East Germany.

We drove to the hardware store in Herr Kaiser's VW Golf. On his roof-rack he could carry Greek columns 15 feet long, he said. Surprisingly enough, I couldn't recall seeing Greek columns in his villa, despite the beguiling catalogue of other ethnic furnishings. He explained the columns were for a friend. 'Greek is not my style.'

Before we even passed the store entrance, a wooden spiral staircase captured Herr Kaiser's attention. 'I prefer cast iron staircases. But this one isn't bad, really.'

The store was the size of several football pitches. Aisles wide enough for two passing cars stretched into the middle distance. Shelves reached so high a fork-lift truck was needed to retrieve shower units, whole swimming pools and power drills on wheels. Much to my amazement, every aisle was brimming with twinkly-eyed home-improvers pushing outsized trolleys. Even on this weekday morning, whole families came to choose between Dulux and Eisoplex paints, or pick a new designer kitchen. Meanwhile, nearby supermarkets were as empty as elsewhere. DIY, I postulated, was the post-communist answer to that nasty capitalist habit, shopping. DIY encapsulated a new Protestant Work Ethic for the unemployed.

Back at the villa, Herr Kaiser gathered his family. The two children could barely walk but were already well versed in the art of DIY. They were growing up with construction toys. The boys built fantasy castles with drawbridges. Brightly coloured plastic tubes and joints were strewn across the matching carpets and floor tiles.

Herr Kaiser liked to be assisted while he grappled with the intricacies of home improvement. Hunched under the sink, he would call out a drill size. Moments later the required drill was put in his stretched-out hand.

But despite the family effort, the fittings kept slipping off. Herr Kaiser needed another power tool. We got back in the car to borrow one from a friend.

Herr Knopf stored in his living room more heavy machinery than had fitted on the plains around Kursk. Herr Kaiser chose an extra long and narrow drill and also borrowed lubrication oil. '*Danke.*'

'Zero problem. There is nothing like vitamin C – connections.'

'You're right. They don't even make this drill any more. That's what friends are for.'

'Just like the old days when you couldn't get any of this in the shops.'

'Those were times! You could wait five years for bricks, eight for timber. And when it came, you had to queue all night to get a piece. One year you got window frames, then had to wait another year for the glass.'

'The first time I walked into a western hardware store after the Wende, I couldn't believe my eyes. Really, what choice.'

The chronic shortages in the socialist economy had often left comic marks on East German landscapes. Paints, for example, were produced one colour at a time. When a new paint shipment arrived, everyone rushed out to snatch a bucket, no matter what they wanted to paint. Soon, the same hue of green or red would appear on garden fences, front doors, bicycle frames, children's paintings and dented Trabbis.

Back in the car, I asked Herr Kaiser: 'Is that why you have completely remodelled your home? Because now you can?'

'In the beginning, yes.'

'And later?'

'People like me, we have lost a lot. I wasn't an SED member or anything like that. But still, it was my state that collapsed. The company I worked for also collapsed and with it my life's work, everything I had built. So I decided to make the house my life's work. When I retire I will have something to show for the years of sweat.'

The Werra and the border squeezed through one more valley mouth. The steep slopes afforded splendid views. At the narrowest point, the town of Philipsthal was perched on one side of the valley, while Vacha hovered across the water. A bridge connecting them had been rebuilt. Red stones framed a memorial inscribed: 'Bridge of Unity, October 3, 1990'. The bridge was erected in the fourteenth century but the wide middle arch kept collapsing. A priest recommended a local child be buried alive in the arch. The desperate builders followed his advice, and successfully joined the towns. It lasted until 1945.

In West German Philipsthal, the pain of division was somewhat lightened before reunification. A white house belonging to a western family stood directly on the border line. In 1951, bricklayers had walled off the only door between the two halves. In the following years, the eastern roof was threatening to fall down as it languished in no-man's-land. But, in 1976, the border was redrawn to put the house entirely on West Germany soil in one of the very few such acts of kindness by East Berlin.

On the Vacha side of the bridge, I spotted a large glass case. It documented the everyday evils committed in the name of expanding the local border fortifications. I read, a family had been deported in a 1973 dawn raid shortly before its riverside home was razed to the ground. In 1984, a fourteenth-century hospital building was flattened despite massive public protests. Even though the exhibition did not name those responsible, the glass case was a prominent reminder. For every Vachaer in the know, a finger was pointed in perpetuity. Nowhere else had I seen a border town washing its dirty laundry quite so publicly. And Vacha's efforts to confront its past went even further. After the Wende, the town had elected to keep some of its Cold War fortifications as if they were as salient as the medieval bridge. A white tower still watched over the Werra and parallel to the river ran one of the longest original stretches of wall. The graffiti on it looked like a leftover from 1980s Berlin, but I doubted the tinted scribbles were more than a few months old. The 10-foot-high concrete barrier remained an irresistible canvas.

Beneath the watchtower, leather-clad figures erected tents for a concert. A banner proclaimed the *Internationales Country Festival in Vacha*. From a loudspeaker, Johnny Cash croaked: 'Freedom's just another word for nutthin' left to lose.' The red and blue colours of the Confederacy troops were pinned to German car roofs. In the shadow of the felled wall, the Civil War flags looked a little less out of place. I lay down on the grass between the tents. Around me, beer cans were being cracked open and a group of dogs chased a bee. For once, I actually felt I was on holiday.

12

AROUND MOORS

'TYPICALLY GERMAN,' MY COUNTRYMEN said, and shook their heads. *Typisch deutsch*. The expression always carried negative connotations. A Londoner might call Nelson or Churchill 'typically English', while a Californian may excitedly exclaim 'Typically American!' upon finding a half-empty jar of Aunt Jemima maple syrup on a visit to an obscure European country. But a German would most likely be reminded of the fatherland with an embarrassed frown. *Typisch deutsch*, one whispered when confronted with a rowdy crowd of beer-guzzling bruisers at the *Oktoberfest*.

The German nation finds it as hard as ever to love itself. During five decades of feeling guilty for Hitler, we developed an extraordinary capacity for self-flagellation. Even now, the ritual whippings still had great popular appeal. Weekend television was endlessly burdened with *Talkshows* weighing the awful state of the unified nation. Hour after hour, brightly suited *ersatz*-Billy Grahams convulsed with cries for self-improvement. Worse still, the mental masochism extended far beyond the realm of politics. Germans had learned to chide themselves for everything from how they danced to what they ate. Where possible, they looked to other nations for guidance. In their eagerness, Germans tirelessly travelled the world to find ethnic replacements for the home-grown. I visited households where triangles of local cheese were commonly referred to as *tapas*, and conversations with overseas guests were exclusively conducted in English. More than once, a host insisted that we – two

Germans – make conversation *auf englisch* as we dined on greasy '*saucissons*'.

Even after the glorious Wende, patriotic pride was still all too often equated with nationalism. The singing of the national anthem ('Unity and Justice and Liberty for the German fatherland' to the same melody as '*Deutschland, Deutschland über alles*') amounted to a near-endorsement of Auschwitz in the eyes of some. While feelings of guilt over the Holocaust were receding as the last survivors and perpetrators died, flag-waving was even more frowned upon now than before unification. The enlarged country, steely and strong, feared being seen as a genocidal threat once again. '*Typisch deutsch*', Germans whispered when they saw a lone neo-Nazi limply kicking a tin can along a pedestrian zone. But it was the misguided observer not the shaven youth who was 'typical' in this scene.

I guess, I was no exception among the flagellants. *Typisch deutsch*, it flashed through my mind daily as I peered over the wheel of the Red Racer, roaming along the border. I had left Germany shortly after unification. My absenteeism might be construed as another form of unpatriotic rejection. But even when I chided the fatherland, I hope it was done with a certain benevolence.

At first, I noticed vibrations. A quiet suburban street in the city of Fulda fluttered past. Next, the car began to sway. When I heard a screeching thud I imagined my bumper had scooped up a poodle. (The thud sounded too gentle for it to be anything bigger.) I looked in the mirror to see if I might be dragging along an elderly lady clinging to a leash. But there was no lady and no poodle. Instead, a tyre had burst. So much for the reliability of Toyotas. Pivoting around the disintegrating rubber, the Red Racer made a sudden swerve, lurching off the tarmac. Before I could tighten my grip on the wheel, the car came to a standstill surrounded by bushes. A gaggle of smirking women pointed at me from the pavement. They seemed greatly amused by my presence. They gestured and laughed and slapped their backs and thighs. Unwittingly, I had parked in a flowerbed, sideways.

'*Typisch deutsch. Nothing but *Schadenfreude*,' I cried out, pounding the steering wheel in a fit of self-pity. None of the bystanders seemed at all worried by my little calamity. To them, I was a source of kerbside entertainment. I opened the door and stepped straight into a muddy puddle. Enter stage left, more uproarious onlookers. A car stopped in the middle of the street. Four windows were wound down and a group of pensioners cheered. The older the bystanders the more they seemed to be taking pleasure in my misfortune. '*Typisch deutsche Schadenfreude*,' I yelled at them. Laughter was drowned out by their squealing engine as they took off again.

I attempted to push the car back through the shrubbery by myself. Two overalled and horny-handed men eventually offered to help. With mounting paranoia, I suspected they were only interested in seeing the next laugh close up. And sure enough, they didn't have to wait long. I slipped on wet roots. But I recovered quickly enough to pretend I was simply shifting my stance. I mumbled something about changing the centre of gravity. They nodded with grins hidden behind flaxen moustaches.

It became obvious that neither could we move the car nor did I have a spare tyre in working order. The Red Racer was doubly stuck. Kindly, my helpers called out a tow lorry, though not without amusedly retailing my predicament. The lorry arrived within minutes. 'I had to come and see this.' The lorry driver circled the car, shaking his head. 'Too funny.'

'What's so funny?' I chided half-heartedly.

My discomfort seemed to cheer him on. 'This is a really good one.'

After a few more chuckles he loaded up. So to the repair shop. I preferred to travel in the piggy-backed Red Racer while my driver probably radioed ahead to relate my situation. And sure enough, gawking mechanics awaited us. By now, I had grudgingly decided to share in the amusement. We exchanged war stories about sliding past garden gates and crashing through garage rear walls. They stood with their horny hands casually planted in their overalls. I almost envied how much pleasure they seemed to derive from my mishap.

The mechanics wanted me to leave the car overnight. They had to check the wheel rim, they said. And anyway, it was almost *Feierabend*, knocking-off time. One of the mechanics, who sported oil stains on his forehead as if he had been wearing a mechanical crown of thorns, called a taxi for me. Having recovered from the shock of my calamity, I cheerfully plumped myself down in the front seat of the Mercedes cab. Mindful of the journalists' adage that taxi drivers are a town's best gossip-mongers, I asked Herr Fricke – a man who primarily chauffeured his own belly – about the latest *Klatsch*.

He paused. 'I don't know about *Klatsch*. A colleague of mine was murdered. The police found his cab near the crime scene.'

Herr Fricke's voice died down before he had finished the sentence.

The almost inaudible Mercedes engine made the silence all the more piercing. I asked if he had known the driver. '*Nein*. Not really. But I had heard the name Plüschke before. Who hadn't?'

'He was well known then?'

'Long story.'

'I see. Are drivers like you frightened the murderer might strike again?'

'Not really. I mean, the police hasn't arrested anyone. But there is no doubt who is responsible.'

Herr Fricke had not told the truth when he said he was not really frightened about further attacks, I decided. He was scared out of his wits. Despite my best efforts, I could not worm any more details out of him and forgot about the incident. A few days later I read the whole story in a local newspaper (perhaps proving that, in Germany at least, papers are still a better medium than cabbies). The headline read: 'Mysterious death of taxi driver – Is former West German border guard a victim of Stasi revenge act? He killed East German officer in 1962.' A grainy picture showed a covered corpse under a crash barrier. The tight layout of German newspapers always gave stories a look of urgency. Dateline Hünfeld. I read:

Is it an act of revenge by underground Stasi agents or murder? The mysterious death of taxi driver and former border guard Toni Plüschke (59) is a riddle to investigating authorities in Hünfeld (Fulda district). The man died from a shot to the head. Now the police task force has to delve into Germany's divided past. More than one hundred clues stretching back to the former guard's period of service have been collected. On 14 October 1962, he killed the East German officer Rudi Arnstadt at the border. Arnstadt had shot at Plüschke and his superior after they passed him on patrol. The then 23-year-old Plüschke said in a statement: 'I didn't aim precisely. I swung around when I heard shooting and blindly returned fire from the hip with my automatic rifle.' Plüschke saved his superior's life. Arnstadt died from a shot to the head. The reason for the armed conflict during which East German guards fired thirty shots was only established later – a botched kidnap attempt. East Germany wanted to abduct the two western guards to exchange them for a modern artillery vehicle which another eastern guard had used to escape. Arnstadt's death was exploited in an East German propaganda battle at the time. Plüschke was convicted in absentia to 25 years imprisonment. For 'safety reasons' he was no longer sent on border patrol duty. He later started a taxi company.

Until reunification, and even afterwards, he was classified as under threat, and permitted to carry a weapon. On 14 October 1997, the 35th anniversary of the incident, Plüschke admitted: 'I always fear for my wife and my children.' The police reject these clues as speculation but investigates them nevertheless. Strange – when Plüschke's corpse was found nothing was missing. Documents and cash were all there, nothing points towards a botched robbery. An autopsy showed he was killed with a calibre .22 weapon, but the bullet as well as the weapon have yet to be found. The head of the task force, Eduard Hampel, has no answer to the question where the 59-year-old was killed – in the taxi or where the body was found, 70 metres away.

Was it possible that former East German border guards or Stasi men had pulled Herr Plüschke from his car and executed him? Herr Fricke must have thought so. Frightened as he was, there had been no doubt in his mind about the circumstances of his colleague's death. I guessed, Herr Fricke feared that by gossiping he might also incur the wrath of these unpredictable killers. After all, they had sought vengeance following a four-decade interval. One day, Herr Fricke, too, could end up under a crash barrier. Or could he?

Like everyone in Fulda, I was curious about the Plüschke case. Even more interesting to me was people's reaction to it. Nobody I questioned about the killing doubted the link with the border. 'The old officers and Stasi agents have gone underground to organize themselves in networks and cells. Now they are ready to strike back,' I heard. According to published intelligence reports, that was utter nonsense. But in West German Fulda, suspicions of violent animosity among East Germans were taken as fact. Nobody seriously considered that Herr Plüschke's killers may have had other motives. Indeed, if a different band of mobsters was responsible, they would find the preoccupation with the taxi driver's past a welcome diversion for the task force. Herr Plüschke was, in a way, an ideal target. The confusion about motives seemed destined to lead investigators in the wrong direction. Fulda, however, did not want to hear that. Hunched behind a half-closed window, another taxi driver told me: 'That was Stasi, one hundred per cent.'

Scanning newspapers for further reports on the case, my attention drifted to an article about Northern Ireland. Yet another peace agreement was apparently in the making. The headline expounded: 'No more Troubles'. Politicians spoke of fading divisions between Belfast's communities. But the accompanying pictures told a different story. Catholics demonstrated in the streets as if fearful of losing the one constant in their lives – hatred. On the opposite page, comically balaclavaed Protestant paramilitaries posed cuddling their weapons.

Northern Ireland was another place where animosity and suspicion had been lingering for decades. And the 'security' wall separating Belfast's Falls Road and Shankill Road stood tall as ever.

I was still waiting for the Red Racer. Every time I phoned the repair shop, a mechanic would say: 'Call tomorrow before *Feierabend*. I am sure it'll be done.' The first day I phoned back I fully expected the car to be ready. This was Germany. Even carrier pigeons arrived on time. But after the third unsuccessful call to Horny Handed & Co., I hatched a new plan. I would leave the car behind. While the mechanics downed their tools and sniggered about their customers' mishaps, I would traverse the border on foot for a few days. Fulda was something of a ramblers' mecca. In 1883, rambling clubs from all over the newly unified Reich had assembled in Fulda to form an *Über*-club, the first national ramblers' association. Under its umbrella, many thousands had set out from here to explore the surrounding fields and *Wald*. So would I now.

My first stop was Geisa, across from Fulda on the eastern side of the border. I hopped off the all-mod-cons bus when the digital noticeboard behind the driver spelled out the town's name. I blinked at the few clouds that busily scurried across the sky. With sun-drenched elation, I began walking towards the border on a deserted highway. The tarmac, glistening and hot, was elegantly tightened over rounded hills like a ribbon on a present. I marvelled at sizzling cornfields wrapped around wooded hilltops. Even though a confirmed city-dweller, I was charmed by this rural idyll. Strangely, the scene even seemed familiar. With every step closer to the border, memories came back to me. Silly German ditties sung on country walks poured forth; the stories of Max & Moritz that my parents had read aloud on family holidays re-emerged after years of being buried under low-brow pleasures and higher education. I was surprised at my sentimental feelings of home-coming. I had never visited Geisa, or for that matter any of the gentle brush-stroke towns we passed in the bus. But the hills of the Rhön, straddling the border south of Geisa, were fast becoming my favourite part of the country. And, of course, the lanky figure of a watchtower now looming beyond the highway had become intensely familiar during the weeks and months I had spent seeking out its ilk.

The tower reminded me of a UFO. Inexplicably almost, someone had planted it in the middle of a sweeping cornfield. Nothing could have looked more alien here. Like a dead soldier still propped up on his gun, the concrete structure towered frozen in time. Around it, the ripe corn stalks jiggled under their own weight. The quick strokes of a light breeze brushed them back and forth in waves. The colour of the field, compounded by the aching sun, seemed to overwhelm an entire painter's palette with a yellow that was as much part of summer as wheat beer with a slice of lemon, and as blonde as absurd Aryan propaganda could have made it, and as wide as a sandy beach that extended all the way from the Greek coast to the Turkish coast. It was a yellow that made me high. This was what the ramblers of 1883 must have sought when they set out from Fulda – the triumphal experience of nature.

Emboldened by my *Sturm und Drang* (or was it the beating sun?) I decided to climb the tower. I waded through the corn with the thumping steps of a Wagnerian figure. The entrance stood wide open. Of all the towers I had seen so far, this was the first open to all-and-sundry all the time. I ignored the spray-painted scribblings discouraging entry. The inside was cool and eerie. Most of the steps on the metal ladder had been ripped out and I bolted up to the second floor in three leaps. The square room was windowless and dank. The guards who had cowered in this cell were prisoners as much as the citizens they aimed to stop from crossing the border. The thought rankled. But it was hard not to feel as sorry for those in solitary confinement in here as for those 'trapped' on the sunny hills outside.

I spurted up another set of metal stairs. The room on the third floor was almost as miserable. I had to crouch to peer out of tiny loopholes. I saw speckles of yellow corn, devoid of its previous glory. Little light trickled in, but the holes were big enough to give guards a clear shot. I raced to the top, still driven by an air of expectancy. How much more overwhelming would the fields and hills look from up high?

I stepped off the rusty ladder and on to broken glass, crackling under the soles of my shoes. The entire floor of the VoPo lair was covered in glass. A breeze banged empty window frames against the concrete walls. The creaking and slapping sounded hollow and lifeless rather than spooky. Jagged remnants of glass stuck out from the edges of the windows, menacingly framing the view of the fields. The sharp fragments pierced the ripe corn. It was a dramatic picture, but it had none of the romance enjoyed below.

Exhausted from exercise and pathos, I slowly climbed back down, using a metal sheet to slide over the stairs. I waddled out of the tower and closed my eyes to the searing sun. My thumping Wagnerian steps from earlier now threatened to give me a thumping headache. I sought rest in the shade.

American soldiers stood in front of barracks near Rasdorf. They were not wearing uniforms or waving Stars and Stripes, but you could tell they were American soldiers. One broad-shouldered GI puffed on a fat cigar. Another towered over a German family, trying to communicate. The diminutive family seemed at a loss what to do with the effusive giant. I thought of photographs of gun-toting American soldiers handing out chocolate from their rations to emaciated and bewildered German children after the war. Only the respective diets seemed to have changed.

The two soldiers looked around. 'Man, we had fun here.'

'Yeah. Goo-oo-ood times.'

'Shit, man. Us should never have left.'

'You crazy? What's there to shoot at now?'

The soldiers were former members of the Black Horse cavalry regiment. During the 1980s, they had been stationed here, at the so-called Point Alpha. The patrol post was NATO's eastern trip-wire. Military planners had identified the 'Fulda Gap', an opening in the hills east of the city, as the strategic key to World War Three. The barracks and observation tower at Point Alpha stood where Warsaw Pact forces would most likely try to break through in the event of an invasion of western Europe. Shots fired here would echo as loudly as those killing Archduke Ferdinand on a Sarajevo street corner in 1914.

The two soldiers introduced themselves as Hipster and Camel. They said they had returned to the Rhön as tourists. 'Man, it's beautiful here.'

Camel, a chain-smoker in a garish tracksuit, offered to give me a tour of the 'greatest campus in the world'. We started on a car park shielded by thick forest. 'Man, heavy-dudy armament was rolling around in our days. We had the whole toy shop.'

Hipster, a khaki vest covering his beer belly, chipped in: 'Yeah, even mini-nukes.'

Three barracks stood lined up along a track going uphill. Camel pointed across the track. 'The gas station. And the BBQ.'

We passed a red line drawn across the track. 'Ach-tung! Ze enemy iz cuming,' Hipster shouted in a fake *Wehrmacht* accent, probably picked up from the Hollywood war epics that made all German soldiers sound as if they had a speech defect.

Camel said, tanks were not allowed to pass the line. Beyond it, 'the reds' could see them. 'We kinda kept a low profile. We teased 'em. But, I mean, let's not start a war or anything.' With no difficulty, I could imagine Camel or Hipster riding across the red line on an armoured vehicle, playing the part of Gavrilo Princip approaching the Archduke's car. I was reminded of Alan Clark's account of a visit to that fateful Sarajevo street corner in 1986: 'I could still smell it, just as one can in a haunted room. A colossal, seismic charge of diabolic energy had been blown, released on that very spot some seventy-two years ago, and drawn its awful price.'

The track emerged from the woods and ended at the top of a rim overlooking the hills to the east. Still inside the perimeter fence and protected by trees was an American watchtower. I followed my guides up the stairs, three steps at a time. The tower stood on stilts with the stairs wrapping around the outside. Across the perimeter fence, we could see a groomed lawn fit for croquet, then the usual 10-foot border fortifications and behind it the solid concrete of an East German tower. By comparison, the American tower appeared light-footed. But the air was heavy. Clark's 'colossal, seismic charge of diabolic energy' seemed for ever invested in the two eyeballing towers, fifty yards apart.

After the US regiment withdrew in 1993, Point Alpha was used as an asylum-seeker hostel for a few years before falling into disrepair. No longer guarded, the barracks fell prey to vandals. Doors and windows were ripped out. Environmentalists planned to 're-naturalize' the Fulda Gap. But at the last minute, local politicians – mostly East German – raised money to preserve the observation post.

Camel lit up again. 'Being a soldier, it's the best.'

'We weren't just soldiers, we were warriors.'

'Killin' machines.'

'Kick ass, man.'

I stayed the night at a private guest house. I arrived late and disturbed the old couple in charge. But the midnight stir didn't seem to bother them. They had already turned off their hearing aids. Dutifully, they asked my name. 'August? But it's only July. Or is it?'

My room, though stuffy, offered a finer collection of books than I had seen in any hotel so far. I picked out several works by Günter Grass and retired. With my heavy legs propped up on the bed, I got no further than the first chapter heading. I fell asleep musing whether an international hotel ranking could be drawn up based on the quality of books available to guests.

The next day's sky hung over the hills like a net curtain. Light streamed down into the fields, but the flimsy clouds filtered out the colour. The dozens of different greens and yellows, carved out yesterday, had been washed away.

I walked through the town of Tann. Cloudy or not, the day was hot. I thirsted for the ever ubiquitous products of the Coca-Cola Company. Unfortunately, the message had not got through from Atlanta, Georgia, that fizzy drinks must be served cold. The local corner store did not even have a drinks fridge. But Tann could be forgiven for being a little backward. The border surrounded the West German town almost entirely. A single highway used to connect it to Fulda. Otherwise, Tann had been caged by VoPos like a cat in a sack. Remarkably, all traffic down Tann's high street still squeezed through a narrow brick gate, framed by two towers. One car could pass at a time. Instead of a Coke, I bought a postcard with a coloured drawing of the gate. 'It's your Brandenburg Gate,' I said to the cashier. She looked at me blankly

A pub served cold drinks, much to my relief. At the bar, I overheard two men. Their sentences were clipped and short. They sounded like soldiers and indeed they were, or at least former conscripts. One had been stationed near the Baltic Sea, the other on the border, taking up residence in the Rhön after quitting.

'So you must have been a VoPo, sorry, a people's policeman, if you guarded the border. Not a soldier,' I suggested.

'How so?'

I had always assumed the entire border was under VoPo control. But the two men explained: '*Volkspolizisten* checked people legally passing through the gates. Fact.'

'Correct. And the NVA [national people's army] protected the border.'

After hundreds of miles of travelling alongside the border, it still bubbled with mystery. Or, maybe, my ignorance had simply fared all too well. I moved swiftly on. 'How are things now?'

'Our army pensions are humiliating.'

I was baffled. 'You receive a pension from the German army, the Bundeswehr?'

'Logically. But not as much as West German soldiers.'

'No equality. *Fakt.*'

'*Korrekt.* We are second-class citizens.'

They recounted the story of an East German general who had asked the West German defence ministry after the Wende if he could call himself 'General a. D.', a retired rank. Even though the general had been honourably discharged when the NVA was dissolved, the ministry said no. The same general then sent a second letter under a different name claiming to have been a *Wehrmacht* lieutenant during World War Two. Could he call himself 'Leutnant a. D.?' 'Logically,' said the defence ministry.

'Worse than Nazis. That's how we get treated. *Fakt.*'

The clipped speech pattern reminded me of Herr Fischer, the border commander in Ellrich where my father grew up. I now realized he, too, must have been a soldier rather than a VoPo.

Like the men in the pub, Herr Fischer had complained about being treated badly. After they left I searched for my notes from my conversation with him. Snapshots emerged: 'We soldiers count ourselves among the defeated not the unified. *So.* Only Wessis get promoted. *So.* No unity. The east is a colony. Unification of armies? More like liquidation. *So.* Wessis get bigger pensions. And nothing works. If this German army was ever challenged, nothing would happen. *So.* The Bundeswehr has eight-hour days. Its soldiers get paid over-time. NVA technology was first-class. *Fakt.*'

I thumbed through my notebook and also came across an earlier interview with a West German lieutenant colonel in Braunschweig. Herr Althoff had commanded a *Panzer* battalion on the fading Cold War front-line from 1988 to 1991. He was an urbane man, unlike the East German soldiers, or the Americans at Point Alpha. We were put in touch through a Rotary Club contact. I remembered him poking his stern forehead out of the officers' mess, beckoning me in. The airy sitting room was fit for a Milanese fashion house. Angular black leather furniture stood in a wide semi-circle round a sleek designer fireplace. Herr Fischer would have taken the officers' mess as further evidence of the Bundeswehr being full of 'softies'. But Herr Althoff thought the rejection of hardship made his troops more effective and loyal. 'All Bundeswehr soldiers eat well. In the NVA, they had separate meals with more meat and better ingredients for officers. That's not a climate we want to create. In the Bundeswehr, everyone gets the same.'

I wasn't sure what to make of the new German army. The blind obedience and Prussian discipline that fired up two world wars had thankfully died out with the demise of the NVA. But could an army be run like a social club?

I left Tann. As I stepped through the town gate into the open greenery, I momentarily deemed myself in Ireland. The Rhön looked deceptively like the Wicklow mountains. The valleys rolled unwrinkled. *Wald*, even trees, were scarce, and tillage surprisingly rare. Hordes of sheep grazed on wet, grassy fields. Nature had a pleasing air, as if pints of Guinness rained from the heavens.

The most curious sight, though, were the hilltops. High above the shorn valleys towered wooded peaks. Trees sprouted unencumbered. The leafy bushes looked like giant mushrooms. Craning my neck, I could see Hilders, five miles south of Tann in the same valley.

And talk about Ireland – the stream running through Hilders was called Ulster.

I staggered uphill to a guest house. The spacious room was a bargain (35 marks), but the choice of bedtime reading questionable. I was bored and complained to my hosts about weak limbs. They recommended taking a sauna. 'Besides, you will meet some more people there.'

I packed a towel and a pair of swimming trunks. I had forgotten that one always sweated naked in mixed saunas in Germany. It was not a mistake that went unnoticed for very long. I swiped off the offending article under the watchful eyes of heaving women and hairy men.

Slumped on a wooden bench, I also came to understand why I had been promised to 'meet more people there'. There was no sexual tension in the hot air. Far from it. The tiny sauna doubled as Hilders' debating chamber. Like Roman senators, togas discarded, the perspiring locals held forth on matters of import. 'What role should Deutschland play in the post-industrial world?' Brows were mopped. 'Do we need a permanent seat on the UN security council?' Sweat trickled. 'First, we have to prove ourselves to the UN in Bosnia.' The temperature rose. 'Let's hope the Bundeswehr doesn't screw up again.' A heated debate ensued over who was responsible for the death of two German soldiers in the former Yugoslavia. They had been killed by a tank shell mistakenly fired by other Bundeswehr personnel. Was the commanding officer to blame? Had the soldiers followed orders?

Sweat welled from heaving bosoms and hairy backs became itchy.

Later in the shower, one man said his son served in the Bundeswehr. 'They gave him fifty marks to go out and buy decent underwear. It's true. All the recruits got money so they can choose their own underwear. Apparently, the standard issue longjohns aren't very comfortable. My son says it's very important for a soldier to have underwear that doesn't scratch.' He ploughed a soap bar through his armpits. 'Under Adolf, things were different, you can be sure of that.'

Over dinner at an Italian restaurant, I browsed through glossy magazines. The cover stories about sport and fashion seemed identical to those on British newsstands. The real treats lurked towards the back. In the 'classified' section huddled countless advertisements for vocational courses. Whatever one desired to learn, there was a school vying to give the requisite tutoring. Naturally, courses such as 'Teach yourself Russian in three minutes a day' took prominence; but hidden in the nooks and crannies of the classified columns I found gems like: 'Learn to build your own igloo. Sign up now for the summer semester.' Or, 'You too can flirt like James Bond. Let us show you how to win any man or woman. Flirting is a skill like driving or cooking.'

Under a picture of a white-knuckled fist, I spotted 'The Ultimate Course for Aggression Release. Come into the ring. We teach how to box all anger and stress out of your system. Ideal for managers, students and soldiers.' Soldiers? I had always assumed being angry and aggressive were basic requirements for being a soldier. To go berserk at a moment's notice, to be unleashed on to the battlefield with blood boiling, to be charged with enough barbaric violence to overwhelm a better-armed enemy – wasn't that the warrior's life? Not if you wore comfy, scratch-free longjohns.

I approached Birx from below. The untidy collection of farms reminded me of a decrepit castle. Stables and barns were bundled together tightly, almost as if one front gate overlapped with the next, one tiled roof melted into the other. The two dozen farms seemed to form one bulky building, enthroned at the tip of a hill range, cramped but imposing. Height bestowed majesty on Birx. Eagerly, I climbed up.

Before the *Wende*, the village had possibly been the loneliest place in East Germany. Like a peninsula, the skinny hill range on which it squatted poked several miles into West Germany. The border fence ran all around the village, cutting off valleys on both sides. For decades, the blinkered village had only known one direction – back along the hill range towards Frankenheim.

Farmers congregated around a football pitch for a village fête. They drank wheat beer while the young organized a penalty-shooting competition. Later, the Birxer XI played a team from Frankenheim. Why not invite a team from Seifert, a village much closer than Frankenheim on the West German side? I asked. 'We've always played Frankenheim. This is an Ossi affair.'

Beyond Birx, the border wound its way around several moors. The Rhön was famous for its upland heaths and I decide to grant myself a detour. A revolving door guarded the Black Moor. I passed through the entrance and walked for an hour on a wooden footbridge laid out across the swampy scrub. If there was a part of Ireland that looked like this, I hadn't seen it. But it wouldn't have surprised me if it existed. From the planks under my feet to the horizon, everything in the Black Moor was sparse and green, not black.

The Rhön moors are easy enough to find on a map. One only needs to run a finger down the border to the point where it made a sharp turn. Instead of cutting through the moors, the border swung left and continued due east rather than south. From here onwards, East Germany was above the divide, and West Germany below it.

Dark stains blotted the sky. Fearing rain, I resolved to retrieve the Red Racer. A call to Horny Handed & Co. confirmed that the car was finally ready. I hitched a lift to Fulda in the back of a brand-new, shiny blue BMW. Two identical white shirts with golden ties and engraved cufflinks sat in the front. Throughout the half-hour journey, they talked non-stop into their shiny black mobile phones. They never spoke to each other or to me. They both had their left arms cocked in the same manner, presumably to fit their identical phones more ergonomically into their identical ears.

Fladungen was my first stop in the Free State of Bavaria. Setting foot in the village heralded my official arrival in southern Germany where life was taken a little less seriously. Bavarians pride themselves on their jolliness. Women big enough to carry four full tankards of beer in each hand sat on a bench in Fladungen, their bodies jolting with laughter.

In Ostheim, I stumbled into a street party. Men sat at long tables covered with tankards. They played a finger wrestling game. The aim was to try and pull each other across the table. Innuendo swirled around and backs were slapped without respite. When one hearty drinker became bored with making frequent trips to the toilet, he relieved himself down his trouser leg, much to the amusement of everyone else.

By comparison, northern Germany seemed almost austere. In Hamburg, say, jokes often came with a warning. People would announce: 'Let me say something ironic . . .' Or they would add: 'Of course, I am being sarcastic.'

Not in Bavaria, land of the jovial brutes.

Many Bavarians were also surprisingly religious. The Catholic church played an important political role; one only needed to see how Bavarians decorated the former crossing points along the border. They erected crosses and chapels instead of memorials or museums. Near the VoPo control point between Mellrichstadt and Meiningen stood a wire crucifix made from parts of the border fence. Below a kneeling Mother Mary with the young Jesus was inscribed: 'In freedom, towards unity. Mother with the heavenly child, step down on German pastures, so that in your footsteps, we will find eternal and true peace. Mother and child joined in love – fatherland, that's how thou must heal.'

At the border in Gompertshausen stood another wire cross, higher even than the original fence.

In Burggrub, a tall 'peace chapel' overlooked the old divide. The spire was intentionally designed to look like a watchtower. Above the door I read: 'The Lord Is One.' The altar had been sculpted from border fence and a sign said: 'This chapel was erected in 1992 to honour God and to show gratitude for the peaceful reunification.'

Herr Peterson from Dresden prayed in the chapel. He told me he was praying for the church itself. 'In the east, religion is not very popular any more. Clergymen are being blamed for the end of socialism. Some people say: "You Christians should all be shot. You betrayed us. You betrayed *den Sozialismus.*" The church leaders who organized the protests in 1989 that led to the Wende are being ignored now, pushed out.'

Shouldn't it be easy to fill the churches in the current climate, given the high unemployment rate?

'Not really. We do get a few new recruits, but of the wrong kind. Old Stasi people are scared of dying, scared of facing their deeds. Often, they live to be very old. The guilt-racked Nazis also lived very long, fighting death till the end. And sooner or later during their agonizing, they all come to us. They don't usually join the parish. They just ask a lot of questions. How to win forgiveness. Is it too late to repent?'

I smiled, no doubt puzzling Herr Peterson. *Typisch deutsch*, I thought. A German dies (so an old folk tale goes) and he wafts away on to the ethereal plane. He reaches the pearly gates where an elderly porter gives him a choice of entry through one of two gates. The German spurns the gate marked Heaven, and sweeps through the gate marked Lectures About Heaven.

13

ALONG THE
FAIRWAY

ON THIS SOUTHERN LEG of my journey, the architectural differences
between east and west faded out. Thuringia and Saxony were indistinguishable from Bavaria across the border. The dilapidation evident in
northern Germany was but a crusty memory. There were no more bare
stretches of scorched land, or houses with pockmarks from the war, or
soulless alleys of prefab dwellings.

Simple gestures made all the difference. In Römhild, vivid window
boxes adorned ancient buildings. In Eisfeld, the old socialist atmosphere
of uniformity was laid to rest with wonderfully diverse cobblestone pavements. A hamlet near Hildburghausen put up a sign, declaring itself a
contestant for the national 'Prettiest Village of the Year' competition, an
event I never knew existed. What *Schwung*.

Was the difference between north and south a question of deutschmarks?
No doubt, Saxony and Thuringia were richer than the northern states. But
I liked to think the south also benefited from a certain generosity of spirit.
Take, for example, the treatment of the Iron Curtain itself. In the far north,
the border, or what's left of it, was largely ignored. One did not want to
be reminded. *Don't mention the Wall*. Down here, however, attitudes were
relaxed to the point that people converted watchtowers on private land into
children's playgrounds. On the whole, many more towers were left standing
and became part of residential living spaces in between lawn-movers and
garden gnomes. Just as the leftover fortifications and their legacy were
incorporated into religious worship, so they became part of daily life.

Maybe the best example of the uninhibited southern attitude to the border, and to the history of division spawned by it, was the *Hotel Grenzgasthof* in the village of Fürth am Berg. The Border Guest House (140 beds, no books on bedside tables) unashamedly exploited its proximity to the former border. A collection of fences and posts with original markings were exhibited in the car park, fifty yards from the old frontier. History buffs could rent rooms overlooking the border for up to 90 marks per night; dogs cost 8 marks extra.

What next? A Disney theme-park of refashioned walls and watchtowers, a post-socialist union of soft drinks and military hardware? 'Borderworld, an action-packed obstacle course. Can you make it past the Commies in the ultimate life and death adventure?'

In Coburg, I rented a room for two nights at the Golden Cross Hotel, a narrow edifice hunched in a corner of the central square like a wily witch. The hotel claimed to be 500 years old and the slovenly receptionist insisted that throughout its distinguished history the minimum stay had always been two nights – probably due to slow service, I grimaced. It was hardly worth staying for just one night given the time it took to book a room.

The receptionist disappeared into the kitchen. Barely before nightfall, she returned with a cigarette and a glass of beer – not for me, but for herself. 'So, you want the room?' I had no choice. Decent accommodation was more difficult to come by than bananas before the Wende. The riflemen of the region were meeting in Coburg for their annual shoot. Besides, the picturesque town always attracted visitors. Queen Victoria once said if she were 'not who she were' she would go and live in Coburg. This was not as far-fetched as it sounded. Her husband Prince Albert was born here, six of their nine children married Germans (as had her father), and as a child Victoria, icon of the stiff upper-lip, had been educated by Johanna Lehzen, a German vicar's daughter.

Coburg, in a sense, was the cradle of the modern British monarchy. Did Prince Charles not seem even more typically German than he seemed typically English in his tweedy ways? His sincerity, his slapstick humour and his interest in environmentalism – derided in Britain – made him a popular figure in Germany. And with Prince Albert, who had masterminded the 1851 Great Exhibition in London's gigantic Crystal Palace, he shared an interest in architecture. One could easily imagine Charles, instead of Albert, painting watercolours sitting on the terraces of the Veste, the family castle that towered over Coburg's gentle green slopes and basked in pastel sunlight.

But so far, Prince Charles and Elizabeth II had studiously avoided visiting Coburg, a town that could claim to have a closer link with their family than Windsor or Balmoral. Until 1914 when the Great War ignited anti-German feelings in Britain, the House of Windsor was known as the House of Saxe-*Coburg*-Gotha. The Windsors may be trying to hide their Germanness now; their beastly subjects may be chanting 'Two world wars and one world cup, doo-dah, doo-dah' and fretting about being subsumed into a German-dominated federal Europe – but standing on Coburg's central square in front of the magisterial statue of a brooding Prince Albert who set out from here in 1840 to become the secret power behind Victoria's throne, it seemed an inescapable conclusion that Britain was already being ruled by Germans. And didn't the ermine beach towels look rather fetching?

Under Albert's stern eyes, riflemen paraded along the central square the next morning. Feather-hatted folk in *Lederhosen* marched to thundering brass music directly below my window. Apart from this nuisance, Coburg was comfortable. It managed to be *gemütlich*, cosy in that German *Bratwurst* way, while being elegant. It was Olde Worlde handsome without appearing to be an urban museum like Bath or Cambridge. The best thing about Coburg was the absence of the British curse of the high street chains. The equivalents of W. H. Smith and Boots were supplanted by family-run stores that smelled of blood and herbal medicines. Prince Charles would approve.

Roaming through the slender streets, I couldn't help but think how un-British the town looked. The chintzy gold ornaments on house fronts were leftovers from an era when the divided pre-Bismarck Germany was innocently parochial compared to the sophistication and strength of the British Empire. To see Coburg was to see why some of the Windsors (né Saxe-Coburg-Gothas) had such difficulty being accepted by their subjects.

Weimar, Germany's dark capital of culture, was by no stretch of the imagination, or the atlas, a border city. It lay a good thirty miles inside East Germany. But my reclaimed mobility, thanks to the successful retrieval of the Red Racer from the clutches of Horny Handed & Co., lured me northwards past Saalfeld. For once freed from potholed patrol tracks, I overtook Trabbis and BMWs alike.

To a cynic, it would seem that Weimar had been designed by American tour operators. In one stop, the voracious travellers from the New World could 'do' Germany. Everything the fatherland was known for abroad – its writers, its composers, its fascists – was tidily show-cased in this sufficiently quaint, post-socialist city. Weimar was a Noah's Ark of German high culture, thanks to the patronage of rulers from centuries past and present. During an afternoon of lazy strolling, I saw Bach's scribbles, Schiller's sarcophagus, Nietzsche's library, Liszt's grand piano, Martin Luther's pulpit, the Bauhaus school once peopled by Paul Klee and Wassily Kandinsky, and Goethe's cottage where the bard sought inspiration in the company of burghers of both sexes.

During the same afternoon, I also found hints as to the residency of a lesser poet called Jakob Lenz. Goethe apparently had him thrown out of the city in 1776 for 'donkeyish' behaviour. I had read about Lenz a decade before, but I failed to remember the exact nature of his misdeed. In 1774, Lenz had published a semi-autobiographical drama called *Der Hofmeister* (The Private Tutor). The five-act play told the story of a male tutor and his doomed love for a female pupil. Lenz wanted to expose the supposedly unfathomable societal chasms spawned by the upper classes who had their children educated at home.

When I was eighteen, I read Lenz's drama at my stuffy grammar school in Osnabrück at the behest of Frau Höfer, the literature teacher. *Der Hofmeister* was her favourite play. Asked if I enjoyed reading it, I blurted something along the lines of: 'What's the problem with private tuition? I'd quite like a tutor to come to my house rather than having to turn up in a crowded classroom every morning. Especially if the tutor is of the opposite sex.'

Frau Höfer took none too kindly to my unorthodox literary criticism. She quipped: 'They still have tutoring at Oxford University in England. Why don't you go there if you think it's such a damn good idea?' With the help of my grandmother, I ordered an Oxford application from the British Council that afternoon, and soon took refuge under dreaming spires. Three years of priceless private tuition did little to inspire any further enthusiasm for *Der Hofmeister* or the 'donkeyish' Lenz.

After my stroll in the city centre, I stepped through the black wrought-iron gate to the Buchenwald concentration camp on the edge of Weimar. Three words were inscribed on the chillingly heavy gate: *Jedem Das Seine*, (To Each His Own). There was little else left of the squalid barracks, the death chambers, or Hitler's élite political academy – the reason why one of the first camps was set up here. Outside the cryptic gate, American tourists bumbled forth from a bus. One more box ticked for the New World travellers on their whistle-stop tour.

When Thomas Mann returned from America to Germany for the first time after the war, in 1949, he too paid a visit to Weimar and said: 'The mixture of Hitlerism and Goethe is particularly disturbing.' To me, the modern Weimar felt claustrophobic rather than outright disturbing. Plaques, statues and former homes of the worthy crowded every leafy street. Tacky souvenir shops – is there any other kind? – squeezed in between. The city centre sparkled with new money. But it didn't seem alive with a new culture. Like soap opera applause, Weimar's vibrancy came from a can, or rather its dusty archives and libraries.

I rested beneath the famous double statue of Goethe and Schiller jointly holding a laurel-wreath. In 1989, while hundreds of East Germans fled across the newly opened Iron Curtain, cheeky socialists put a hand-painted sign on the wreath, saying: 'We're staying here.' And indeed, ten years later, the two poets still stood in front of the historic theatre where Goethe's *Faust* premiered in 1829 and the liberal constitution of the Weimar Republic was born in 1919.

Later, I went to a bookshop in search of a modern-day Goethe or Schiller. Would Weimar be where the bards of the post-unification era prospered? Frau Meitner, the shop assistant, gestured busily towards the bestseller shelf, carefully ranked and ordered. The shelf did not include a single book written by a German. At a time when high fashion was dominated by Italians, luxury cars were invariably built by some of my more mechanically gifted countrymen, and stereos usually came from Asia, bestsellers had become the sole preserve of English-speakers: John Grisham, Ken Follett, Peter Mayle and Michael Crichton hogged the German book charts. Not a single rip-roaring yarn about life after the Wall penned by a German had made it on to the current bestseller list. In vain, I looked for, say, a Stasi thriller.

Almost as an afterthought, Frau Meitner handed me *Simple Stories*, an English-titled novel by Ingo Schulze. 'It sells quite well,' she mused. The blurb emphasized that Herr Schulze 'writes in the American tradition of Cheever, Carver and Ford'. Then she offered me *Helden Wie Wir* (Heroes Like Us) by Thomas Brussig. Again, the blurb assured us that Herr Brussig was writing like an English-speaker. He was a German 'Charles Bukowski, Philip Roth and John Irving,' all in one. But no Goethe or Schiller.

Exhausted, I followed the street signs for private accommodation out of the centre. I finally came to a rest on a convertible sofa at the Schmidt family's home. Herr Schmidt taught at a primary school. A wispy-bearded giant of a man, he had hands that could enclose one of his pupil's heads. He acknowledged Germany's literary output was flagging – why, he couldn't say. But the country's many classics were still popular. Running his big hand over shelves of yellowed East German paperbacks, he said: 'I used to be worried that our children will find it difficult to handle all the wickedness in our world. They get exposed to so much so early. Especially after the Wende, with the rise in crime and the arrival of tabloid horror stories which we didn't have before. I was really scared. But there was no need to worry. The children have heard it all before in the bedtime classics and Grimm Brothers stories their parents read to them. Take any awful news, they will understand.'

'What about public hysteria over the Stasi?'

'The children have heard of the evil stepmother that banishes Snow White. Sinister figures are nothing new to them.'

'And sexual harassment, even rape?'

'Take Rapunzel.'

'Child abuse?'

'Hansel and Gretel. The German classics prepare children for everything. Recently we talked in class about the dangers of chain letters and pyramid schemes. I told them to imagine they were the rats in the story of the Pied Piper.'

On my way back from Weimar, I crossed the border at Mödlareuth. The village of a dozen houses and two dozen BMWs had for decades literally been cut in half. A concrete wall, rather than just the usual fence, blocked the view between eastern and western kitchen windows. East German rulers wanted to prevent all contact across the divide. Villagers were not supposed to see each other, let alone talk. The divided hamlet earned the nickname Little Berlin.

I had read that Mödlareuth was the home of a dog called Bubi, the only known canine *Republikflüchtling*. A year before the Wende, the young mongrel slipped through the fortifications from east to west. He seized his chance when a small gap was left open during engineering work to redirect the Tannbach, a stream running alongside the border. Having successfully made it past the guards, Bubi proudly lifted a leg to mark his new territory. I asked to be introduced but nobody could find him. Apparently, he still liked to criss-cross the border. Some 100 yards of the original 700-yard concrete wall had been left standing as a memorial. The roaming mongrel must have been grateful.

I inquired, had Little Berlin overcome its division? Yes, I was told. Except, the West German villagers still said '*Grüss Gott*', or Greetings to God, while across the Tannbach they continued to say '*Guten Tag*', or Good Day. Such were the lasting influences of Catholic Bavaria and atheist East Berlin.

South of Mödlareuth, I drove through Hof. The collapse of the Wall, and reunification a year later, had their origin in this once sleepy Bavarian city. Not Berlin or Leipzig, but Hof could lay claim to having been the place where the most dramatic scenes of the Wende were played out. When Ossis and Wessis danced in front of Berlin's Brandenburg Gate in November 1989, the battle was already won. A month earlier, the first trainload of East Germans had arrived in Hof. These first few thousands ripped the original hole in the Iron Curtain, right here. They had fled to Hungary and Poland during summer holidays, and, in anticipation of a visit by Mikhail Gorbachev, East Berlin eventually approved their departure to the west. Floodgates were opened that eventually swept away the entire socialist regime.

Ben Bradshaw, a BBC correspondent, witnessed the dramatic scenes in Hof. He described them as follows on the *From Our Own Correspondent* radio programme:

It is quite difficult for an Englishman to understand the emotions that were unleashed on Hof's railway station in the early hours of Sunday morning. We do not have a minefield and fences running down the middle of our country . . . It was not just the arrivals at Hof who wore their emotions on their sleeves. The local people turned out in their hundreds to welcome them; stout men and women in their Sunday best, twice or three times the average age of those getting off the trains, wept as they clapped. 'These are our people, free at last,' they said . . . Those arriving at Hof report people lining the route of the trains in East Germany waving and clapping and holding placards saying: We're coming soon.

And so they did.

Both Mr Bradshaw and Hof have come a long way since. The former BBC correspondent is now a Labour Member of Parliament for Exeter after defeating Dr Adrian Rogers, the sitting Tory MP, who had said about him during the 1997 election campaign: 'He's a media man, a homosexual, he likes Europe, he studied German, he lived in Berlin, he lives in London and he rides a bike. He's everything about society which is wrong.'

Meanwhile, in milder climes, Hof re-established its role as an ancient trading post. The city had once been Bavaria's commercial centre. In the Middle Ages, major trading routes crossed here and local manufacturers exported textiles all the way to India and China. But with the onset of the Cold War, the city fell asleep. Hemmed in by East Germany in the north and by Czechoslovakia in the east, its potential as a market town withered away.

When I tried to find a parking spot now, I sensed Hof had clearly risen once again. Not a single cobblestone stood idle. Beaming metal crawled through gilded lanes. Lorries turned off the trampled Munich–Berlin autobahn straight into the city centre to shovel more construction toys, power tools and assorted kitchen knives into thronged stores. The many Turkish guestworkers in the midst of the rampant commerce gave Hof the well-trodden appearance of a Byzantine bazaar.

Stuck in traffic on a steep incline, I could read a sign mounted on the pavement advertising local couriers, rental cars and postal services. Confirmed in my belief that Hof had fallen on its feet, I drove straight back out of the city without making a stop. There was no room for me here. But I didn't mind. I left the frenzy of Hof to the merchants and winners of the Wende.

The Red Racer and I approached the very last stretch of the border. We had passed, I don't know, a hundred, maybe several hundred leftover watchtowers. Soon, the months we had roamed together would end. Czech territory loomed. What was once the Iron Curtain continued past Pilsen and all the way to the Black Sea. But the scar of German division – easily the most fortified part of the Iron Curtain before 1989 – ran out in Hof's backyard. Or rather, it ran out on a golf course.

Strung along the last few miles of the border were immaculate fairways. Green baize stretched across the former death strip. Where border posts, draped in national colours, had marked the Cold War line in the sand, flags now flew over eighteen holes. Minefields to sand bunkers, I thought, rather than swords to ploughshares. What better symbol for the region's change from incarcerated backwater to commercial hub.

The golf course teemed with feisty businessmen in ill-fitting Italian suits. Wielding mobile phones they made spurious deals in the car park. An

East German salesman and proud owner of a bright red BMW with white leather seats bantered uneasily with a West German machine-tool buyer who leant against his black BMW with tinted windows. *'Take it easy.* We Hofers are very relaxed human beings.'

'Because you can be. If an Ossi is relaxed, Wessis call him lazy. But you Bavarians can even be proud of being relaxed or lazy.'

'We are not Bavarians.'

'What are you then?'

'We're Franconians.'

And so they bickered. The old duchy of Franconia had long been absorbed into northern Bavaria. But regional conflicts continued to simmer, even if Germany was no longer divided down the middle.

I quietly snuck off the premises of the *Golfclub Hof e.V.* The next cheapest car in the parking lot probably cost ten times more than the trusted Toyota.

Down a gravel track, I reached the point where the territories of Czechoslovakia, East Germany and West Germany once met. I parked on the West German side. There was no visitors' car park on the East German side – of course, there never had been one.

The location was known as *Dreiländereck*, or three-country-corner. Even though there were no longer two Germanys, the name surprisingly still appeared on road signs. It was an unspectacular place, and completely empty. In front of me, three fizzy streams flowed together shaded by trees. Dogs barked in the distance and I felt uncertain whether I had ended up in Peter Mayle's garden in the Provence or the site of a SS mass grave on the Polish plains. A breeze brushed over tree tops. Rain came suddenly as I climbed out of the car.

I failed to find a memorial, except for the war grave of an 'unknown soldier'. A rusty steel helmet, not unlike the helmet with the bullet hole I had found as an eight-year-old on the Baltic coast, sat atop a wooden cross, curiously dated July 1945 – two months after the end of hostilities and the start of Germany's division.

I headed back to the autobahn. Berlin – 300 kilometres, said the signs. The most famous stretch of border had always stood in Berlin. What was left of Checkpoint Charlie, the graffitied Wall around the Brandenburg Gate and the empty corridor that sliced through the heart of the German capital? I felt I had not yet finished my journey. Berlin was my final destination.

I didn't get very far. The Red Racer was caught up in a colourful traffic jam, locked between hundreds of Trabbis. A convoy of two-stroke engines stretched up a hill in front of us. The stinking box cars spluttered as we came to a standstill. Many of them had been custom-painted and structurally redesigned by their owners. Next to me bobbed a convertible Trabbi with pink racing stripes. The edges had been highlighted and fur headrests put on leather seats. I didn't know much about the Ossi old-timers but I was sure the unsmiling East German bureaucrats had not wasted scarce resources on producing a luxury convertible.

'What's going on?' I yelled across to the tanning driver in the roofless Trabbi.

'Maybe an accident. Hope it won't take too long.'

'*Nein, nein.* I mean, why are all these exotic Trabbis here?'

'Big festival in Zwickau. The opening is today.'

'An exhibition?'

'A parade through the city centre of all the best Trabbis.'

'Well, I hope you won't be late.'

'I bet the traffic jam was caused by an old Type P 601. Never good on the hills.'

Indeed, a steaming Trabbi blocked the right lane – or at least half of it, given the car's modest width. Other Trabbis passed by and honked. The stranded driver clutched a wrench and waved back, not the least bit distraught.

In a matter of minutes, I overtook a bizarre collection of cannibalized but still boxy vehicles. One Trabbi had been converted into a Midwest-style pickup truck, another was painted in the colours of the Union Jack. Every car had an individual note. Gone was the uniformity that once dominated East Germany's highways and byways. At the Zwickau exit, traffic again came to a standstill. I could have bypassed the avalanche of plastic (for that's what the cars were made of), but I decided to follow the Trabbi trail and queued up behind a Trabant P 601 done up as a fire engine.

Zwickau, fifty miles inside East Germany, was the Trabbi capital. The cars had been built at the local Sachsenring plant. 'Sachsenring instead of wedding ring,' read a bumper sticker. Production came to a halt in 1991; like most East German products, the 'plastic bombers' could not compete with western goods. The Trabbi was no match for the VWs and BMWs, the Mercedes and Audis. Compared to Sachsenring, the West German companies really had the much-advertised *Vorsprung durch Technik*, or advantage due to technology. But although ridiculed by Wessis, the Trabbi remained a cult car. Ossis seemed genuinely attached to the ugly duckling, maybe out of nostalgia, or because they'd had to wait an average of fifteen years for delivery.

Today, the streets of Zwickau bulged with Trabbis from across Germany and as far as Hobart, Indiana. One American enthusiast had travelled 4,000 miles to show off his vanity licence plate spelling out TRABANT.

I parked the Red Racer – for once a real grown-up among the multi-coloured midgets – and walked the last mile into Zwickau's centre. Street corners hummed with two-stroke engines. Trabbis raced with baited breath. Parents were well advised to keep children indoors so the cars could play safely in the streets. 'I didn't think I would ever see a day like this,' sighed a nostalgic Herr Bolinski as tyres squealed. He had just arrived from Berlin in a Type P 50: 'A fine car. A masterpiece.'

Some 100,000 people lined the streets. So said the papers the next day. The crush felt like all 16 million East Germans had congregated to see the Trabbi parade. As we waited for the start, old Trabbi jokes were recycled. I must have been the only one in the vicinity who didn't know why Trabbi drivers were great thinkers.

'We *think* we drive a real car,' chortled Herr Bolinski. 'And why were there no bank robberies under socialism?' I grinned helplessly. Herr Bolinski announced: 'Who wants to wait fifteen years for the get-away car!'

The thub-thub-thub of two-stroke engines eventually hailed the start of the parade. Most vehicles were mutants of the variety I had seen on the autobahn. Every fantasy was indulged. One owner had kitted out his spotted Trabbi for safari. Black grates protected the open-topped vehicle against larger mammals on the autobahn.

The crowd revelled in technical details. The occasional cheer went up, but most spectators quietly gawked at the outlandish modifications on display. A stretch limo Trabbi rolled past, at least twice its original length. '*Mensch*, you can't do that with plastic. That chassis must be reinforced with steel.' Such sacrilege left Herr Bolinski breathless.

At the climax of the parade, the 'Trabbi-Queen' swept down the aisle of goggling fans. Janine Lehmann, a crop-topped eighteen year-old blonde, rode in a sleek, black convertible. She draped herself over the boot with her feet on the back seat. She waved, but most onlookers were too preoccupied with the car. 'Did you see the leather bench in the front, instead of individual seats.'

'Oh, and the bonnet-mounted wing mirrors.'

'And the free-standing windshield.'

'The chrome door handles.'

After the parade, city officials unveiled a Trabbi statue nearby. Where Goethe and Schiller held hands in Weimar, a Trabbi cut from stone towered in Zwickau. Enthusiasts crowded around the pedestal after the departure of officials, photographers and camera crews. 'Now, is that a P 601 or a P 50?'

The rest of the fifth annual Trabbi festival took place on a suburban field. The three-day celebration of the good life under socialism was fuelled by Goldbrand, the favourite cognac of pre-Wende days. Apparently, a brand of East German canned dog food had carried the same name.

Music stages, tents and cars galloped across the field for hundreds of yards. My favourite Trabbis were a Formula One racer built by Herr Saupe from Wilkau-Hasslau, and a double-decker caravan with sleeping quarters driven by Herr Lindner from Chemnitz. Both men won prizes.

Then there were the Trabbi-lovers from Blighty. Richard Overton, an accountant from Cambridge, shrieked 'Do you mind?' when I leant against his vehicle. Later he invited me to a Trabbi meeting in Mildenhall, Suffolk. 'The Germans own traditional British car-makers like Rover. But what a joy these two-strokers are.' He said his UK Trabbi club had 150 members.

Another British bastion of Sachsenring car-lovers hid among the peaks of Derbyshire. Graham Goodell, a bearded and bespectacled mechanic, had amassed thirty-eight Trabbis at his 'Trabant Centre UK' in the village of Middleton. 'Mine is the biggest collection outside Germany.' I asked what attracted him. He mumbled something about '70 miles to the gallon'.

Behind a swap centre for spare parts, Herr and Frau Knocken vigorously scrubbed down their P 601. 'Sparkles like a new one,' I admired.

'*Danke schön*. But it never was this clean when it came out of the factory.' Frau Knocken shook my hand while her husband redoubled his efforts.

We watched him. 'Seems like a matter of life and death,' I said.

Herr Knocken scrubbed. Frau Knocken grinned. 'Oh, it's much more important than that.'

Guiltily I admitted I had not once washed the Red Racer since setting out in Travemünde. What heresy! I would make up for it on the way to Berlin.

14

ALL ALONG
THE WALL

A WEAPON MADE FROM CEMENT, that's how the world knew the Berlin
Wall. A metaphor for lifeless existence. To the Berliners who saw it
every morning from their kitchen window, it was much more. The gash
wiggling through the streets of the German capital had been a mirror to
their *Befindlichkeit*, or spiritual location, as the German dictionary has it.
Crossing Checkpoint Charlie or glancing at the Brandenburg Gate, one
saw not just the hollow eyes of the watchtowers, the cold mouth of a gun,
the pricked ears of listening antennae. Here, in the rosy dawn, the romantic
imagined the love that would unite the city; the fearful painted pictures
of an erupting nuclear war; the avid thriller-reader suspected a spook
under every crinkled trenchcoat; the thirsty glimpsed a glass half-full on
the other side while the Cold Warriors insisted it was half-empty. The
border was defined not by geography but by people; the people it caged,
the people fighting it and the people who controlled it.

I had tried to find all types on my journey. I met indignant West
Germans who rolled up their sleeves to wipe away all traces of 'that
barbaric border'. I saw them clash with East Germans who never approved
of the border but objected to being 'colonized' after its fall. Some of
them felt overwhelmed now that bricks and mortar, fences and barbed
wire no longer sheltered them from the prevailing westerly winds. Then
there were the Wende winners, the czars of the burgeoning trade in
second-hand cars and third-rate dreams. But most of all, I met countrymen
who were grateful. History, in post-Hitler Germany, had been a byword

for evil and guilt. Now, history had for once been good to Germany.

The people I had wanted to meet the most were the border guards. Without them, the highest wall or the fiercest dogs would not have held back 16 million East Germans for long. On the whole, I found the guards to be surprisingly pleasant. If not remorseful, most were at least humble. Someone like Herr Fischer, the border commander in Ellrich, had not benefited personally from his post. That counted for something in my book.

But there were leaders above Herr Fischer who built their entire careers on the Iron Curtain. It protected their privileged positions. It even entitled them to extra rations of West German milk chocolate. They had had the power to prevent the death of almost 1,000 people along the border between 1961 and 1989; they chose to do nothing. I was curious how they lived now and who they were. According to Herr Fischer, the whole border had been under the ultimate command of General Baumgarten, the East German deputy defence minister. Apparently, he still lived in Berlin. I resolved to find General Baumgarten, the man who had watched the watchtowers.

Arrival in Berlin was sudden. Unlike London or New York, the city of four million lacked a suburban belt. Poppy-spotted fields stopped and across the road the first blocks of flats started. There was no sprawling sponge of prefab commuter homes and soulless shopping emporia. Life in Berlin still happened inside the city, mainly because the Wall had restricted expansion during the Cold War, but also because there was so much room in the centre. Some 70 per cent of the city had been destroyed in 1945. More bombs fell on the few square miles around the Führer bunker than on the whole of England.

For the first few miles, the urban border was easy enough to follow. It shadowed roads and waterways in long parade-ground lines. The Red Racer spurted along Schönefeld airport on the southern city edge. On the Schönefelder Chaussee I passed one of the earliest attempts to puncture the emerging Iron Curtain. In 1955, the CIA dug a tunnel under the border and tapped into the Soviets' secret phone network. But the tunnel was betrayed by the British spy George Blake even before it was finished. Berlin still brimmed with such tales.

After passing a railway bridge and a Siemens plant, the border became bogged down in a residential thicket, zig-zagging through blocks of flats. For a while, I amused myself trying to spot the shifting direction of the divide, second-guessing the coming turns. There were dozens of little clues. A rare piece of graffitied Wall still fenced in a school yard. I followed it around a street corner. On the eastern side, house fronts had remained windowless. Blocks directly by the border had been torn down, creating a 100-yard-wide strip. In the empty space between washing lines and flower pots, the Cabuwazi Circus pitched its tent.

I stayed on the border trail. Derelict houses offered new clues. Buildings by the border had deliberately been left to rot since 1961. The fewer people lived near the border, the better. After three decades, the buildings stank.

Eventually my trail went cold and I lost the border among new high-rises. Like the pounding sea, the city slowly reclaimed its territory. Now I needed my map. Thankfully, the Wall – even in its non-existent form – was deemed enough of a landmark to be pencilled in. The street grid showed a red line roughly shadowing the River Spree from south to north. In the centre it cut a steamroller track through the original government quarters and buried old corporate head offices under minefields. Imagine a concrete barrier running down Regent Street and Whitehall. The building of the Wall (an entirely self-inflicted wound, Moscow only reluctantly gave permission) had decapitated Germany's capital. Berliners bemoaned this sad fact for decades. As long as the border existed, their city was defunct.

The events of 1989, however, gave them the chance to reinvent Berlin. The opportunity was almost without precedent. Empty spaces were vast. Plans for the 'new capital of the new Germany' were drawn up and executed in the decade after reunification. In one fell swoop, a new face was invented.

Would I encounter grand façades and imposing gables built by a newly confident nation? Or the unassuming shelters of no import befitting an age-old *angst*? I had witnessed a comic fretting about the new German identity everywhere I went. It blossomed into something of a national pastime. 'Who are we, oh, who are we now that we're one again?' The cries rose from newsprint in Lübeck as much as from bars in Bavaria. Berlin promised an answer.

Most days, I would be inclined to describe a rain storm as harsh and relentless, in turns as icy and fever-pitched, or simply as awesomely ferocious. Especially when it came down as on the day of my arrival in Berlin. Dark pellets splattered on the red bonnet. Chicanes a foot deep welled up on the streets. But today I reserved all my adjectives, kept my ammunition dry. I needed a stock of the meanest, most fearsome vocabulary. For I had entered the Stalingrad of the service industry, an area where consumer sovereignty was an unknown concept. Berlin's waiters were famously rude, nay, harsh, relentless . . . worse than a force 10 gale.

I had unfortunately forgotten this. To see the border properly, I ventured out into the rain on foot, clutching my Irish umbrella (what nation would be better prepared to make umbrellas than the Irish?). I intended to dash from shelter to shelter. I knew in the city I'd never have more than a few hundred yards to go between bars, cafés, restaurants and *Kneipen*. And while I waited to dry over a glass of Pils, I would have ample opportunity for a friendly chat about General Baumgarten, where I might find him and how he was thought of today. It seemed a perfect plan. But, as a German proverb has it: *Ich hatte die Rechnung ohne den Wirt gemacht*, I had added up the bill without consulting the waiter.

I parked next to a dozen trailers assembled in a circle. Judging by the colourful war paint on the barricade of waggons, a hippie commune had taken over this border strip. I sought shelter under the yellow and red canopy of a small hut. '*Hallo und Willkommen*,' a deep voice spoke up. 'Welcome to the Tennessee worm farm.'

'The what?'

'You see in front of you a fine specimen of the Tennessee worm.' The man wore a wide-brimmed carpenter's hat. 'Don't worry. They bite – but not much.'

'It's a long way for a worm. I mean, travelling from Tennessee.'

'Tell you a secret – we gave them a little help coming over.'

'How generous of you.'

'Oh, not at all. We now exploit them mercilessly.'

'What – you make them work on a building site, help refurbish the Reichstag?'

'Not quite. We give them cardboard to eat. They turn it into humus.'

The worms' lair formed a circular concourse. The side walls were a foot high.

'So, how fast do they run?'

'The boys are phenomenal. They're practically racing. Rotating Roland here is leading the pack, second is Worming Wolfgang, followed by Phlegmatic Phillip. But any of them could win the race.'

I soldiered on, sword-fighting the rain with my umbrella. A watchtower graced a public park near Pushkin Allee. The fortifications looked less

out of place here in the city than on a field somewhere between Travemünde and Hof. Berlin and the Wall had merged into one mental picture
over the years. I still held on to that picture. It seemed soothing and
familiar.

Gusts of cold rain sneakily slipped under the umbrella, splashing
straight into my face. At Schlesisches Tor, I needed my first pitstop. The
foodstuff of choice in this part of Berlin was kebab. The district of Kreuz-
berg probably harboured more Turks than most cities in Turkey. The
nearest kebab shop, however, was unfortunately run by a gruff woman of
decidedly Prussian complexion. Her blonde hair hung limply into the food
she was preparing while she quarrelled with a Turkish man. 'Mustafa,
your mother in her village in Anatolia might put onions in a kebab. I
don't. Onions stink. This is *Deutschland*.'

'*Bitte*. But you've got onions right there.'

'I fry them.'

'They don't stink after frying?'

'Of course not.'

'Can I have fried onions in my kebab?'

She looked at him, then she looked at me. She said: 'And?'

I said: 'I can wait.'

'But I can't,' she said.

I ordered a Turkish coffee. 'Milk, no onions.' She frowned. The coffee
was Kenyan, it turned out. But most importantly it was warm and the
kebab shop dry.

'Ever heard of General Baumgarten?'

'General who?'

I crossed the Oberbaum Bridge over the Spree. The red-brick monument
had been destroyed in the war and wasn't repaired until 1995, one of
Berlin's countless wounds, open for five decades. The two ornate brick
towers on bridge piers formed a city gate. On an upper deck, trams now
once again rumbled from east to west and back. Cars and pedestrians
shared the sumptuous lower deck.

Starting at the eastern end of the bridge, a stretch of Wall ran alongside
the river. The mile-long barrier had been renamed 'East Side Gallery' in
March 1990. Artists adopted a few yards each. They painted a continuous
mural, hoping their art would prevent a felling of this historic monument.
A decade later, they could celebrate a rare artistic victory in the murky
world of city politics. The East Side Gallery had become the biggest

surviving piece of *Berliner Mauer*. Paint was peeling but plans to tear the Wall down were roundly defeated.

I passed a painting of a giant Trabbi crashing through the Wall, bursting into the Free World. A gap opened up next to another Wall section depicting a combined German and Israeli flag. On the water's edge rose a six-storey warehouse, converted into a beer hall: 'Der Speicher – dance & more.' The windowless granary with flashing red lights could have been mistaken for a brothel, But the '& more', in fact, referred to 'live TV: boxing, football, Formula One'.

'*Ein Bier, bitte*,' I said. Propping up the bar, I wondered in how many languages I could say 'a beer, please'. It was something of a traveller's mark of distinguished service. I fumbled the sixth: '*Pivo, pajulsta . . .*'

By now, I had been waiting ten minutes for my beer. I waited another ten before raising my arm to the barman. He nodded calmly. 'I'm busy. If you got eyes you might see that.' He was slicing lemons. A whole grove.

A man at the other end of bar let out a smoker's gurgle which I took to be a laugh. 'I'll buy the young man a beer,' he croaked.

'If you say so.' The barman filled a glass with foam. 'Seven minutes, no less. That's how long it takes to draft a good German beer.' I waited another six minutes and fifty-eight seconds for the foam to settle. The waiter mockingly held up his watch.

Eventually, I raised my glass to my benefactor. 'Thanks. *August ist mein Name.*' I stretched out my hand. One exchanged surnames not first names in a German *Kneipe*.

'Stritzka.'

Herr Stritzka was in his fifties. I doubted he would make it into his sixties. Cigarettes seemed to have toasted his voice and probably the rest of his body, too. His handshake was stiff, like a corpse, rather than firm. He had driven city buses all his life.

'I'm looking for a man called Baumgarten, General Baumgarten. I don't know if you've heard of him.'

'The old Nazi, you mean?'

'No, he wasn't a Nazi.'

'Sounds like one, though.'

'He was a general in the NVA, controlled the Iron Curtain.'

'Close enough to a Nazi then.'

'He was deputy defence minister in 1989.'

'They're all the same. Nazis, *Mauerschützen*.' (*Mauerschütze* literally means Wall-shooter.) 'I doubt you'll find him. Probably sipping rum and cokes in South America by now.'

'I heard he was still in Berlin,' I said, mostly to reassure myself.

The border crossed the Spree again at the other end of the East Side Gallery. Squatters lived in a building rotting in no-man's-land. They had scrawled across the side of the house: 'The border runs not between different peoples but between the poor and the rich.' A canal had divided a row of houses here called Bethaniendamm in the last century. Later the waterway was filled in and turned into a park. After the war, the level strip, 100 yards wide, served as a convenient place to erect inner-city fortifications. None of the houses was removed on the eastern side. Essentially, I trotted through pre-war Berlin. The strip – now once again a park – curved past St Thomas church and fattened into a square called Engelsbecken, once a terribly smart address.

I hurried through the rain, too dejected to talk to anyone. Apparently, the inhabitants on the two sides of the Bethaniendamm had not exactly taken to one another after the Wende. 'A line had been drawn, invisible but still effective,' I had read in a book called *Wo die Mauer war* (Where the Wall was).

It rained and rained. I caught a cab back to the car and drove past the Bethaniendamm. At Dresdner Strasse, I pulled on to Heinrich Heine Strasse. Right here had been one of the border crossing points for West Germans visiting East Berlin. The checkpoint barracks were long gone. Cars drably queued in front of a light. I snuck the Red Racer's snout into a gap in the queue to get across. I checked there was no traffic coming from the right. Then, nudging ahead, I turned to look the other way. Before I could see past the car to my left in the queue, the Red Racer winced, lurched sideways, ducked into its suspension and back out, shuddered once more, and came to a halt, all in a split second. The delayed sound of shattering glass brought me back to life.

'That was your fault, clearly.'

'My fault? You crashed into me. How can it be my fault?'

'But you shouldn't have waited there.'

'No, you shouldn't have driven there.'

'No, you . . .'

Herr Bachbrunn, the gentleman I was arguing with, had come barrelling down the other side of the queue, in effect overtaking it. He was practically queue-barging – how could this accident not be his fault? And if it wasn't, it should have been.

We exchanged insurance details and filled out the usual forms in triplicate. Herr Bachbrunn said he worked at the finance ministry.

'In that case, you should have enough money to pay for the damage,' I said.

'I don't print the money. All I do is refurbish the building, the old Nazi air ministry.'

I probably needed a Schnaps now. Clutching accident reports and insurance cards I stumbled into a dark bar with wooden benches on Oranienstrasse. 'Can I order a Schnaps?' The waitress grimaced. 'I have no idea if you can. But do you want to?'

Now I definitely needed a Schnaps.

I had brought with me a travel guide I acquired on a school trip to Berlin in 1986. The section on East Berlin started with the words: 'The east is different.'

Today, it was still cheaper.

I took refuge from the rain at a friend's flat in East Berlin near a street still named after Karl Marx. Anusch and I knew each other from school. She was a child of the leisurely west and all it had to offer in terms of the good life. She had studied at an art college in West Berlin, Germany's capital of hedonism. I admired her gift for seeking pleasure.

A few years ago, however, she moved to the poorer, sooty half of the city. The bargain was irresistible. The rent for her palatial residence in the east came to a pittance. The heating system in her high-ceilinged flat was the only drawback. Or rather, the lack thereof. Most East German blocks of flats only had coal heaters. Every morning one raced down to the icy basement, brought up a bucket of coal bricks and fired up. A dusty ritual to be repeated twice more in a day. The coal barely lasted eight hours. The afternoon I arrived we made three trips to the basement to build up a reserve for the night. Anusch was sweating as she shunted the buckets behind a heater. But she didn't complain. She had come to accept the grimy ritual. Nonchalantly, she wiped the coal dust from her face and smiled. To me, she suddenly seemed ten years older, wiser even.

Later, I found a phone book in the hallway and looked up Baumgarten. The list was daunting. I picked out a few addresses in the vicinity. Maybe one of these Baumgartens would at least be a relative of the general. But even then, would they still be in touch with someone so reviled?

Seemingly no. I gave up after the fourth attempt. As soon as I said the words 'Wall' and 'NVA commander', doors closed. Hastily.

At Schreinerstrasse, I found a store selling old East German products. I tried out a version of Trivial Pursuit with questions like 'How many *Mark* cost a pint of milk in the old days?' and 'How many years was the average waiting time for a fridge?' I had no idea. Nor was I convinced by the old East German map of Berlin that showed the whole of West Berlin as a white, featureless desert. Surely, not even diehard socialists had believed that. Finally, I bought a pre-1989 bumper sticker: '*DDR – Deutsche Demokratische Republik.*' The Red Racer went undercover.

Few buildings rose directly west of the Wall during the Cold War. Building work was generally taboo. East Berlin was very sensitive about the whole area. And who would want to live in a walled-off dead-end where guard dogs barked through the night?

One man, however, aggressively pursued a presence on the superpower edge. Axel Springer, publisher of the West German flagship newspapers *Bild* and *Die Welt*, held robustly right-wing views. These included a strong commitment to German unity. One day, the east would be forced to abandon its childish isolation, the tycoon believed. In 1960s leftist circles, his views were denounced as an endorsement of the kind of nationalism that swept Hitler to power. But despite massive public protests, Springer never let up on his crusade against socialism and the division of Germany.

In an audacious gesture, he erected an eighteen-storey office tower only a few feet away from the border in 1961. The Wall ran directly past the windows. Springer wanted his journalists to look out from the newsroom every morning and see the horror of the border, the cocked rifles, the fortified minefields, the deserted houses. It was to be an inspiration to his journalists. The tower was also a reminder to East Berliners how wrong their blank, featureless maps of West Berlin were, and what they were missing out on.

When the tower went up, East German leaders fumed. The ongoing propaganda war escalated. They retaliated by erecting a battery of twenty-five-storey tower blocks directly opposite. This battle they won. Springer's view east was blocked.

Four decades later, however, his publishing empire looked better than ever. Not only did his offices now overlook the centre of the new Berlin. But his maverick position on German unity (strictly on western terms) had become respectable.

I had arranged to meet Herr Döpfner, editor of the *Welt* newspaper, at the tower. I waited by his panoramic office window. The view no longer resembled a cabinet of horrors. The once empty strip bustled. On the other side of Zimmerstrasse garish new developments sprouted. This was a prime location now. Springer had triumphed. His steadfastness would give his papers added weight in the emerging *Berliner Republik* (as journalists liked to call the reunified Germany, comparing it to the *Weimarer Republik* of the 1920s and the postwar *Bonner Republik*).

Like many senior German journalists, Herr Döpfner sported a Ph D. His secretary referred to him as 'Dr Döpfner'. In marked contrast to Fleet Street, German editorial offices still had the relaxed feel of a university common room. The tone was professorial. The hacks were quiet like librarians.

Unlike his casually attired colleagues, Herr Döpfner wore a three-piece suit and amber cufflinks. As he strode through the door I remembered to call the thirty-five-year-old editor 'Dr Döpfner'. To omit a title was the height of rudeness.

'For decades,' he said, 'Axel Springer was reviled as a reactionary, the hate figure of the 1968 student protests. From the historical perspective, we now see that the supposed reactionary turns out to be a visionary. His so-called "essentials" which the journalists had to sign as part of their contracts – and which included an iron-clad commitment to German unity – are as common as A, B, C today.'

I asked about General Baumgarten and drew yet another blank. The acerbic disdain on Dr Döpfner's face matched the ferocity with which his paper must have battled the general. But he was no longer the subject of breaking news.

I took one last look out of the editor's window and left. Springer's political triumph had bequeathed his journalists arguably the finest lunch-eon spot in Berlin. The top floor housed a breathtaking staff restaurant and clubroom. Windows on the eighteenth floor reached from floor to ceiling. Splendid food and wine were served at elegant wooden tables. Even the waiters seemed pleasant, almost borderline charming.

After a meal of *Saumagen*, Helmut Kohl's pork belly favourite, the firebrand writers would sip high-percentage typewriter fuel in deep leather armchairs. From up here, they observed their four million subjects below. Welcome to the moral high ground.

I lunched with Herr Haubrich, the paper's architecture critic and to the best of my knowledge a 'Herr' rather than a 'Dr', but I wasn't sure. On balance, I thought it ruder to ask whether he had a Ph D than to muddle up his title. Nevertheless, I felt uncertain how to address someone only six years my senior. While he critiqued the rebuilding of Berlin, pointing out of various windows, I found myself switching between the more formal third person singular *Sie* and the informal *Du*. Journalists the world over called each other by their first names, but I had entered a different stratosphere. Herr Haubrich (or should it be Rainer?) magisterially surveyed the good ship Berlin anchored below us with the steely eyes and dark brows of a Peter Mandelson. He answered my every question, and avoided the third person singular altogether. He was too attentive a host to trip up.

On our way out I lingered by a large portrait photograph. It was carefully mounted in the centre of the wood panelling like the altarpiece in a shrine. The resolute old man in the picture seemed familiar.

'Who's he?'

'Oh, that is Axel Springer himself.'

He had died in 1985, four years short of his greatest victory.

Even without Springer, Zimmerstrasse had been a political battleground. East and west picked up juicy ideological bones here. The antagonized public on both sides salivated.

In June 1962, the East German border guard Reinhold Huhn died from shots fired by a man about to sneak his family into a tunnel leading west. Huhn had stopped the group a block away from Zimmerstrasse and asked for their papers. The man, later identified as Rudolf M., pulled a gun and killed Huhn at point-blank range. The family successfully escaped. The incident received tremendous publicity in the east and resulted in tightened border controls. The street where Huhn died was named after him and his memory was conveniently kept alive.

Two months later in August 1962, the eighteen-year-old Peter Fechter bled to death only a few yards from where Huhn died. Fechter had fled more than halfway across the death strip when he was mown down by gunfire. The East German guards left him lying there for almost an hour. 'Help me,' he cried. Passers-by in the west heard him moan but couldn't help. Like Huhn in the east, Fechter became a *cause célèbre* in the west. A large cross draped in barbed wire went up just beyond the Springer tower. Regular memorial services were held within earshot of his killers.

I rounded the Springer tower and went looking for Huhn and Fechter, but soon I realized their ghosts were no longer politically convenient. The new Berlin desperately wanted to meld its two halves back together.

Memorials divided. I stood in front of a brand-new office complex. It had swallowed the Fechter cross.

A block east, the Reinhold-Huhn Strasse had been given back its original name, Schützenstrasse. What irony. In German, *Schützenstrasse* literally means 'street of the shooter'. Rudolf M. had had the last laugh.

Well, almost. I later read in Dr Döpfner's paper that the Berlin county court had just indicted him on murder charges, almost four decades on. Fechter's killer had already been dragged before a judge. But Rudolf M.'s case marked the first time that a *Republikflüchtling* had been prosecuted.

I retired to the Café Adler further along Zimmerstrasse. For a moment, I entertained the hope of encountering a well-spoken and charming waitress, someone who could lift my spirits. The delightful luncheon at the Springer tower had raised entirely false expectations. My conversation with the frumpy apron at the Adler began with my question: 'Can I order?' It ended with her answer: 'Yes.' She continued her plodding path without further ado.

While I was desperately formulating an alternative strategy for ordering a Pils, a theory started to foment. Berlin's charmless bar-tenders and waitresses, I decided, were the root cause of what Dr Dopfner had labelled the city's continued division. He told me: 'Nowhere was the tension between east and west as strong as here. The ideological poles had faced each other anew every day during the Cold War. When the writer Wolf Jobst Siedler said after the Wende it will take twenty-five years to complete unification, people laughed. But ten years on it seems he was too optimistic. It'll take rather longer than that.'

But why? Was it because Berliners still worshipped different ideological gods? Maybe. But I preferred a different explanation. Berliners never felt welcome when they strayed across the former divide. In their neighbourhood pubs they were usually treated well by staff who knew them, but only a desperate man would dare to enter unfamiliar drinking territory. The death strip had been replaced by a giant killer beer mat, I mused. And then I finally ordered my Pils.

Café Adler sat on a street corner directly opposite Checkpoint Charlie. By a stroke of genius it opened in 1988, in time for its busiest day and craziest night ever. On 9 November 1989, thousands streamed across. Today, the dark, smoke-swaddled room crammed with intense talkers had the feel of an Eastern European émigré haunt. The historic location seemed to inspire existentialist 'conversation'.

'It reaches deep inside.'

'Almost like a mother-daughter relationship.'

'*Ja*. Father-son dynamics don't catch the nimbus.'

The couple at the next table referred to Ostler and Westler. Berliners used these terms instead of Ossi and Wessi.

Meanwhile, the waitresses gossiped by the bar, each holding a full tray of drinks.

The checkpoint itself had long been scrapped. New office towers swallowed up the land. A single, stubbly watchtower remained, but only because the development supposed to take its place fell through. Soon the new capital would devour it, too. All that remained was the sign with the Allies' famous warning: 'You are leaving the American sector.' It was repeated in Russian and French, and, as if intended as a punishment, in smaller print in German.

An unusual work of art commemorated the twenty-eight-year armed superpower stand-off here. Mounted on a 20-foot pole in the middle of the street, stood a large picture. The side facing east showed a colour photograph of an East German guard. His clean features, his loftily balanced helmet, his neatly creased uniform, his glaringly innocent eyes, his stiff composure – it was all a mirror-image of the photograph of the American soldier on the other side. Both were equally young, obviously recruits. These fresh faces were what one saw when approaching Checkpoint Charlie between 1961 and 1989.

A few houses down from Café Adler I squeezed into a museum devoted to the checkpoint. Countless exhibits documented the Wall and the many attempts made to cross it. Hundreds of visitors besieged the building and tour buses delivered yet more. To me, the museum was a celebration of German courage and inventiveness. Berlin had attracted those who didn't accept the limits put on their freedom by the border. I was surprised how many had risked their lives.

They tried wonderfully outlandish schemes to reach the west. I marvelled at hollow car engines that provided enough room for someone to hide in. There was a plethora of balloons and pedal-power planes. People hid in cable drums and industrial transformers. Elaborate tunnel systems gnawed at the Wall. One woman smuggled her baby son across in a shopping bag. One man slipped through the checkpoint in an extremely low sports car by flipping down the windshield and passing under the pike. A cabaret manager carried acrobats through the checkpoint one by one in a suitcase. A snorkler built an underwater engine to motor across the border just below the waterline. *Vorsprung durch Technik*. Here were heroic acts around which the united Germany could rally. Here was a piece of the new identity the country so desperately clamoured for.

Being German, though, the situation was more complicated. I saw a woman absorbed in a booklet. Curiosity roused, I looked over her shoulder at the poem she was reading:

> Unforgotten are
> Those murdered on this border
> Chiselled in stone
> Their names live on
> Imprinted on the memory
> The image lives on.
>
> We stand
> Where they fell
> What they loved
> We love more deeply
> What they hated
> We hate more strongly
> Wherefore they died
> We now live.
>
> Unforgotten are the murdered
> Unforgotten the murderers!

By the softly-softly literary standards I grew up with, the poem sounded unusually martial. But it echoed my feelings when seeing museum photographs of Peter Fechter crouching under barbed wire.

I said: 'I like the poem.'

'Me, too,' the woman replied in a strong Saxon accent. 'It was written by a border guard.'

I was stunned. I re-read the lines 'We stand/Where they fell,' and I noticed the difference in nuance from the museum. The writer was eulogizing the Huhns, not the Fechters. He was talking of armed men revenging the 'unforgotten' comrades.

All along I had relied on maps. Some showed the border clearly, often predictably in blood red. One visitors' map actually had a miniature wall running through the streets. But none of the maps could capture the haphazard way in which the Wall had disfigured Berlin.

Beyond Checkpoint Charlie I picked up the trail of a red line painted on the tarmac. Now, my journey became easy. The line was meant to guide travellers like me. For a few years after the Wende confused tourists had wandered around aimlessly because Berliners longed to be rid of the beastly barrier. They succeeded to the extent that when they finally came to paint the line, nobody could remember exactly where the border once ran. Aerial shots had to be consulted to pinpoint locations.

I traversed Zimmerstrasse. Whenever the red line crossed the street, it turned into a double row of cobblestones, apparently a recent addition. Motorists had complained about the irregular paint markings on the tarmac. Some orderly soul or other always stopped at the red line as if it was still a state boundary. Bless them.

The last continuous piece of Wall in the city centre fenced in the former headquarters of the Gestapo, Hitler's army of henchmen. Allied air raids had razed the building. Fragments of the basement were displayed in an outdoor exhibition called 'topography of terror', but it amounted to little more than a row of rubble.

The adjoining stretch of Wall had fared only marginally better. Souvenir hunters had chipped away at it. In thousands of homes from Hamburg to Honululu, there must be odd crumbs of concrete. Grandchildren will crowd around them for years to come. 'A real piece of the Berlin Wall,' grandpa will say. He had chiselled a piece of history. Future generations might accord the crumb the same status as a brontosaurus bone.

The chiselled-down Wall looked as if it had been gnawed by Ted Hughes' Iron Man. A few inches of concrete had gone missing. Metal beams reinforcing the concrete were sticking out like broken bones and mangled limbs. Every few yards the chisels had broken through to the other side, leaving gaping punctures. I thought it a terrific monument to how individual people had brought down this barrier, not a state treaty or a war, but chisel-wielding men and women. Hence, I was all the more aghast when I read 'international human rights activists' planned to replace the mangled concrete with a new memorial Wall, fresh from the factory.

I felt frustrated. I had seen miles and miles of General Baumgarten's old garden fence, but the man himself remained elusive. Few people still remembered him, even at the Checkpoint Charlie museum. Those who did, brought me no closer.

As a last resort, I called Herr Fischer in Ellrich. 'Do you remember telling me about General Baumgarten? I am trying to find him.' Herr Fischer seemed reluctant. General Baumgarten apparently was in prison. That would explain a certain lack of public visibility. 'But where?' Herr Fischer didn't want to give me the address. 'But he's in Berlin, as you said, no?' He really was. Herr Fischer thought it might be permissible to give me the name of the prison, but not the address. Düppel Penal Institution. I thanked him and got the phone number from directory inquiries. I dialled.

'Düppel.'

'*Guten Tag.* Could I please speak to General Baumgarten?'

'That's not possible.'

'Why, is he not there?'

'Maybe.'

'And?'

'We never confirm the names of inmates. Who knows who you are?'

That was the one answer I had not expected. '*Who pays your salary?*' I phoned back. 'OK, listen. I know you won't tell me if Baumgarten is one of yours. But if I send him a letter and he really is there, will he get the letter?'

'Yes.'

I rejoiced – but not for long. What does one say in such a letter? 'Herr Baumgarten, I would like to inquire what it feels like to conduct state-sponsored murder?' Hardly. But to use subterfuge would mean lowering my standards to his own.

I ended up describing my meetings with ex-border guards on my journey and how I had heard about him from Herr Fischer 'as we talked one sunny afternoon in his garden'. Maybe it was all in vain anyway. Maybe the general had long left prison and really was sipping rum and coke in South America.

I now approached Potsdamer Platz, the bustling hub of pre-war Berlin. This was the city district I most wanted to see. The busy square had always been the face of the German capital, the shop window of the nation, a fountain of identity and inspiration to the rest of the Reich – for better or worse. Since Travemünde, I had carried around with me a newspaper cutting that recounted its place in history's maw. I pulled out the yellowing scrap now:

In 1895, 20,000 vehicles a day passed through the square. It was the Times Square of Europe. There were three stations, 25 tram lines, eight bus lines and an underground railway. In 1924, the first German traffic lights were installed there. Its hallmark, a large clock, an appropriate symbol for Potsdamer Platz, set the pace of the city. The stress of 1920s Berlin was relieved by the square's other function as an entertainment district. The caricaturist Georg Grosz and the satirist Erich Kästner, well known for the quintessential Berlin children's book, *Emil and the Detectives*, lingered in the Café Josty. The more elegant Berliners held their rendezvous in the Fürstenhof or Esplanade cafés. On one corner of the square, the Haus Vaterland provided a huge entertainment complex big enough to hold 2,000 people. The Nazis were drawn to the area. The so-called People's Court, presided over by the merciless hanging judge Roland Freisler, was housed in an old grammar school. The square was close to the centre of Nazi power. The SS bunkers were dug underneath its paving stones and it became a target of Allied bombing. The square was flattened within a few days. Nothing was left apart from a wine shop and the shell of the Esplanade. The Cold War made the square a macabre tourist attraction. On a wooden platform one could peer over the Berlin Wall that split the square and study the East German border patrols and their dogs. Wolf Jobst Siedler, the critic, called the square a desert dividing ramshackle socialist emergency architecture from western New Brutalism.

I goggled. Berlin had fully reclaimed its old heart; that much was immediately obvious. Instead of a bypass, the capital's planners opted for a full-blown transplant. A young Potsdamer Platz pulsated. A cluster of new high-rises bustled with vigour like greased lightning. A swerving bus whirled me round, a surging loudspeaker spun me the other way; a tray laden with *Kuchen* passed above my head while a troupe of Peruvian pipers straddled my legs.

A scene to get drunk on meandered through the stubbly postwar carnage of socialist emergency architecture and New Brutalism. On my walk, I had seemingly rounded an island cove, nothing but pines in the supine sea air, only to find an urban armada camped in the shallows once sheltered by the Wall.

Berlin's empty backwater now bulged with newly arrived vessels. The deserted cove suddenly brimmed and hollered. Those anchored in the formerly treacherous waters made a living as traders, carting their wares ashore, hawking Benetton shirts and fur mittens and undies of the sexy kind. Others portside were pirates in the moneyed world of mergers and acquisitions. They strode aloft in pinstripes that seemed to carry on up the façades of the new temples of power in long lines of smoked-glass windows. The biggest name plate read *DaimlerChrysler*, a company too busy and greedy even for a hyphen.

The new Potsdamer Platz mimicked the dormant old, where Liza Minelli had sung in *Cabaret*, Christopher Isherwood said *Goodbye to Berlin* and the hard faces of prostitutes leered from the paintings of Otto Dix. Now the corporate throne of the Sony music empire cut an entirely different figure. The glass exterior sloped forwards like a tilted cookie jar.

Since the war, entertainment had grown by a whole dimension. Crowds panted at the 3-D IMAX surround cinema. Later they passed the frighteningly sleek marble walls and stainless steel interior of McDonald's. One caroused at the reopened Esplanade. The bartender uncorked another infatuating vat of power and glamour. Cocktails, everyone.

I observed the goings-on from the rather more grimy Imbiss across the square. Herr Langrzik catered for the tastes of the high-rise master builders. He wiped the counter with his stained apron. 'Thuringia Bratwurst DM 3.50. Jagdwurst 150g. Mars, Twix DM 2.00. Becks with everything.'

Herr Langrzik today fried sausages where Kennedy had stood in 1963 and declared: 'All free men, wherever they may live, are citizens of Berlin, and therefore, as a free man, I take pride in the words *Ich bin ein Berliner*.' After the fall of the Wall, Herr Langrzik had more free time than he ever desired. He lost his job as a lorry driver in East Berlin. Selling fast food became his American dream. 'Business was slow at first. Even if Kennedy once stood here.'

'And now?'

'Lots of builders. The tourists come and ask where exactly the Wall stood.'

'Must have been a touch further east.'

'To tell you truth, I'm not so sure myself any more.'

Herr Langrzik had new customers. Gary, a Glaswegian welder, ordered Becks. 'I could get used to this brew.' I offered to pay for the drink but Gary said he could afford his own. 'I get paid a bundle 'ere.' He worked as a specialist underground and underwater welder. Hundreds of British labourers helped to feed the square's renewed appetite for concrete and steel. By German wage standards they were cheap.

Another world apparently lurked underneath us. Gary and his mates were building a cobweb of subway and inter-city train stations. From below Potsdamer Platz, tunnels were under construction that would put it at the centre of the city and national rail network once again. 'I've never seen anything like it. Building 'ere is hideous.' Most of his work was done in diving suits. Ground-water levels could not be lowered as was the norm with such projects. The nearby Reichstag building had no foundations but instead rested on 3,000 wooden poles. If water levels dropped, the poles would rot and the German parliament most certainly subside. 'You don't wanna do that, mate.'

Later, Gary saw me gazing uncertainly at the new metropolis. It seemed so discordant. The dozen or so buildings of different height, shape, colour and style lacked any kind of common denominator. 'What a change from the old Berlin,' I said.

'The Führer would have been proud of your lot now.'

The remark sounded odd to me, rather than downright offensive. I knew of the plans of Albert Speer, Hitler's chief architect. With the Führer's approval, he wanted to rebuild the city centre including the Potsdamer Platz. Grand-standing monuments were to dominate the unitary capital of Europe, a granite mainstay for the vast *Lebensraum*.

But today's Potsdamer Platz had turned out completely different. It was a patchwork of sloping glass triangles, stainless steel cutaways, touches of the Centre Pompidou next to a playful adaptation of the Rockefeller Center, fuzzy glass cubicles in stairways of frameless windows and a collage of spicy orange, galling green and rubber yellow. City planners obviously wanted to avoid any comparison with Speer's heavy-handed monotony. Nothing was repeated and everything seemed in some way *en vogue* and illustriously international. Of course, that should come as no surprise. The city had invited an all-star roster of architects from Rome, London, Tokyo and Chicago to redesign its market square. Richard Rogers, Renzo Piano, Arata Isozaki, Jose Rafael Moneo – they were all given a plot on the Potsdamer Platz. Each built a little monument to his own style with irregular glass cutaways and dissonant colours.

The city planners could now point to the new Berlin and say: 'Look, no more heavy brick castles, no more squat monotony. Albert Speer is dead. This is the new Germany.' But, of course, Speer lives on in the fears of those who think they must eternally distance themselves from the likes of him with everything they do. The new Germany epitomized in Berlin still defines itself through the things it doesn't want to be: not Nazi, not martial, not heavy and, ultimately, not German. However, bundling together parts of Rome, London, Tokyo and Chicago does not build a new identity.

I checked my messages. Still no response from General Baumgarten. Yet he seemed strangely present. I had after all inspected his oeuvre daily. I wondered whether he ever travelled the length of the border. Probably not. Generals sat in bunkers. Or in prisons. Or in Hollywood swings in South America.

From Potsdamer Platz one looked out on to the Brandenburg Gate. Everyday traffic rushed through. Street vendors flogged Russian fur hats and VoPo caps and flags with hammer and sickle. The supply from the frozen east seemed to be limitless. Stockpiles reaching back to 1917 were being tapped.

I walked towards the triumphal gate along an imponderably large expanse. Right at Berlin's heart yawned a disused space the size of several football pitches. The ground was bulldozed. Craggy lumps alluded to historical significant. Hitler died in his bunker right here. A robust fence stood guard. But who was being protected from what? Did vandals threaten the demonic ground? Or was the fence protecting us from what lay behind it?

This peculiar strip had been reserved for a memorial to the European Jewry sent to the gas ovens from this very spot. Astonishingly, no such memorial had previously been conceived in the German capital. Germany never built a central Holocaust memorial – I had to repeat that sentence to myself. But it still sounded false. Of course, the concentration camps had been preserved. Yet, during four guilt-gagged decades of division, the nation had gone without a central stone of apology and sorrow.

After the fall of the Wall, Berlin's most open space was picked for this purpose. But ten years later, the plot remained empty. The fence reined in the ghosts of the past, while politicians, planners and intellectuals were locked in disagreement. The rest of the new capital rose around the plot, yet they argued: 'What nation would come up with the idea of putting the most horrible acts of its own history in such an exposed position in in its capital?' So spoke the right; the left echoed: 'The concentration camps are better monuments.'

Hence, Germany still had no Holocaust memorial. Instead, the empty plot of ulcerous boulders and funereal soil became a memorial of a different kind, a memorial to the country's lingering paralysis when directly confronted with its past. And an astoundingly ugly memorial at that.

Beyond the Brandenburg Gate, the new German government quarter struggled to its feet. The Reichstag has received a facelift, courtesy of Sir Norman Foster. The British star architect placed a glass dome on top of the building torched by Hitler's henchmen. Light and inspiration flood into the parliament now returned to its original habitat. A futuristic new Chancellery has risen behind it. The narrow glass complex is placed on a bend in the Spree and crosses over the river twice like a beached whale in fenland.

I passed through the Brandenburg Gate and started down tree-lined Unter den Linden. Embassies and ministries jockeyed for position. The bulging stonework made them look gauche. But the surging electricity of power had returned to Berlin's centre.

I had drinks at the reopened Hotel Adlon where Chaplin, Garbo and T. E. Lawrence met the likes of Roosevelt and Kaiser Wilhelm II. In years to come, political levers will once again be pulled here. The Adlon with its siren nooks and crannies suited the bawdy art of politics much better than the bland glass palaces across the Brandenburg Gate. 'Our party cannot afford the right leader,' said a fat fellow at the bar. He sat comfortably. The stools were curiously oversized. They measured almost two square feet. The dowdy deckhands in the bowels of the bar worked hard.

I passed the Russian embassy. On its steps, an attempt on Bismarck's life was made in 1866, five years before he first unified Germany. How that could have changed everything in European history. Without a strong Germany, the twentieth century might have taken an entirely different course. But the assassin's bullet bounced off the Iron Chancellor's ribcage.

At Friedrichstrasse train station I wished for one brief second I could be back in divided Berlin, just to taste that ghoulish excitement again. Friedrichstrasse in East Berlin was really neither east nor west in those days. The train station operated a segregated platform. Westerners could stop off, buy duty-free goods and return on western subway trains that barrelled through eastern tunnels without stopping. The trains slowed down when passing through one of the deserted stations close to the Wall. Potsdamer Platz was one of them. In the dimly lit ghost stations, one could see 1940s advertisements still on billboards, frozen in time. And occasionally, one could glimpse Graham Greene: 'The border means more than a customs house, a passport officer, a man with a gun. Over there everything is going to be different; life is never going to be quite the same again after your passport has been stamped and you find yourself speechless among the money-changers . . .'

It had turned nine in the evening now. Much to my surprise I found a bookshop still open. Outside, on what Germans aptly called a 'grab table', I saw a book of jokes called *10 Jahre sind zuviel* ('Ten Years are Too Much'). A sample on the back read:

Ostler: 'Waiter, what wine do you recommend for the tenth anniversary of German unity?'

Waiter: 'That depends, *mein Herr . . .*'

Ostler: 'On what?'

Waiter: 'Well, do you want to celebrate or forget?'

I bought a novel called *Magic Hoffmann* by Jakob Arjouni, a Turk writing in German. According to the blurb, Arjouni was Philip Marlowe's *Doppelgänger*. In the book, Arjouni's protagonist, Hoffmann, travels from the West German provinces to Berlin to look for old friends. On his way, he meets a Westler who points at decrepit Ostler houses and tells him: 'Look at them! It's all rubbish! Of course, we knew we weren't getting Switzerland, but it could at least have been Austria.' Hoffmann's Westler friends live in East Berlin. One of them says she feels like a white woman in the bush; she often intentionally puts on dirty clothes and is always ready to give advice to the 'indigenous people'. The friends are miserable here. Hoffmann gets into a fight with a rude waiter. Hoffmann, the country lad, concludes that in Berlin it is bad form to be in a good mood.

I checked into the Hotel Unter den Linden on the corner of Friedrichstrasse. Once upon a time, when the Trabbi was deemed a luxury car, this was the best guest house in East Berlin. The socialist crown jewel had been reserved for party leaders. The location remains unbeatable to this day. But the new clientele at the concrete bunker was decidedly more working class now. So was the service.

In my boxy room, I flicked through my stacks of notes. I had filled five books and countless loose scraps. They were my personal map of Germany, my new bond with the country. When I started the journey at the Baltic Sea, my scribblings had been 90 per cent in English and 10 per cent in German. Re-reading them, I noticed the ratio was now reversed. The occasional throw-away remark or off-the-cuff observation had flown from my pen in English, my working language for the last decade, but the most heart-felt jottings – ink-stained and unconstrained by page margins – were *auf deutsch*. And so were the anecdotes and the jokes. Seen through German eyes, the country was not as humourless a place as it is so often portrayed. My journey had yielded something amusing every day. Sometimes I had laughed with my countrymen and sometimes at them.

Often, maybe too often, I recorded snide remarks in my notebooks.

Flicking through the books, I felt the notes read like love letters, full of comic tiffs and scraps. But the letters described an ongoing love affair. My journey was a story with a happy ending. Sipping a Pils at the cosy hotel bar, I decided I liked the new Germany for all its warts. I felt at home here.

My mother Tini arrived to pick up her car. I would miss the Red Racer. Nevertheless, my fondness obviously had its limits. I realized at the last minute that I had forgotten to clean the car despite my vow in Zwickau to do so. And I had failed to repair the front lights damaged in the accident. An overalled man at a Toyota garage said it would take weeks to order the parts 'for such an old model'. I prayed for a maternal pardon.

I had asked Tini, short for Christine, to accompany me along the last stretch of Wall in northern Berlin. In 1963, she and her friend Axel had organized the flight of Axel's girlfriend Ruth across the border. I wanted to find the exact spot. Tini thought it was probably on Bernauer Strasse, but she wasn't sure. She had not thought much about the incident since the day it happened. The fear made her forget as much as possible. She hadn't seen Axel and Ruth for years.

We pulled out of the hotel car park and drove past Friedrichstrasse train station. Tini said: 'Axel asked me to carry a walkie-talkie across to Ruth in the east. They needed to be able to communicate on the night of her flight.'

'Why didn't he carry it across?'

'Axel himself was a fugitive from the east. He was wanted there.'

'And he had left without Ruth?'

'I think so.'

'So you took a walkie-talkie through the checkpoint. Wasn't that dangerous?'

'I was very naive at twenty-two. Axel had put it in a box of chocolates, supposedly a gift for Ruth. I just put the box in my coat and went to the checkpoint. I had never been searched before. But this time they called me into a small room. I hung up my coat. They searched me – but not the coat. Then I put the coat back on again and a minute later I was on the street here. I can't remember giving her the walkie-talkie but I must have done.'

We crossed the bridge at Invalidenstrasse. Sandstones marked the dividing line. The border hugged the Spree. On the bank across from the Reichstag, a short segment of Wall stood near an eco-memorial called 'parliament of trees'. Harbour cranes unloaded barges as they had done for centuries. Cemeteries broke up the industrial wasteland.

'The whole business, I think, started earlier when Axel asked me to go across and just call Ruth.'

'Seems exciting.'

'It was. And I wanted to help. I met Axel on a university trip. A group of us architecture students from the Technical University went on a tour of Britain in 1962. We went to York where my grandmother was born. In Scotland, we bought a roll of tweed cloth and founded our own clan. We made tartan ties and suits from the cloth for every clan member.'

'And how often did you go to East Berlin?'

'A few times, usually to call or meet Ruth.'

We passed under a railway bridge at Gartenstrasse. Tini said: 'I remember, there were tracks near where Ruth was supposed to come across. But it looked somehow different from this street.'

We turned left into Bernauer Strasse. Directly after the Wall was built, spectacular scenes took place here. Whole families climbed down ropes of knotted bedlinen. The eastern houses then stood right on the border on Bernauer Strasse. Soon, the blocks closest to the street were pulled down. The resulting corridor still cut through the neighbourhood.

'Do you recognize the spot, Tini?'

'There were definitely blocks of flats, but much closer to the street. And they looked older. Maybe it was further down the street.'

We ploughed up and down Bernauer Strasse. A second-hand car dealer occupied part of the corridor. Somewhere else a sign read: 'Private property.' A young woman took pictures of the border desert. At Ackerstrasse, a longer Wall segment was framed between two even taller slices of corroded metal. The memorial space blocked off in the middle could be seen only through slits in the back. One glimpsed a VoPo view.

We stopped again. Tini examined the house fronts. I could see she tried to juxtapose them with a mental picture. But the picture was fuzzy and punctured by time. She shook her considerable head of silver hair. 'The business with the walkie-talkie was really quite stupid. The guards obviously sought to catch the helpers as well as those fleeing. Afterwards, I got scared. For many years I only ever flew in and out of Berlin, never took the train or car where they could stop you. I remember, even twenty years later in 1984 I was almost too scared to go across at Friedrichstrasse. So oppressive.' She scrutinized the buildings once more. 'I think we actually knew someone in the house from where Ruth started. I was there that night. But I repressed a lot of memories. Afterwards, I just wanted to forget. We should ring Axel.'

'You've got his number?'

Until today, she had never mentioned his name.

We sat on a black leather sofa under a photograph of the World Trade Center in New York, toasting the reunion with Prosecco. Axel and Ruth Busch, now married, lived near West Berlin's old US Army base. The border had only been a few hundred yards away. Ruth, wiggling unruly strands of curly hair, recounted: 'Before the Wende, we used to hear the guard dogs bark at night, trotting along those long leashes.' Axel and Ruth chose to live close to the monstrosity that had almost kept them apart. It was oddly romantic.

Axel, bespectacled and bearded with a professorial aura, was a well-known Berlin architect. After the Wende, he conducted a planning survey of the territory along the Wall. He would have liked to turn the strip into a park running the length of the city. Put greenery where death and destruction had ruled. But the DaimlerChryslers won the day.

I explained my interest in the events of 1963.

Ruth said: 'I think we still have newspaper cuttings from back then.'

'I'd love to see them,' said Tini.

Ruth disappeared into the bedroom to look for the cuttings. The story-telling fell to Axel. 'I myself came over in 1962. I crawled from district Treptow in the east to Neukölln in the west through a tunnel. Seventy centimetres wide, unsupported. Around forty people were in my group. I tried to get Ruth in as well. But it didn't work. On previous occasions, informers had infiltrated groups that way and everyone was arrested. In my case, of the forty, only seventeen made it across. The rest were caught because the guards became suspicious about all these people arriving and nobody leaving. They searched the house where the tunnel started. Luckily, I was one of the first to go through. The tunnel was closed after that.'

Tini must have known all this at the time, but fear had buried the memories.

Axel's eyes were wide open but unfocused. 'Once in the west, I tried everything to get Ruth out. She was my girlfriend. I considered forging papers, or smuggling her through a checkpoint hidden in a big American street cruiser, or driving up to the Wall with a lorry and throwing a ladder across. But all too risky. Then I heard about an eastern family who lived right by the Wall and wanted to come over. That's when I had the idea to fasten a cable across the divide. They could slide across on a handle or harness. The group that was to come across consisted of Ruth, the family who lived in the house, another friend of mine and his girlfriend. I carefully checked out the territory across from the house on the western side. There were railway tracks.'

'But there are no tracks on Bernauer Strasse,' I interrupted.

Axel's voice was urgent and sped on. 'The house was north of Bernauer Strasse, on Korsörerstrasse above the Gleimtunnel. *So*. I found somewhere to fix the cable. I built special metal handles to slide down the cable and Tini took them across in the trunk of her car. And then, of course, the famous walkie-talkie. We watched the weather and the moon. We agreed a date. It was very well planned. But everything went wrong nevertheless.'

Axel briefly clung to a pained pause. 'Well, first, things went *wunderbar*. It was dark and dry. From the east, they had to start the operation by throwing across a hook with a string attached. We would then put the cable on the hook and they would pull it back and attach it to the roof of the house. Unfortunately, the father of the family insisted that he must throw the hook. My friend was an athlete and could easily have thrown it far enough. But the father couldn't. It fell short and crashed into the Wall. Smack against it. Enormous loud noise. Oh, God, we thought. Oh, God. We agreed over the walkie-talkies to pause for an hour. Eventually, they got the hook across and pulled the cable back. But we still had to fasten it. The cable was attached to a drum. We wound up the drum with a lever. But the mechanism made a loud clicking noise. To silence it, I rolled a carpet around it. Then the carpet got caught in the drum. I tried to cut it out but failed. It slowed everything down further. By this stage it was getting late. We had been there half the night. Everything took too long. The group was already up on the roof. At that moment we were spotted. And before they could ride across, the guards went up there and arrested them.'

'Including Ruth?'

'Her too.'

'And when did you see Ruth again?'

'The whole group was interrogated for a long time. They kept them in solitary confinement. Played mind games with them. Telling them the others had confessed everything. Nobody outside knew what had happened to them. Not even Ruth's mother heard anything. For weeks. Even when she asked, the police pretended not to know.'

Axel was angry. 'Ruth was tried and sentenced. Meanwhile, I checked out our legal options. I heard of a certain type of *Menschenhandel* [trading of human beings]. Officially, this sort of thing never happened. But through back channels, the West German government fed East Berlin millions from secret pots of cash to release *Republikflüchtlinge*. I put Ruth's name forward and after a few months she was given a legal exit visa. Officially, the whole business was called "family reunification". We had claimed to be engaged.'

'And then got married here and stayed here.'

'We didn't want to leave Berlin.'

'You weren't scared of the Wall? Didn't want to leave it all behind?'

'Well, one still had an interest in all that. Today, as an architect I look at the Wall strip that remains. With a devil-may-care attitude, everything is being paved over and wiped away. That's a shame.'

Finally, Ruth found the newspaper cuttings. 'Fantastic flight attempt,' read the headline. Axel's cable had glistened in the border lights. That's how the guards spotted them, according to the paper dated 31 July 1963. It was only five weeks after Kennedy's visit. *'All free men, wherever they may live, are citizens of Berlin . . .'*

The next day I said good-bye to Tini and the Red Racer. They returned to West Germany and, I headed for Korsörerstrasse. From Bernauer Strasse, I walked past the rebuilt Jahn sports stadium. Part of the old fortifications now formed the stadium's back wall. But the graffiti on the porous concrete looked new. Bright sunlight reflected in the silver paint. Caged crowds roared inside.

Just as Axel imagined it, here at least a short border strip had been turned into an ever green *Mauerpark*. Children massacred each other in playgrounds. Residents argued across picket fences on small allotment gardens. The rail tracks Axel spoke of ran on the far side of the park. They were overgrown and had long since been decommissioned. Further north, I found the reopened Gleimtunnel. Cars passed through it under the border.

One block up, Korsörerstrasse hit the tracks at a right angle. The house on the corner still sported East Germany's national colours, grey and brown in innumerable shades. Next to the rotting door, someone had sprayed: 'How can I win the heart of a princess?' The five-storey apartment building overlooked the border. The front windows and roof were no more than fifteen yards away from the tracks. Axel had been very lucky to find this spot. Ruth had been very unlucky not to make it.

However, Axel had not been the only person to recognize this as the perfect escape hatch. I realized, I now stood on the exact location of the final scene in John le Carré's *The Spy Who Came in from the Cold*. Alec Leamas, the British agent, and Liz, his girlfriend from the Bayswater branch of the Communist Party, headed for this spot in the last five pages of the spy novel. They're in East Berlin, on the run from they don't know who. They need to cross over to the west quickly.

'Where are we?' Leamas whispered. 'We crossed the Leninallee, didn't we?'
'Greifswalder Strasse. Then we turned north. We're north of Bernauer Strasse.'

Le Carré immortalized the human drama that surrounded the Wall. Nobody described it better. When Leamas approaches the border, he steps up to 'the white demarcation line which lay across the road like the base line of a tennis court'.

A mile further north, the tracks had been refurbished. Commuter trains once again ran from Bornholmer Strasse station to Wollankstrasse, Schönholz and Wilhelmsruh. Each station was directly on the border, a border that now only separated the districts Pankow and Wedding.

I boarded a S2 line train at Bornholmer Strasse. The old checkpoint at the railway bridge here was the first along the entire Iron Curtain to open on the night of 9 November 1989. A plaque commemorated the genesis of German reunification. From the northbound train, I had a last look at the reclaimed border. There were pleasant garden ponds, industrial storage areas, raucous goal-scorers. Every neighbour, every shop, every community along the way nabbed a piece of land. You could say the socialist death strip was 'collectivized' after the Wende. At Wilhelmsruh, I got off and made the return trip from the opposite platform. For me, this was the end of the line, *Endstation*. I would go to the Hotel Unter den Linden and pack my bags.

'There's a fax for you. It's from a Frau Baumgarten.'
'Frau Baumgarten?' Could women rise to the rank of general in the East German military? I grabbed the fax. The sender was clearly identified as Frau Hannelore Baumgarten. '*Sehr geehrter Herr August*,' it started. The typed script was tidy, the signature squiggly. How very curious.
Frau Baumgarten had sent the fax via my father whose number I was

using while I travelled. It read: 'On behalf of my husband, I would like to tell you that we have received your letter. My husband is happy to talk to you. However, he is in prison and only seldomly at home. Once a week, he is allowed to receive visitors. But I'm afraid these dates are booked up for the foreseeable future. Friends, former comrades-in-arms and many people whom we don't even know wish to visit him in Düppel. It therefore seems impossible to arrange your visit. But maybe you could ask the warden Herr Ihle to make an exception and grant you a special visit. Best regards from myself and my husband, H. Baumgarten.'

I couldn't help but feel fobbed off. It seemed the general was hiding behind prison officials and guards. As border commander he had always been shielded by men in uniform. Maybe he still preferred it like that.

Frau Baumgarten had put her phone number at the top of the fax. I dialled. We exchanged odd pleasantries, almost as if I was asking to see her healthy new-born baby rather than her husband in the slammer. 'By all means,' she said, 'call Herr Ihle.'

And so I did. By the standards of his profession, Herr Ihle was helpful. He promised to speak to Herr Baumgarten. But he didn't sound hopeful.

I called back the next day. 'Baumgarten says he's happy to see you.'

'He does?' I sounded like an idiot. I was offered what I had asked for and still I was surprised. 'And it's OK with you?'

'See no reason why not.'

'So when can I come?' This was all happening so fast.

'Why, I can't decide that.' Of course, there had to be another bureaucratic hurdle, another layer of fortification for the general to hide behind. 'You have to speak to Herr Hein. Baumgarten is in an open prison. Herr Hein is the warden there. I'll let him know you'll call.'

When I got through to Herr Hein he had no idea who I was. 'Really? Herr Ihle said you could see Baumgarten? *Nee*, don't know anything about it.' Again, I would have to call back the next day. *Morgen, morgen, keine Sorgen.*

I thought I should finally start packing my bags. Even at economy room rates, the Unter den Linden was cannibalizing my bank roll. I had seen all there was to see of the border. Or had I? I would stay for one more night. And for one more breakfast served by waiters hired straight from the VoPo training academy.

'Herr Hein, any news from Baumgarten?'

'Oh, Herr August.'

'I guess that's a no.'

'*Nee, nee . . .*'

'It's OK?'

'*Ja, ja.*'

'OK, but then today?'

'Sure, sure.'

Sure?

I put the phone down but held on to the receiver. 'Wait, wait,' I wanted to shout. 'That was too quick, too easy. And, by the way, what should I ask him?' I probably knew more about the godforsaken border than the man who used to crack his whip over it. What could he possibly add? Would I find a sad, broken figure uncomfortably baying for my pity?

Before I could compose a mental list of questions I had already arrived in a leaf-strewn residential street. The prison building was pleasant enough. The sculpted sandstone walls had remarkably big windows. Next door was a school. I gathered the general was not sharing a cell with the rougher element, the rapists and rip-off artists; this had to be more of a gentlemen's club.

Indeed, it was probably more difficult for an outsider to be admitted to the Reform Club in London than to the Düppel Penal Institution. I rang the quaint brass bell and was admitted by a guard who really was more of a porter. He returned to his cosy lodge and inquired as to the purpose of my visit. 'Very well, I shall call Herr Baumgarten.' In here, the general had lost his title. He was plain 'Herr'. But when his bulky frame bounded past the front door, it was almost as if the guard was standing to attention. His spine stiffened and his eyes took on the beaming inflexibility of a set of train lights. Still, it wasn't quite servile enough for the general. '*Na*, what's wrong with you today?'

'Not enough sleep, I think.' The guard shuffled sideways to make room.

'But you have all day to rest.'

There was little doubt who was in charge. The guard might have control over the door buzzer, but the general had the skin-deep charm of a man who naturally commanded the parade ground. At heart, both were men in uniform. And they both knew how to treat the different ranks.

The general stepped past the guard. 'Herr August, so nice you could come and see me.' He acted as if I was doing him a favour. He shook my hand effusively and then pointed down the hallway with a short wave. 'After you.'

We walked into a roomy cell on the ground floor. He said something apologetic about not being able to play host in grander surroundings. It was his defence ministry office he probably had in mind. I felt distinctly more comfortable meeting him here. But the general didn't seem uncomfortable here himself. There was no lock on the cell door and the inmates didn't wear prison garb.

A coke machine hummed in the corner. Ever hospitable, the general offered to get me a drink. 'I'm sorry, no alcohol,' he said in a tone of voice that suggested they had only temporarily run out of booze. The butler would for certain be dispatched on the morrow to replenish the decanters in the library.

The general leant back in his chair. He was mentally preparing himself for a sermon. A belly, surely impermissible among the lower ranks, protruded. His shirt was tucked into white undergarments. The waistband visibly rose above his belt. Cartoonists had been fond of depicting John Major thus. But in the general's case, the practice seemed deliberate, borne out of military rigour. In preparation for all eventualities, a shirt needed to be fastened securely.

Without prompting, he suddenly said: 'You know that Mikhail Gorbachev offered to come to my trial. He was going to be my defence witness. But the judge wouldn't let him.'

'Why not?'

'Oh, I can tell you why not. Gorbachev would have made things more difficult. After the judge announced the verdict – six and a half years – he said: "We wanted to convict and we did convict." I later heard he really rather would have put me away for life, but couldn't.'

I suggested every prisoner around the world probably thought his trial unfair. But he couldn't see why the death of almost a thousand people along the border should be dragged into court. 'The accusations against me are a settling of old scores, *oh ja*, a destruction of an alternative Germany. Against the rules of international law. Even a breach of the German unity treaty.'

Here we go again, I thought. He had acted in the name of a 'higher truth'. The philosophical kingpin of any totalitarian system whirred into action. But the general was manoeuvring on much simpler ground. He needed no thinking man's construct. He served up humbug. 'The border was not fortified to prevent the escape from our side. That's simply slander. I know. I was an insider.'

'How can you say that? I travelled along the entire 1,300 kilometre border and ...'

'May I correct you? The border ran for 1,600 kilometres, plus another

160 kilometres through Berlin.' I thought about interrupting him. He saw me thinking. 'Let me give you the facts. I served in my post from 1979 to 1989, no, 1990. On 27 January I retired, with honours. During these eleven years, there were 2,905 arrests. Shots were fired 148 times. Seventeen dead. Twenty-one injured. This was not a gun-crazy force.'

'Let me see. Seventeen and twenty-one, that's thirty-eight. And you said 148 shots were fired. Did they miss the other 110 times?'

'Of course not. Those were warning shots.'

'Of course.'

'The force was highly trained. Four years officer training.'

'And you never felt sorry thinking about the victims?'

'I was pained, terribly hurt by it.'

I looked up from my notepad. His forehead beamed red under a mat of white hair, swept back. Private grief engulfed him like clouds around a hilltop. But something was wrong.

'I thought a lot about . . . Klaus-Peter Seidel and . . . the little one from Plauen . . . I'll think of the name in a minute. They were shot by Weinhold – a criminal in the NVA. I remember, Jürgen Lange, that was the name of the little one.'

'And they were killed while escaping?'

'*Nein, nein.* Weinhold was on the run. He fired on them. They died in the line of duty. I was their commander at the time. When you see such a crime, I tell you, one is for ever committed to prevent further injury.'

The cell was shrinking around me. I felt sick. The heat from the radiator and Baumgarten's rhetoric combined had the intensity of an infernal fire. So, he really thought of the dead guards as the primary victims. And it got worse. He continued: 'The private citizens who tried to cross the border knew what they were doing. They knew there were risks. They acted carelessly by approaching the guards.'

Baumgarten sensed my disbelief. 'I can understand if you view all this with some scepticism,' he purred. 'But you have to believe me. I'm telling you the truth. You can read the documents on this. I have great respect for the sanctity of life. I'm very proud that the use of guns continually declined, that no shots were fired at anyone on West German territory. I'm very proud of the border troops. They are unique over the last thousand years. At the Wende, not a single shot was fired.'

The general became animated. He pointed at me as he spoke. He would lift one hand, then a minute later use the other. I couldn't help but stare at his hands, for he pointed at me with stumps. The index fingers on both hands were missing. Rounded finger butts jabbed the air.

He eventually noticed my embarrassed glances.

'I used to be a carpenter before I joined the force in 1949. The fingers stayed behind on a building site in Ellrich after a sawing accident.'

A sympathetic response would have been in order. But I couldn't muster one. *Ellrich?*

'I knew your father, you know.'

'You did?' I had hardly recovered from the last blow. What now?

'I was born in Werna in 1931, not far from Ellrich. I went to primary school in Ellrich at the same time as your father.'

'He, too, was born in 1931,' I stammered.

'See, I'm telling you the truth.'

'But he never mentioned you.'

'Well, I don't forget people.'

I kept staring at his jabbing stumps. They were surreal. But at the same time, they were real. I could see them. I even touched them when I shook his hand. What Baumgarten said, however, seemed ever more fantastic. I only half listened now to the story of his childhood. A certain fear and loathing had permeated our conversation. 'My father – an officer in the Wehrmacht – died in Belgrade in 1944. He quite literally committed suicide. My mother taught me human beings must be treated decently. Inmates from the concentration camp in Ellrich built an air raid shelter three hundred yards from our house. My mother would send me over to these haggard figures with a few sandwiches. Another time, I brought them some soup . . . I was a committed member of the Hitler Youth. But I knew human beings could not be treated like that . . .'

This was not so much the Nuremberg Trials as a dazzling soap opera.

I put my pen down. 'You must be hot,' he said, still the perfect host. He opened the cell window. I wondered whether the cells where arrested fugitives like Ruth were held had windows that could be opened at leisure. I didn't ask. I wanted more than an open window. I wanted out. But not before I had made a last attempt at asking tough questions. Wasn't that what one is supposed to do in my situation? Or was it enough that the general had already been judged in a court of law. Aimlessly, I inquired as to 'justification . . . guilt . . . aggression . . .'

The general took off his military cap and put on his politician's hat. So spoke the ex-deputy defence minister: 'The Russians didn't want the division of Germany; all resulted from the Potsdam Agreement . . . The division was caused by West Germany and its currency reform in 1948 ... Churchill's speech in Zurich was really the start of the Cold War.'

Every inquiry hit a dead end. There was a textbook answer to every one of my textbook questions. The same clichéd exchange of opposing views must have taken place at countless UN sessions and student meetings during the Cold War. We both knew our conversation had come to an end. I felt relieved.

He escorted me to the door while we chit-chatted about holiday destinations. 'Greece is nicest in the spring, you know.'

The irony of the subject was not entirely lost on Baumgarten. 'In the old days, we could never travel. And now, I still can't go.' He sounded amused rather than upset.

At the door, he wished me good luck and said: '*Passen sie auf sich auf*', ('Take care of yourself'). Almost as if I was the one to be pitied. Me, who had to brave the harsh world outside the safety of Düppel.

It would have been easy for him to walk out of the door behind me. In fact, next Sunday he would visit his wife at home. Baumgarten was a prisoner in only the legal sense. Nobody would have trained a rifle on him from a watchtower behind barbed wire. He could easily run away.

But he just stood there in the door. Waving. Smiling. Waving again. Like a host who wanted to be sure his guest got off to a good start on his journey back home. Then he stepped back, shut the door and locked himself in.

I walked away bewildered, yet enlightened. I had glimpsed an answer to the question that puzzled me all along: How could the Wall have lasted so long and why were so few East Germans openly defiant? On Baumgarten's smiling face, I detected a certain comfort, an appreciation for his reassuring lack of options in prison. It seemed, the general welcomed the regularity of life behind walls. 'Take good care of your self out there,' he had said – out there where no walls protect you and nobody watches over you from a tower.

Thank goodness, I thought, and headed for the nearest *Kneipe*.

INDEX

PLEASE NOTE

To save dollars . . .

No overdue notice(s) will be sent on thi
material. you are responsible for returning
by date on card in pocket. Otherwise you
will be billed.

Board of Managers
East Hampton Library
159 Main Street
East Hampton, NY 11937

GAYLORD M

Hitler and Stalin

Parallel Lives

Alan Bullock

Fully revised second edition

'It is practically unprecedented to take two such monsters as Hitler and Stalin, who never met, and interweave their lives chronologically, chapter by chapter, often paragraph by paragraph, as Bullock has done. It sounds like a recipe for confusion, irritation and indigestion. In fact, it works brilliantly. The book is a triumph of organisation, lucidity and perspective.'
JOHN CAMPBELL, *The Times*

'A magnificent piece of historical writing which, despite its massive size, makes for compulsive reading. The sweep is broad and the information concisely conveyed without any sign of pedantry. The judgements are sane and balanced . . . The grasp of the biographical material is matched by a multitude of interpretations which are the mark of a master historian.'
ZARA STEINER, *Financial Times*

'A magnetic chronicling . . . which, by dint of its distillation of a vast amount of matter, and by virtue of its author's consummate powers of analysis and narrative, becomes a standard work from the very instant of publication.'
MARTIN FAGG, *TES*

'Lord Bullock has carried out to perfection an artistic revenge on Public Enemies Numbers One and Two. This enormous book is a fitting tombstone to their world.'
ANDREW ROBERTS, *Spectator*

0 00 686374 4

FontanaPress
An Imprint of HarperCollins*Publishers*